# The Fix 3

# The Fix 3

*K'wan*

www.urbanbooks.net

Urban Books, LLC
300 Farmingdale Road, NY-Route 109
Farmingdale, NY 11735

ISBN 13: 978-1-62286-770-7
ISBN 10: 1-62286-770-X

First Mass Market Printing February 2017
First Trade Paperback Printing February 2016
Printed in the United States of America

10 9 8 7 6 5 4 3 2 1

*This is a work of fiction. Any references or similarities to actual events, real people, living or dead, or to real locales are intended to give the novel a sense of reality. Any similarity in other names, characters, places, and incidents is entirely coincidental.*

Distributed by Kensington Publishing Corp.
Submit orders to:
Customer Service
400 Hahn Road
Westminster, MD 21157-4627
Phone: 1-800-733-3000
Fax: 1-800-659-2436

# PART I

## *SO MANY TEARS*

# CHAPTER 1

*One week earlier*

"Jesus, Li'l Monk, why can't you seem to sit still?" Sophie asked from the passenger seat of Li'l Monk's Bonneville.

"Because I'm uncomfortable." Li'l Monk rolled his broad shoulders beneath the blazer he was wearing, trying his best to tear the seams and give himself a bit more room. He hadn't worn a suit since sixth grade graduation, and even then he hated them.

"Because it's a suit jacket and not a dope boy leather, and should be worn according to your actual size and not be falling off you," Sophie told him. "Stop complaining, Li'l Monk. You're only going to have to wear it for a few hours."

"Yeah, but those few hours are gonna feel like a lifetime, considering the circumstances," Li'l Monk said. Suddenly they were both reminded of where they were going and why they were going there, and the mood darkened. A few minutes later, they were pulling up at their destination, Unity Funeral home.

The minute Li'l Monk crossed 126th Street and Eighth Avenue, he felt the ball of ice forming in his gut. It was the same feeling he got whenever he was within spitting distance of a funeral home. It was odd to him that he could murder people out in the streets without losing sleep over it, but being around them laid out properly gave him the creeps. His mother's was the first and last funeral he had ever attended. He could remember, as if it were yesterday, seeing her stretched out in that satin-lined box like she was only sleeping. They had done an excellent job with her makeup, except for the raised patch of skin on her forehead that appeared slightly darker than the rest of her face. Gunshot wounds to the head were slightly harder to cover than most causes of death.

At the urging of his father, Monk, he'd approached the casket to pay his final respects. When he touched her hand, it felt different. It wasn't the same hand that had held his while walking him to the bus stop for school, or the hand that stroked his face and told him he was handsome when he would come home crying over the mean kids in school calling him ugly. What he held was a room-temperature shell that had once housed his mother's spirit. From then on, Li'l Monk refused to attend another funeral, even for someone he loved; yet that day he found himself going back on his word for someone he barely even liked.

There were cars parked and double parked on both sides of the street, but Li'l Monk was able to squeeze into a spot near the bodega on the corner. His was the only car without a funeral sign in the window, so he was leery about leaving it there for fear of being ticketed or towed by some thirsty traffic cop. The last thing he wanted to do was have to go down to Pier 76 to retrieve his car over some parking fines. Had it been up to him they'd have circled the block once or twice more looking for a spot, but they were already pressed for time and he didn't want to hear Sophie's mouth.

After giving a brief look around to make sure there was no danger looming, Li'l Monk walked around the side of the car to open the door for his lady. Sophie stepped out of the car looking like a woman ready for the world in a stylish skirt that hugged her hips, and the matching jacket. On her feet was a pair of modest heels that gave her just enough lift to show off her toned calves. Her hair was freshly done in a tight French braid with a gold butterfly clasp at the base. It was one of her favorite hair pieces. It wasn't much, but Li'l Monk had given it to her one day on the humble, so she loved the thought behind it more than the value of it and wore the clasp all the time.

After helping Sophie onto the curb, Li'l Monk took a minute to adjust his jacket so that the gun tucked in the waist of his slacks was concealed.

When Sophie spotted it, she frowned in disapproval.

"Nigga, I know you ain't bring no gun to a funeral?" Sophie asked with an attitude. "Li'l Monk, you're disrespectful as hell for that."

"Call me what you want, Sophie, but this here pistol can be the difference between being a spectator and the guest of honor at a funeral," Li'l Monk told her, while continuing to button his jacket.

When they reached the funeral home, Li'l Monk had to do a double take. There was a horse-drawn carriage driven by a man decked out in white gloves and a coat with tails. Two beautiful horses stood erect and tall, waiting for the coach driver's command. It reminded Li'l Monk of a scene from a movie Sophie had forced him to watch called *Imitation of Life*. From the looks of things no expense had been spared on the funeral, and from what he remembered of the family of the deceased they surely didn't have it like that.

In front, clusters of people gathered; some needed a breather from seeing their loved one off for the final time, and others had more sinister intentions. Li'l Monk's focus was on the latter group. He gave Sophie a look, and she knew what was on his mind without him saying. She excused herself and went to talk to a girl she knew from the block and left Li'l Monk to his business.

Several pairs of eyes turned toward Li'l Monk as he approached. Some of them he knew and others he had only seen around the neighborhood. Standing in the center of them was a man who was no doubt their leader. Even if you didn't know him, you could tell from the way the men surrounding him seemed to hang on his every word. He looked like was holding court the way he walked up and down the line, speaking sharply. His dreads whipped back and forth every time he changed focus on who he was speaking to. He looked like a mighty lion king holding court. When he noticed he had lost the attention of some of the men, he turned to see what they were looking at. The anger immediately drained from his face and his lips parted into a wide grin.

"What up, gangsta?" Omega embraced his friend. "I'm surprised to see you here. I know how you feel about funerals."

"I started not to come, but Sophie wouldn't leave me alone about it. She says it would've been disrespectful if I didn't come," Li'l Monk told him.

"Well, y'all did grow up together."

"True, but it wasn't like we were good friends or no shit. I know why I'm here, but what's your excuse?"

"Ramses insisted I show up. He said that seeing me and a few of the guys there would show people that the family was respected in the neighborhood," Omega told him.

Li'l Monk frowned in confusion. "Why does he even care?"

Omega shrugged. "Beats the hell out of me. Maybe he was just protecting his investment, since he did foot the bill for the funeral."

This bit of information shocked Li'l Monk. It wasn't unheard of for Ramses to help out financially if someone from the neighborhood needed a proper send-off and their families didn't have the money to do it, but it never went further than an envelope of cash or maybe a nice floral arrangement. Sending one of his field commanders to represent personally was an honor usually reserved for members of their organization or an affiliate. Li'l Monk wondered what kind of attachment Ramses had to the deceased or the family to make him show such respect.

"So what's up with you and that situation? The thing with the Italians?" Omega asked.

"Ain't nothing up with it. Ramses said it was dead and I shouldn't worry about it. Why, did you hear something different?" Li'l Monk asked suspiciously.

"Nah. I mean, I only know what the streets are saying, ya know?" Omega explained.

"No, I don't know, nor do I give a fuck." Li'l Monk snorted. "I didn't have nothing to do with what happened and Ramses said he'd tell Frankie as much. If Ramses's word ain't good enough for him then I can tell him myself."

"Be careful with how you handle that, Li'l Monk. Those Italians are dangerous," Omega warned.

"Any nigga with a gun is dangerous and I got a few of those on deck," Li'l Monk said confidently.

"Damn, I never thought I'd actually ever see a real monkey in a monkey suit." One of the men Omega had been speaking with came over. He was dark skinned, and wore his hair in long cornrows. He had moved so silently that Li'l Monk hadn't even noticed him at first. Typical of a snake like King Tut.

"I ain't no monkey. I'm a full-blown gorilla and you'd do well to remember that." Li'l Monk's voice was neutral, but the threat in his words wasn't lost on Tut. King Tut was one of Ramses's newest field commanders and a general pain in Li'l Monk's ass. They tolerated each other out of respect to Ramses, but there was no love lost between them.

Tut sized him up briefly, before smiling so wide that you could see all thirty-two of his perfectly white teeth. "C'mon, you know I was only joking with you, Li'l Monk."

"Last dude who called himself being funny ended up in the emergency room," Li'l Monk reminded him, referring to Chief. Chief was one of Tut's boys who had run afoul of Li'l Monk. As a result, Li'l Monk fractured his cheek and had broken several of his ribs.

The smirk faded from King Tut's face. "Yeah, old pretty-ass Chief ain't so pretty no more after that ass whipping you put on him. I can't say that I wouldn't have done the same if a nigga almost took my bitch."

Li'l Monk took a step toward King Tut, but Omega stepped between them. "You know this ain't the time or place."

Li'l Monk clenched and unclenched his fist. He wanted to pummel King Tut, but Omega was right. It wasn't the time or place, but their reckoning would come. "You got it, O."

"Let me holla at you right quick though." Omega led Li'l Monk out of earshot of the rest of the group. "You heard what happened uptown last night?"

"Nah, I been at Sophie's since yesterday morning. Everything good?"

"Afraid not. We lost two soldiers last night," Omega said solemnly.

"Damn, that's fucked up. Anybody I know?" Li'l Monk asked.

"Probably not. They were two low-level runners from Tut's crew," Omega explained.

Li'l Monk snorted. "Sounds like Tut's problem, not ours."

"Tut's with us, so that makes it our problem. We gotta take care of our own no matter how high or low they sit on the totem pole. Niggas dying on our watch is bad for morale. Cats will start feeling like it ain't safe to work for us and seek employment elsewhere."

Li'l Monk didn't like it, but he understood Omega's point. "Do we know who was responsible for it?"

"The streets are saying it was some of them Clark boys," Omega told him. He was speaking about Shai Clark, heir to Poppa Clark's multimillion dollar heroin empire. His predecessor, Poppa Clark, had been a reasonable man and had no problems coexisting with the other bosses, but his son lacked his diplomatic skills. According to Ramses, Shai Clark was a ruthless and power-hungry brat who was conquering drug territory in the tri-state area like Hannibal sweeping across Europe.

"If we know who it is, why don't we arm up and go bang on this nigga?" Li'l Monk asked heatedly.

"Because that's not how Ramses wants it done. He says this situation involving the Clarks has to be handled with diplomacy," Omega told him.

Li'l Monk shook his head. "I don't get it, Omega. In the short time we been riding with him Pharaoh has crushed at least a half dozen upstarts, but when it comes to these Clark niggas he starts dancing around the issue. Word life, it's looking like he's scared."

Omega gave him a look. "You and I both know that fear don't live nowhere in Pharaoh's heart, but the Clarks are a different animal. These guys aren't some crew of thugs armed with machine guns and heart. Shai's family is old-school organized crime."

"And that's what makes the situation even more bizarre, O. If them niggas coexisted all these years, why the sudden blowup between them?"

"Listen, you reading too deep into this, Li'l Monk. All we need to know is that Pharaoh don't fuck with these niggas so neither do we!" Omega said definitively.

Li'l Monk wasn't feeling it, but he didn't bother to try to argue the point with Omega. He was a loyalist and the only thing that mattered to him was the will of Pharaoh. "I need to pay my respects. I'll see you inside." Li'l Monk stalked off.

"What the fuck is his problem?" Tut asked once Li'l Monk had gone.

"Li'l Monk is just being Li'l Monk." Omega downplayed it. "And why are you always antagonizing him? You're like a kid throwing rocks at a stray dog then cries about getting bit."

"This dog bites back. Unlike most of these niggas, I ain't scared of Li'l Monk," Tut said defiantly.

"That's because you ain't smart enough to be scared of him. Li'l Monk is a good dude, but he is also a monster. When provoked he becomes a creature of pure rage and will destroy anything or anyone he feels is a threat. You might wanna keep that in the back of ya mind the next time you go talking shit to him."

"I hear you, O," Tut said like he agreed, but he really wasn't heeding Omega's warning. Tut lived by the law of the gun, meaning the quickest on the draw was the one who'd likely come out of the fight on top. "Any new word on that thing?" Tut changed the subject.

"I told you that I've got a plan, so stop worrying," Omega said.

"That's easy for you to say. You weren't the one who tortured and killed the nephew of a man who could wipe out our entire bloodlines with one phone call," King Tut shot back.

King Tut was referring to the ambitious move Omega had orchestrated, which turned into a heaping pile of shit dumped in Tut's lap. Omega had enticed Tut into whacking a dealer named Petey who controlled a small piece of territory situated just across the 145th Street Bridge into the Bronx. Omega wanted to expand, but Petey was in the way so he had to go and he called on King Tut to do the deed. As far as King Tut knew Petey was a nobody, a relative blip on the underworld radar who wouldn't be missed, but what Omega failed to mention was that Petey was the nephew of a cartel boss named Suarez. Suarez was furious when he discovered his nephew had been murdered, and since it happened in Pharaoh's backyard he suspected that one of Pharaoh's people was behind it. The only reason Omega and King Tut were still alive was because Suarez didn't have any proof. Pharaoh had charged Omega with assisting Suarez's right-hand man Felix to investigate the murder. If Omega played his cards right he could keep the Puerto Ricans chasing their tails until the situation blew over or they found a believable patsy to pin the murder on. Until such time, Omega's and Tut's survival rested in them keeping their cool.

"Be easy, Tut." Omega draped his arm around King Tut's shoulder and lowered his voice to a whisper. "Them spics can't prove it was us who laid Petey out. Right now they're just flexing, hoping that we crack and start turning on each other. So long as we keep our heads we'll get through this."

"I hope so, O. Just remember that if I burn, you burn with me," King Tut reminded him. He had been the killer, but it was Omega who authorized the hit so their fates were intertwined.

"Have no fear, King Tut. Somebody is gonna feel the fire behind this, but it ain't gonna be us." Omega gave a sinister laugh.

# CHAPTER 2

By the time Li'l Monk made it inside the funeral was wrapping up. There were two lines, family and friends, stretching from the front of the funeral home to the back. This was the opportunity for people to say their final farewells to the deceased.

From where he was standing Li'l Monk could see the beautiful ivory casket that held Karen's shell. There were too many people for him to catch more than the occasional glimpse of Karen's face and he dared not move closer. Li'l Monk wasn't sure he would be able to take seeing her laid out in a box. It wasn't that he was squeamish or even overly saddened by the loss, but he was having trouble processing it. Li'l Monk had lost plenty of homies but Karen's death was different. Karen was someone Li'l Monk saw damn near every day of his life because they grew up in the same hood and he was best friends with her brother Charlie; and now she was gone, snuffed out before even hitting the prime of her life. They had never really been friends, but they were cool and her death made Li'l Monk start to think on his own mortality. At the rate he was going he doubted he would make it to a ripe old age, but being at Karen's funeral made this real to him for the first time. He pictured himself lying in that casket with people crying and falling out over him, and it rattled him.

Down in front Li'l Monk spotted Karen's family. Her mother and some of Karen's other relatives were there. Karen's mother was normally loud and brash, but sitting mere feet away from her daughter's body had taken all the fire out of her. She sobbed uncontrollably while friends and relatives tried to no avail to console her. Sitting on the end of the bench, trying to look everywhere except at the casket, was Karen's brother and Li'l Monk's best friend, Charlie. He was trying to hold it together, but you could tell from the redness of his eyes and the solemn look on his face that he was going through it. Charlie and Karen had different fathers and more often than not they disrespected each other like total strangers, but Li'l Monk knew firsthand how much the siblings loved each other. Li'l Monk's heart went out to his friend in his time of grief.

Charlie must've felt Li'l Monk staring at him from the back of the funeral home, because he picked his head up and looked in his direction. Li'l Monk pounded his chest in salute, to let Charlie know he was there for him, but to his surprise Charlie turned his back and acted as if he had never seen him. Li'l Monk figured he was so deep in his grief that he didn't notice him and left it at that.

Li'l Monk contemplated letting the conversation he needed to have with Charlie keep until another time, but he knew that it couldn't. Li'l Monk's reputation and potentially his life could've been on the line. Ramses was specific in his instructions to Li'l Monk to go alone when he'd sent him to pay a call on an old wise guy named Mr. D, but Li'l Monk had taken Charlie with him. He was trying to help his man get back on his feet and maybe gradually integrate him into Ramses's street crew, but that plan got derailed when a few days later Mr. D was found dead in his apartment and the contents of his safe were stolen. Since technically Charlie wasn't supposed to be there, as far as everyone was concerned Li'l Monk was one of the last people to see him alive. It didn't take a rocket scientist to know how it must've looked to the Italians. All Li'l Monk had in the world was his name and his word, and he refused to see either dirtied. He knew the best way to clear himself and not wind up on a mafia kill list was to fill in the blanks of the mystery he was caught up in. This was why it was so important that he spoke to Charlie.

Li'l Monk picked his way through the throngs of mourners, nodding and shaking hands of different people he knew from the block. It seemed like everyone came out to pay their respects to Karen, including the drug addicts. At the end of the aisle he spotted an old crack fiend who went by the

name of Neighborhood. Neighborhood had traded
his usual crackhead gear of outdated clothes for a
suit that had probably fit him once upon a time, but
was now two sizes too big. He had even combed
his bush of nappy hair and made his shapeless afro
look somewhat presentable. Neighborhood was
normally a mess of a man who was always high on
this or that, but for the first time in all the years Li'l
Monk had known him he looked relatively sober.

At the time Neighborhood was speaking with a
woman who looked familiar to Li'l Monk, but he
couldn't place her right off. She was older, probably somewhere in her early fifties and well dressed.
She sported some expensive pieces of jewelry on
her neck and fingers, but they didn't completely
hide the unmistakable look of someone who had
once danced with drugs. It wasn't obvious to the
untrained eyes, but Li'l Monk dealt with addicts
day in and day out. For all intents and purposes
there was nothing special about the woman, but
the local fiends seemed to have a great deal of
respect for her.

After their exchange the woman said good-bye
to Neighborhood and made her way toward the
exit. As she passed Li'l Monk she paused and gave
him a look of recognition. She opened her mouth
as if she was about to say something, but thought
better of it. Instead she gave him a warm smile and
continued on her way.

A few seconds later, Neighborhood came walking up the aisle. When he saw Li'l Monk he managed to muster his signature yellowing smile, but the pain beneath was apparent. "Sup, young blood?"

"Not too much. Here to pay my respects like everybody else. Seems like everybody in the hood showed up to see Karen off." Li'l Monk looked around at the crowd.

"Nothing like a funeral to bring the vultures and gossipmongers out," Neighborhood said in disgust.

"Say, who was the old bird you was talking to?"

"That wasn't nobody but Queen. You're probably too young to remember her, but your dad might know her. All the young boys wanted a shot of that old pussy, but she wouldn't give you the time of day unless you were handling. I tried to take a crack at her back when I was clean and sober, but my money wasn't long enough," Neighborhood said.

"The way the crackheads were crowding around her you'd think she was holding a bag as big as Pharaoh's," Li'l Monk joked.

Neighborhood laughed. "Queen ain't never held no bag, at least not that I know of, but she held the heart of many big-time players, including your boss. The way I hear it, Pharaoh used to worship Ms. Queen."

This surprised Li'l Monk. "Wait, so you mean that old lady has actually seen Pharaoh? I been working for him for months and never laid eyes on him. Some of us were debating whether Pharaoh really exists or if he was a ghost story Ramses made up to keep the heat off himself."

"Nah, Pharaoh is real. I've never had the pleasure, but I know a few who have. Queen was one of them. That old bitch was so bad back in the day that she turned some of the hardest niggas I know into love-struck basket cases, and Pharaoh wasn't no different. Queen could've put herself in a position to be a major player, but she had larceny in her heart and that's what ruined her."

"How you mean?" Li'l Monk asked curiously.

"Well, like I said, Queen's pussy was like magic. Pharaoh had it so bad for her that he'd have killed you just for looking at her. The problem was Pharaoh was married, so trying to juggle his home life and his money on the streets didn't leave much time for Queen. A woman like that needs constant attention or she'll stray, and that's exactly what ended up happening. Word got out that Queen had lain down with a Trinidadian named Poppa who was also on the come up. When Pharaoh found out Queen let somebody else dip in he lost his damn mind. As far as he was concerned, wife and kids be damned. Queen still belonged to him. Her tipping made him look like a sucker, so he had to punish her and he did so in the most vile way he could think of, and that was by getting her strung out.

He kept Queen around long enough to see her hit rock bottom then kicked her to the curb. It crushed Pharaoh to do it because he still loved her, but she had betrayed him and he had to save face. They say that to this day he's never forgiven himself for what he done to her. I was around back then so I know how ugly things got for Queen. Does my heart good to see her back on her feet."

"That's one wild-ass story, Neighborhood," Li'l Monk said.

"The streets are full of wild-ass stories, young blood. Just not all of them have happy endings." Neighborhood looked back at Karen's casket. "I'm trying to hold it together, but I'm fucked up, man. Real fucked up. They didn't have to do Karen like that."

According to the police report, Karen had been beaten, raped, and sodomized before the killer put a bullet in her head. "I heard," Li'l Monk said solemnly. "They got any leads on who did it?"

"You know the police don't give a fuck about what happens to kids in the ghetto. They ran a bullshit investigation then tossed it in a pile with the rest of the cold cases," Neighborhood spat.

Li'l Monk shook his head. "That's some cruel shit."

"That's the life we live, young blood. If the police ain't killing us, we're killing each other. Karen was just another example of that. The police might not know who did it, but I got my own ideas about who the shooter might've been."

"What you talking about?" Li'l Monk asked

"Dig, you know they found Karen in Pennsylvania, right?"

"Yeah, and I never could understand what she was doing out there. Karen never struck me as a chick who would ever venture out of the hood," Li'l Monk said.

"She wasn't. Word is that she was down there trying to get her life together, but I call bullshit. Karen was about as concerned with getting her life together as I am," Neighborhood said.

"Then what was she doing out there?"

"Running," Neighborhood informed him. He lowered his voice so that only Li'l Monk could hear what he was about to say. "Word is that Karen knew who killed Ramses's man Boo and dropped a dime."

This surprised Li'l Monk. "To who, the police?"

"Worse; she told Ramses. Why do you think Ramses went all out to try to have Chucky killed?"

"I thought because he was a traitorous snake and an undercover smoker," Li'l Monk said.

Neighborhood laughed. "Chucky been a snake and a closet addict for years; that ain't nothing new. It was only a matter of time before Ramses or someone else laid a claim on his life, but when he killed Boo that sped up the clock."

"But Chucky has been MIA for months. I hear he's hiding out down South somewhere," Li'l Monk said.

"Don't go believing everything you hear. All Chucky knows is New York, so even if he did go into hiding he didn't go too far from the city. I got a feeling he's been somewhere lying in the cut and waiting."

"Waiting for what?"

"To settle old scores." Neighborhood glanced back at the casket. "Chucky is a creep and a piece of shit, but he knows how to hold a grudge. Ain't no way he'd have vanished without settling up with anybody he feels crossed him, especially Karen."

"Neighborhood, I know Chucky is a killer, but even he ain't cold-blooded enough to do Karen like that. She was tortured and that ain't his MO."

"One thing being around your daddy all these years should've taught you is that drug addicts are unpredictable. When you're strung out on that shit you ain't yourself no more. Look at me. I was a made man once upon a time. If you had told me twenty years ago that I'd be willing to do anything short of sucking a cock for a blast I'd have laughed at you, but the fact that I'm standing here broken and strung out says that anything is possible."

Li'l Monk thought on what Neighborhood was saying. "So you really think Chucky killed Karen?"

"I'd be willing to bet my next high on it," Neighborhood said seriously. He looked up and spotted one of the corner boys in the doorway of the funeral. Just seeing him brought on the cravings. "Well, I've paid my respects and now I gotta go get my head right. You stay safe out there, Li'l Monk. And watch your ass. These streets don't love nobody, not even good-hearted li'l niggas like you." He gave Li'l Monk dap and continued up the aisle.

Li'l Monk stood there watching Neighborhood amble up to the corner boy and whisper something in his ear. The corner boy nodded and dipped into his pants pocket to serve Neighborhood right there in the doorway of the funeral home. "No fucking respect," Li'l Monk grumbled before continuing down the aisle.

Charlie was standing now. He was talking to one of his uncles about something that didn't seem to interest him. Every so often he would cast a nervous glance in Li'l Monk's direction. He looked almost skittish, as if Li'l Monk was the Grim Reaper coming to call his number. If Li'l Monk wasn't sure before, he was sure then that something was off about Charlie.

Li'l Monk had almost reached the front of the funeral home when a woman popped up seemingly out of nowhere. She was moving so fast that she wasn't paying attention to where she was going and collided with Li'l Monk. When she looked up and he saw who it was, Li'l Monk's mind went black and for a moment. Charlie and everything else in the world became afterthoughts.

# CHAPTER 3

Persia lay on the queen-sized bed looking up at the cracked ceiling. The bare mattress was so worn and beaten up that it had lumps in it the size of golf balls. They were uncomfortable, but tolerable compared to the loose springs. Several times when she'd moved the coils bit into her soft skin. It was best just to lie still and pretend she wasn't there.

On the nightstand a cheap dollar store candle burned. It was meant to set the mood but fell horribly short. Next to the candle was a pack of Newports and an ashtray with a half-smoked cigarette in it. Persia's eyes stayed fixed on the pack of cigarettes, or, more accurately, what was wedged under the pack. There was a small Baggie full of white powder. Persia tried to tear her eyes away, but couldn't. It was as if she could smell the cocaine through the plastic and it caused a familiar drip in the back of her throat.

Without even realizing it, her hand moved to the nightstand. She traced a line along the edge of the chipped wooden nightstand. Her fingers stopped just short of the cocaine. She could've sworn she could taste it on the back of her tongue. The familiar beast called addiction reared its head and began scratching at the walls of Persia's insides. She wanted it so bad. She needed it. Persia closed her fingers along the edge of the Baggie and was sliding it from under the cigarette pack, but then her eyes landed on the tennis bracelet on her arm. Her mother had given it to her when she made six months clean. Persia abruptly withdrew her hand and rolled over on her side, crying.

For the millionth time she wondered how she found herself in such a predicament. Persia had been born into privilege and like most kids born wanting for nothing she took what she had for granted until she hit rock bottom. The time she spent battling her cocaine and crack addictions was one of the darkest periods of her life. Persia had foolishly put her trust in a man who she thought would be her salvation; but he ended up being her undoing. She rued the day that the chocolate devil walked into her life. There were times during her struggle when she had sunk so low that she felt like she would die. Every time that crack pipe touched her lips it was like an out-of-body experience. It was like she was sitting on the sidelines watching herself load up and blast off into the stratosphere. The man she loved had truly dragged her to the bottom of the barrel and it was a long and hard fight to climb out.

After months of rededicating herself to life and extensive counseling, Persia was able to start pulling it together. Things were good at home, she was about to graduate high school and go off to college, and she had even managed to garner the attention of a young man who wanted to change her life. Persia had it made; then her past caught up with her and this was what had her sprawled out on a dirty mattress thinking about relapsing.

The bedroom door opening sent a cool breeze across Persia's back. She didn't have to turn around to see who it was. It was the same person who had been coming in and out of the room for the last few hours. Persia imagined that if she closed her eyes super tight she would be invisible and he wouldn't see her. When she felt his weight behind her on the bed she knew she'd have no such luck. He leaned over and tried to kiss Persia on the mouth, but she moved so that his lips landed on her cheek. There was a time when she looked forward to his kisses, but now the smell of stale cigarettes and malt liquor repulsed her. As he ran his ashen hands between her legs and slipped his chipped fingernails inside her, Persia had to resist the urge to vomit. She couldn't believe that once upon a time she had loved this man.

"What the fuck is your problem?" Chucky asked, noticing Persia stiffened at his touch.

Persia kept her face pointed at the wall when she replied. "Nothing, I'm just a little sore. It's been a long time and I'm not used to something that big anymore," she said, stroking his ego.

"Yeah." Chucky sat up on his knees. "I'll bet that football nigga ain't hung like this." He slapped his half-hard penis against her thigh.

"I wouldn't know. I told you we haven't slept together," Persia said. She and Vaughn were still in the beginning stages of their relationship and had only been on one date, two if you counted the night they'd run into each other at the gala.

"Bullshit," Chucky said angrily. "You expect me to believe a hot in the ass dog bitch like you got a millionaire chasing her and ain't fucked him yet? You either a liar or a dummy, and you ain't never been dumb, Persia."

The fact that she had let Chucky touch her again after all he'd done to her contradicted his accusation, but she let him rant.

"It's probably that superstar dick you taking that's keeping your pussy from getting wet from me anymore." Chucky unexpectedly jammed his fingers inside Persia, making her sit bolt upright.

"Chucky, you already blackmailed me into coming here and fucking your creep ass; haven't I been humiliated enough?" Persia snapped.

Chucky grabbed her by the throat and pinned her to the headboard. "First of all, you little slut, watch your mouth when you talking to me. You think you somebody because you're clean now, but never forget I know you for the lowlife base head you are. Or have you forgotten all the good times we had?" He leaned in to kiss her, but Persia turned her head. "Yeah, that's what it is. You need to be properly motivated to get that thang wet for ol' Chucky." He reached over and picked up the

Baggie with the cocaine in it. Chucky held it in front of her face and plucked the bag. "Is that what you need, Princess P? A little liftoff to get you in the mood?" He sprinkled a bit of powder on the flap of skin between his index finger and thumb. Chucky let his hand linger under Persia's nose.

"Stop it, Chucky. I told you I don't fuck around anymore." Persia tried to turn her face away, but Chucky was holding her in place.

"Li'l bitch, them few months of sobriety you got under your belt ain't enough to quiet that monkey pounding on your back." He tried to force his hand to her nose, but she continued to struggle.

"Chucky, I told you I don't want to!" Persia shoved him.

Chucky's eyes flashed with anger. "Oh, you a big shot now so you're too good to take a bump with me?"

"No, it's not that. I gotta go to Karen's funeral in a little while and I don't wanna show up high." Persia half lied. It was true that she had to attend Karen's funeral, but the real reason why she didn't want to take a bump was because she knew that she wouldn't be able to stop at just one. Drugs had always been Chucky's way to control her and she promised no matter what she'd never give him that kind of power over her again.

At the mention of Karen's name a look crossed Chucky's face that Persia couldn't quite place. He slowly climbed off her and lay back on the bed.

"Fuck you then." He snorted the coke off his hand. "More for me."

Persia took that opportunity to start gathering her clothes and getting dressed as fast as she could.

"What's the rush? I figured we could fuck one more time before you go," Chucky said, stroking his dick. The cocaine was already working its magic and he could feel it swelling.

"I told you that I had to go to Karen's funeral. I don't want to be late," Persia told him while stepping into her skirt.

Chucky slithered off the bed and eased up behind Persia. "That bitch is dead, ain't like she'll notice if you're a little late." He pressed himself against her.

Persia shoved him away. "Why don't you show some respect for the dead? Karen might've had her bullshit with her but she was still my friend. You don't have to mourn her loss, but at least you don't have to be a dick about it, especially since you were fucking both of us at the same time." She flipped her hair and turned to the fingerprinted, stained mirror on the wall to finish fixing herself up.

Chucky moved so fast that Persia didn't even have time to mount a defense. He grabbed her by the back of the head and forced her face against the wall. "Little bitch, you must've forgotten who the fuck you're talking to!"

"Stop, you're hurting me," Persia cried.

"You're lucky I ain't killing you." He added a little more pressure. "Now you're gonna curb that fucking mouth of yours and remember who's in charge; or have you forgotten what I'm in possession of and what it can do to your new little life?"

Persia had tried to forget several times, but Chucky wouldn't let her. It was her moment of drug-induced stupidity not so long ago that had her in her current bind. Persia had worked extremely hard to get Chucky out of her life and keep him out, but a damning piece of dirt he had on her allowed him to worm his way back in. One night when she was whacked out of her mind on crack Chucky had secretly videotaped her doing some shameful things. She hadn't even remembered that particular night and wouldn't have believed him had he not e-mailed her a clip of the video. Even as Persia watched herself on camera performing all kinds of sexual acts and doing drugs, she couldn't believe it was her. Chucky had threatened to leak the tape if she didn't go along with whatever scheme he was cooking up. Not only would the leaked tape be utterly embarrassing to Persia and her family, it could've done major damage to Vaughn's professional image. The media would surely crucify the young football star for his affiliation with an ex-junkie. She couldn't bear to do that to him or her family. To spare the people she cared about, Persia once again found herself a slave to the man she once loved.

Persia hated Chucky for the hold he had over her, but she hated herself more for allowing herself to be put in such a position. Persia was so mad that tears welled in her eyes. She would've killed Chucky if she'd had access to a gun at that moment, but she didn't. All she could do was suck it up and go along with whatever Chucky said until she could figure out a way to get rid of him once and for all.

Chucky wiped away one of the tears rolling down her cheeks and tasted it. "Even when you trying to be sour, you're still sweet." He chuckled.

"Chucky, why don't you stop torturing me and just tell me what you want so we can end this?" Persia fumed.

"I told you what I want." Chucky stroked her cheek. "Revenge. One by one everybody who crossed me is going to feel my wrath, starting with you." He pulled her skirt up.

"What are you doing?" Persia tried to turn around, but Chucky held her against the wall.

"Just giving you something pleasant to think about while you're at the funeral boohooing over a skank bitch who didn't give a shit about you anyhow." He yanked her panties down. Chucky spat in his hand and rubbed it over his dick.

"No, not in there. It'll hurt," she pleaded when she felt Chucky's dick dancing near her anus.

Chucky grabbed her hair and yanked her head back. "That's the general idea." He laughed before forcing his dick into Persia's ass.

# CHAPTER 4

After Chucky was done violating Persia he finally freed her to take her leave. Before dressing, again, she took a quick shower in the dirty bathroom. The bathroom was just as much of a mess as the rest of the house. The floor tiles were dirty, and the tub had a nasty ring around it. She had a good mind to jump in her clothes and run to the funeral as is, but she needed to wash away the mess that Chucky had made.

Persia had never had anal sex before and her first time was even more horrible than she imagined. Vaginal sex with Chucky had always been a task for her because he was so well hung, but she was totally unprepared for the pain that awaited her when he entered through the back door. Chucky was brutal in his technique, jamming himself inside her instead of easing it in. Ignoring her cries he pumped himself in and out of her, stretching her asshole beyond its limits. At one point she thought she felt something tear. She had never felt so violated in her life and having her ass brutalized by Chucky only made her hate him more. If it was the last thing she did she would make him pay for everything he had done to her and then some.

After washing the blood and semen from her legs and ass, Persia came back out into the bedroom to prepare for the funeral. She was pleased to see that Chucky was no longer in the room. She got dressed as fast as she could fearing that he would come back into the bedroom and make her fuck him again. Though Karen's funeral was a sad occasion, it would at least allow her a few hours to be away from Chucky, which was a blessing.

Persia came out of the bedroom and walked into the living room to find Chucky sitting around scheming with his two new minions, Maggie and her sister Rissa. Maggie was an older chick, even older than Chucky. She was a tall chick with chocolate skin, and thick black hair that stopped short of her shoulders. She was wearing a yellow halter top and tight-fitting black skirt that showcased a body that had once been firm and succulent, but was starting to sag slightly in certain places. Maggie had once been a looker, but hard drugs and harder living had started to take their tolls. From the time they'd first met it was obvious that Maggie didn't like Persia. Part of it was because she knew that no matter how fucked up Chucky treated her, he still had a tender spot in his heart for his old boo. Persia not only represented a threat to her position with Chucky, but she was also a constant reminder to Maggie of what she used to be.

Rissa was Maggie's younger sister. Rissa was a cute girl who wasn't much older than Persia.

Unlike her bitch of a sister she was kind of cool and easy to talk to, at least when Chucky wasn't paying attention. Persia always got the impression that Rissa didn't totally agree with what Chucky and her sister were doing, but she dared not speak against them. She was an addict like her cohorts, but her habit hadn't gotten to the point where Chucky's and Maggie's had. She was like Persia had once been, a chipper, someone who occasionally dabbled in hard drugs, but it would only be a matter of time before her occasional fixes became daily ones, especially keeping company with the likes of Chucky.

The moment they noticed Persia in the living room their conversation stopped.

"I'm leaving," Persia announced.

"Good riddance," Maggie mumbled under her breath.

Chucky cut his eyes at Maggie and silenced her. "About how long you think you gonna be?" he asked Persia.

Persia gave him a look. "As long as I need to be. I'm going to my best friend's funeral, not running to the weed spot," she said sarcastically.

"Ain't no need in getting smart. I'm just trying to make sure your priorities are in order. You know you got a date with our boy Mr. Tate tonight," Chucky reminded her.

"After what you put me through this morning the last thing I wanna do is be in the company of a man. Nah, after the funeral I'm going home to soak. I'll call him after the funeral and cancel."

"You'll do no such thing," Chucky informed her. "You're going to keep that date with our new potential meal ticket. I got big plans for that boy."

"Chucky, it's bad enough that you got me out here playing myself, but I won't pull Vaughn into this bullshit. He's got nothing to do with it."

Chucky tapped a cigarette out of his pack of Newports and fired it up. "Persia, you might've missed the memo, but I'm making the rules in this little game. Now you've managed to snag the golden goose and I ain't gonna sit by and watch you piss it away, even if you're too damn stupid to realize what you got. Vaughn Tate can be our meal ticket for a long time to come, so you're gonna do whatever you have to in order to keep him happy."

Persia rolled her eyes. "Whatever you say, Chucky."

"Fucking right it's whatever I say. And in case you get any ideas about going off and doing what you wanna do anyhow, I'm gonna give Rissa the car and have her roll with you for the day," Chucky told her.

Rissa didn't like it. "Chucky, how you just gonna volunteer me for some shit? This is your side chick, so why can't you chauffer her around?"

"For one, I'm hot as a firecracker on these New York streets. And, for two, because I told you to.

Besides, I got some other shit I need to handle while y'all are doing that. Now stop asking so many fucking questions and put on something presentable and get your ass in gear."

"How much longer you gonna keep that bitch around?" Maggie asked from the couch where she had deposited herself when Persia and Rissa left.

Chucky was sitting across from her in the arm-chair, using the bottom of a beer bottle to crush the crack rocks he had tucked in a folded dollar bill. "For as long as I say." He flipped the dollar open, deemed the crack wasn't ground fine enough, and went back to his crushing. "Why do you keep riding my back about Persia when I done already told your ass why we need to keep her close? I got plans for Persia." He picked up the dollar and dumped the contents over a waiting pile of weed in an open cigar.

"You and these damn plans. I'll be glad when you come up with one that actually works." Maggie rolled her eyes.

"You roll them eyes at me again, and I'm gonna snatch them out your damn head," Chucky warned while licking the ends of the cigar to close the blunt. He noticed he had some cocaine residue on his thumb and rubbed it over his gums. "And I don't know why you sitting over there talking shit like I ain't been taking good care of you and your sister since we been back in New York. Shit, it's my money that been keeping your ass in drugs and whiskey for a week straight."

"You mean the old man's money that you ripped off, with your thieving ass," Maggie quipped.

The old man she was referring to was Mr. D. Charlie had hipped Chucky to the old man and his bedroom safe after visiting the apartment with Li'l Monk. At the time Charlie had no idea Mr. D was mobbed up; he just saw a score. Knowing he couldn't bring Li'l Monk in on the caper, Charlie turned to Chucky. It was supposed to be a simple robbery, but Chucky was high on coke and took things too far. The next thing anybody knew, Mr. D was dead and every mobster in the city was looking for his killer.

Chucky's head snapped up as if someone had just poked him with a hot iron. "What did I tell you about that mouth of yours? You know the walls have ears."

"Boy, bye, can't nobody hear us in this slum-ass apartment but the roaches," Maggie told him.

"Shit, for enough money even the roaches will drop a dime on us behind killing that dago," Chucky said, drying the coke blunt with his lighter.

"If killing him could bring so much grief, why do it? We could've just robbed him and kept it moving," Maggie pointed out.

"Because I don't believe in leaving anything to chance. That's one killing don't none of us want coming back on us, and as long as you did like I told you to we shouldn't have to worry about it."

"You know I did. I went in and told the man with all the jewelry exactly what you told me to," Maggie said proudly.

"That's my girl," Chucky said, handing her the blunt and the lighter.

When Chucky found out who it was that they'd killed in that apartment he knew it would only be a matter of time before the Italians put pressure on the streets to find out who did the old man. In order to keep it from coming back around to him, Chucky would need a fall guy. He could've pinned it on Charlie, but it wouldn't take much pressure to get him to start talking, so he needed someone else. This is when he got the idea to kill two birds with one stone. Chucky had Maggie go and see Ramses, posing as an eyewitness to the crime, and fingered Li'l Monk as the person she saw leaving Mr. D's apartment following the murder. After that, all Chucky had to do was sit back and watch the pieces fall into place.

"One thing I don't get." Maggie put the blunt in her mouth and prepared to fire it up. "From what you say, you've got a ton of enemies in the city you could've put this on, so why the kid?"

"I got my reasons," Chucky said sinisterly. Chucky had never liked Li'l Monk, but he liked him even less when he had unwittingly exposed a skimming operation in Ramses's crew, orchestrated by Chucky and executed by his best friend Benny. They had been skimming drugs right under Ramses's nose and planning to become the new kings of the hill. Unfortunately for them, their plan was uncovered when Li'l Monk and his partner Omega foiled one of their robberies and killed the perpetrators. One of the shooters was traced back to Benny. Chucky, being Benny's best friend, was naturally a suspect as well. By sheer luck Chucky was able to worm his way out of it, but fate wasn't as kind to Benny. Ramses had Benny executed and Chucky demoted. Things went downhill from there and the next thing Chucky knew, he and Benny were out and Li'l Monk and Omega were in. He hated Li'l Monk for taking his spot, but he also held him responsible for Benny's death. Chucky vowed one day that he would avenge his friend and settle the score with Li'l Monk.

Chucky was brought out of his twisted little thoughts by Maggie handing the laced blunt to him in her limp hand. She had a spaced-out look in her eyes that let him know she was slipping into her zone and he needed to catch up. Chucky held the blunt at eye level, watching the cherry and the end crackle and spark from the crack-cocaine he'd married to the weed. It reminded him of his childhood when his mother had taken him to Coney Island to watch the fireworks. With this thought in his mind, Chucky put the blunt in his mouth and took a deep pull. The smoke rolled over his tongue and down into his lungs, leaving an icy numbness in its wake. A groovy feeling spread throughout Chucky's body and crept up into his face. There was a slight popping noise in his ears and he heard faint trumpets playing "The Star-Spangled Banner." He had officially entered the zone.

Halfway through the laced blunt Chucky was too stuck to move. His head lolled back in ecstasy as he enjoyed the high. Chucky had only been in the chair for a few minutes but it felt like he'd been there for days. His face had gone completely numb and his eyes felt like he could see through walls. There was a tugging at his pants and he managed to compose himself enough to pick his head up and look down. At some point Maggie had crawled between his legs and was working to get his pants undone. She always got horny when she was high. Chucky started to swat her away until she managed to get his pants open and slipped his dick into her waiting mouth.

Maggie took her time running her tongue up and down the sides of Chucky's dick, pausing every so often to tickle the head of it. When it was good and slick she opened her throat and let his shaft explore it.

Chuck felt the head of his dick hit the back of Maggie's throat just before a secret passage opened up and allowed him farther inside. When Maggie swallowed his whole cock and started tickling his balls with her tongue Chucky let out a slight gasp. It wasn't the first blow job Maggie had given him, but that time seemed more passionate than the others.

Slowly, Maggie removed Chucky from her mouth and began to stroke him tenderly, looking up at him with dreamy brown eyes. "How's that feel?"

"That feels real good, baby." Chucky looked down at her with a silly grin plastered across his face.

"I'll bet." Maggie flicked her tongue around the rim of his penis. "You know that young bitch can't make you feel the way I do." She grabbed his cock as if it was the handle of a sword and his balls the hilt, and began squeezing and yanking it, applying a slight amount of pressure. The mixture of pleasure and pain made him swell in her hands. Maggie dipped her head and took him in the back of her throat again. She bobbed up and down ferociously, letting his dick stab her tonsils to the point where she began gagging. Maggie took a minute to catch her breath before spitting on Chucky and repeating the process once more.

"You're playing dirty." Chucky caressed the back of her head.

"Nah, I'm just marking my territory." Maggie gave him a little slurp before releasing his cock and standing up.

Chucky sat in the chair watching Maggie as she wiggled out of the halter and tight skirt. Seeing her standing there in all her chocolate glory reminded Chucky of African art they used to sell on the Avenue. Maggie had big breasts with silver dollar–sized Hershey's kisses for nipples, and they always seemed to be hard. She had a bit of a stomach and a few stretch marks, but the older woman was still stacked enough to entice any man with eyes.

Maggie approached the chair Chucky was sitting in and threw one of her legs over the arm. She lowered herself far enough to where his dick grazed against her pussy, but not far enough to let him enter her. With one hand locked on the back of the chair and the other on Chucky's lap, balancing herself over him, Maggie began swaying back and forth, letting her wet pussy brush over the shaft of his dick. Chucky tried to pull her down all the way, but Maggie resisted.

"Stop playing and let me hit that," Chucky said anxiously.

"You don't want this old pussy, Chucky. Your nose is busted wide open for that young trim," Maggie said playfully before easing away from the chair. Drugs had dulled her skills at most things, but she still knew how to seduce a man.

Chucky grabbed Maggie's waist and pulled her back. "I see you're in a game-playing mood this morning. Well, let me show you how I like to play." He pulled her down on his dick roughly.

Maggie cried out as Chucky's thick cock shoved the curtains of her sweet spot open and invited itself in for a look around. She braced herself against the chair so that he couldn't shove it all in her at one time. Gradually she allowed him in, deeper and deeper still. When Maggie felt the jolt of electricity run up her spine, she knew he had hit her spot. This is when she settled in and did her work.

By then the laced blunt had kicked all the way in and Chucky was fading in and out of himself. The only things he was aware of were that he was high and trying to go balls deep inside of what was feeling like the best shot of pussy he'd ever had. He locked one hand behind Maggie's neck and the other at the small of her back and began stroking her. Maggie's hole was warm and adhered to his dick with almost perfect suction. He could feel her clenching and unclenching her pussy muscles while she rode him. Chucky's vision blurred momentarily and when it cleared he didn't see Maggie riding him, but Persia. With his brain playing tricks on him Chucky thought he heard Persia's mocking laughter. All he wanted to do was make her feel good and remember why she'd loved him, but she laughed at him and this angered Chucky.

Maggie smiled when she felt Chucky pick her up out of the chair, with his dick still planted firmly in her. He was into it now and about to take her where she needed to be. She expected Chucky to pin her against a wall, or circle the room while stoking her, as was his norm, but she was surprised when he dropped her on the floor. Maggie banged her head on the ground and was momentarily dazed. When she looked up she saw Chucky descending on her with a strange look on his face. It wasn't a look of passion, but one of rage.

"You wanna laugh at me? Let's see if you find this shit funny." Chucky swooped in.

Maggie was confused by his sudden change. "Chucky, what are you talking a—" Maggie began but her breath caught in her throat when Chucky entered her. His dick hit like a jackhammer when he plunged to the depths of her nether regions. He began stroking her viciously and grunting obscenities. "Baby, wait. You're hurting me," she tried to tell him, but her pleas fell on deaf ears. She looked into his eyes trying to see where his head was at, but Chucky had completely checked out.

She managed to push him off her and tried to scramble across the floor, but Chucky was on her ass. He grabbed Maggie about the waist and pulled her back toward him. "Yeah, you running from this dick, huh? I'll bet that football nigga don't work your pussy like I do." He forced her head to the floor and entered her from behind. He stoked her so hard Maggie felt like he was trying to liquefy her insides. A barrage of dirty words fell from Chucky's mouth as he approached his climax. Just before he popped he pulled out and sprayed his seed all over Maggie's back. Just as suddenly as Chucky's madness had come it had gone, leaving him breathing heavily, leaning against the couch, and Maggie lying on the floor trying to figure out what had just happened.

Chucky lay on the floor with his head resting against the couch, while he watched Maggie struggle painfully to pull herself into a sitting position. "Damn, that was some good shit, baby."

"Fuck you, Chucky," Maggie spat. She touched her fingers to her pussy to make sure she wasn't bleeding.

Chucky gave her a look. "After the fucking I just put on you I'd think you'd be a little more appreciative. What the fuck is your problem?"

Maggie's eyes flashed with anger. "Nigga, you can't be serious." She climbed to her feet and limped toward the bathroom.

Chucky got off the floor and went after her, grabbing Maggie's arm when she was just shy of the bathroom door. "Girl, where the fuck is your head at this morning?"

"I could ask you the same thing," Maggie shot back.

"And what's that supposed to mean?" Chucky asked with a genuinely confused expression on his face.

Maggie shook her head sadly. "That young bitch has got you so caught up that you don't know whether you're coming or going."

"You still got your panties in a bunch over Persia? I told you I go that under control," Chucky told her.

"So much under control that you don't even know who you're fucking?" Maggie snorted. "I hear that hot shit, Chucky. Let me lay some game on you; I didn't let you drag me and my sister from Philadelphia to New York to have us die in the streets or go to prison because your head ain't in the game no more. Since you brought your little girlfriend on board she's been a liability. Do what you gotta do and get rid of the bitch."

Chucky felt like Maggie was trying to give him an order and he didn't like it. "And what if I decide I wanna keep her around awhile longer?"

"Then I'll do what your tender-ass heart is keeping you from doing," Maggie said seriously before disappearing into the bathroom.

# CHAPTER 5

Even with the delay having to wait for Rissa to change, Persia still made good time getting to the funeral. She'd expected them to be riding in Chucky's BMW, but instead they rode in a slightly dinged-up blue Buick that sported temporary plates in the rear window. According to Rissa it had been a gift to her from Chucky. Where a drug addict got the money for a car, even a used one, was a mystery to Persia, but it rode smooth and the radio worked so she wasn't complaining.

Rissa tried to make small talk with Persia on the ride over to break the awkward silence. Most of it revolved around Chucky. Her tone when she spoke of him reminded Persia eerily of how she sounded when she was caught up in his spell. From what Persia could tell Rissa was wise enough to know Chucky was a piece of shit, but she also had feelings for him. Persia was willing to bet that somewhere in the back of Rissa's mind she thought that she could change Chucky. The poor girl had a hard lesson coming her way in the near future.

Persia was surprised at the number of people who had turned out, especially considering that Karen wasn't the most well-liked person in the neighborhood. Persia scanned the crowd for familiar faces. She didn't want to go in alone. Standing off to the side smoking cigarettes were her old friends Meeka and Ty. Persia, Karen, Meeka, and Ty had been best friends until things went sour and the group had been divided. She and Karen had been enemies toward the end, but she was still taking her death hard and could only imagine what Meeka and Ty were going through, especially Ty.

"Chucky order you to come inside with me, too?" Persia asked Rissa sarcastically.

"Yeah, but I think I'll pass. I didn't know her so I don't think it'd be appropriate," Rissa lied. She might not have known Karen, but she had seen her before. Rissa had been there the day Chucky tracked Karen down and killed her. Chucky beat Karen like a dog before raping her over and over. His assault on her was so vicious that Rissa was actually relieved when Chucky finally killed her. He'd left Karen's body to rot in the apartment but it had been Rissa who secretly called the police to tell them where they could find the body. That day constantly haunted her and seeing Karen in the casket would be nothing but a grim reminder of how little Rissa had done to try to stop what had happened to her.

"Cool. I guess I'll see you when I come out." Persia slid from the car and joined the crowd on the curb.

Ty spotted Persia first. She was an itty bitty thing with dark skin and short hair. She looked like a little girl on her way to church in her floral dress and patent leather shoes. She threw her frail arms open and pulled Persia in for a hug. "What's good, P?" she greeted Persia in her squeaky voice.

"Missing your little ass. Are you staying out of trouble?" Persia asked with a smile.

"I'd be lying if I told you that I was, but I'm doing better than most," Ty said.

Persia looked over at Meeka who had been staring at her the whole time she spoke with Ty. You could almost feel the tension in the air. When Persia and Karen were beefing it split their group. Ty never really picked a side. She stopped hanging with Persia to keep Karen from getting mad at her, but Ty would still speak to Persia when she saw her in the streets, and even called to check on her while she was in rehab. Meeka sided with Karen. Though she too still spoke to Persia when they saw each other in the streets, there never seemed to be any love in her tone. It was like she was speaking more out of being civil than actually wanting to keep ties with Persia. Meeka and Karen had always been closer than any of the others, so Persia kind of expected it, but it didn't make it hurt any less. The girls were like the sisters she never had and losing their friendship was almost as painful as kicking her addiction had been.

The awkward silence lingered for a few moments longer before Persia decided to be the bigger person and speak first. "Listen, Meeka—" Persia began, but Meeka cut her off when she grabbed Persia in a tight embrace. The sobs Persia could feel racking Meeka's body as she buried her head in her chest said what her mouth couldn't. In light of why they were all there, the beef between the two girls was unimportant.

"She's gone, P. They took our girl," Meeka finally managed to get out between sobs.

"I know." Persia rubbed her back. "I know." Meeka had always been the most emotionally removed of the group so it was strange seeing her so broken up.

After a few moments Meeka was finally able to compose herself. "So, how's recovery been treating you?"

"It's a pain in the ass. Everything that I used to love to do is now 'bad for me.'" Persia made air quotations with her fingers.

"Even weed?" Ty asked.

"Especially weed," Persia confirmed. "My counselors say it's a gateway to heavier shit."

Ty shook her head sadly. "That sucks. I don't know what I'd do if I couldn't smoke chronic. How can you stand it?"

"It's really not that bad. I mean, at first I missed getting blazed but after a while it got easier. Since I been clean and sober I been able to focus on more important things like school," Persia told her.

"I hear you're leaving for college soon," Meeka said.

"God willing, I'll be enrolled in somebody's university next year. Being that I took some time off I won't get my diploma until January so it kinda put me behind schedule," Persia said.

"Don't matter if you get there late, so long as you get there," Ty said.

"Amen to that," Meeka chimed in. "You know, Persia, I'm glad to see you're doing good again. You know there was a time when some of us thought . . ." She let her words trail off.

"Yeah, me too, Meeka, but it's gonna take more than a crack habit to take me out of the game," Persia joked. It was the first time the three of them had laughed together in a while and for a minute it felt like old times.

"So, when is the last time you saw Chucky?" Ty asked, unintentionally darkening the mood.

"I haven't seen him since the night he left me for dead," Persia lied.

"Good riddance," Meeka spat. "I was never a fan of his. A nigga that handsome always comes with baggage."

"Is that why all the dudes you fuck are butt ugly?" Ty asked with a smirk.

"Fuck you," Meeka said playfully.

"Persia, can I ask you something?" Ty suddenly became serious.

"Sure, what's up?"

"Well, I don't mean to pry and you can tell me to mind my fucking business if you don't want to answer." Ty was trying ease into it.

"Girl, just ask the fucking question!" Meeka snapped. She knew what Ty wanted to ask and was a bit curious herself.

"Okay, okay." Ty rolled her eyes at Meeka. "Persia, we all heard about what happened, you know, when Chucky left you in the house." She shook her head sadly. "All them people ended up dead because of Chucky's snake ass, but you survived. I . . . we"—she glanced at Meeka—"were just wondering how you got away."

Persia took a few moments before answering. That night was still somewhat of a sensitive subject. "Honestly? I have no idea." Persia absently ran her hand up and down her arm as she recalled the night. Chucky had them held up at his aunt and uncle's place in Mount Vernon while he plotted their next move. Chucky was running the streets doing God only knew what and had left Persia at the house. She had been high out of her mind on crack when the men came looking for Chucky to hand down the death sentence that had been passed on him. When they couldn't find Chucky, everyone in the house was made to pay for his crimes. "I can remember hearing the most terrible screams as all those people were cut down like dogs, and thinking how I didn't want to die in a crack house."

"So what happened?" Meeka asked.

Persia shrugged. "God stepped in. One minute I'm fleeing for my life out of a second-story bathroom window and the next I wake up in the hospital in more pain than I would've thought humanly possible. I was in bad shape when they brought me in. Apparently I had fallen, broken a few bones, cracked my skull, and had some internal bleeding. They wasn't sure if I would make it, but through some miracle I lived."

"How did you get to the hospital?" Ty asked.

"That's the craziest part of the story. According to the doctors a man brought me into the emergency room unconscious and half dead. He waited until they stabilized me then disappeared. The police searched high and low, but my savior vanished without a trace. It's like he never existed, but the fact that I'm here to tell the story says that he did. I hope to find him one day so I can thank him for giving me a second chance."

"Damn, you're one lucky bitch!" Ty said.

"Nah, I'm not lucky. I'm blessed," Persia said seriously.

"Well, we're glad you didn't cash out," Meeka said, giving her a hug.

"Me too." Persia laughed.

"Is that Meeka over there?" someone called. A chubby young man with thick glasses came ambling over. He adjusted his frames to make sure he had the right woman. "What's good, baby sis?"

"Hey, Boogie." Meeka greeted him with a hug. Boogie was short for Boogie Blind, a nickname he had acquired because of his poor eyesight. "What you doing here?"

"I came to pay my respects," Boogie said, hiking his oversized jeans up so that his boxers weren't showing.

"I didn't even know you knew Karen," Meeka said.

"I knew her in passing, but her mother and my mother go back a taste. Mama-love insisted on coming so I rolled too to support her," Boogie said.

"Boogie, you know it always fucks me up how you run around like the hardest niggas in the streets, but you're really a mama's boy," Meeka teased him.

"You only get one mother in life, Meeka. Never forget that." Boogie pointed the water bottle he was holding at her for emphasis.

"What's in the bottle, Boogie? I know it ain't no water." Ty eyeballed the slightly murky liquid in the bottle.

Boogie gave the bottle a shake and smirked. "This here is grown folk's business."

"Well shit, I can use something to take the edge off right about now. Let your girl get a sip." Ty reached for the bottle, but Boogie moved it away.

"Shorty, this ain't no liquor. What I got in this bottle might take you on a trip you can't come back from and I don't want that on my conscience," Boogie warned. Just then his eyes landed on Persia as if he was noticing her for the first time. "Yo, don't I know you from somewhere?"

"You probably seen Persia around the neighborhood. She used to run with us and Karen," Meeka answered for her.

"Nah, that ain't where I remember her face from." Boogie tapped his chin. Then it hit him. "I think I saw you in one of them gossip papers or something. Might've been the *Enquirer*."

"Boogie, you don't strike me as the type who reads those types of things," Ty said.

Boogie shrugged. "My moms always gets them from the supermarket and leaves them in the bathroom. The articles are mostly bullshit, but it makes for good reading when you're taking a dump. If I remember, you're that football nigga's girlfriend, right?"

"No, Vaughn and I are just friends," Persia corrected him.

"Well I wish I had your kinda friends. I hear that boy just signed for like $80 million!"

*$16 million.* Persia wanted to correct him, but instead just shrugged as if she didn't know.

"Stop acting like a groupie, Boogie," Meeka scolded him.

"Hey, ain't every day I get to stand next to the girlfriend of a celebrity," Boogie said honestly.

"I'm not his . . . You know what, never mind." Persia sighed.

"Bernard, bring your ass on!" An older woman wearing a large church hat called from the funeral home doorway.

"I'm coming, Ma," Boogie called back with an attitude. He hated when people called him by his government name. "Let me get up in here before this old bird makes me show my ass out here. You coming through later, Meeka? Christian has got a birthday coming up so we gonna do something for him at the spot tonight."

"That sounds like a plan. I'm gonna hang on the block for a while in case Karen's mom needs me to do something, but I'll slide through the spot later tonight."

"That's a bet. If she ain't doing nothing"—Boogie thumbed at Persia—"bring the celebrity with you, too. I'm gone." He saluted Meeka and went to escort his mother inside.

"Boogie is off the chain," Meeka said after he'd gone.

"Tell me about it," Persia added. "I seen him before with those kids from the Polo Grounds. I hear they're out here robbing and killing everything moving. Meeka, I didn't know you knew them dudes like that."

"Meeka is practically a member of their gang," Ty volunteered, which got her a sharp look from Meeka.

"It ain't that serious, Persia. Boogie and Christian just let me get a little money with them when I'm strapped for cash. No big deal." Meeka downplayed it. In truth she was getting in deeper than she let on with Boogie's crew of hitters. When Meeka was down and out Christian and Boogie had been the only ones who helped her stay above the poverty line by allowing her to earn her keep with their team. "But enough about Boogie and them." She changed the subject. "What's up with you and this Vaughn cat? I wasn't gonna ask you about it, but since Boogie already brought it up, spill."

"Oh my goodness." Persia sighed. "Vaughn and I are just getting to know each other and people are acting like we're engaged! Why is everybody making such a big deal out of some pictures a few thirsty-ass tabloids posted? They're not even credible sources."

"Ah, I saw the picture of you two in the *Daily News*. I think they're pretty credible," Meeka said. "Look, Persia, no need to be modest with us. We ain't no haters. After all you've been through you deserve a come up more than anybody. I'm just happy to see you back on top of your game. You can give us all the dirty details later, but we should probably get inside. Looks like they're about to start."

Persia, Meeka, and Ty were able to find three empty seats a few rows back from the front of the funeral home, not far from where Karen's family was sitting. Persia thought about approaching

Karen's mother to offer her condolences, but she didn't look like she was in the shape to receive them. She was in bad shape, wailing uncontrollably and crying rivers of tears. A time or two Charlie and his uncle had to restrain her from rushing the casket. Persia could only imagine the pain a mother experienced when she had to bury her child. Seeing Karen's mom all broken up like that made Persia think of her mother and the grief she had put her through over the past year.

For as long as Persia could remember her mother had always been her rock. When Persia's father, Face, went to prison it was Michelle who stepped up. Long before she met and married Persia's stepfather, Richard, it had been Michelle who held the family down. Even when Persia had run off on a crack bender with Chucky and gave her mother her ass to kiss, Michelle refused to give up on her. Persia couldn't see it when she was caught up, but being clean gave her a whole new perspective and an even greater respect for her mother.

They came to the point during the service where the pastor had invited the friends and family to say their final farewells to Karen. Persia stood to fall in step with Ty and Meeka as they filed out to the aisle. One by one, friends and family said their good-byes. Meeka handled it like a G, but Ty went to pieces over the casket. She fell on the floor and began crying uncontrollably. Two funeral home employees pulled her to her feet and helped her to a chair, where Meeka tried with little success to console her. It was Persia's turn to say her good-byes.

Persia had been purposely avoiding looking at the casket, but she couldn't put it off any longer. The moment she looked down at Karen her eyes welled with tears. She'd heard the killer did a number on Karen but seeing her up close told the tale of how much she must've suffered before she died. Karen's face was swollen, either from the beating or post-death bloating. Persia wasn't sure which. They'd caked her face with makeup, but some of the bruising was too deep to do more than tone down. On her head sat a cheap wig that nobody had even taken the time to style. The young woman in that box was not the girl Persia had grown up doing dirt with. It couldn't be.

Persia felt ill. Her stomach lurched and she knew she was going to have an embarrassing episode if she didn't get out of the funeral home. She doubled back the way she came, shoving people out of her way as she tried desperately to make it to the exit before she threw up. She was in such a rush that she wasn't paying attention to where she was going and bumped into what felt like a brick wall made of flesh and bone. She cast her eyes up to offer an apology and found herself at a loss for words.

# CHAPTER 6

"Hey," Li'l Monk said once he was finally able to find his voice.

"Hi," Persia offered back.

"Been awhile, huh?"

"Yeah, quite awhile. I wasn't in the best shape the last time we bumped into each other." She thought back to her time running with Chucky and how she must've looked to Li'l Monk and everybody else who had known her.

"You look like you bounced back nicely." Li'l Monk let his eyes roam over her.

Persia blushed. "Taking it one day at a time trying to get my life back in order."

"So I've been told."

"I'll bet the whole hood is talking about me," Persia said, embarrassed.

"People are always gonna talk. It's when they stop talking that you should start worrying, Princess P," Li'l Monk said reassuringly.

For the first time that whole day Persia laughed. "I haven't heard you call me that in long time."

"That means you need to come around more often."

"I wish. My life has been extremely hectic between school and everything else," Persia told him.

"I can only imagine. I was glad when I heard you went back to school. You always were smarter than most," Li'l Monk said.

"If I were that smart then I wouldn't have gotten myself into all that bullshit." Persia huffed.

"Ain't no shame in making mistakes, Persia, but there's plenty of shame in not learning from them," Li'l Monk said in a serious tone.

"Jesus, you sound like my stepfather." Persia rolled her eyes.

"How is old stiff-ass Rich? He still walking around with that broomstick up his ass?" Li'l Monk joked.

"You are terrible. Richard isn't that bad."

"This coming from the same chick who used to give him shit every chance she got?" Li'l Monk raised an eyebrow.

"Yeah, yeah, I know. I probably gave Richard more hell than he deserved, but sometimes people can change your opinions of them. Richard changed mine of him during my recovery. Next to my mother nobody went harder for me than him. There were a few times when I wanted to quit, but Richard wouldn't let me. He pushed me to do better, to want better."

"Well I'm glad that you guys are getting along now. I wish I could say the same about my dad," Li'l Monk said, thinking of his last remaining parent and namesake.

"Y'all still at it?" Persia asked. She wasn't really surprised. The father and son had been butting heads since Persia and Li'l Monk were kids and things got worse once Big Monk got strung out on drugs.

"For as long as he's out here on that bullshit we're always gonna be at it," Li'l Monk said.

Persia took his hand in hers. "Li'l Monk, I know Monk hasn't been the best dad, but try to be patient with him. Monk is an addict and when you're caught up with drugs they can make you lose focus of who you are. Give him time and he'll come around."

"If you say so, Persia."

"I know so. Take it from somebody who was once a slave to addiction."

Their moment was broken up when just behind them one of the mourners collapsed in the aisle, crying and reminding Persia and Li'l Monk of why they were there.

"Sorry about what happened to Karen," Li'l Monk offered.

"Yeah, a real tragedy." Persia reflexively cast a glance back at the casket. "You know, even though Karen and me were going through a rough patch it still fucked me up when I heard she died. I'll always feel like there was so much that went unsaid between us."

"My mom used to always say if you give people flowers while they're living you don't have to weep for them when they pass." Li'l Monk recalled the quote his mother would always recite when someone passed.

"That's some very good advice," Persia agreed. Remembering she still had to meet Vaughn she looked at her watch and checked the time. "I gotta make moves, but it was good seeing you."

"Good seeing you too, Persia. We need to link up one of these days," Li'l Monk suggested.

Persia would've liked to have taken Li'l Monk up on his offer, but in light of Chucky popping back up in her life she wasn't sure it was such a good idea. "We'll see." She mustered a weak smile.

Li'l Monk felt slighted, but didn't show it. "I guess I'll catch you when I catch you then, Princess P."

"See you around, Li'l Monk." Persia wrapped her arms around his thick neck and hugged him.

Li'l Monk stood there watching Persia as she walked up the aisle and disappeared through the funeral home doors. Long after she had gone his heart was still aflutter. Li'l Monk had loved Persia ever since they were kids, but the feeling was one sided. Despite his best efforts to impress her she still barely noticed him. Persia looked at Li'l Monk more like a big brother than a potential lover and he was reminded of it every time she brushed him off.

Li'l Monk had considered confessing to her that it had been he who spared her life the night of the massacre at the crack house in Mount Vernon. Ramses had ordered them to kill everyone in the house, but he couldn't bring himself to hurt Persia. Even strung out and looking like death warmed over she was still the most beautiful girl he had ever seen and his heart wouldn't let him hurt her. When Persia fell from the bathroom window trying to escape the death sentence passed on the house, Li'l Monk feared he'd lost her for good. He knelt in the snow, weeping as he cradled Persia's withered frame in his arms. Li'l Monk had never been very big on religion but that night he prayed to God to spare Persia, and to his surprise God answered him and Persia stirred. Li'l Monk abandoned the mission and rushed Persia to the nearest hospital. Huck called him a fool for risking his neck over a crackhead, but he didn't understand. To Li'l Monk Persia was more than just a smoker; she was the center of his universe.

Had Li'l Monk revealed all this to Persia then just maybe she would've been a bit more receptive to his feelings, but he didn't want her to love him out of obligation; he wanted her to love him because she felt it in her heart.

When Li'l Monk was done daydreaming about something he would never have he turned his mind back to the business at hand: Charlie. He needed answers that only his friend could provide. He looked down to where Charlie had been sitting with his family, but he was no longer there. His mother and uncles were but there was no sign of Charlie. Though Li'l Monk didn't see Charlie he saw Sophie, glaring at him with her nostrils flared.

"What was that all about?" Sophie asked as she and Li'l Monk walked toward the exit. They'd wanted to leave before the procession started making their way out with the casket.

"What was what about?" He faked ignorance.

Sophie stopped and gave him a look. "You know what I'm talking about. I saw you and the little Miss Thang making goo-goo eyes at each other."

Li'l Monk sucked his teeth. "Wasn't nobody making eyes, Sophie. Me and Persia just haven't seen each other in a while so we were catching up."

Sophie snorted. "Looked like more than that to me. You all smirking in her face and shit." She mimicked the love-struck look he'd been wearing when he was talking to Persia.

"Sophie, how come you get your panties in a bunch over every broad I speak to in the streets?" Li'l Monk asked.

"Not every broad, Li'l Monk. Only the ones you were once in love with," Sophie shot back.

"That was a childhood crush." Li'l Monk downplayed it.

Sophie cupped his face in her hands and looked him directly in the eyes. "We've known each other for a long time. We were friends long before we became lovers, so don't put me in a position to think poorly of you by trying to play on my intelligence. Now I know how you feel about Persia and though I might not like it I've learned to accept it, but don't you ever forget that what she saw as trash has always been my treasure. You understand?"

Li'l Monk nodded.

"Good, because I'd hate to have to beat the breaks off that bitch for fucking with what's mine." Sophie gave him a peck on the lips and strode toward the exit.

Li'l Monk followed his lady outside and took a deep breath. The fresh air felt good after spending so much time breathing the smells of death and sadness that clung to the funeral home. The sidewalk was now crowded with mourners who had filed out, while cars idled double parked at the curb waiting to follow the procession to the cemetery. Li'l Monk saw Omega leaning against a familiar black SUV. Huck sat behind the wheel, smoking a cigarette, while Omega spoke to Ramses through the open back window. Li'l Monk nodded in greeting. Huck returned the gesture, but Ramses did not, which Li'l Monk found odd. He was about to approach the vehicle when Ramses gave Huck the signal to pull off.

"What the fuck is his problem?" Li'l Monk approached Omega. He watched as Ramses's truck hit the corner and vanished.

"Job-related stress. Don't take it personal." Omega downplayed it.

"So what brought him out here? I thought Ramses don't fuck with funerals," Li'l Monk said.

"He don't, but he had to bring me a message that couldn't be delivered over the phone," Omega told him.

"What's good?" Li'l Monk asked.

"Something light. A nigga who we do business with is out of bounds and Ramses needs him put back in bounds."

"Well you know I'm with you if there's dirt to be done," Li'l Monk said, ready to ride out with his partner.

"Not this time. Ramses wants me to put somebody else on it," Omega confessed.

This took Li'l Monk by surprise. "What's the matter, my gun don't go off loud enough for him anymore?"

"Nah, it ain't that. We're upper management now, so he don't want us getting dirty unless we got to," Omega lied. In truth Ramses never gave

Omega an explanation as to why he didn't want Li'l Monk involved. He just specified that Li'l Monk was to have no part in the job. Of course Omega didn't want to tell his friend that and further bruise his ego. He was aware that Ramses had been feeding Li'l Monk with a long-handled spoon since the Mr. D situation. Though Li'l Monk never came out and said it, Omega knew him well enough to know that he felt slighted by it.

"If you say so, O," Li'l Monk said, not really believing the excuse Omega offered. "I'll catch you on the block." He gave Omega dap and went to catch up with Sophie.

Li'l Monk walked away with mixed emotions about his exchange with Omega. Something was obviously going on. Li'l Monk didn't like to be kept in the dark and it especially bothered him coming from someone who he trusted with his life night in and night out. It was very possible that Omega was as clueless as he acted, but it was also possible that Ramses had ordered him to play his hand close to his chest. Either way Li'l Monk wasn't feeling it. He spared a glance over his shoulder and caught King Tut watching him and smirking. If Ramses's abrupt departure and Omega being cryptic wasn't enough to tell Li'l Monk that something was wrong, the look Tut was giving him confirmed it.

# PART II

## *ULTERIOR MOTIVES*

# CHAPTER 7

After the funeral Li'l Monk and Sophie went back to her place where they changed out of their funeral clothes and put some weed in the air. It had been a trying day for both of them and they needed to mellow out.

After smoking a blunt they jumped in a taxi and went to BBQ's on Seventy-second Street to grab a bite. The whole time they ate Li'l Monk's mind seemed to be elsewhere. Sophie inquired as to what was troubling him. He shrugged it off as if he was okay, but he wasn't. He was thinking about the strange treatment he had received from Ramses. Lately Ramses was becoming increasingly distant. Li'l Monk knew he was under an enormous amount of pressure over the escalating beef with the Clarks and the deteriorating relationships with several of their allied crews, but Li'l Monk felt like there was something else. His dad had always taught him to trust his gut and his gut told him that something was brewing.

Sophie wanted to catch a movie afterward, but Li'l Monk had to get back on the clock. He had been away from the block all day and felt disconnected. He needed to plug back into the streets and see what was going on in the neighborhood.

The first person he saw when he got out of the taxi on the corner of 138th and Seventh Avenue was Droopy. They called him Droopy because his sagging jowls and lazy eyes made him look like the cartoon dog Droopy. Droopy was a thirteen-year-old juvenile delinquent who had been running the streets since the time he could walk. Droopy was a troublesome kid who was likely to be murdered or end up in prison if someone didn't bring some direction into his life. Li'l Monk had become his unofficial mentor and the only one who gave enough of a shit to try to keep him out of trouble. Droopy reminded Li'l Monk a lot of himself at that age, alone and trying to navigate the world without getting killed or starving to death. Li'l Monk wasn't much in the way of a role model, but he did what he could to keep the young boy fed and alive.

As usual Droopy was dressed in jeans that were at least two sizes too big and a New York Giants jersey that swallowed his frame. A black du-rag was tied so tight around his head that it pulled his eyes back making him look Chinese. He was snacking on a bag of BBQ potato chips, with a pineapple Tropical Fantasy soda sticking out of his back pocket.

Li'l Monk watched as a fiend approached Droopy and said something to him before slipping Droopy what looked like some crumpled bills. Droopy gave a cautious look around before digging in the bag of chips and handing the fiend something, before snatching the money and shooing him along. If Li'l Monk couldn't depend on anyone else to be out chasing money twenty-four/seven, he could depend on Droopy. Ever since Li'l Monk put him down with the team all Droopy did was chase paper.

"What I tell you about making sales out in the open like that?" Li'l Monk walked up on him.

"Man, ain't no cop gonna catch me in them flat-ass shoes they gotta wear." Droopy gave him dap. "Besides that, ain't been no signs of police in the hood for the last few hours unless they're just passing through on their way downtown. They got their hands full."

"What's going on downtown that made it legal to sell drugs in Harlem today?" Li'l Monk asked.

"Some teacher at a school on 108th Street lost his job and didn't take too kindly to it, so he came back with a machine gun and took the school hostage," Droopy informed him.

"With the kids in it?" Li'l Monk asked in shock.

"Word life," Droopy confirmed. "I heard they got SWAT teams out there and all that. Because it ain't been no cops it's been like Candy Land in the hood all day. The block been jumping! No disrespect to them kids, but I'm trying to get this money while I can."

"You got a point," Li'l Monk agreed. "You seen Omega and them out here?"

"I seen that bitch-ass nigga Tut ride off in a cab about an hour ago, but Omega is on the stoop." Droopy pointed across the street.

"I'm about to go check him in a few. How things been looking out here? Any problems?"

"Nah, everything been quiet. It's so much money flowing ain't nobody had time to beef."

Li'l Monk nodded. "That's a good thing. Beef is always bad for business. I'm gonna slide over here and check O right quick. You gonna be good over here by yourself?"

"I'm straight, my nigga. I'm on this money," Droopy assured him.

"A'ight, but still keep your eyes peeled. Anybody roll through the hood you don't recognize, let me know," Li'l Monk told him.

Droopy laughed. "If a nigga come through here I don't recognize the only thing I'm gonna let you know is where to find the body." Droopy lifted his oversized jersey and showed Li'l Monk the Beretta shoved in his pants. From the oversized clip he estimated it held about thirty rounds.

"Where the fuck did you get that?" Li'l Monk questioned.

"Don't ask questions you really don't want the answers to." Droopy winked and disappeared down the block.

Just as Droopy had said, Li'l Monk found Omega sitting on the stoop of one of the buildings they kept a stash apartment in. He was sitting on the steps between the legs of a chocolate-colored girl who was braiding his dreads into plaits. Li'l Monk thought he knew her face, but couldn't place it.

Flanking the stoop were three young shooters who Omega had taken to running with lately. There was a time when Omega was a cat who moved with as few people as possible, but lately he kept an entourage around him. Dudes in the streets were getting murdered left and right and he wasn't taking any chances. The dudes with him were cruddy cats who would let their guns blast on command.

The eyes of the young shooters turned in Li'l Monk's direction as he approached. He nodded in greeting before giving Omega dap. "Sup wit' you, O?"

"Ain't shit, just out here enjoying life." Omega smiled, taking a sip from the Hennessy bottle that had been resting on the step near his leg. He wiped a bit of spillage from his chin with the back of his hand and offered the bottle to Li'l Monk.

Li'l Monk accepted the bottle and took a deep swig. It was his first drink of the day and the cognac's slow burn made his nerves come alive. "I needed that." He handed the bottle back to Omega.

"I imagine so after this morning. That funeral was sad as hell," Omega said.

"Yeah, death is never easy, especially when it hits so close to home." Li'l Monk thought back to seeing Karen in a casket.

"Man, I heard they did shorty dirty, hit her like twenty times," a young man wearing a blue Dodge cap said. This was Blue; he was new to the fold and had a bad habit of saying the wrong thing at the wrong time.

"Nah, it wasn't twenty times; it was only like five," a kid who wore his hair in braids corrected him. His name was Paulie and he was just as ignorant as Blue.

Li'l Monk gave them a dirty look that expressed his displeasure with the nature of their conversation.

"My fault, I forgot that was ya peeps," Blue offered by way of an apology.

"Blue, you always saying the wrong thing at the wrong time." A bald youth spoke up. His name was Dre and he had arguably the most common sense out of the knuckleheads Omega kept around him. "No disrespect, my nigga," he told Li'l Monk.

"It's all good. If I felt disrespected you'd know about it," Li'l Monk assured him.

Dre smirked, but didn't reply to the statement. "I'm about to go to the store to get something to drink." He stepped off the stoop and started up the block. Blue and Paulie looked to Omega for the nod of approval before falling in step behind Dre.

"The blind leading the blind." Li'l Monk shook his head. "Where did you dig those knuckleheads up again?"

"Ramses recruited them. I just put the niggas to work. Blue is kind of a dick, but Dre and Paulie are okay," Omega said.

"I don't like either one of them," Li'l Monk said.

Omega laughed. "That's no surprise. You don't like anybody. You need to learn to relax."

"That's kinda hard to do when niggas are getting their wigs pushed back on a nightly basis. How shit been looking out here today?"

Omega shrugged. "All quiet, except for the crackheads running back and forth. The streets been good to us today."

"Droopy told me. How much we clock?" Li'l Monk asked.

"Enough for us to call it an early night and have a little fun." Omega gave him a wink and rested his hand on the thigh of the girl who was braiding his hair. "This is a friend of mine, Stacy," he said, introducing the girl.

Li'l Monk nodded in greeting.

"Stacy dances at that new spot they got down on 116th Street, the after-hours joint. I was thinking we could go through and pop a bottle or two," Omega told him.

Li'l Monk knew just what Omega meant by that. "Nah, I'm good. You go do ya thing."

"Stop acting like that, Li'l Monk. The block ain't gonna go anywhere if you leave it for a few hours. You been wound up tighter than a thong on a fat bitch lately and you need to blow off some steam before you hurt somebody. Let's go look at some ass and titties."

"Yeah, Li'l Monk. Tonight is amateur night and I got a friend named Tiffany who's coming through to do her thing. I think you'll like her," Stacy said as if she knew Li'l Monk well enough to know what he liked and he didn't.

"I got a girl," Li'l Monk told her.

"And she's got a man so it's an equal playing field," Stacy shot back.

Li'l Monk still didn't look convinced.

"Stacy, baby, do me a solid and go upstairs to the spot and grab my jacket. I need to holla at my man for a minute," Omega said.

Stacy quickly caught on. "Okay, Omega." She got up and went into the building.

"What's up with you lately, dawg?" Omega asked once Stacy had gone.

"I just got a lot on my mind lately, O. That's all," Li'l Monk responded.

"Li'l Monk, I dig it, since the bodies started dropping things been tense for all of us. But you know what? Death is a part of the game we chose to play. For as long as we out here on these corners there's always gonna be somebody gunning for us. Stressing ain't gonna change shit. What that nigga Jay-Z said? 'Fuck tomorrow, as long as the night before was sweet!'" He hoisted his bottle of Hennessy, splashing liquor on himself and Li'l Monk.

For the first time all day Li'l Monk laughed. "You wild as hell, O."

"Call me what you want, but you know I'm right, Li'l Monk. Man, we ain't little niggas hustling no more; we run the block! These are supposed to be some of the best times of our lives. It's time we started living accordingly, and that means having some fucking fun. Besides, I been trying to fuck this bitch Stacy for weeks and I need you to run interference with her homegirl while I crack."

Li'l Monk shook his head. "I knew you had an agenda."

"Don't I always?" Omega asked with a smirk. "Not for nothing, you might even enjoy yourself. I've seen her friend Tiffany and that's a bad little bitch!"

"O, I'll hold you down, but I ain't cheating on Sophie, especially with no stripper bitch," Li'l Monk told him.

"It's only cheating if you get caught." Omega laughed. "But on some G shit, I don't care if you fuck her or read the bitch bedtime stories as long as you keep her busy long enough for me to get mine."

Omega and Li'l Monk continued to sip Hennessy on the stoop and lay plans for the rest of their night. They were deep in conversation when Li'l Monk spotted a man with a hood pulled over his head walking in their direction.

"On point," Li'l Monk whispered to Omega, before drawing his trusty Desert Eagle. He didn't point it, but made sure that it was visible. Li'l Monk kept his eyes on the hooded man as he drew closer.

The hooded man drew to a stop when he saw the gun in Li'l Monk's hand. "Easy, fellas," he said with the faintest trace of an accent. He raised his hands to show they were empty. The backs of them were covered in tattoos written in a foreign language. Moving very slowly he pushed the hood from his head and revealed the face hiding beneath. He was an attractive man with an angular chin, and skin the color of unprocessed chocolate. The same kind of tattoos that covered his hands also covered his neck from collar to jaw. Kinky hair that looked like it hadn't seen a comb in a while covered his head. On both his cheeks, just below his eyes, were what looked like small burns but upon closer inspection you could see that they were brands of some kind. Eyes so dark that they reflected no light drank in Li'l Monk and Omega. "I'm not looking for any trouble."

Omega rose from the stoop and regarded the man. "What you're looking for and what you've found are two different things. State your business, or make your peace with God." He glanced at Li'l Monk, who was ready to pop off at a moment's notice.

The dark-skinned man assessed both of them and deduced they were both killers, but being that Li'l Monk was the only one who appeared to be armed he was the immediate threat so it was him who he addressed. "I'm looking for a dude named Monk."

"Well you've found him." Li'l Monk stepped forward. "Whether that's a good or bad thing remains to be seen."

The dark-skinned man sized him up and smirked. "Unless time moved in reverse while I was away, you're a little young to be the Monk I'm looking for. Sorry to have wasted your time." He turned to walk away, but Li'l Monk stopped him.

"What you want with my pops?" Li'l Monk called after him. "He owe you money or something?"

The dark-skinned man stopped and turned back. "Nah, nothing like that. I just came home from a bid and a mutual friend on the inside suggested I look Monk up when I got back into the world."

"My daddy ain't got no friends," Li'l Monk said.

"Well, Face seems to think different," the dark-skinned man said.

Face was a name that hadn't been spoken on the streets in quite a while. Face was Persia's father and had been like an uncle to Li'l Monk. He had been Big Monk's best friend and business partner back in the days. When Face was on the streets he ran the neighborhood, but he was currently serving fifteen to life for killing a man. It had been a self-defense shooting but because of Face's reputation the jury rejected that defense and he blew trial, which was what led to his lengthy sentence.

"You know my uncle?" Li'l Monk asked.

"We shared a cell for a time," the dark-skinned man said, but you could tell there was something more to it. "One day when you ain't feeling so aggressive," he said, and glanced at the gun, "I'll give you the rundown, but for right now I need you to get word to your dad that I need to holla at him. It's important."

"And who should I say is looking for him?" Li'l Monk asked.

"Tell him Kunta came calling," the dark-skinned man told him and headed back the way he came.

"What was that all about?" Omega asked.

Omega watched Kunta hit the corner and vanish. "I don't know, but I'm gonna find out."

# CHAPTER 8

Chucky cruised in his candy red BMW through the crowded New York streets with all the windows down. A slight chill had settled over the city when the sun went down, but it didn't bother him. He needed to smell the stale city air and hear the sounds of the streets to let him know that he was officially home.

He knew that he was taking a big risk by parading himself out in the open like that, but it was a necessary evil. He had something that he needed to deal with that would require a personal touch. To accomplish his task, he needed to put his ear to the ground and gather a bit of information. There was a time when he could've tapped any number of resources for information, but these days there was only one person he could depend on to keep him abreast of what was going on. This was what made him desperate enough to gamble with his life and venture back into the lion's den.

Maggie sat in the passenger seat, in and out of a nod. After their earlier session Chucky had gone out and scored them a bottle of cheap cognac and some beers. He told her it was a reward for how she had put it down when they were fucking, but it was really a way for him to keep her more under control. Maggie could smoke or snort up anything you put in front of her and still walk a straight line, but she had no head for liquor.

His newest accomplice had been talking real reckless lately and Chucky wasn't feeling it. Maggie had a sharp tongue whether she was drunk or sober and Chucky normally ignored her, or slapped her around to remind her who was running the show, but when she started kicking dirt on Persia it got under his skin. In truth, the game he was playing with Persia was a dangerous one. By coming back to New York and playing her so close, Chucky was putting himself as well as his traveling companions in jeopardy. She was the missing link between Chucky and all the dirt he'd done before fleeing New York; and she was the only living person who could link him to some of his most heinous crimes. The smart thing would've been for Chucky to take the money they'd ripped off from Mr. D and get in the wind, but he couldn't. There was too much he had left undone and he meant to finish what he started.

Chucky had convinced Maggie and Rissa that he had come back to settle old scores, which in part was true, but Chucky also still had designs on Persia. For as bad as Chucky treated Persia he loved her in his own twisted way. Of all the girls he had run through in his young life, Persia was the one who was most unlike the rest. She was fine, had an education, and was totally down for him. Persia loved Chucky more than he loved himself and instead of nurturing and appreciating that love, Chucky corrupted it and bent Persia's will to his own fucked-up ways. To those on the outside looking in, Chucky probably appeared to be a devil and, in part, they were right, but Chucky really didn't know any better. The only way he knew to express his love was through control.

In trying to control Persia he brought her down to his level instead of him elevating to hers. As a result, he pushed her away and possibly out of his reach. Still Chucky was determined to try to rope her back in. He would either win back Persia's heart or cut it from her chest. If Chucky couldn't have her, no one would . . . especially Vaughn.

A car blaring its horn behind him let Chucky know that he had slipped into a daze. He managed to floor it through the intersection as the light was turning from yellow to red. Their destination was coming up so Chucky parked in the first spot he saw, which was several blocks from where they'd agreed to meet. He was sure he could've found a more convenient place to park that was closer to the spot, but he'd be expected to drive up. If he arrived on foot he'd be better equipped to see trouble before it saw him.

"Wake up." Chucky hit Maggie with a sharp elbow.

Maggie snapped up as if she had just been elec-
trocuted and looked around frantically. "Where
the hell are we?" She wiped a bit of drool from the
corner of her mouth.

"We are where we need to be. Now get yourself
straightened out and try not to look so much like a
damn junkie," Chucky snapped and got out of the
car. He took a minute to shake the loose cigarette
ashes from his black suit jacket that had accumu-
lated there during the ride over. The shoulders
and sleeves of the jacket, which had at one time
been tailored to fit him, now seemed frumpy and
loose, reflecting his recent weight loss. Chucky was
overdressed for his meeting, but appearances went
a long way and he wanted to project the illusion
that he was still doing well.

Chucky had his arm hooked in Maggie's trying
to keep her standing upright. The whole time his
eyes darted this way and that, in search of signs
of danger. He was a man with a price on his head
and there was no telling who could be enticed to
try to collect, including the person he was meeting.
As planned Chucky spotted him way early. He was
standing outside, pacing and sucking the life out
of a cigarette, still wearing the ill-fitting suit from
earlier.

"Sup wit' it?" Chucky crept on Charlie, startling
him to the point where he dropped his cigarette.

"Damn, you scared the shit out of me. I didn't see you walk up," Charlie said, fishing out his pack of cigarettes and lighting another one.

"Then maybe you need to be paying more attention to your surroundings." Chucky took the cigarette from Charlie and started smoking it.

Charlie took out a third cigarette and lit it. "Got a lot on my mind."

Chucky nodded in understanding. "I'll bet. Listen, I'm sorry I didn't make it to your sister's funeral. You know mine ain't the most welcome face in the hood."

"So I been hearing," Charlie told him. "They say Ramses dropped a bag on your head."

"Something like that." Chucky laughed it off. "I'd kick double to the family of anybody fool enough to try to collect. They gonna need it to bury him." He looked Charlie in the eyes when he said it. He wanted to make sure Charlie picked up on the threat he had laid down.

"I feel you," Charlie said in a tone that let Chucky know the threat had been received.

"So, you got something for me?" Chucky changed the subject.

"Yeah." Charlie looked around cautiously as if he was afraid someone would overhear what he was about to say. "Like I was telling you before, I'm fucking this bitch who was laying down with this clown-ass nigga whose name ain't even worth mentioning. Like I said, dude is corny, but the cats he runs with are supposed to be heavy out here, on some real murder for hire shit."

"I know plenty of nigga who kill for profit, but tell me what you and this blabbermouth bitch got to do with me?" Chucky said in an irritated tone. He hated the way Charlie could be so roundabout when telling a story instead of getting to the point.

"Give me a minute. I'm getting to it," Charlie told him. "So according to her, the nigga gets drunk and starts trying to impress her by shooting his trap off about all the high-profile hits him and his squad have been behind. That's when your name came up. What's on the wire is that these niggas picked up the contract on your head."

Chucky shrugged. "Them and every other thirst bag trying to fatten their pockets or shove their tongues further up Ramses's ass. Charlie, niggas been trying to kill me all my life and I'm still here to talk shit about it."

"I respect your gangsta, Chucky, I'm just trying to pull your coat. Even the Dominicans uptown use them when they come across problems they can't handle. These ain't no knockoff shooters; they're the real deal."

Chucky felt both flattered and leery. He knew Ramses felt betrayed and would send shooters at him, but he hadn't expected him to drop the kind of bread it would take to hire actual assassins. Apparently Ramses placed greater value on Chucky's life than he did. Street niggas popping shots to try to fatten their pockets Chucky could either evade or knock off, but trained assassins would be much harder to deal with. The way Chucky figured it, the best defense was a potent offense and striking first would give his would-be killers food for thought.

"You done good, Charlie. Now tell me, how much do you know about these niggas who been sent to take my life?"


It had been a busy day for Adam. Not that all his days weren't busy, but when he rose that morning it was the first time in a long time he rose with a purpose other than chasing a dollar. He picked out his most crisp pair of jeans and a polo shirt he had caught on sale at Macy's and a brand new pair of white-on-white Air Force Ones. It was a big day for him and he wanted to make sure he looked the part.

Adam began his mission around 10:00 a.m., picking up his girl for breakfast. He smiled when she answered the door wearing tight blue jeans, a fresh pair of Jordans, and a shirt cut close enough to show off her curves. Their day started with steak and eggs at a local diner, before they hopped a bus to Rye Playland. Amusement parks weren't really Adam's thing, but Bess loved them. She squealed like a schoolgirl when the pirate ship ride suspended them upside down, spilling all the change from Adam's pockets.

When Bess had her fill of rides and cotton candy, they hopped a bus back to the city and headed to downtown Brooklyn. Adam had made them dinner reservations at the Hanging Gardens, but they had about a twenty-minute wait before they were to be seated, so Adam suggested they take a walk along the promenade. He figured that would be as good a place as any.

"So, are you having a good time, Bess?" Adam asked her as they strode down the promenade, looking at the city skyline across the water.

"The best time!" Bess exclaimed, hugging the large teddy bear Adam had won for her at the amusement park. "I can ride roller coasters over and over and never get tired of them. Feeling the wind whip across my face makes me feel so free." She twirled with the bear in her arms excitedly. In many ways Bess was much like a child and the simplest things made her happy.

"Well enjoy it while you can. In a few months you ain't gonna be able to go on those rides anymore for a while. Can't have my son coming out with a scrambled brain." Adam rubbed her stomach. He could feel the first hints of her baby bump.

"How you know it's gonna be a boy? It might be a girl. What you gonna do then?" Bess asked playfully.

"Whether it's a girl or a boy, I'm gonna love it just the same," Adam said proudly.

Bess smiled. "Adam, you're the best boyfriend I ever had. You never get mad because I ain't smart and call me names like the other ones." Her voice took on a sad tone. Being slow Bess didn't have the easiest time growing up and often found herself victimized by those closest to her. From her father to boys she dated, they all took what they wanted then abandoned her like trash. Adam had been the only man to ever show her genuine kindness and love.

"Bess, you know you're my favorite girl." Adam draped his arm around her. "I would never be anything but a good man to you."

Bess smiled. "I know, Adam. You always been good to me, so you don't have to tell me."

"You're right. I don't have to tell you, but I would like to show you." Adam dug in his pocket and pulled out a small velvet box. He popped it open and inside was a small diamond ring. It wasn't the grandest stone, but it was what his pockets could afford. "My daddy wasn't never around and

I want to make sure I'm always there for my kid by making an honest woman of you."

"Adam, are you serious?" Bess asked excitedly.

"As a heart attack, baby. I want you to be my wife. Please say yes."

"Of course I will!" Bess threw her arms around him and planted kisses all over his face.

Bess and Adam strolled hand in hand, talking about their plans for the future. It was a happy moment for both of them and nothing could ruin it, or so they thought. As they were walking, Adam noticed an unfamiliar man leaning against a car. He wouldn't have paid it any mind if it hadn't been for the way the man was staring at them. There was something in his eyes that made the hairs on the back of Adam's neck stand up. Adam tightened his grip on Bess's hand, keeping his eyes on the glaring man.

"What's wrong, baby?" Bess asked, noticing Adam had tensed.

"Nothing," Adam said calmly, so as not to frighten her. The man who had been glaring at them was now walking in their direction. Adam had been in the streets long enough to know when something was about to pop off, and he went for his gun. Before he could clear it from his waist, something smashed into the back of his head.

The world swam and for a minute Adam had trouble focusing. He thought he might've been falling, but wasn't totally sure until his face hit the concrete. His ears were clogged, like he was underwater, but he could hear Bess screaming. He tried to push himself off the ground to help her, but someone kicked him viciously in the mouth. He spat blood and teeth onto the ground as he rolled over onto his back. Standing over him he saw two people; one was the unfamiliar man who had been watching them, and the other was someone he had seen only in a picture.

"So, you and your punk-ass boys are the ones who picked up the contract on my life, huh?" Chucky stood above Adam, twirling an aluminum bat. "I hope they gave you a nice retainer, because y'all are gonna need every dime to pay for all them funerals!" Chucky snarled before tearing into Adam with the bat.

Bess crawled over and threw her body over Adam to protect him. "Please, you're gonna kill him," she pleaded.

"That's the general fucking idea." Chucky tried to kick Bess away, but she held fast to her lover, taking some of the licks with the bat that were meant for Adam. When Chucky was done caving Adam's skull in he drew his gun.

Bess looked up at him. Her face was bloodied and one of her eyes was now swollen shut from being hit with the bat. Even being mentally slow, she was smart enough to know what was about to happen. "Please don't. I'm pregnant." Bess tried to appeal to Chucky's sense of humanity, but Chucky had stopped being human a long time ago.

"Then I'm doing you a favor by making sure he'll never be born into this fucked-up world." Chucky tapped the trigger twice.

Chucky left the bodies there for the police to find, beaten and shot to death. When they found them, Bess was still hugging Adam's corpse. She loved him so much that even as she took her last breaths she was still trying to protect him. In the police report one officer wrote it up as one of the most heartbreaking crime scenes he had ever come across.


"Chucky, what the fuck did you do, man?" Charlie asked nervously as they sped away from the crime scene in Chucky's BMW. Rissa and Maggie sat in the back seat in stunned silence.

"I was practicing my swing for the upcoming little league season," Chucky said sarcastically. "What the fuck does it look like we just did?"

"We?" Charlie asked in shock. "Man, I never laid a hand on either one of them!"

"Don't matter, you were there. Same as when I knocked that old Italian out the box. You might not have gotten your punk-ass hands dirty, but you helped me with both. That makes you an accessory and that's sure as hell the story I'm gonna tell if you ever get to running your mouth and this shit comes back to me."

"Chucky, my mother just had to bury my sister and I don't think her heart would be able to take it if I went to prison over some shit with you," Charlie told him.

"Nobody is going to prison if you do like I tell you and keep your mouth shut. Now keep your ass quiet so I can think!" Chucky barked. Steering with his knees he tapped a cigarette out of his pack and lit it. Killing the young couple had been a bad move because of the heat it was going to bring on him, but he had to do it. For a whole year he had been dodging one threat or another and it was time for him to go on the offensive. He wanted word to get out to anybody with big ideas that he was still willing and ready to kill. This would make them think twice. The only problem with that was word would quickly spread that Chucky was back in town and he would lose the element of surprise. It would only be a matter of time before he ran into someone who was quicker on the draw than he was or, worse, Ramses. There was no longer time to carefully orchestrate his plan; he had to do what he had to do and get back in the wind.

# CHAPTER 9

"How many times do you plan on changing your clothes?" Asia asked. She was stretched across Persia's bed, flipping through a magazine and watching Persia try on outfit after outfit.

"As many times as it takes for me to find something that doesn't make me look like I borrowed it." Persia turned to the side, looking in the full-length mirror to see how the lavender dress made her ass look. It, like everything else she tried on, didn't seem to fit quite right. She had gained some of her weight back during her recovery, but she was still a bit on the thin side compared to where she used to be.

"You have got to be kidding me." Asia put the magazine down and got up to stand next to Persia. "I know chicks who would kill to have your figure, including me." She looked at herself in the mirror. Asia was a beautiful girl, but didn't have much in the way of hips or ass. She was a tall and thin girl with just enough of a figure to entice a man, but could hardly be considered thick. "I envy you, Persia, and women like you. You have curves, and curves are beautiful. Me, on the other hand . . ." Asia turned herself this way and that in the mirror.

"I'm cursed to be a walking billboard of what society believes is the perfect size."

"You could stand to put on a few pounds," Persia joked.

Asia rolled her eyes. "I wish. The last time I got heavier than one hundred and twenty-five pounds my mother tried to check me into fat camp."

"Damn, Nya don't fuck around when it comes to your career," Persia said, speaking of Asia's mother/manager.

"She takes it more serious than I do." Asia sat back on the bed and crossed one long chocolate leg over the other. "Most times I feel like my mother pushes me so hard because she's trying to relive her glory years through me, but I'm not her and this isn't the eighties. Being rail thin is cool for white models, but in today's industry there's also a place for Black women with curves."

One of the reasons Persia loved talking to Asia was because she always spoke her mind. She was one of the rare people in Persia's life where what you saw was what you got. There was nothing fraudulent about her. Lately Asia had been one of her closest confidants, but it hadn't always been like that.

Persia and Asia actually started out as rivals. Persia was one of the few Black girls at the prestigious St. Mary's Academy, and one of the most popular girls at school until Asia's arrival at St.

Mary's. She and her family had just moved to the States from Germany and her celebrity status as one of the most popular young models in Europe made her a quick favorite among the other girls. Persia didn't like Asia; she felt like she was stuck-up and had entitlement issues while Asia felt the same of her. The fact that Asia's mother had purchased one of the biggest houses in Persia's neighborhood didn't help their rivalry. It was inevitable that Persia and Asia would bump heads, but ironically when they did it was over something that didn't involve either of them directly.

Two white trash sisters who ran with Asia by the names of Vickie and Jean dropped a dime on Persia's best friend Sarah over some pills she had sold them and Sarah ended up in serious trouble. As payback Persia busted Vickie's nose. Instead of handling it on her own Vickie ran to Asia and made up a lie to get Asia on her side. Things got ugly between Persia and the girls from Asia's crew, with an incident when they even tried to jump her at the bus stop. When the truth finally came out and Vickie and Jean had been exposed as liars Asia turned her wrath and her mob on her one-time friends. Asia realized she had misjudged Persia and as a peace offering she extended an invitation to Persia to attend a celebrity auction that her mother was hosting in the city. That was the beginning of their budding friendship. As the girls spent more and more time around each other they realized they had more in common than just going to the same school and living in the same neighborhood.

"So, where are you guys off to tonight?" Asia asked.

"Probably just dinner and a movie, nowhere special," Persia said as if it was no big deal.

"Girl, it's always special when you step out with a man like Vaughn Tate," Asia said.

"You sound just like my homegirls from Harlem." Persia sucked her teeth. She stepped out of the dress she was wearing and grabbed another one from the closet. "Vaughn is just another guy."

Asia gave her a look. "Persia, the last dude I dated was just *another guy*. The fine-ass dude who drives the UPS truck is just *another guy*. Vaughn Tate is about to be the face of a sports franchise. I don't think he qualifies as just *another guy*. You better stop thumbing your nose at that wealthy piece of meat and get with the program before some other bitch does. Especially after all I did to hook you guys up!"

Persia cocked her head to one side. "You? Asia, I knew Vaughn long before he got drafted and before I bumped into him at the auction."

"Yes, but you weren't checking for him!" Asia shot back. "I knew from the minute the way Vaughn was looking at you that he had it bad, but your naïve ass couldn't even see it. I felt it was my civic duty to help you not squander the opportunity by passing him your phone number, because I knew you weren't going to do it."

Persia laughed. "You're right about that, because I sure wasn't trying to get caught up with no dudes after my ordeal with Chucky." It was true, Vaughn was checking for Persia but she wasn't trying to give him the time of day. It took a hell of a lot of work on his part to get her to agree to go out with him with a divine intervention from Asia.

"Persia, you can't compare a crackhead, no offense, to a man like Vaughn. Now I've come across an athlete or three in my day and I've found most of them to be arrogant sons of bitches with mommy issues, but I don't get that from Vaughn. He seems like the genuine article," Asia said sincerely.

"Vaughn is cool peoples, but I wouldn't go planning any weddings just yet. I'm only eighteen years old and I'm more concerned with graduating high school and going to college than I am with trying to get some nigga to wife me," Persia said.

"Ain't nobody telling you to settle down just yet, Persia, but what I am telling you is to go into this with an open mind. Most girls will never meet a real millionaire, let alone one who doesn't just want to fuck and drop them back off. Vaughn likes you, and I know you're digging him. This thing y'all got going may or may not go anywhere, but have fun with it while you can. Stop worrying about your past and learn to live in the moment."

Three outfit changes later, Persia was ready to go. She chose a simple black dress with the matching heels to wear out on her date. She wasn't sure where they were going for dinner so she didn't want to overdo or underdo it. When she came downstairs with Asia, they found Persia's mother Michelle and her stepfather Richard sitting on the living room couch watching *Sparkle* on their big-screen television.

Michelle and Richard made an odd pair, with her being a reformed hood chick and him being a square who had probably never held a gun in his life, but they made a dynamic couple. In the beginning Persia didn't like Richard. She looked at him as the man who was trying to take her father's place and she resented him for it. It took a long time before Persia came to the realization that Richard, much like her real father, only had her best interests at heart. They didn't have a father-daughter relationship, but Persia respected him for stepping up and being a good husband to her mother and provider for their family.

"Looks like someone's got a hot date," Michelle said when she noticed Persia all dressed up. Michelle looked like a slightly older version of Persia except she was a shade or two lighter and had bigger breasts and hips.

"It's not a date. Me and Asia are going into the city with her mom to catch a Broadway show," Persia lied. She felt bad about telling the fib, but she wasn't ready to tell her mother about Vaughn yet.

"Really, which one?" Richard asked. He was giving her his usual accusatory state. Persia hated when he looked at her like that because it reminded her of how her teachers in school looked at her when they were about to chastise her for doing something wrong. With Richard being a college professor, she guessed it must've been a practiced look among educators.

The question caught Persia slightly off guard, but luckily Asia was quick on her feet. "*A Raisin in the Sun*."

"Really?" Michelle's eyes lit up. "Richard took me to see it a few years ago. I loved it."

"The book was better," Richard mumbled.

"Hush." Michelle elbowed her husband. "I can't wait until you're back so we can compare notes. I wanna hear how the younger generation feels about what's hailed as a literary classic."

"Sure thing, Mom," Persia said, wondering how the hell she was going to pull that off considering she wasn't really going to a show. "Listen, I gotta go. We gotta get back to Asia's house so she can get dressed." She leaned down and kissed her mother's cheek.

"Okay, you be safe out there, baby, and don't come in too late," Michelle told her daughter.

"I won't, Mom," Persia said and hurried out the door. "That was some quick thinking," she said to Asia once they were outside.

"You know I'm always saving your ass." Asia winked. "And don't worry about the play-by-play your mom is expecting. I've got the 1961 version on DVD."

"That's why you're my girl." Persia high-fived Asia.

# CHAPTER 10

Traffic wasn't bad so it only took Persia about an hour to get from her house in Long Island City to Midtown where she was meeting Vaughn. He offered to come by and pick Persia up, but she shot that idea down. She was hesitant about having him meet her mother because she wasn't exactly sure where their relationship was going. She was okay with taking public transportation into the city, but Vaughn wasn't trying to hear it so he sent a car for her. She had the driver pick her up a block away from her house because she didn't want her mother getting suspicious. She wasn't worried about her mother following up with Nya, because she was currently out of the country so her lie was airtight.

As they drew near their destination Persia felt the butterflies in her stomach. She had been on a few dates with Vaughn already, but she still got nervous whenever they were out. Before she'd found out he was famous she had looked at Vaughn as a regular dude, but after the auction things had changed. Riding through Midtown in the back of a Town Car Persia reflected on how she had met Vaughn and how they ended up at the point where they were.

Persia had first met Vaughn at a club she had gone to with Chucky. Back then Vaughn wasn't a superstar yet. He was fresh out of college and there as a member of the entourage of the rappers who had performed and Persia was there with Chucky, and her friends Marty and Sarah. Vaughn wasn't like the rest of his crew. The rappers were loud, arrogant, and thirsty while Vaughn was very laidback. He and Persia made small talk that night and there was definitely a spark between them, but Persia was there with someone. When they parted company Marty and Sarah left with the rappers while Persia slid with Chucky. A few weeks later she would find out about the brutal rape of her friend Marty at the hands of the rappers. She received the news shortly after Marty committed suicide.

The next time Persia's and Vaughn's paths would cross would be months later at a record store in the city. Persia was fresh out of recovery and seeing Vaughn again caused mixed feelings in her. Vaughn wasn't there at the time of the rape and had stopped hanging around the rappers when he found out what they had done, but Persia still had a hard time disassociating him from the rappers. Speaking with Vaughn that day in the record store gave her a better idea of what kind of man he really was, but she was still leery of him. It wasn't until the third meeting when the ice would finally be broken.

The third time Persia's and Vaughn's paths crossed was at the auction. Persia was a guest of the hostess so that explained her presence at the gala, but she wondered how somebody like Vaughn had gotten in. At the time Persia was still clueless about his newfound success. Spending the few hours together Vaughn was finally able to get her guard down enough to let him prove that he was a good guy. To Persia's surprise, Vaughn actually made pleasant company. Persia noticed that people seemed to be paying extra attention to them, snapping pictures and acting like they were a big deal, but it didn't hit her as to why until the point in the night when they began the celebrity auction. Persia was stunned when they called Vaughn up on the action block, and introduced him as the recent second-round draft pick of the Philadelphia Eagles. It was then that the pieces finally fell into place.

Persia was so frazzled by the revelation that she didn't know what to say to Vaughn so she slipped out of the gala without saying good-bye. The next day the newspapers were running with the pictures taken of her and Vaughn at the auction. Persia had heard through the grapevine that Vaughn had been searching high and low for Persia but she avoided him like the plague. She was still trying to deal with life after addiction and wasn't sure if dating a celebrity would've been the healthiest thing for her at the time. Persia had no plans on pursuing Vaughn, but little did she know he had no intention of giving up on his pursuit of her.

She was surprised when she answered her bedroom phone one day and found Vaughn on the other end. Persia questioned how he had gotten her number but Vaughn refused to reveal his source. It didn't take long for Persia to figure out that it had been Asia who gave it to him because she was the only person they had in common. Vaughn pleaded with Persia to go out on a date with him, but she refused. This was when the deliveries started. Every day for a week a large floral arrangement was delivered to Persia's house with a card that read JUST ONE DATE. Persia's mother was beginning to think she had a stalker, but Persia knew who was behind the deliveries. Vaughn vowed that the following week he'd start sending two per day until Persia agreed to go on just one date with him. Finally he broke her down and Persia agreed. Two weeks and several dates later they were at the scratch line of what could've only been described as a budding relationship.

Vaughn was into Persia and she liked him too. Because of the baggage she brought with her she had yet to tell Vaughn that she was in recovery and she was afraid of how he might react. She knew she would have to tell him one day, but it would be on her terms and in her own time.

Chucky reappearing in her life might bring her secret out sooner than she planned.

"We're here, Ms. Chandler," the driver said, snapping her out of her daze.

The driver got out and came around to open the back door for Persia, extending his hand to help her out of the back seat. She looked up and saw that they were in front of a fancy-looking steak house. Something about it struck a chord with Persia, but she was pretty sure she hadn't been there before.

The moment Persia stepped inside the establishment she felt out of place. There were older white people dressed in all their finery, enjoying meals and drinks. She self-consciously tugged at the bottom of her skirt feeling like it was too short.

The hostess greeted her with a lukewarm smile and asked if she had a reservation. She gave Vaughn's name and suddenly the hostess's demeanor changed. She went from borderline sour to pleasant and accommodating. The hostess led Persia through the spacious dining room to a booth nestled in the corner and sectioned off from the rest of the tables. It was there where she found Vaughn.

Vaughn was busy on his cell phone so he didn't see her at first. This gave Persia a few seconds to admire him. He looked good in a dark-colored suit jacket and plain white shirt with no tie. His hair was freshly faded close on the sides, with thick, rolling waves on the top. When he finally noticed Persia he smiled, showing off his near perfect white teeth.

"Let me hit you right back," Vaughn told whomever he was speaking to before ending the call and standing up to greet Persia. "Hey, pretty lady." He hugged her.

"Hey, yourself," Persia responded, drinking in the sweet smell of his cologne.

Vaughn dismissed the hostess and pulled the chair out for Persia. Once she was seated he sat back down across from her. "So, how was the ride out?"

"Traffic was light so it wasn't too bad," Persia told him.

"It would've been even better if you'd let me come scoop you in my new toy. Think about it: me and you on the open highway, blasting Mary J. with the top down and the wind blowing in our hair." Vaughn painted the picture for her.

"Sounds like a blast." Persia smiled.

"Feels even better," Vaughn quipped back. "I don't know why you never let me come and pick you up. I feel kinda like a creep by not coming to your doorstep and presenting myself to your mom like a proper gentleman."

"I think it's sweet and I respect the fact that you're even willing to do it, but I think it's a little early for all that," Persia said, trying to take as much of the sting out of her words as possible.

"Damn, you act like I'm coming to ask for your hand in marriage," Vaughn said sarcastically.

"I'm sorry, I didn't mean that how it sounded. Me and my family just have some unresolved issues we're trying to work through and I don't want you caught in the crossfire of our bullshit," Persia half lied.

"I can dig that, Persia. Just know that the offer was extended," Vaughn said. "So are you hungry?" He changed the subject.

"Starving!"

"Good to know, because we're about to eat like freed slaves," Vaughn joked, lightening the mood. "I hope you don't mind, but I took the liberty of ordering for you."

This took Persia by surprise. "Is that right? And how would you know what I like and I don't?"

Vaughn shrugged. "I took a stab in the dark."

"Well I hope your stab was accurate, because I'm too hungry to send my food back for something else." Persia faked an attitude.

"You didn't know? Accuracy is my middle name." Vaughn rolled up one of his napkins and held it in a throwing position like he would a football.

"I don't see how you fit that ego of yours into a helmet every Sunday night," Persia teased him. "Speaking of football, how was practice?"

"Oh, it was an off day. Thank God." Vaughn sighed. "My regiments in college ain't got shit on these pro workouts. The coaches work you until you die, resurrect you, and work you until you die again."

"Well with all the money they pay you guys I guess they're trying to get their worth out of you," Persia said.

Vaughn laughed. "You don't know shit about football outside of what you read in the newspapers, do you?"

Persia shrugged. "Never had a reason to pay much attention to the sport until now."

"Well, let me school you right quick. First of all, I didn't go very high in the draft so my signing bonus wasn't as heavy as people think. On top of that it's not like I'm getting everything at one time; it's broken up into payments. Factor that in with taxes and other shit and you'll look at balling in a whole different light."

"I never knew all that," Persia said sincerely.

"I know you didn't and that's why I'm telling you. Now don't get it fucked up; I'm doing way better than a whole lot of other athletes, but I ain't where I need to be yet. Right now it's all about getting out on the field and proving my worth and then I can hit them in the head for the long paper."

"Sounds like you've got it all mapped out."

"Everything you strive to do in life requires a plan, at least if you intend to be successful at it.

I might only be a rookie, but I've heard enough horror stories about dudes who come into the league ill-prepared and wash out. That ain't gonna be me," Vaughn said confidently.

"I'll drink to that." Persia raised her water glass.

"Cheers." Vaughn touched his glass of wine to her water glass. "You sure I can't get you something stronger than water?"

"No, I'm cool. I stopped drinking awhile back. I had a bad experience," Persia told him.

"I feel you. I can remember back in college after we had this game against Texas. A bunch from the team thought it would be a good idea to creep across the border into Mexico for a night of fun. I got so wasted on tequila that I was up all night and half the morning puking my guts out. When Coach found out what happened he made us run until we damn near died."

"Aww, poor baby." Persia patted the back of Vaughn's hand. "Sounds like your coach was a real prick."

"No, he was actually one of the single most positive things in my life. Coach was a taskmaster, but I learned a lot from him about discipline, hard work, and an appreciation of beautiful things." Vaughn laid his hand over Persia's. She blushed and pulled her hand back. "Persia, can I ask you something?"

"Sure, what's up?"

"Why you keep dogging me like this?"

"What do you mean?" She was confused.

"I think you know what I mean, ma. I'm crazy about you and I know you're digging me, but every time there's even the smallest spark between us you go pouring water on it. What is it, does my breath stink? Do you think I'm ugly or something?"

"No, I think you're very handsome and your breath always smells nice. Well, except for that one time when you had that pizza with anchovies," she joked.

"I'm glad you can find humor in my heartache." Vaughn frowned.

Seeing he was serious Persia felt bad about laughing. "I'm sorry. Your feelings are not a joke. I like you, I really do."

"Then why am I still sitting in the friend zone?"

"It's complicated," she said. "I haven't had the best of luck with relationships. Things didn't end so well with the last guy I was seeing."

"Who, that fake-ass gangster you were with that night we met at the club? I can't say I'm surprised. I don't know him, but from what I saw he seemed like a real grease ball."

"How can you say that about somebody you don't know?" Persia asked.

"For two reasons: for one, I'm a good judge of character; and for two, any man who would treat you wrong obviously ain't about shit. Dig, Persia, I can understand why the way things ended with him would make you hesitant, but I'm not that dude. I'd really like to see where we can go with this."

"But you hardly know me," she pointed out.

"Because you won't give me a chance to get to know you! I'm not asking for your hand in marriage or no shit like that, just the opportunity to show you that I have nothing but the best intentions."

"We'll see, but I can't make any promises."

Vaughn smiled. "Fair enough, baby. Fair enough."

Persia had to admit, Vaughn was persistent when it came to something he wanted. It was one of the things she found attractive about him: his determination.

The wait staff finally arrived with their appetizer: a dozen large oysters on a bed of ice. Vaughn picked one up, and squeezed a lemon slice on it with a dollop of horseradish and a few drops of Tabasco sauce. He fed it to Persia, who seductively slurped it from the shell. A split second later when the horseradish hit her nasal cavity her eyes began to tear up. She downed her water while Vaughn tried to stifle his laugh. Their next course consisted of cold-water lobster and two rib eye steaks that were so tender Persia's knife glided through hers like butter. For dessert they shared a chocolate mousse. It was shaping up to be one of the best nights Persia had ever had; then the other shoe dropped.

Vaughn and Persia were making small talk and cracking jokes when she heard a voice that made her head snap up. There was a group of men passing their booth, laughing and talking among themselves. The leader was a slightly older, but very well-built man, who had traces of gray peppering his low-cut hair. His ears, wrists, and fingers were flooded with diamonds, and hanging from his neck was a huge gold chain. The eight-inch bust of an Egyptian queen bounced off his chest while he moved.

When Persia spotted the man all the color drained from her face and her mouth suddenly became very dry.

"You okay?" Vaughn asked in a concerned tone, looking back and forth between Persia and the passing group.

"Yes, I'm fine," Persia lied. She tried to shrink herself in the booth, hoping the man with the big gold chain didn't notice her. The men had almost made it past the booth without giving Persia or Vaughn a second look, and then her luck ran out.

"Yo, ain't that the kid who play for the Eagles?" a man who had been bringing up the rear asked loudly. This made the whole group stop and turn their eyes toward the booth.

When the man with the big gold chain spotted Persia she saw the light of recognition go off in his eyes and felt a tinkle of pee squirt down her thigh.

She didn't know him very well personally, but his exploits in the hood were legendary. His name was Ramses. He was the eyes, ears, and executioner's sword for a drug lord named Pharaoh. More importantly he was the man Chucky had robbed before he and Persia made their great escape.

"How you doing tonight, fellas?" Vaughn greeted them like a man who was used to getting approached by strangers, not too inviting but not standoffish either.

"Man, I told y'all it was him!" the man who spotted them told his companions excitedly. He walked over to the table and shook Vaughn's hand. "I saw you in that game when you came off the bench against Chicago. They were kicking y'all asses until you went on that two score drive in the fourth. That's one hell of an arm you got."

"Thanks," Vaughn replied.

"I'm surprised to see you in New York. You thinking about requesting a trade and coming up this way?" the man asked.

"My heart is New York." Vaughn glanced at Persia. "But my contract is in Philadelphia."

The man continued to badger Vaughn with questions and even asked him to pose for some pictures. Persia could tell Vaughn was getting annoyed, but he just smiled and was as accommodating as possible. The whole time Persia could feel Ramses's eyes on her. She dared not look his way out of fear of not knowing what he would do or say. Chucky had been the one who betrayed Ramses, but Persia had been his unwitting accomplice. There was a standing bounty on Chucky's head and Persia wasn't sure where she stood. She knew how Ramses dealt and feared that she had now also put Vaughn's life in jeopardy.

"I know you, don't I?" Ramses asked, startling Persia to the point where she jumped and almost knocked over one of the water glasses.

"Huh?" Persia asked for lack of a better reply.

"I said, I know you," Ramses repeated. "Your name is Persia, right?"

Persia was stuck on stupid. She thought about lying and telling Ramses that he was mistaken, but that would raise a red flag with Vaughn. Ramses glared at her, waiting to see how she would respond, while Vaughn looked back and forth between them trying to figure out what the connection was. The secrets Persia had sought to keep were about to come out and there wasn't anything she could do about it. "Yes, my name is Persia," she answered softly.

"I thought I recognized you." Ramses rubbed his hands together as if he was planning something sinister.

Vaughn finally got tired of playing the guessing game. "How do you two know each other?"

"Vaughn, there's something I need to tell you," Persia began, but was cut off.

"You're Face's little girl," Ramses said.

"Um, yeah," Persia said trying to hide her shock. She thought sure that Ramses was about to expose her in front of Vaughn or worse.

"I thought so." Ramses gave her a knowing nod. "Your dad was a good dude, a stand-up dude. Not like some of these larcenous fucks who are running around calling themselves hustlers these days. The kids today have no honor and would steal from the very pockets that feed them," he said coldly.

Vaughn noticed the uncomfortable look on Persia's face so he intervened. "Look, fellas, I don't wanna be a dick or anything, but I'm feeling like I'm being rude by neglecting my lady." He let them know subtly that it was time for them to move on.

Ramses looked down at Vaughn. For a minute Persia thought that he was going to make a move, but instead Ramses just smiled. "Sure, you're right, kid. I can respect a man who knows when he's got a good thing and tries to do right. Oh, but before I go I was wondering if you could sign an autograph for my son." He helped himself to one of their cloth napkins and slid it across the table to Vaughn.

"Sure, I'm happy to do it." Vaughn fished a pen from the pocket of his suit jacket. "What's his name?"

"Make it out to Pharaoh," Ramses said glancing at Persia.

"No problem." Vaughn began scribbling on the napkin. "Is li'l man a fan?"

"Nah, we don't fuck with the Eagles in my house. We're Giants fans, but I figure seeing a kid from the gutter who made good with his life can inspire my boy to do the right thing with his."

"Right," Vaughn said awkwardly. "Well, here you go." He handed him the autographed napkin.

"Appreciate it." Ramses tucked the napkin away. "You kids enjoy your evening." He turned to leave with his men.

Persia was thinking how she had just dodged a bullet when Ramses stopped and turned back.

"One more thing." Ramses hovered over the table. "Persia, I'm trying to catch up with a mutual friend of ours. You remember Chucky who drove the red Beemer, right?"

"Yes, but I haven't seen him in I don't know how long," Persia said, but she couldn't bring herself to meet Ramses's gaze.

Ramses leaned over and rested his knuckles on their table, causing his heavy gold chain to clank against a discarded saucer. "Are you sure? It's real important that I get a hold of him."

"Yes, I'm sure," Persia lied.

Ramses stared at her for what seemed like an eternity before nodding in approval. "Okay." He stood erect. "But if you do happen to run into him, let him know that I haven't forgotten about him." With that Ramses led his men from the restaurant.

When the fear that had been gripping Persia during the whole conversation finally let go, Persia grabbed her water glass with trembling hands and emptied it in one gulp.

"You okay?" Vaughn asked in a concerned tone.

"Yeah, I'm fine. I just need to go home," Persia said, not able to hide the nervousness in her voice.

Vaughn looked at his watch. "It's not even nine o'clock. I was thinking we could hit up Times Square and keep the night going."

"Maybe some other time. I'm suddenly not feeling very well."

# CHAPTER 11

King Tut sat on the passenger side of his black-on-black GMC truck. He had his seat pushed back so far that he might as well have been sitting in the back, and the heavily tinted window was lowered just enough for him to flick the ashes from the blunt he had been smoking. He loved that truck. It was the first big purchase he had made since Ramses put him in the position to make some real money.

Several years prior King Tut had been a soldier working under one of Ramses's lieutenants named Benny. He was on the come up, but his ascension was derailed by a prison sentence. A situation jumped off and Tut had taken one for the team. Most men only sent letters full of empty promises to their comrades in prison, but Benny sent cash and made sure Tut was taken care of during his entire bid. He also promised when Tut came home he would still have a place within the organization. By the time Tut was released from prison, Benny was dead and there were two new kids running the block.

King Tut was skeptical that his time in prison had caused him to miss his opportunity, but Ramses stayed true to the promise Benny had made and put him on when he touched down. It didn't take long for King Tut to prove that he was an efficient earner, but he was also a very capable killer. There was no hesitation or remorse on Tut's part when it came to taking a life. For him it was as simple as turning a light switch on or off. His bloodlust made most give him a wide berth, but Ramses saw value in a man with Tut's unique skill set and as a reward he gave him his own crew. Tut now had money and power, but he still craved more and was willing to do whatever it took to achieve it, even if it meant stepping on a few toes.

"This is the spot right here," Ed said from behind the wheel. Ed was an older dude who was down with Ramses's crew. He wasn't much of a thinker and suffered from a serious lack of motivation, which explained why he was almost twice as old as most of them but had never made it very far up the ladder in their organization. Tut didn't really care for Ed, but he had his uses, mostly running errands and driving for whoever needed him because he was one of the few of them who had a clean driver's license, or a license at all for that matter.

King Tut sat up and peered out the window. They were in front of a small storefront that had been converted into a soul food restaurant by the current owner. The words GEORGE'S CHICKEN were scrawled across the brown awning. "It would be another fucking restaurant." He chuckled to himself, thinking about what had happened the last time somebody sent him to handle business at restaurant. Tut punched in what appeared to be a series of random numbers on the in-dash stereo system and a hidden compartment popped down from beneath the glove box. From it he retrieved a small Glock.

Ed looked at the gun skeptically. "What's that for? I thought Ramses just wanted us to talk to him."

"We are going to talk. This"—he brandished the gun—"is my translator. Now bring your scary ass on." He got out of the car.

King Tut walked into the soul food joint with Ed hot on his heels. It was the dinner rush so they were crowded. He weaved his way through the tables full of diners on his way to the kitchen area, plucking a chicken wing off the plate of a stunned patron. Halfway there he was stopped by a young woman wearing a T-shirt that bore the company logo.

"Can I help you?" the woman asked, standing between King Tut and the kitchen.

"Yeah, sweetie. I'm here to see George," Tut said, munching on his stolen chicken wing.

"He's not in right now," the woman said, but she didn't sound convincing.

"Is that right?" Tut peered past her toward the swinging doors that led to the kitchen. He saw someone peek through one of the little round windows and disappear. "Look out." He brushed past her.

"Wait you can't go back there!" the woman shouted, but Tut ignored her and kept going.

He pushed through the doors and stepped into the kitchen area, which was slightly larger than the dining room. Wait staff and cooks milled back and forth between the rows of pots and pantry shelves, preparing meals for their hungry guests. King Tut took his time strolling down one of the aisles, drawing the occasional glance from a surprised employee but no one moved to stop him. It didn't take him long to find George. He was standing near the deep fryer, pretending that he was so busy with the chicken and fish that he didn't notice Tut.

"What's up, Chicken George?" Tut said his name with a smirk. It was a play on the shucking and jiving slave turned cock-fighter in the movie *Roots*. George hated to be called that, and Tut knew it, which was why he did it.

George turned around with a manufactured look of surprise on his face. "What's going on, Tut? Didn't realize you were here."

"I'll bet. I need to have a word with you, George."

"Okay, can you maybe come back later? We're hella busy right now," George said, pulling a hot strainer full of fried chicken from one of the deep fryers.

"No, it can't wait. Our mutual friend is wondering why your orders have gotten smaller and smaller over the past few weeks," King Tut said.

George wiped his hands. "What can I say, things have been tight lately."

"That's funny, because I've had one of my boys watching this place for the last couple of days and it's still looking like business as usual; discount dinners out the front and cocaine out the back. What gives?"

George looked nervous.

"Is everything okay back here, Mr. George?" A large black man wearing a dirty apron appeared behind them. He was easily taller than King Tut by a foot, and wore a scowl on his face. In his hand he held a meat cleaver.

"Yeah, everything is cool, Ant," George said in a nervous tone. His eyes pleaded with Ant not to leave, so he lingered while George finished talking to his guests.

King Tut gave the scowling Ant an amused look before turning his attention back to George. "Look, George, it's too hot in this fucking kitchen to mince words with you so let's get straight to it. When you were selling five dollar dinners out of the trunk of your car Ramses put you in position to open this joint and is compensating you very well for the drugs you move through here, but lately you been on some brand new shit. It doesn't take a genius to know that something is funny, and I'm just trying to figure out what it is."

George thought about lying, but the truth would've come out eventually. He was sure King Tut wasn't going to like what he had to say, but doubted he would be foolish enough to try anything right then and there with Ant having the drop on him.

"Okay, fuck it," George began. "One of those Clark boys came by here and made me a business proposition. The coke they're giving me is twice as potent as what Ramses was hitting me with and the numbers are better."

"George, I'm disappointed in you." A look of sadness crossed King Tut's face. "We're supposed to be a team and as soon as things get a little complicated you go crawling to the other side and start sucking Clark dick. I always took you for a stand-up dude, but that's some real bitch shit. To top it off, you dropped a body on Ramses's streets without getting the nod. You're out of pocket, old man."

"Now you hold the fuck on," George snapped. "I don't know nothing about no murder, so you can miss me with that shit. Furthermore I been on these streets since you were still pissing yourself in grade school, so I'm gonna need you to show me some respect, especially in my damn establishment. You're right, we're supposed to all be a team but we can barely eat with that stepped-on shit Pharaoh been putting in the streets lately. This thing that's brewing between Pharaoh and the Clarks ain't got nothing to do with me. I'm just out here trying to make a dollar and they came with a better offer. Ramses of all people should be able to understand that. This wasn't personal; it was all business."

"All business, huh?" Tut smirked. "Well, this is personal." He grabbed one of the fryers that had been submerged in the hot grease and tossed the contents on Ant. The big man howled as the greased melted away the skin on his face and chest. George tried to run, but Tut grabbed him by the back of his apron and pulled him back. He wrapped his hand around the back of George's neck and forced his face down just inches above the deep fryer. "Now you listen to me, you chicken frying piece of shit; when you were flat on your ass and selling five dollar plates Ramses put you on your feet and this is how you repay him?" He pushed his face closer to the grease.

"Please, Tut, don't do this to me!" George pleaded. Grease popped up, stinging his face.

"That's King Tut to you, you traitorous muthafucka!" He squeezed his neck tighter. "Let me tell you something and you better listen loud and damn clear, Chicken George. For as long as niggas like me are still behind the triggers these streets belong to Pharaoh!"

"Yeah, King Tut, whatever you say!" George assured him.

After holding him there for a few more moments to make sure he got the message Tut let him up. "Get the word out to your people, Chicken George, and you let them know about our little chat, you hear me?"

"I hear you." George panted, trying to catch his breath. For a minute he thought he had fried his last batch of chicken.

"That's good." Tut patted George on the shoulders reassuringly. "Not for nothing, I kinda like heart attack food y'all serve up in here and I'd hate to have to come back and burn the joint down. So long as we understand each other, everything is cool. Are we cool, George?"

"Yeah, we're cool," George said, leaning against the fryer while trying to compose himself. He hated Tut even more now than he did before, but he was willing to agree to whatever he said just to get him out of his restaurant.

"Good, so you won't take this personal." Tut grabbed George by the wrist and dipped his hand to the knuckle in hot grease. Tut laughed hysterically while George shrieked. When he felt like he suffered enough he released George and shoved him on the floor.

George cowered on the floor while clutching his ruined hand to his chest. "My hand. My fucking hand," he whimpered.

"Next time I gotta come back it'll be your fucking head going in instead of your hand." Tut kicked him in his ass for good measure. "Spread the word, Chicken George." He stepped over Ant on the way out. "You buy from Pharaoh or you're out of business."

King Tut strolled casually back to the truck and climbed in like he didn't have a care in the world. The same couldn't be said for Ed. He was clearly rattled, looking around nervously as if he was expecting someone to jump out and grab them. Ed was in such a rush to get away from the scene of the crime that he almost sideswiped a delivery truck when he pulled away from the curb.

"Why don't you be the fuck cool?" Tut plucked the weed clip he had been smoking from the ashtray and relit it.

"Tut, how can you expect me to be cool when I just watched you deep fry two people?" Ed asked, steering with both hands wrapped tightly around the wheel. "Ramses said to talk to George, not maim him!"

"I prefer a more hands-on approach." Tut snickered, thinking about George's burnt hand.

"This could cause us some unwanted problems if George's people make a stink about what happened. We got enough problems as it is without bringing more beef to the table," Ed said.

Tut sat up and looked at him. "What is it with all this 'we' and 'us' shit? You ain't no shot caller, nigga. You're a fucking flunky. Now do your job and drive the fucking car before you find yourself unemployed; and I think you know what the severance package is hitting for." He patted his waist.

"I didn't mean nothing by it. I was just trying to look out for you," Ed said nervously.

"Last nigga tried to look out for me ended up whacked. You remember that, Ed," Tut warned.

"Whatever you say, *King* Tut." Ed turned his eyes back to the road.

Tut shook his head. "These niggas and their fucking opinions," he said to no one in particular. Tut pulled out the small recorder that he'd had stashed in his pocket and hit the play button. "Ramses of all people should be able to understand that. This wasn't personal; it was all business," he heard George's voice play back. With a triumphant smile on his face, Tut whipped out his cell phone and placed a call.

# CHAPTER 12

Meeka got out of the taxi in the meatpacking district in downtown Manhattan and double checked the address Boogie had texted her. She was in the right place, but from the looks of the drab warehouse she was standing in front of it didn't look like much of a party was going on. In fact it didn't look like there was anything going on at all. She didn't hear any music, and there was nobody on the deserted street. It looked like more of a spot for an ambush than a birthday party.

Meeka tried to flag down the taxi she had just gotten out of, but it was already bending the corner. There was no traffic in sight so flagging down another one was out of the question. She could've called one, but standing on the empty street gave her the creeps. She decided it was best to move to a more populated and better lit area and figure out her transportation issue from there. Meeka was about to start making moves up the block when she heard something.

"Pssst. Pssst."

Her hand dipped inside her clutch bag and came out holding a small .22. She scanned the darkened street looking for signs of life but didn't see any.

"Yo, Meeka!" a familiar voice called from somewhere to her right.

Meeka strained her eyes to pierce the shadows near the front of the warehouse. She didn't spot it on the first sweep, but on the second she saw it: the burning ember from the end of a cigarette attached to a silhouette. "Who that?" Meeka called, chambering a round into her gun.

The shadows parted and from them stepped a large man dressed in a black leather blazer and black turtleneck. His name was Frank, but his friends had nicknamed him Frankenstein from his striking resemblance to Mary Shelley's character. Frank stood at least six foot five with shoulders wider than Meeka's entire body. Incredibly long arms hung down so far that he barely had to bend over to tie his shoe. Frank was a physically imposing man, but it was his face that made him the stuff of nightmares. He had a large, block-shaped head, and a jaw that looked like it had been carved from stone. His thick, blackened lips always seemed to be pulled back into a sneer, baring his crooked yellow teeth. A scar that was shaped like a lightning bolt stretched from his forehead and stopped just above his eyes. Frank had a face that only a mother could love, and even that was up for question.

"Jesus, Frank, you scared the hell out of me!" Meeka snapped.

"Sorry about that," Frank said sincerely. "You here for the party, right?"

"Yeah, but it doesn't look like there's any partying going on down here." Meeka looked up at the still warehouse.

Frank laughed, sounding like a car with a bad muffler. "You know with Christian nothing is ever as it seems. C'mon, I'll walk you up."

Meeka followed Frank around the side of the warehouse to a secondary entrance. It was an iron gate that stood well over twelve feet from the ground. She assumed it was used for loading and unloading. From the looks of it, it would've taken Meeka and two more people to lift it, but Frank did it effortlessly with one hand. She dipped under the opening he had provided and found herself standing in a large room that smelled like something had died in it. The only light was coming from the space under the gate Frank had opened and as soon as he closed it, Meeka found herself engulfed in total darkness. She almost jumped out of her skin when she felt one of Frank's rough hands engulf hers.

"Stay close and watch your step," Frank told her.

Nervously Meeka allowed Frank to pull her along through the warehouse, hoping to God she didn't trip over anything and break her neck in the heels she was wearing. Meeka couldn't see her hand in front of her face, but Frank navigated the darkness with ease. After a few seconds of walking, Meeka saw a light in the distance. As they got closer she could see it was another door. When

Frank pushed it open Meeka was temporarily blinded by the bright halogen lights that illuminated the adjoining hallway. From there Frank took her to a freight elevator and motioned for her to step inside.

"Aren't you coming up?" Meeka asked when she realized Frank wasn't getting on the elevator with her.

"I'll be up in a few. Christian has got something that needs handling," Frank told her before slamming the elevator gate shut.

Between the shaky elevator and her already shot nerves, Meeka felt her stomach churn. She had been running with Boogie and his crew for a while, and for the most part they had all embraced her, treating her like one of the fellas, except Christian. So far he had been the least receptive to her presence, sometimes acting as if he didn't even notice her. Because he was their leader Meeka wanted to gain his approval most of all, but Christian wasn't easily swayed. He was a very different kind of man from the others; in fact, he was like no one Meeka had ever met.

The freight elevator came to such a rough stop that it almost knocked Meeka off balance. She kept her hand close to her pistol, ready for whatever she might encounter. When the freight elevator gate was pulled back, Meeka was speechless.

It was like crossing through the gates of hell. The elevator opened up into a large room that had been converted into a pop up–style night club. There were about 300 people crammed into a space equipped to host half that number. Strobe lights flashed in multiple colors making it hard for her to focus and the music played so loud that it felt oppressive. Shielding her eyes against the light, Meeka timidly started making her way across the dance floor in search of her party.

Meeka's head swiveled left and right taking in the circus unfolding around her. People of all races, shapes, and colors paraded around the room, dancing and drinking like it was their last night on earth. In the middle of the floor two women wearing way too much makeup tried to suck the breath from each other's mouths, while gyrating against each other to the heavy pulse of the music. A man wearing a wrinkled business suit strolled up and watched the girls intently. They took a break from their kissing and invited him to join them. The duo was now a trio of interlocking lips and moving body parts. In a dark corner Meeka spied a pretty, pale woman who wore her hair in a half-shaved blond mob, and wore dark lipstick, sharing a six-foot bong. It was the most unlikely collection of people Meeka had ever seen in one place. From the freaks to the chic and everything in between, Christian had brought them out for his birthday.

It took Meeka nearly fifteen minutes to pick her way from one side of the room to the other. She spotted Boogie sitting in a private section that rested upon a four-foot platform, giving those seated a bird's-eye view of the entire room. He was whispering into the ear of a man Meeka only knew as Ghost. Meeka had met Ghost a time or two, but he never spoke and always seemed to vanish just as suddenly as he popped up. The level of respect Boogie and Christian showed him told Meeka that he was someone important, but she didn't dare pry as to how important. Ghost frightened her and whenever she saw him she gave him a wide berth.

There were several girls occupying the space with them. Half looked like streetwalkers and the other half were confused young girls who hadn't realized what they signed up for. They flocked around the crew, drinking their liquor, doing their drugs, and compromising their integrity in hopes for a shot at the brass ring. Before the night was over a lucky few would be chosen, but most would end up with cab fare and a story to tell.

Sitting in the center of the chaos was the birthday boy, Christian Knight, or to those who knew the darker side of him, Principe de La Noche, which translated to Prince of the Night. If Meeka had to sum Christian up in one word it would have been "beautiful." He was almost a perfect shade of cherry wood, with soft, moist lips that always seemed to be curved into the faintest hint of a smile. He wore his hair tapered on the sides with deep, rolling waves on the top, highlighted over one temple with a splash of color that usually

matched whatever outfit he was wearing. That day
gold was the theme. He wore a shiny gold blazer,
with a black and gold Versace with the top buttons
undone showing off his well-defined chest.

Sitting at his feet were two buxom women,
one of chocolate with rich dark hair, and the
other of vanilla with golden curls. Two chains
were attached to the diamond-studded dog col-
lars around their necks, with Christian holding
the ends of the chains like leashes. They were
Christian's playthings, Ebony and Ivory, who he
brought out on special occasions.

Meeka watched Christian run his manicured
fingernails through Ivory's blond curls while whispering into Ebony's ear. Ebony giggled as his hand
traced a line from her face down the length of her
body and disappeared between her legs. Ebony's
eyes rolled back in her head as Christian explored
her insides in plain view of anyone watching. She
was officially caught in his thrall, as were most
women who came in contact with the Prince of the
Night.

Christian was a club promoter by trade, but
a criminal by nature. He always had the line on
the best drugs and the hottest women, and had
all access to the hottest spots. He was a man who
didn't limit himself to one hustle; he had his hands
in a bit of everything. To those on the outside
looking in the well-dressed and somewhat eccen-
tric youngster made an unlikely leader of the

hardened killers who followed him. Christian was soft-spoken, flamboyant, and took more time and care with his appearance than a woman. Rumors circulated about Christian's sexual fetishes but those who tested him found out that looks could be deceiving. Christian was as much of a predator on the streets as he was in the bedroom, and would end you without thinking twice about it. He was as cold-blooded as he was pretty.

Christian must've felt Meeka watching him because he pulled himself from the nape of Ebony's neck and looked at Meeka. A smirk appeared on his face as he continued to play inside Ebony's womb. Without taking his eyes off Meeka, he got the attention of one of the bodyguards and whispered something in his ear. A few seconds later the bodyguard was escorting Meeka up onto the platform.

Boogie was the first to greet her. "Glad you could make it." He stood and hugged her.

"You know I had to come out and show love on the homie's B-day," Meeka told him. "Happy birthday, Christian." She handed him an envelope from her purse.

Christian regarded the envelope before taking it from her. "You shouldn't have, but I'm glad you did." He proceeded to slice the envelope open with his pinky nail and examined the contents. When he saw what was inside, two tickets to a Knicks game, he looked genuinely surprised. "Wow, thank you so much! The Knicks are my favorite team."

"Even though they ain't had a winning season in damn near a decade." Boogie snickered.

Christian frowned. "It would be a half-blind nigga like you who'd try to devalue such a thoughtful gift. Thank you, Meeka. Real talk, I appreciate these."

"No problem. I figured you can take someone special with you." Meeka cut her eyes at Ebony.

Christian caught the look and smirked. "Sadly, there isn't currently anyone in my life who can seem to occupy me for more than a night or so at a time." He patted the tops of both girls' heads like they were simple house pets. Unexpectedly he grabbed two fistfuls of the girls' hair and yanked their heads back. "They all here for a season, while I try to find reasons." He released them. Christian turned his soft brown eyes to Meeka. "Well don't just stand there like some gate-crasher." He patted the empty seat opposite him. "Sit, drink, and be welcome, honey. Tonight, the world is your oyster."

One thing Meeka could say about Christian was that he was a man who knew how to party. Bottles flowed, blunts were passed, and a good time was being had by all. One of the girls came by with a glass bowl containing an assortment of colorful pills. Boogie greedily snatched a handful and popped two of them, drawing a distasteful look from Christian. When the bowl came to Christian he plucked two of the pills from it and placed them on his tongue. Seductively, he leaned in and planted kisses on the waiting lips of Ebony and Ivory, slipping the pills into their mouths. He picked up a champagne glass and gave each of them a sip to wash them down.

Christian took two more pills from the bowl, and held them between his fingers in front of Meeka. "So what's up, Alice? You ready to venture down the rabbit hole?"

Meeka sat there looking at the pills as if she was trying to figure what to make of them. Meeka could smoke and drink with the rest of them, but pills were out of her league. "Thanks, but I'm going to have to pass."

"No need to be frightened, baby. This is just a little pick-me-up. It's all the rage with the young party crowd. This little pill will make you feel like you're on a roller coaster while sitting perfectly still," he tried to persuade her.

"I'm not afraid, I just don't rock like that. Designer drugs have never been my thing," she said honestly.

"The lady is as wise as she is beautiful." Christian smiled and tossed the pills back into the bowl. "I don't indulge either, but I do love to watch. Nothing wrong with a little weed, but I frown on people in my origination who do more than that. Boogie is the rare exception because he's easier to deal with when he's in his happy place. Had you taken the pill there would've been no way I could've accepted you into my flock, little sheep. You've passed the test."

"You were testing me?" Meeka asked in surprise.

"Everything is a test," Boogie said from the sidelines. A dopey grin was plastered across his face, courtesy of the pills he'd popped.

Frankenstein appeared seemingly out of nowhere, looming silently over Christian. There was an irritated expression etched across his hard face. In one hand he held a black leather doctor's bag. Christian waved him forward and Frank leaned down to whisper something in his ear. Meeka couldn't hear what it was, but whatever had irritated Frank seemed to amuse Christian.

Christian stood, tethering the leashes of Ebony and Ivory to his chair until his return. "Walk with me, Meeka. I have something I want to show you." He extended his hand.

When Christian laid those dreamy eyes on her she felt like she was powerless to resist and went with him without question.

Christian led Meeka across the warehouse, through the throngs of partygoers, with Frank and Boogie bringing up the rear. A burly man wearing woman's clothing and a face full of makeup staggered into their path. Frank made to step forward but a dismissive gesture from Christian stopped him.

"Christian, dear boy, I've been trying to get a word in with you all night," the cross-dresser said in a deep voice.

"My apologies, Beatrice. I've been otherwise occupied," Christian said politely. "I trust you are enjoying yourself?"

"Hell yeah! Me and my girls have been having a grand old time." Beatrice danced in place.

"Glad to hear it. With that being said, have you given any thought to my proposal?" Christian asked.

"Indeed I have and you can count me and my girls in," Beatrice told him.

"Well this is excellent news indeed. You and I are going to make quite a bit of money together. This is cause for a celebration. Tell your girls the drinks and drugs are on me for the rest of the night."

"Thanks, Christian. I appreciate that, but before we get to celebrating we still have to address the elephant in the room," Beatrice reminded him.

Christian took one of Beatrice's hands in his. "No need to worry about that. I'll pay a call on your former employer and deliver the message personally."

"Bless your heart." Beatrice kissed the back of Christian's hand. "You truly are a prince among savages. Enjoy the rest of your night. Oh, and happy birthday." Beatrice smiled and walked off.

"Fucking fag," Boogie mumbled once Beatrice was out of earshot.

Christian turned toward Boogie. "What was that?"

"Nothing, man," Boogie said, realizing his mistake.

Christian walked over and stood directly in front of Boogie. Christian was taller, but Boogie outweighed him by quite a bit. Still, Boogie seemed small in his presence. "No, it sounded like you had something to say. I believe 'fag' was the word you used."

Boogie sucked his teeth. "C'mon, man, I'm just saying I wasn't feeling the way that thing was all up on you. Nigga was acting like he wanted to fuck you."

Christian raised an eyebrow. "If I didn't know any better I'd say you were jealous. What's the matter, Boogie, you thinking about taking a crack at Beatrice?" he teased him.

"Fuck no! I rock with bitches, not no chumps!" Boogie declared.

"And that is exactly my point. A man who is confident in his own sexuality shouldn't be made to feel uncomfortable by the preferences of others. You know my rules about those who choose to party under my roof. I don't care if a person chooses to lay with man, woman, fish or foul, they're all welcome so long as they can pay to play, and that includes the 'children,'" he said, using a term that was usually reserved for members of the gay and lesbian community. "Do we understand each other?"

"Yeah, man," Boogie relented.

"Good." Christian patted his cheek. "I have no tolerance for bigots, Boogie, even the ones in my own family." He walked off.

Meeka looked over at Boogie, who was watching Christian and seething. From what Meeka knew for a fact Boogie was a raging bull and it usually took little to nothing to send him into a murderous rage, yet he had taken the scolding from Christian with the grace of a child who had just been disciplined. The display didn't make Meeka question Boogie's gangster at all, but it did raise some questions in her head about what kind of hold Christian had over those who followed him.

The rest of the walk was taken in total silence. At the back of the warehouse level they were on there was a door that led to a short flight of stairs. As they were walking up the stairs Meeka's nose picked up on a familiar stench. She couldn't quite put her finger on what it was, but it had the scent of something rotten. When they stepped out onto the next level it finally hit Meeka what she was smelling: death.

The tiled walls of the room they entered had once been white, but those days were long gone. Time and lack of care had made them a sickly shade of yellow. Along the walls were a few rusted stalls and there were drains cut into the floors. It hadn't occurred to Meeka until then that the spot they'd picked to host Christian's party had once been a slaughterhouse. She looked at the old and dried blood on the floor and wondered how many animals had met their ends in the room.

Christian brought the small group to a stop in front of one of the stalls. He leaned against the wall, arms folded and a disappointed look on his face. Boogie looked inside and made a face like he wanted to throw up. Frank just looked on with his usual emotionless expression.

"Don't just stand there gawking. Come and have a look." Christian waved Meeka forward.

Meeka sheepishly walked up and peered between the two larger men to see what they were looking at. The sight before her caused Meeka's stomach to lurch and she almost vomited on Christian's designer boots.

Inside the stall a man was suspended by his ankles from a chain hanging from the ceiling. His naked body was a mess of bruises and cuts. As Meeka's eyes traveled the length of him and landed on his face she realized she knew him. His name was Robbie and she had met him earlier on in her dealings with Boogie and Christian. Robbie had been like a little brother to Christian so what he had done to land himself in that situation was beyond Meeka.

"Right now you're probably wondering, what kind of man am I to have someone who I claimed to love hung like cattle, waiting for the slaughter, huh?" Christian asked as if he was reading Meeka's mind. "To answer your unspoken question, I am a man who will not tolerate disloyalty. You see, young Robbie here let his ego get in the way of his better judgment and got to running his mouth to some people who he had no business talking to. As a result, something that I've been planning for months has potentially been compromised and we lost two of our own, Adam and Bess."

Meeka was surprised and hurt to hear this. She liked Adam and Bess. They were two cute kids, barely out of high school and so madly in love with each other that Meeka sometimes wondered if the world outside of their relationship even existed to them. Adam was cool, and always kept a smile on his face, but would bust his gun on command. Meeka often got the impression that he wanted out of the life, but his fear of disappointing Christian kept him in it. Bess was a bit of a different case. She had no taste for the lifestyle they had chosen, but hung close to Christian's crew because Adam was a part of it. Mentally, she wasn't the sharpest knife in the drawer, but Bess had a heart of gold. Adam and Bess were like the crew's unofficial children and everybody took turns looking out for them. Even Frank, who didn't seem to like anyone except Christian, did his part when it came to Adam and Bess.

"Adam was a soldier," Christian continued. "He understood the rules of the game, but Bess . . . My sweet, dimwitted Bess." His voice was heavy with emotion. "She was an innocent. That girl wouldn't kill a mosquito if she caught it sipping from her arm. Bess and Adam died in a most cruel way all because you whispered into the ear of a bitch, who whispered into the ear of a nigga who tipped our target off."

"Christian, that bitch was lying! Her and that other nigga twisted my words!" Robbie tried to explain.

"So says the man who is standing in the shadow of the end of his life; well, in your case, hanging in the shadow," Christian said with an amused smirk. He eased off his golden jacket and handed it to Boogie. "Frank, my bag please." He rolled his sleeves up. Frank handed him the bag, which Christian placed on the floor before Robbie and popped it open. "What I've found is that a man who thinks he's about to die will build a dam of lies to try to prolong the inevitable flood of what's coming, even if only to extend his life for a few moments." He retrieved a pair of rubber gloves from the bag and slipped them on. "But a man who knows he's about to suffer," he said, and removed several nasty-looking blades from the bag to spread them out on the floor, "will spill the truth in rivers."

"Boogie, don't let him do this to me," Robbie begged. Boogie just turned his back. "Frank." He turned to the bigger man. "This is me, your li'l homie. Help me out!" Li'l homie was the nickname Frank had given him.

Frank shrugged his broad shoulders. "You ceased to be my li'l homie when you went against the grain." Frank then turned his back also.

Robbie continued to try to appeal to Christian, but his pleas fell on deaf ears. Christian selected two blades: one with a nasty curve at the end and the other thin and sharpened to a razor-fine point. "I once met a man by the name of Kaplan, and had the pleasure of spending an evening with him at the craps tables in Atlantic City. While I watched him gamble away every dime in his pocket he told me something that I still hold dear to this day. He said that the most satisfying debts were those collected in blood. You, my one-time protégé, will be a testament to that." He struck the blades against each other, causing them to spark.

"I can't watch this." Meeka made to turn away, but Christian's cold voice stopped her.

"Don't you fucking move," Christian hissed, pointing one of the blades at her accusingly. "You will watch and you will remember," he told her before starting in on Robbie with the blades.

Christian began slicing off strips of Robbie's flesh, starting with his thighs, while firing off questions. Meeka had to give it to Robbie, he lasted almost a full minute into the interrogation before he was telling Christian everything he knew and then some. Robbie rattled off names, dates, and addresses while Christian stripped him of his skin. He even confessed to cheating on his girlfriend in the tenth grade. For the most part the information Robbie's babbling didn't mean much to Meeka, but two names he spoke made her pay closer attention: Chucky and Ramses. She had no clue what the connection could've been between them, but she dared not ask.

"This is bad. All bad." Boogie shook his head in disappointment while he processed Robbie's confession.

"Indeed it is, my overweight friend." Christian placed his soiled blades back into the bag. "Robbie fucked us, but this changes nothing. A retainer paid is a contract honored."

"So what do you wanna do about that?" Frank asked, nodding at what was left of Robbie. Christian had turned him into the victim in a slasher flick, reducing Robbie to little more than six feet of open cuts and mumbled prayers.

"There's nothing more to be learned. This piece of shit wanted a pat on the head so bad, give him one; right between his fucking eyes," Christian spat.

Frank reached inside his leather blazer and pulled out his .45, ready to put young Robbie out of his misery, but Christian stopped him.

"Not you, her." Christian pointed a bloody finger at Meeka.

"Me?" Meeka was shocked.

"Yes, you," Christian insisted. "Meeka, since Boogie brought you around all I've heard you scream is how you're trying to come up, so I'm giving you an opportunity to prove you're serious about it."

"Christian, she ain't ready for this kinda shit. Let me do it," Boogie offered.

"Then you should've thought about that before you brought her in," Christian told his friend. "Don't keep me waiting, Meeka."

"Christian, I'll admit that you guys have been there for me when nobody else was and plenty of nights you kept me from starving. For this you will forever have my gratitude and my loyalty, but to be honest, I don't think I'm built to catch no body," Meeka said honestly. Hijacking and busting heads was one thing, but murder was a whole different ballgame.

"Maybe you've mistaken my statement for a request." Christian took the .45 from Frank and went to stand in front of Meeka. "I'm not asking you to kill a man. I'm telling you what's required of each and every member of this dysfunctional little family of ours. You gotta pay to play, baby, and the price of admission is blood." He extended the gun to her. "Unless you're ready to go back to living in that one-room shack and putting your name on the orange juice and mama's house?"

Meeka felt every eye in the room on her, including Robbie's. There was a good chance that if she refused she would still be allowed to leave, but it wasn't a bet she felt confident in taking. It was just like Boogie had told her earlier: everything with Christian was a test and Robbie was an example of what happened to those who failed.

"Okay," Meeka said, taking the gun from Christian. She stood there for a time, aiming the gun at Robbie. Meeka had fired a gun before, but never at a living target.

Christian eased up behind her, standing close enough to Meeka that she could feel his body heat. He slid his hands down her arms. She was trembling so bad it was a wonder she didn't drop the gun. Christian wrapped his delicate yet sure hands around hers to help steady the gun. "Just relax," he breathed into her ear, causing the hairs on her neck to stand up. "And fire." He tapped her finger.

Meeka's eyes instinctively closed when the gun kicked. The retort of her gun was like someone letting off a firecracker near her head and it took a few seconds for the ringing in her ears to pass. The smell of gun smoke singed her nose and throat giving her the urge to cough. All was silent save for the fading echo of the .45. When Meeka finally opened her eyes she beheld her handiwork . . . her price of admission.

Robbie hung there, lifeless eyes staring out and seeing nothing. A section of his throat and shoulder were missing, exposing his now bare collarbone. She wanted to turn away from the gruesome sight, but couldn't. A man was dead and she was now a murderer.

Christian cupped her face lovingly in his gloved hands. "My little rose has sprouted her first of many thorns." He kissed her on the forehead. When he removed his hands from her face there were bloody fingerprints on her cheeks. "Frank, take care of the mess. Me and Boogie are going to take Meeka back to Boogie's place to get cleaned up. Meet us there when you're done."

Meeka and her newfound family went back to Boogie's house where she stripped and put her clothes in a plastic bag for disposal. They wanted to make sure they destroyed any and all trace evidence that could connect them to the murder. Meeka had loved that outfit when she bought it, but after what she'd done she doubted she'd ever be able to look at it again let alone wear it. *Good riddance.*

She stood naked in Boogie's shower, letting the water wash over her as she reflected on what she had done and where her actions would leave her. Christian was like the sly spider who had caught her in his web. It baffled her how someone so beautiful could have such an ugly heart.

Meeka looked down watching the water and soap carry Robbie's blood down the drain. Blood washed away from the skin easy enough, but it left a permanent stain on one's soul.

# CHAPTER 13

The club where Stacy danced was surprisingly nicer than Li'l Monk had expected it to be considering the neighborhood it was in. They were stopped at the door and patted down by a beefy white guy wearing a police badge. Li'l Monk was nervous at first until Omega explained to him that sometimes off-duty cops moonlit as security for different clubs. Li'l Monk was somewhat of a novice on the club scene. He had been to a few, but clubs really weren't his thing. He hated crowds, even more so when he wasn't allowed to carry his gun. He expressed to Omega how uncomfortable he was with leaving the guns in the car, but Omega assured him that they'd be good. They were parked right out front and besides that Omega had two razor blades taped to the collar of his shirt.

Omega seemed to think that being guests of Stacy's would've gotten them some special treatment, but it didn't. Their policy was in order for them to get a private table they had to buy two bottles at $300 each. Li'l Monk wanted to tell them stick their policy and overpriced bottles up their ass, but Omega dropped the bread so they could party comfortably. That's how Omega was.

He didn't mind dropping money on a good time. Li'l Monk was more conservative, choosing to fly under the radar and stack his bread, but Omega lived out loud. He spent his money just as quickly as he made it, and made no apologies for it. Li'l Monk had once tried to check him on his reckless spending and Omega simply said, "I live every day like it's my last, because I never know when the streets will call me home."

When they finally got inside Li'l Monk found the place to be smaller than he expected. Several small tables littered the main floor while the booths were set against the walls. The main stage was situated behind the bar and boasted three twelve-foot poles, two of which were occupied with young women trying to earn their keep. It was quaint, but what it lacked in size it made up for in décor and choice ladies. Every time Li'l Monk thought he had seen the baddest chick in the spot, one even more beautiful would walk by. Li'l Monk had been reluctant to come with Omega, but now that he was there he was glad he did.

While Li'l Monk nursed his Hennessy and Coke, watching asses of all shapes and sizes walk past, Omega sat with his phone to his ear. It must've been an important call because Omega had been totally ignoring the beautiful Dominican chick with the huge ass who was trying to get his attention. When Omega was done with his call he slipped his phone back in his pocket and smiled like the cat who had swallowed the canary.

"I take it that was good news?" Li'l Monk asked.

"Great news," Omega informed him. "Tut handled that piece of business from earlier."

"Seems like Tut's been handling a lot of business lately," Li'l Monk said slyly.

Omega looked at him, knowing his friend well enough to read between the lines. "C'mon, man. You still on that? Dawg, it was Ramses who bumped him up not me. Even still, we're the ones who brought the strip back to life when we took it over; me and you, not me and him. What me and Tut got going on ain't got nothing to do with our thing."

"Sure feels like it when you're giving Tut and his maggot-ass crew slices of our pie," Li'l Monk shot back.

Omega waved him off. "That was about business, nothing more. Tut did me a solid so I let him stretch his legs a little bit, that's all."

"Right, and you never did give me the rundown on exactly what it was that was big enough to earn him a whole block in our territory."

The statement caught Omega off guard, but he recovered quickly. "Just some shit that needed to be handled that couldn't be traced back to me or you."

"I've noticed lately that there's been a lot going on that I'm not involved in," Li'l Monk said. It was merely an observation, but it sounded like an accusation.

Omega regarded Li'l Monk for a time. They hadn't been friends that long, but circumstances and mortal sins had forged a brotherhood between them stronger than most friends who had known each other all their lives. Li'l Monk had pulled Omega's ass out of the fire more times than he cared to remember and vice versa. If Omega couldn't depend on anyone in the world he could depend on Li'l Monk and that meant something. He knew he hadn't been keeping it one hundred with his friend and decided to come clean.

"Okay, check it." Omega leaned over the table and spoke in a hushed tone. "I know I ain't gotta tell you that what I'm about to say stays between me and you, right?"

Li'l Monk gave him a look that said he was offended by the question.

"I don't think all is as well as we're being led to believe in the kingdom of the Pharaoh," Omega confessed.

"What makes you say that, O? Did Ramses say something?" Li'l Monk asked, thinking of his own suspicions.

"It ain't about what he's saying; it's about what he isn't saying. Ramses has been acting differently lately. He ain't never been the most friendly muthafucka, but it's like he's always sour about something these days. He don't even come around like he used to. Most of the time I communicate with him through Huck or one of his other flunkies. Then you got all these new niggas he's bringing in. Every time I turn around he's recruited some fucking knucklehead I gotta babysit. It almost feels like he's preparing for something."

"Something like what?" Li'l Monk asked.

Omega shrugged. "I wish I knew. Ramses don't tell me shit no more unless it's got to do with the strip or a muthafucka needing to die. He's on some real secretive shit lately. I can't quite put my finger on what's going on, but over the last few weeks things have changed. I'm thinking that maybe it's because of all the problems popping up he's under a lot of stress. We go through enough holding these corners and strips down so I can only imagine what Ramses gotta deal with trying to keep Pharaoh's shit in order."

Li'l Monk scratched his chin. "Could be that, could be something else. You speak to anybody else about this?"

"Nah, only you," Omega assured him.

"Good, and make sure you don't. That kinda talk whispered in the wrong ears can get you clipped," Li'l Monk said seriously. "For now just keep your eyes open and your ears to the streets, and I'll do the same."

"Fo sho, Li'l Monk," Omega agreed. He knew just what his partner was thinking and he couldn't say that he was surprised, especially since it had been he who planted the seeds. What he said about Ramses acting different was true, but what he left out was the part he had contributed to Ramses's behavior. The stunt he and King Tut had pulled with Petey and the Puerto Ricans had put a strain on the relationship between them and Ramses, but so had Li'l Monk and the Italians. They were two peas in the same pod, trying not to end up in the boiler; and in their circumstances Omega saw a potential solution to each of their problems. If either one of their situations went sour the odd man out would need an ally. Omega was sure he'd stand tall and die with his lie about what had happened to Petey, but he couldn't say the same about King Tut. If it came down to it Omega knew the best way to put a vicious dog down was to sic a rabid one on it.

"You gonna finally pay me some mind and tip me or keep whispering to your friend?" Stacy threw herself on Omega's lap. She had changed out of her street clothes and was now wearing her work attire: a black lace bra top and black lace thong. With a face full of makeup and a platinum blond wig she looked totally different from the girl who had been braiding Omega's hair on the stoop.

"Damn, baby, you look good enough to eat."
Omega cupped her ass.

"That's what I'm hoping." Stacy twirled one of
his dreads around her finger. "Oh, this is my friend
Tiffany." She motioned to a girl who had been so
quiet that she was almost invisible standing there.

Li'l Monk looked up and was confronted by a
caramel beauty, who couldn't have stood taller
than five foot five and that was in heels. She had
big, dreamy brown eyes and full lips that curved
at the ends as if she was going to smile at any
moment. Unlike the rest of the girls, who were
parading around in elaborate outfits, she wore a
simple green two-piece bathing suit that rode up
on her high hips. Her face looked like it had been
professionally made up, but you could still tell that
she was young, probably one of the youngest girls
working the joint. She stood there twirling a cherry
Blow Pop between her lips, looking at Li'l Monk. It
wasn't a sexual look, but to him it felt like one.

"Nice to meet you." Li'l Monk spoke up to break
the sexually tense silence.

Tiffany popped the candy from her mouth to
say, "Likewise," before putting it back in.

"So what's up?" Stacy interrupted. "Y'all sitting
around like you just lost your best friend. I thought
y'all was trying to have a good time." She grabbed
one of the bottles from the table and helped herself
to a glass.

"You heard the lady." Omega picked up the bottle of Hennessy and placed it in front of Li'l Monk. "Let's get this party started."

For the next twenty minutes Stacy and Tiffany danced for Omega and Li'l Monk exclusively, much to the dismay of some of the other patrons. A few haters even tried to complain to management about the preferential treatment, but the way Omega was throwing money they let the girls rock out. Li'l Monk was tipping too, but not like Omega. True to his word he was in there living like a man on his last day.

One of the scantily clad waitresses came over with a bottle of champagne on a silver tray. The sparkler sticking out of the mouth of the bottle rained sparks on the table as she set it down. "Compliments of the gentlemen over there." She pointed across the room, answering the question that was on both Li'l Monk's and Omega's faces.

Li'l Monk looked in the direction where she had pointed and saw three men sitting in a booth on the other side of the room. One of them, a young dude who wore his head completely shaved, raised his champagne glass in salute, acknowledging that it had been his party who sent the bottle over. "You know them niggas?" he asked Omega.

Omega looked over and frowned. "Yeah, those are some of Shai's peoples," he said in disgust. "I don't know the other two, but they call the one with the bald head Nut."

"Send that shit back and tell them we good," Li'l Monk told the waitress in a sharp tone.

The waitress looked back and forth between Li'l Monk and the party that had sent her over, not particularly sure what to do.

"Bitch, are you hard of hearing?" Omega spoke up. "You heard my friend. Send it back or pour it out. Either way I don't want that shit on this table."

Li'l Monk watched the waitress as she went back to the table to deliver the bad news. The one Omega had identified as Nut looked their way and smirked, nodding his head. One of his people made to get up from his seat, but Nut stopped him.

"Bitch-ass niggas." Omega sneered at them and took a swig from the Hennessy bottle.

As the night wore on Li'l Monk slowed down on his drinking, but Omega was throwing them back. Between him and the two girls they had polished off the first two bottles and were now doing shots. Omega kept ordering shots for Li'l Monk, which he pretended to drink, but he mostly poured them on the floor. He didn't like the dirty looks the kid Nut and his people were shooting their way and wanted to be on point if something went down.

"Damn, I gotta take a leak." Omega pushed himself up from the table. He wobbled a bit as he stepped out of the booth.

"You good?" Li'l Monk asked, noticing a glazed-over look in Omega's eyes. He was clearly drunk off his ass.

"Yeah, man, I'll be straight once I piss all this old liquor out and make room for some new booze." Omega laughed drunkenly.

"You want me to roll with you?" Li'l Monk asked, seeing Omega was having trouble keeping on his feet.

"Nah, I can hold my own dick." Omega staggered off toward the bathroom.

"Your drunk-ass friend is probably gonna be in there for a while so I'm gonna hit the main floor and try to get some of this money." Stacy slid from the booth. "You coming, Tiff?"

"Nah, I think I'm good right here." Tiffany nestled closer to Li'l Monk.

"Suit yourself." Stacy sauntered away.

While Stacy was chasing dollars, and Omega was likely in the bathroom throwing up, Tiffany kept Li'l Monk entertained. She had finally loosened him up enough to let her give him a lap dance. Tiffany straddled Li'l Monk's lap, finding a comfortable position before getting into her routine. Li'l Monk found himself surprised because Stacy had said it was Tiffany's first night dancing, but she moved like a veteran, throwing her lower regions on Li'l Monk and causing his dick to rise. For as short and light as Tiffany had been on conversation all night, when her number was called she proved heavy on moves.

Li'l Monk had been good at keeping his hands to himself all night, but Tiffany was turning him on.

He let his rough hands explore the length of her body, and cupped her nice-sized breasts. Tiffany reached her hand between her legs and played with Li'l Monk's dick through his jeans, causing it to swell to the point where he thought he might nut on himself. Li'l Monk loved Sophie, but Tiffany was making him weak. He was about to throw caution to the wind when there was the sound of breaking glass somewhere behind them.

The first place Li'l Monk looked was in the direction where Nut and his crew had been sitting, and he found it empty. "Omega." He gasped, pushing Tiffany off his lap and heading toward the bathrooms.

# CHAPTER 14

Omega had barely made it through the smoked-glass bathroom door before all the liquor he consumed came pouring out. He leaned over in one of the stalls, stomach lurching, and painted the toilet seat with everything he'd eaten that day. After a few minutes the sickness had passed and Omega was starting to feel more like himself.

After taking a minute to create more of a mess for the cleaning crew by pissing all over the toilet seat, Omega went to the sink to try to get himself together. He washed his hands and rinsed his mouth out with cold water. As he was rinsing his mouth Omega heard the bathroom door open and close. He looked up in the mirror and saw Nut and his two boys roll into the bathroom.

"Sup, Omega?" Nut approached him.

"You tell me, nigga," Omega replied coolly, drying his hands on one of the rough brown paper towels.

"C'mon, man. Why all the hostility?" Nut asked in a calm voice. "I sent you a bottle and you send it back. I try to come in here and talk to you like the stand-up nigga I always heard you were and your body language is telling me to go fuck myself. If

I didn't know any better I'd think you didn't like me."

"Probably because I don't," Omega shot back.

"Man, fuck this nigga." One of Nut's boys stepped forward, but Nut waved him back.

"Listen, Omega," Nut began. "You don't like me and in truth I ain't no big fan of yours, but my boss Swann seems to have a high opinion of you. He's the one who asked me to talk to you."

"Talk to me about what?" Omega asked.

"About the future. Look, dawg, ain't no need to mince words or sugarcoat this shit because we're both on the streets and we both see what's happening. The eighties and nineties are gone and Pharaoh's reign is coming to a close. The pickings are about to be real slim on that side of the fence. This doesn't mean that all y'all gotta starve with that old relic. Cats like you, Benny, Li'l Monk, even Chucky's smoked-out ass, y'all young dudes were the ones really holding the streets down while men like Pharaoh and Ramses sit back in their big houses reaping the benefits and handing the soldiers whatever scraps fall off their tables. On our side, everybody eats the same."

"Yeah, I can tell y'all ain't missing no meals," Omega said sarcastically, looking at the overweight young man who was with Nut.

Nut shook his head at Omega's immaturity. "Look, man, you can make jokes all you want but, like it or not, this thing is going to happen. You're a good earner, Omega. Don't let pride and misplaced loyalties leave you out in the cold with everyone else. Fucking with the Clarks you'll be balling on a level you never dreamed possible."

"Is that right?" Omega raised his eyebrow.

"Swann got big plans for you, Omega. No foot soldier shit while you're waiting to make your bones. Your rep speaks for itself so you'd come in as a boss; your own crew and an entire housing project to run instead of some bum-ass corners," Nut told him.

"That's a damn sweet offer," Omega said mulling it over.

"And it's only gonna get sweeter, Omega. Shai doesn't just want to rule the city; he's got his sights set on the world. You ain't gotta answer right now, but think on it and come see me when you make up your mind." Nut extended his hand.

Omega shook Nut's hand. "No need to wait, I got an answer for you now. You, Swann, and Shai Clark can suck my dick!" he said before snuffing Nut.

In a flash Nut's crew was on Omega, trying to pack him out. Omega put his back on the wall and defended himself as best he could. Nut's crew weren't the most skilled fighters, but Omega was drunk and his reaction time was off. Someone managed to land a solid blow on the side of his head, dazing him. Omega went down to one knee, and tried to protect his head as they rained punches on him. Omega spied Nut making his way toward him with his leg drawn back. He waited for the kick to come and grabbed Nut's leg. Calling on his adrenaline, Omega picked Nut up and dove with him through the glass bathroom door.

The fight spilling over onto the main floor caused a panic inside the club. People were scrambling to get out of the way of the warring combatants. Nut and his crew outnumbered Omega so they should've been whipping his ass, but he was holding his own, until a bottle crashed into the back of his head and sent him sprawling face down to the ground. Once Omega was at their mercies, Nut and his crew began viciously stomping and kicking him. Security had now gotten involved, but Omega couldn't tell if they were trying to break it up or help Nut's crew stomp Omega out. Omega thought they were going to kill him until he heard an unmistakable voice.

"The fuck off my homeboy!" Li'l Monk roared, charging Nut's crew. He was like a mini wrecking ball bowling through security and enemies alike. Li'l Monk paused long enough to help Omega to his feet, which allowed Nut time to kick him in his back. Li'l Monk flew several feet and crashed into an unoccupied chair. Before they could swarm him, Li'l Monk was back on his feet and armed with the chair. In a show of brute strength he ripped two of the legs from the wooden chair and wielded them like clubs. He and Omega stood back to back as they were surrounded by Nut's crew and almost a dozen angry bouncers and staff members.

"See, I told you we'd have fun tonight," Omega said over his shoulder.

"Fuck you, O! Every time I turn around I gotta pull your ass out of the fire!" Li'l Monk shouted back.

"That's one of the perks of being my best friend." Omega laughed. "You know this is gonna end bad don't you?"

Li'l Monk surveyed the numbers and knew they were about to take a beating. "Fuck it; live every day like it's our last right?" he quoted Omega before lashing out with the chair legs.

Li'l Monk and Omega lasted all of thirty seconds before they found themselves at the bottom of a dog pile getting the shit kicked out of them.

After getting tossed out of the strip club Omega and Li'l Monk ended up back at Stacy's where the girls tended to their wounds. Omega ended up losing several of his dreads and suffered a bruised cheek in the brawl, while Li'l Monk felt like his rib was cracked. They had taken an ass whipping of epic proportions, but it was worth it. They had succeeded in causing a full-scale riot that everyone in the streets was sure to be talking about for weeks, including the Clarks. Omega sent them a loud and clear message that they were loyal to Pharaoh.

Stacy was angry because being that they had dropped her name at the door, the club owners blamed her for bringing them. Omega patched things over by promising to give her a few dollars to keep her afloat until she landed another gig. Tiffany didn't too much care about not being able to dance there anymore. It was her first night and she hadn't developed any attachments to it.

Once Omega and Li'l Monk's injuries were tended to they kept the party going. Omega had some weed on him and Stacy managed to scrounge up a big-ass bottle of cheap vodka that had been in her refrigerator. Normally Li'l Monk wouldn't have mixed light and dark liquor, but all the fighting had completely blown his buzz from earlier. Besides that he needed something to numb the pain of his aching ribs.

The liquor and weed brought Tiffany all the way out of her shell. She pranced around the living room still dressed in her stripper outfit, dancing seductively to the slow jams CD Stacy had put on. While everyone else seemed to be mellowing out, she seemed to be getting more out of control. Stacy had to check her when she attempted to pull her bikini top off in front of Omega. Had Li'l Monk not known any better he would've thought she was on something more than weed or alcohol.

As the night wore on things got a bit more intimate. Omega was damn near molesting Stacy in the middle of the living room for all to see. Eventually he took her in the bedroom, leaving Li'l Monk and Tiffany alone.

Tiffany parked herself on Li'l Monk's lap with a drink in one hand and a blunt between her lips. She ground back and forth on Li'l Monk's lap, blowing weed smoke in his face. "You know, Stacy told me that you were off the chain, but seeing it for myself was something else."

Li'l Monk shrugged. "I do what I do when necessary."

"Strong and modest, huh?" She leaned forward and whispered in his ear. "I got so wet when you split that kid's skull with the chair leg." She licked his ear.

"Chill, ma." Li'l Monk pushed her back a bit to put some distance between them.

Tiffany looked hurt. "Why you acting like that? I thought you liked me."

"I do. I mean, you're bad as shit, but I got a girl," Li'l Monk told her.

"Well, she ain't here right now is she? And I don't know the bitch so you won't have to worry about her finding out, so what's the problem?"

Li'l Monk didn't answer. Internally his heart and his dick were locked in a heated argument. Having Tiffany playing him so close was dead wrong, but it felt so right.

"I know what it is." Tiffany raised her cup between them. "You need some more to drink to loosen you up." She sipped from her cup, leaned forward, and spit the liquor into Li'l Monk's mouth before kissing him. It wasn't a passionate kiss like those he shared with Sophie; this was one of pure lust. The next thing Li'l Monk knew he was kissing her back.

He and Tiffany sat on the couch kissing and sharing vodka. Li'l Monk wasn't sure if it was the cheap liquor or the fact that he had been drinking heavily earlier, but his head began to swim. Heat spread through his face and worked its way down his body, settling in his dick.

"That's what I'm talking about." Tiffany stroked his dick through his jeans. She slid down the length of his body and began undoing his pants.

"Stop, don't do that," Li'l Monk said weakly. His brain told him to push her away but his body wouldn't cooperate. "What the fuck is wrong with me?" he wondered out loud.

"Nothing, baby. You're just riding the E train." Tiffany winked at him before making his dick disappear in her mouth.

Li'l Monk looked at the nearly empty cup of vodka in his hand and it was then it hit him. Tiffany had put something in their drink.

Tiffany crawled back up his body and he could feel her trying to put his rock-hard dick into her soaking wet pussy. "Wait, a condom," he babbled.

Tiffany placed her finger over his lips. "Don't worry, I ain't got nothing. Besides, it feels better this way."

Every fiber of Li'l Monk's being screamed for him to get Tiffany off his ass, but he was too far gone in the throes of whatever Tiffany had slipped him. When he felt her warm pussy slide over his dick, Li'l Monk's whole body went rigid. Without even realizing it a drug-induced smile spread across Li'l Monk's lips.

"That's right, baby." Tiffany got comfortable on him. "Just relax and let mama ride this dick 'til it spit."

# PART III

# *STRANGE BEDFELLOWS*

# CHAPTER 15

Meeka stepped out of her building wearing a pair of baggy gray Juicy sweats, Moschino sneakers, and a graphic T-shirt. A Gucci scarf was tied on her head, Aunt Jemima style. Since it was chilly out that day she wore a light wool jacket that she had gotten from the thrift store for a fraction of its retail price. What she was wearing wasn't too far off from the street uniform she'd worn all her life, only the brands had changed.

Meeka had never been a chick who cared about brands or what something cost. If it was comfortable and presentable she was okay with it, but when Christian came along everything changed. Whether he was going to handle some hood shit or host a gala, Christian was always sharp, and it reflected in the people he kept around him. It wasn't that he enforced any sort of dress code, but Meeka noticed that those lucky enough to inhabit his inner circle carried themselves a certain way: always clean. Even Boogie could throw it on when he needed to. Even when they were slumming their label game was up. The more time Meeka spent around them, the more she got tired of feeling like the dusty hood bitch who hung around the beautiful people, so she invested a good chunk of what she made into her wardrobe.

As she strolled her block she found it relatively dead, which was odd. Normally at that time there was always someone out either trying to buy drugs or sell them, so to see her neighborhood deserted was strange. She wasn't complaining, just a bit surprised. Goodness knew she welcomed the calm.

Meeka walked to the bodega two blocks away to get her morning coffee and a pack of cigarettes. The bodega on the corner of her block was closer, but the one two blocks away sold Newports for almost half the price. They were from other states and didn't have New York State stamp so they could be sold for cheaper than suggested retail cost. It wasn't legal, but it was lucrative.

She was making her way back to her block, sipping coffee and smoking a cigarette, when she noticed a red Corvette parked in front of her building. As she got closer the driver got out and walked around to the curb. It was Christian. She almost didn't recognize him dressed in loose-fitting jeans, a pair of construction Timberlands, and a black-and-white varsity jacket. The only trace of his normal flash was the black baseball cap he wore, with big gold metallic letters across the front that spelled out G.O.D. In his hand he held a Burberry umbrella, despite the fact that there wasn't a cloud in the sky.

"Morning, sunshine!" Christian waved the umbrella.

"Good morning to you too. What brings you up to this end of the ghetto?" Meeka asked, surprised to see him in front of her house unannounced.

Christian turned his face upward and spread his arms, basking in the sun shining overhead. "It's a beautiful day, so I thought I'd come out and water my garden." He opened the Corvette's passenger door. "Take a ride with me, little rose."

"I'm not really dressed to go anywhere," Meeka said, motioning toward her outfit.

"You look fine, love," Christian assured her. "Besides, where we're going how well you pay attention will matter more than what you're wearing. Now get in."

Meeka tossed her cigarette and got in the passenger's side, while Christian got behind the wheel and they peeled off. As they drove Meeka kept casting curious glances at Christian.

"What's on your mind, sugar?" he asked, noticing her looking.

"Nothing. I was just thinking how much different you look when you're dressed down," Meeka said. "You look so . . ."

"Manly?" he finished the sentence for her. Christian laughed. "Let me let you in on a little secret: for as much as I love to glamour up, it's not my everyday thing. Believe it not, I enjoy a comfortable pair of Tims and jeans more than I do leather and silk."

"Really?" Meeka couldn't hide her shock.

"Yes, really. Why do you seem so surprised?"

"You don't seem like the type."

"What you really mean is I don't strike you as butch enough to dress like an everyday street nigga. It's okay to say what's on your mind. You're family now," Christian told her.

"I didn't mean any disrespect. Whatever your sexual preferences are ain't none of my business. You're a good dude and that's all that really matters to me," Meeka said sincerely.

Christian laughed hysterically, banging his hand on the steering wheel. He was laughing so hard that tears were coming out of his eyes and he was having trouble catching his breath.

"What's so funny?" Meeka asked, not picking up on the joke.

"Did you think I was gay?" Christian asked, trying to compose himself.

"Maybe not gay, but at the very least bisexual," Meeka admitted.

"No, I'm not. I got a kid, a girlfriend, and two mistresses. I've never lain with a man or had the urge," he informed her.

"My bad. I just thought that with the way you dress, the wild parties with trannies . . ."

"What can I say? I'm a sucker for fine fabrics and fabulous people." He chuckled. "But seriously, don't be so quick to believe everything the world shows you. Most of it is just smoke and mirrors, baby."

"So you go through all the theatrics just to throw people off?" Meeka was still trying to process it.

"Not entirely. He is me, yet he is a stranger." Christian waved his hand over himself like he was pulling down a curtain. Meeka looked even more confused now, so he elaborated. "The vibrant and strikingly handsome piece of man meat you girls fawn over in the clubs is but one side to a coin. I'm a mama's boy through and through, and I make no apologies for who I am. I picked up more game catering to the hags at my mother's Saturday night poker games than I ever could standing on a corner with the other boys my age. These neighborhood women, who had less than we did, would dress up in all their finery and prance into my mama's house like it was the Ritz-Carlton. When you looked at them, you didn't see a woman living under harsh conditions; you saw a lady of wealth and influence. If only for one night they could forget who they really were and be whoever they projected. It was these women who planted the seeds in my head that would grow and take me to the top. See I was never the toughest kid on the block or the biggest, so brute strength was never an option for me. I would have to find another way to get where I needed to be. This was where the art of perception came into play. I didn't want to be just a player in the game or a boss. I wanted to be a god. But Christian Knight was no deity; he was no different than your average hood nigga trying to get a dollar. If I wanted to be praised, I had to give people something to worship."

"Principe de La Noche." Meeka finally caught on.

"The smart girl gets a cookie." Christian nodded approvingly. "The man my mother birthed is plain and unassuming, but the one those old women at the poker game spawned is larger than life. He is the lover of fine clothes, fine women, and fine drugs. More importantly he is the last person you'd expect to walk up on you and put a bullet in your head. An enemy who'll never see you coming is an enemy who doesn't have a chance to mount a proper defense."

Meeka had to admit she was impressed by his logic. Dolled up in his fine clothes, with his big words and colorful hair, you were more likely to mistake Christian for a queen than a cold-blooded killer. It was a brilliant strategy and she had a whole new respect for him. "So, who is the real Christian?"

Christian gave her a sly smile. "Stick around long enough and you might find out."

He drove them farther uptown and turned down a dead-end street. He parked his Corvette by a hydrant and grabbed the umbrella from the back seat. He tested it to make sure it was working properly before getting out and motioning for Meeka to follow him. Christian led her into the courtyard of a run-down building where several women were loitering. From the way they were scantily dressed Meeka knew they were working girls. Their eyes all followed Christian curiously as he passed them.

Sitting on the bench at the far end of the courtyard was a man who looked like he had just stepped out of a seventies movie, dressed in a crushed red velvet suit and matching apple jack hat cocked on his head. Hovering behind him was a dark-skinned man wearing a too tight T-shirt and a scowl. He must've been the pimp's bodyguard. The dark-skinned man whispered into the pimp's ear, causing his head to snap up. When he saw Christian, his body tensed and his hand drifted to his jacket pocket. No doubt he had a weapon hidden there. Ignoring the hostile gesture Christian continued to approach.

"Sup, Red?" Christian extended his hand, but Red didn't shake it. A sad look crossed Christian's face. "Looks like somebody woke up on the wrong side of the bed this morning."

"Don't you be worrying about what side of the bed I woke up on, snake. What you doing 'round here?" Red snapped.

"I came to pay a call on an old friend and hoped that we could do some business," Christian said.

"Christian, we ain't never been friends. The one and only time I was ever fool enough to break bread with you, you had me drugged and made off with two of my bitches. I should smoke your larcenous ass for having the audacity for even coming to my place of business on some funny shit," Red spat.

"Red, you can't fault me for the decisions your girls make. You know the rules of the game. And as far as you doing even the slightest bit of harm to this gorgeous body of mine, I think we both know that if it were that simple you'd have tried your hand ages ago. You can front for people you don't know, but you can't front for someone who has heard the dirty little whispers of your heart. You're a pretty chatty fellow when you're on that Mind Candy," Christian said, referring to the pills Red had been on that night. "Now can we skip the pissing contest so I can make my proposal and get out of this cesspool you call a ho stroll?" He looked around distastefully.

"Speak your business and be gone, freak!" Red demanded.

"Very well." Christian twirled his umbrella. "Beatrice and some of her lady friends have decided they're ready for a change of scenery and would like to explore the greener pastures of my organization," he said flatly.

Red opened his mouth to protest, but Christian raised his umbrella to silence him.

"Now," Christian continued, "before you go into giving me the whole pimp speech about trying to knock your bitches, let me just say that I didn't come to her. She and some of her girls came to me and wanted to join my circus. Now I understand that as well as this being a bruise to your ego it's also going to hurt your pockets, so I have come prepared to compensate you."

Red frowned at the word because he didn't know what it meant.

"It means I'm willing to pay you, Red." Christian sighed at his ignorance. "I think paying you the sum of five thousand dollars for Beatrice and, let's say, fifteen hundred per head for each girl who defects with her is fair. This way when word gets out that they're with me it won't look like you got knocked for your ladies; it looks like you sold them. It allows you to save face and make a few extra bucks for your trouble. How's that sound?"

"Sounds like you been taking them happy pills you sell," Red capped. "You've got some nerve coming over here and spitting in my face, dressing it up like you're doing me a favor. That he-she bitch Beatrice makes more for me on a weekend than you're offering."

"Indeed, so. Beatrice's client list of businessmen makes her quite a valuable piece on the chessboard, which is all the more reason you should've taken better care when she was with you. See, the problem with niggas like you is that you think you've got to keep your foot in a chick's ass to make sure she stays productive. Ain't nobody gonna be a punching bag forever, man nor woman."

Red stood. "And the problem with niggas like you is you can't seem to keep your nose out of other people's shit." He jabbed his finger into Christian's chest. "First you're a stick-up kid, then a drug dealer, and now you wanna be a pimp! Nigga, you can't even make up your mind which sport you wanna play! You think because you got them team of killers running with you that you can muscle your way into other people's rackets, but I ain't going to be muscled by nobody, especially your sugary ass!" He jabbed him again. "Now I'm gonna let you prance on outta here only because I need you to deliver a message to Beatrice for me. You tell that abomination that his asshole is mine to rent out until I say different. Now get the fuck from around here before I put you in a dress and have you selling your shithole for me too." He popped his collar and strutted back to where his bodyguard was standing. They slapped each other five and laughed.

Christian let out a deep sigh. "I was really hoping we could've put our past differences to the side and handled this like gentlemen, but obviously there's no reasoning with you." He opened his umbrella, and held it over his head.

"Damn right there ain't no reasoning with me. Now fly your ass away, Mary Poppins," Red dismissed him.

"Meeka, you may want to stand a little closer so you don't ruin your clothes." Christian pulled her under the umbrella.

Meeka wasn't sure what Christian meant until she heard something whistle by her ear and a split second later Red's head exploded. Christian tilted the umbrella just in time to keep blood and brain matter from splashing on them. Red's bodyguard took off running, but he didn't make it very far before something slammed into his back and he too fell over dead. When Christian lowered the umbrella, Meeka looked up and saw Boogie perched on the roof holding a rifle.

"You should've taken the money," Christian said to Red's corpse before strolling back to the center of the courtyard. He climbed up on one of the benches and addressed the stunned prostitutes. "As you can see by the mess over there, Red is out of business. Those of you who want to go rogue or choose someone else are welcome to do so, but those of you who wanna get your shit together and make some real paper get with Beatrice. You bitches are now liberated and I am your messiah!"

***

Meeka was silent during the ride back to her block. It amazed her how Christian could turn from sweet and fun-loving into a cold-blooded killer in the blink of an eye. She wasn't sure why she was surprised. What he had done to Robbie the night before had shown her how much value he placed on human life, and it wasn't much. Christian had ordered the deaths of Red and his bodyguard with a simple gesture, which further demonstrated the kind of power he had in the streets. He said he wanted to be a god, and Christian was certainly playing the part.

Christian made a sudden move and Meeka damn near jumped out of her skin. She looked down to see he had produced a lavender handkerchief and was handing it to her. "You've got a little blood on your cheek," he pointed out.

"Oh." Meeka looked in the mirror and saw the speck of red just below her eye. "Thanks." She took the handkerchief and wiped her face. Once she'd cleaned the blood off, she busied herself staring out the window. Christian was a puzzle she wasn't sure she wanted to solve.

"Something is obviously on your mind, so you might as well spit it out," Christian said, picking up on her mood. "You've been through quite a bit over the past twenty-four hours so the least I can do is give you the courtesy of some candor."

"What the fuck was that back there?" she asked.

"A power move. Red was standing in the way of progress," Christian said as if it was nothing.

"That was about more than the purchasing of some whores to fatten your stable. You never intended on making that deal with Red. You planned on killing him all along," Meeka accused him.

Christian raised his hand. "Guilty as charged, your honor. We went over there under the guise of brokering for Beatrice's freedom but I was really collecting the contract that had been placed on his life. Beatrice and the girls scraped up a nice chunk of change, but couldn't cover my normal retainer. Luckily for them I never cared much for Red so I didn't mind eating the loss."

Meeka sat up in her seat and looked at Christian. The revelation caught her off guard. As far as she knew Christian made his money running girls and selling drugs. She had seen him at work so she knew he was more than capable of murder, but would never have pegged him for a paid hitter. Her new boss was proving full of surprises.

"Don't look at me like the girl who just went home with the guy at two a.m. and then gets offended when she realizes that he just wants to fuck. Niggas take lives for free to hold drug corners, so why shouldn't I turn a profit from it? The name of the game is get rich by any means necessary and I'm doing just that."

"I ain't no killer," Meeka told him.

"You'll be whatever is necessary if and when the need arises, or have you already forgotten Robbie?" he sneered. He pulled the car to a stop in front of Meeka's building and threw it in park. "Listen, honey, I like you, truly I do but this game me and mine are playing isn't for the faint of heart. If you don't have the balls or the desire to be remembered, then you best get your cute ass out this car and be forgotten."

Meeka remained seated.

"That's what I figured. Look, if you're worried about me having you running around clipping people, you needn't be. My vices are my vices, and I'd never expect you to take a life unless it was absolutely necessary. What I had you do to Robbie was about trust. I couldn't very well fully let you in on my business unless I had something to use as insurance that you'd never turn on me if you were ever pressed."

"I'm a loyal bitch. I'd never turn on you," Meeka said, offended that he would even think such a thing.

"I'm not a man who believes in taking chances or blind trust. We are a family bound by blood and secrets, and now you are too, little flower."

"I'm so over this." Meeka made to get out of the car, but Christian grabbed her about the wrist.

"Before we part company, I need to ask a small favor of you."

"What, do you need me to drown some puppies or something?" Meeka asked sarcastically.

Christian chuckled. "That was cute, but no, nothing quite so extreme. It's just a small task." He ran his finger down her arm. Christian leaned forward and whispered something in Meeka's ear that made her recoil.

"I can't do that," she told him.

"Oh, but you can. This is far too delicate of a situation for me to entrust to Boogie or Frank. In fact you're probably the best person qualified for the job because of your familiarity with the parties involved," he told her. Meeka still looked unsure. "Whether you agree or not, it's still going to happen. I just thought I'd give you the courtesy of letting you know and maybe helping this all go a little smoother." He ran down his plan to her.

Meeka sat there contemplating what had been asked of her while Christian watched her, waiting to see how she would answer. If she refused he'd likely just have Boogie or Frank take care of it and there was no telling how they would handle it, but it would likely end up messy with a lot of unnecessary people getting hurt. Going along with Christian's request was likely the lesser of the two evils and the safest course of action. "Okay, I'll do it," she agreed.

"Excellent." Christian smiled. "Thank you, Meeka. I won't forget how much you've done for this family."

Meeka didn't reply; she just got out of the car. "Christian." She leaned in the window. "After this, no more bullshit. I'm about getting money, not playing these sick-ass games of yours."

Christian placed three fingers over his heart. "Scout's honor, baby. Now go on upstairs and get pretty for me."

Meeka walked up the stairs of her building with mixed emotions. Her grandmother had always told her that nothing in the world was without costs, and for her place among the beautiful people she was paying a heavy price. The irony of it all was no matter how much she tried to escape her past it always seemed to catch up with her.

# CHAPTER 16

Persia's night had been a fitful one with very little sleep. Every time she closed her eyes she saw Ramses. Bumping into him at the steak house had been unexpected and frightening. The whole time he was at their booth Persia kept thinking that she was going to die and take Vaughn with her for the ride. She had never been more relieved than when he left.

The whole ride back to Long Island City Vaughn kept asking about her relationship with Ramses. Persia downplayed it like he was just a guy from the old neighborhood, but she could tell Vaughn didn't believe her. The incident with Ramses was just another reason that Persia couldn't commit to Vaughn. She really liked him, but her life was far too complicated. Vaughn had everything going for him and she feared that her bullshit would only bring him down.

After a few minutes of lying there and feeling sorry for herself she finally managed to get out of bed. She checked her bedroom phone and found the light on the answering machine blinking. She had eleven messages, mostly from Chucky no doubt. He had been blowing her phone up to the point where she finally turned her ringer off. After the night she'd had the last thing she wanted to deal with was his crackhead shit.

Pushing thoughts of Vaughn and Chucky out of her head she went into the bathroom to take a shower. She felt much better after washing the previous night's drama off her. She pulled her hair into a ponytail and grabbed her favorite pair of old sweatpants and an oversized T-shirt from the drawer. Persia didn't plan on doing anything that day except lounge around the house and watch movies.

She was just about to leave the bedroom when she saw her phone lighting up. Persia was about to let it ring thinking it was Chucky, until she peered at the caller ID and recognized Asia's number. "Hey, girl," she answered.

"Hey, yourself," Asia replied. "You didn't call me last night after your date so you know I need the play by play."

"It was okay, nothing to write home about," Persia lied. "I got sick after dinner so he brought me home."

Asia sucked her teeth on the other end of the phone. "I swear you could fuck up a wet dream."

"Blame it on my stomach, not me," Persia said.

"Well I guess it was your stomach's fault that another bitch was trying to mark your territory last night," Asia informed her.

"What you talking about?" Persia asked in a confused tone.

"Well I was listening to the radio this morning and rumor has it while you were home nursing your tummy ache, Vaughn and some other ballers ended up at the Golden Lady. I hear they were throwing around garbage bags full of money!"

Asia's revelation stung, but Persia tried not to show it. "So? He's not my man and I'm not his girl. What's that supposed to mean to me?"

"It means you're cutting your nose off to spite your face!" Asia fumed. "Let's keep it real between us. I feel like you're in the way of your own happiness. You have a man who has his shit together and is head over heels for you and everybody except you seems to see it!"

"I do see it, trust me I do, but I can't get serious with Vaughn like that. I mean, you're one of the few people who know my story so you should understand why I don't wanna track that mud into his backyard."

"How long are you gonna be beholden to those old ghosts?" Asia asked seriously. "Your past is your past and should have no bearing on your future. If Vaughn cares for you like he acts like he does then he'll be able to accept all of you, as you were and as you're striving to be. What kills me about you is that you're not even putting it on the table to find out. Why are you so damned opposed to giving love a chance?"

"Because I've seen what love can do." Persia huffed. "I've only loved two men in my lifetime, my father and Chucky, and both of them claimed to be something they weren't."

"Kind of like what you're doing with Vaughn," Asia shot back. "I know you like Vaughn and you're just trying to keep from hurting him but lying ain't gonna do much to spare his feelings when this hits the fan, and trust me it will. If he has a problem with your past then fuck it and fuck him, but don't deny him the freedom of choice."

"I gotta go," Persia said, wanting to get off the phone. In truth Asia's words were hitting too close to home.

"Okay, but promise me you'll at least consider what I'm telling you."

"I promise, I will," Persia agreed.

"Cool, call me later if you need to talk," Asia said and hung up.

Persia took a few minutes to process her conversation with Asia. Though she hated to admit it, Asia was right. Persia had been beholden to the ghosts of her past for far too long and it was time to finally lay them to rest. The thought of losing Vaughn scared her, but the thought of hurting him scared her even more. He was the only man since her father to ever show her even a shred of kindness and not expect anything in return.

Vaughn was a good guy and deserved to know the truth. Persia decided that the next time she saw Vaughn she would lay it all on the table and let the chips fall wherever they may.

When Persia came down the stairs she was greeted with the smell of bacon frying. Her mom was making breakfast. Persia hadn't even realized how hungry she was until the smell of food made her stomach growl. She went into the kitchen to find her mother standing over the stove flipping pancakes.

"Hey, baby," Michelle greeted Persia when she noticed her standing there.

"Hey, Mom." Persia kissed her on the cheek. "I see you're in here throwing down." She looked over the spread: eggs, bacon, pancakes, and fresh fruit.

"I was up a little earlier than usual for my morning workout and decided to whip something together for the family," Michelle said proudly.

"Mom, your figure looks great but you still exercise like you're training for a triathlon," Persia teased her.

"Honey, unlike you young girls Mama gotta work to keep this figure popping." Michelle pinched one of her love handles. "What I wouldn't give for a body like yours, Persia."

"That's gotta be a joke. I lost so much weight that I look like a ten-year-old boy now. I hate my body," Persia said sadly.

Michelle stopped her cooking and gave her daughter her undivided attention. "Baby, don't ever let me hear you say that again. Self-hate is a terrible thing, and I've always taught you to love yourself. Yes, I know you've lost some of that ass you were carrying, but you're wearing this new weight well. You are beautiful, Persia, whether you're thick or slender; never forget that, you hear me?"

"Yes, Mom," Persia said, mustering a smile. Her mother always had a way of making her feel better when she was down.

"Do me a favor and go tell your stepdad that breakfast is ready. I think he's in the study."

"Okay, Mom." Persia left the kitchen and went to fetch Richard.

Persia crossed the living room and approached the closed door of Richard's study. She listened for a few seconds before knocking softly.

"Enter," Richard called from the other side of the door.

Persia pushed the door open and entered Richard's private sanctum. Richard's study was the one place in the house that was off-limits to everyone but him. He didn't even allow Michelle to clean it for him. Persia would sometimes joke about Richard secretly being a terrorist and was probably building a weapon of mass destruction inside. It was a small room furnished with a writing desk, a small sofa, and wall-to-wall bookshelves. She found him sitting on a folding chair hovering over a chessboard, deep in thought.

"Mom says to tell you that breakfast is ready," Persia told him.

"I'll be there in a sec," Richard said, not bothering to look up from the chessboard. There were pieces set up on both sides, but he was the only one playing.

"Doesn't chess usually require two players?" Persia asked.

"Technically, but not necessarily." Richard moved one of the white pieces. He looked up at Persia and saw her staring curiously at the board. "Do you play?"

Persia frowned. "Jesus no! Chess looks about as much fun as watching paint dry."

"Chess is more about strategy than fun. It's a thinking man's game," Richard informed her. "Come over here for a second, Persia."

With a sigh Persia went over and stood over the board.

"What do you see here?" Richard motioned toward the board.

Persia shrugged. "Looks like a game of checkers with fancier pieces."

Richard chuckled. "To the uninitiated, maybe, but chess is far deeper than a game of checkers. Chess is a game of life."

"How do you mean?" Persia asked, now very interested.

"Each piece," Richard said, waving his hand over the board, "has a very unique purpose. From the king to the pawns." He tapped his finger on the pieces respectively. "Each piece is pivotal to the survival of the king." He plucked a piece from the board and held it up for her to see. "This is the queen, who the king leans on most heavily. Her ability to move anywhere she likes on the board makes her the strongest piece." He moved the queen across the board this way and that. "The queen has one purpose: protect the king."

"Seems like the queen has all the real power," Persia remarked.

Richard smiled. "And therein lies the lesson. Let's go eat before the food gets cold."

As Persia and Richard were coming out of the office the doorbell rang. Her mother was already on her way to answer. As they neared the foyer Persia heard her mother talking to someone. The closer she got the more familiar the voice became. Persia's heart dropped as she knew it wasn't who she thought it was. Not at her house. Not like this.

# CHAPTER 17

Li'l Monk awoke with a splitting headache. His tongue felt like he had been licking a shaggy carpet and his eyes stung. He was disoriented and for a minute couldn't figure out where he was. When he tried to move, he found himself weighed down. He looked and found Tiffany lying on his chest snoring. That's when the memories came flooding back to him.

Guilt suddenly rained over Li'l Monk like a ton of bricks as he thought back on his night of wild sex with Tiffany. Whatever she had slipped into the drink they shared brought out a side of Li'l Monk he never knew was there. He was an animal, taking her in several positions and sticking his dick in every hole in her body. Li'l Monk had done things with Tiffany that he couldn't even talk about with Sophie and the worst part was that he enjoyed it. Sophie was a good chick and had never stepped out on Li'l Monk, and in return he had betrayed her. He felt like shit and wasn't sure he'd be able to face her, but eventually he would have to.

Li'l Monk slid from under Tiffany, careful not to wake her. He tiptoed around the living room, gathering his clothes from the various places they had been thrown. He was able to track down everything except one of his socks. Only God knew where it had gotten off to and he wasn't about to stick around to find out. He didn't even bother to check on Omega, who was likely still in the bedroom sleeping it off. He just wanted to get out of the apartment and put the whole crazy night behind him.

When he got outside Li'l Monk flagged down a taxi to take him back to the block. He was tired, hung over, and had to take what felt like the worst dump in his life. All he wanted to do was get back to his apartment so he could shit, bathe, and take a nap.

Li'l Monk got out of the taxi and of course the first person he saw was Droopy. The young man was sitting on a milk crate in front of Li'l Monk's building, sipping a twenty-two ounce bottle of beer and watching the block.

"Damn, you look like shit," Droopy greeted him.

"I feel like shit," Li'l Monk replied. "I had a rough night."

"So I've heard. The streets been buzzing about how you and Omega put it down last night at the strip club. I heard y'all backed down like thirty niggas on some Jet Li shit." Droopy starting mocking some moves he had seen in a karate movie.

"It wasn't thirty, nigga, more like ten or so. You know how stories get exaggerated when they pass through the grapevine."

"They say y'all put in on two of them Clark boys too and their friends wasn't none too happy about it. One of they peoples came through twice already looking for you. He asked for you by name. Some nigga named Swann," Droopy informed him.

Li'l Monk didn't know too many people in the Clark crew, but Swann's was a name he was familiar with. He was a high-ranking member of the Bloods street gang and Shai's second-in-command. "What'd he say? Was he on some bullshit?"

"At first I thought he was, but he said he was just looking to talk to you about some unresolved issues," Droopy said.

"What'd you tell him?"

"What you think I told him? I told him get the fuck off our block before something bad happens to him." Droopy lifted his shirt to show he was still carrying the Beretta with the extended clip.

"I admire your dedication to the cause, Droopy, but be more mindful about who you threaten. Swann is connected," Li'l Monk told him.

Droopy sucked his teeth. "The only thing he would've been connected to was one of these hollow points if he had tried to get crazy out here. I don't give a fuck about a nigga's rank; if he can bleed then he can die."

Li'l Monk shook his head. "Young and foolish. I'm going upstairs to take a shit and a shower. You gonna be out here for a while?"

"Where the fuck else would I be going?"

"A'ight, I'll come check you in a few." Li'l Monk started to walk in his building.

"Yo, what you want me to do if Swann comes back through? Should I air that nigga out?" Droopy asked, hoping Li'l Monk gave him the green light.

"Don't do shit. You hit my phone if you see him, but don't try to play no hero. You hear me, Droopy?"

"Yeah, I hear you." Droopy nodded. When Li'l Monk went inside the building he added, "That don't mean I'm gonna listen."

As soon as Li'l Monk reached his door he smelled it: the unmistakable odor of burning chemicals. It was the stench of someone smoking crack. His father was home.

Inside the apartment the smell was even more potent. Li'l Monk rounded the corner and found his father sitting on the couch, but he wasn't alone. On her knees in front of him was a brown-skinned woman dressed in nothing but her bra and panties. She had a nice shape, and a large, round ass that looked like it would jiggle when slapped. Li'l Monk couldn't see her entire face because it was buried in his father's lap, but from her profile she wasn't bad looking. She didn't have the look of a crackhead, but she was obviously on one drug or another if she was keeping time with Li'l Monk's dad. The girl had Monk's cock tonsils-deep in her throat while he free-based rocks from a glass cylinder.

Seeing his father that way filled Li'l Monk's heart with both anger and sadness. You wouldn't know it by looking at what he had become, but at one time he was a great and powerful man. With his partner Face, Monk had the streets on lock. Face was the brains, but Monk was the brawn. Monk was a merciless brute who had little to no respect for human life, and he made sure everyone knew it by spilling blood every chance he got. When Face went to prison it was left to Monk to keep things going, but between his partying and getting high it didn't take long for their little empire to start crumbling. Things took a turn for the worse when his girlfriend Charlene, Li'l Monk's mom, was killed. That's when Li'l Monk's father lost his way and his will to go on.

Charlene was the center of Monk's universe and someone had taken that from him the night men came to rob the boutique she owned. In addition to taking her money they had also taken her life, leaving Li'l Monk with no mother and a shattered father. In time Monk would eventually catch up with his girlfriend's killers. With his young son, Li'l Monk, at his side he tracked them down and unleashed the wrath of the gods on them. The last one he saved for his baby boy. Li'l Monk was very young at the time, far too young to understand the long-term ramifications of taking a life. His hatred for the man for taking away his mother and his need to please his father drove him to pull the trigger.

The sin the father and son had committed should've brought them closer together, but instead it drove them further apart. Monk slipped deeper into depression and drugs, while his son learned to fend for himself in the streets. All his life Li'l Monk had vowed he would never be the kind of man his father was, yet he found himself walking a mile in the shoes of his namesake.

"I thought I asked you not to smoke that shit in here," Li'l Monk spoke up, startling the girl, but his father barely budged.

Monk's glazed-over eyes landed on his son and a smirk formed on his lips. "What's up, junior? I didn't hear you come in."

"Probably because your ass is in here blasting off. That shit stinks." Li'l Monk fanned the smoke.

"Listen to you sounding all judgmental and shit. Do I complain when you're in here smoking that hydro? God knows that crap smells like old flowers that been dragged through dog shit when you burn it. Back in my day they didn't have all them different strains. It was either good weed or bad weed," Monk recalled.

"Well this ain't back in your day," Li'l Monk said with an attitude.

"I'd better get my stuff and go," the girl said, looking embarrassed. She made to get up, but Monk grabbed her about the wrist.

"You're still on the clock, love. So you sit tight until I tell you to get gone or my money runs out," Monk told her. "Why don't you go on in the bathroom and get that pussy nice and fresh for me while I talk to my boy."

The girl hurriedly did as she was told. As she passed Li'l Monk on the way to the bathroom she was so embarrassed that she couldn't even look him in the eyes.

Li'l Monk looked at the setup on the coffee table. There were empty beer bottles, an ashtray full of cigarette butts, and a Baggie with at least $500 worth of crack in it. "Looks like somebody had a good night."

"I guess you could say that. I caught these two pussies slipping at this rock house uptown and helped them get rid of some of that product and money they were sitting on," Monk told his son.

"You make a clean getaway?" Li'l Monk asked.

Monk shrugged. "All depends on who you ask. One of them tried to get cute, so I had to make him ugly, feel me?" He patted the barrel of the shotgun that was propped against the couch.

"You better be careful out there, old timer," Li'l Monk warned his father.

"I could say the same to you, youngster." Monk lit a half-smoked cigarette that he'd found in the ashtray. "I heard about you and that sneaky-ass Omega getting your asses kicked at that strip club last night."

"Damn, I guess news does travel fast in the hood."

"Son, let me hip you to something." Monk exhaled a cloud of smoke. "Two of the best sources of information pertaining to what's going on in the streets are prisons and crack houses. Don't too much happen that I don't know about especially when it involves my boy getting the shit kicked out of him."

"There were more of them than there were of us," Li'l Monk explained.

"Don't matter. A pistol always evens the odds in a fight, but considering I didn't hear about nobody getting shot I take it you don't have yours with you." Monk's face suddenly became serious. "What's the first two things I taught you when you decided to start playing with guns?"

Li'l Monk lowered his eyes like he was ten years old again and was about to get a spanking. "Never pull one unless you plan to use it and never leave home without one."

"Well your memory is working fine so that rules out brain damage, so we're gonna chalk this up to you being a damn idiot."

"Don't call me that!" Li'l Monk said sharply. He had always been sensitive about people making jokes about his intelligence, which his teachers and other kids did his whole time in school. It wasn't that Li'l Monk was actually stupid, he just had a lot of issues that he didn't know how to deal with so his natural reaction was to rebel against any and all authority. His guidance counselor had diagnosed him as having a learning disorder, but Li'l Monk had a social disorder.

"Don't get your panties in a bunch, junior. I'm only giving you a hard time," Monk told him. "But on the real, you and your dumb-ass friend Omega might've opened a nasty can of worms by putting your hands on them Clark boys. I keep warning you that Shai Clark ain't some sucka-ass niggas like Pharaoh and Ramses who hide behind their soldiers. They'll get out in them streets and get with your little ass."

"I ain't scared of Shai," Li'l Monk said confidently.

"I know you ain't, son, but that don't mean you gotta be stupid about it either. There's a difference in going up against some street crew versus a real, organized crime family," Monk warned him.

"Whatever, man," Li'l Monk said as if he was no longer interested in what his father was saying.

About that time the girl was coming out of the bathroom. She was wearing a bathrobe and slippers, but it didn't look like anything underneath. When she passed Li'l Monk she smelled fresh and sweet like soap. As he looked at the print her large ass made in the robe he couldn't help but to wonder what something so tender was doing with a man like his father.

"Listen." Monk got off the couch and came to stand in front of his son. "You're with Pharaoh and Ramses, so I know you're loyal to them. I understand loyalty better than you might think, but I also understand staying in my lane. If Pharaoh and Shai got some kind of pissing contest going on, you leave that to them to sort out. Soldiers ain't got no business involving themselves in disputes between bosses unless y'all at war and, the way I hear it, things haven't gotten that far yet. For now, you keep your head down, get your money, and if it comes down to it make sure you blast first. Ya dig?"

Li'l Monk nodded.

"Good." Monk patted him on the shoulder. "We might not always get along, but never forget that you're my son and I love you. If something were to happen to you out there I'd have to make these streets feel me and the police would be cleaning up Clark blood and Pharaoh's alike. Now go on in your room for a few ticks and let Daddy get his nut off."

Li'l Monk felt better after he dropped his load and washed his ass. When he came in he wanted nothing more than to lie down, but talking to his father had him so wired that he wasn't tired anymore. He figured he might as well hit the block and get back on top of his money.

After changing his clothes he strode back into the living room to tell his father he was heading out. The girl was gone and Monk seemed halfway sober by that point. He was sitting on the couch, smoking a cigarette and going through a shoebox full of old pictures.

"What you got there?" Li'l Monk asked, sitting on the couch next to his father.

"Just some old memories." Monk handed one of the pictures to his son. It was an old photo of a much younger Monk. He was shirtless, wearing a huge gold rope chain and standing in front of a bodega that no longer existed.

"Shit, Dad, you were big as hell back then!" Li'l Monk examined the picture. Monk looked like a squat mountain of muscle.

"I could bench press four hundred pounds back then. I was the only one in the crew who could get that much weight up back then," Monk said proudly.

"I can see why niggas has so much respect for you back in the day," Li'l Monk said.

"Nah, they feared me, but they respected him." Monk handed him another picture. It was a photo of him and Face leaning on a BMW, posted up in front of Willie Burgers on 145th. "Me, I never had the patience to be diplomatic about shit. My gun did all my negotiating, but Face had a way about him that when he spoke, people listened. Face was the last of the stand-up guys in Harlem."

"Do you miss him?" Li'l Monk asked.

"Every single day," Monk said sincerely. "Face was more than just my business partner; he was my brother. Face was the one dude who had my back no matter what. Whether I was right or wrong he always rode out with me. My biggest regret is never getting a chance to tell him how much I appreciated his friendship."

"There's still time, you know? Ain't like Face is dead; he's locked up. I got a car now, so maybe we can take a road trip," Li'l Monk suggested.

Monk thought about it and shook his head. "I ain't seen Face in over a decade. I'd rather he remember me as I was rather than see what I've become."

"Well if you ever change your mind the offer still stands," Li'l Monk said sincerely. "That reminds me, you ever hear of a nigga named Kunta?"

"Who hasn't? *Roots* was a must-watch in every black household," Monk said, referring to the movie based on Alex Haley's timeless novel.

Li'l Monk sucked his teeth. "Not Kunta Kinte, fool. I'm talking about some dude who rolled up on me last night. He says he knows Uncle Face."

Monk ran his hand over the stubble on his chin searching his memory. "I do remember Face writing me a couple of times and mentioning some crazy-ass African kid he had become fond of in prison. His name started with a K, so it could've been Kunta."

"What's his story?" Li'l Monk asked.

"Wait a sec, I think I got the last letter here." He dug around in the shoebox of pictures and came up with a folded piece of paper. Monk scanned through the letter. "Here it is." He tapped the page. "See, Face had always been a smart muthafucka, not just streetwise, but book smart too. Quiet as kept he even had a college degree."

This surprised Li'l Monk because he had only ever known Face to be a drug dealer and killer. "No shit?"

"No shit. He got an associate's degree in English while he was on the streets and received his bachelor's in prison. Him continuing his education was a secret; only me, him, Michelle, and your mom knew about it. He kept it from the guys because it wouldn't have gone over well with some of them. Face feared it would've made him look weak."

"How could a man wanting to better himself have been looked at as weak?" Li'l Monk was confused.

"Because on the streets it ain't about smarts, it's about slugs. In our line of work men are more inclined to follow someone who can outshoot rather than someone who can out-read them. Now are you gonna shut your hole and let me finish or what?"

Li'l Monk nodded for him to continue.

"Like I was saying," Monk continued, "Face was a borderline genius and because of his smarts he was able to land a job as a teacher in prison. He taught some of the younger inmates to read and write. One of the inmates he taught was this Kunta kid. Face wrote me about a couple of the young guys he'd been helping, but the reason Kunta stuck out is because he was one of the hardest to reach. The kid was real damaged: hadn't been in the country long, no family to look after him while he was on the inside, and having a rough time adjusting to American culture. Being in prison didn't help. Face once described him as something like a feral animal, real skittish and defensive. He'd pop off in a heartbeat when he felt threatened. A lot of the inmates gave him shit for him being foreign and all, but Face kinda took him under his wing and tried to help him adjust. Face never said, but I suspect he tried so hard to help this kid as a way of compensating for not being there for Persia all these years. Face never forgave himself for leaving his lady and kid alone in the world."

Li'l Monk took a moment to process what he had just learned. "Okay, that explains his connection to Face, but why is he anxious to talk to you?"

Monk shrugged. "Beats the hell out of me. Maybe he thinks I'm Abe Lincoln and wants me to sign off on his freedom papers." He chuckled.

"Look, kid, Face has helped a lot of people over the years, in and out of prison. Some of them feel like they owe him, and it's probably the same with this Kunta character. Knowing Face he's probably got this kid out here wanting to save my immortal soul," he said sarcastically.

"Well what should I tell him if he comes around looking for you again?" Li'l Monk asked.

"Tell him to fuck off." Monk retrieved his glass cylinder from the table and reloaded it with a crack rock. "As you can see, I ain't quite ready to be saved."

# CHAPTER 18

"Persia, you didn't tell us you were expecting a guest," Michelle said, standing there looking back and forth between her daughter and the visitor.

"I, ah . . ." Persia tried to find her voice.

"I'm afraid that's my fault," Rissa spoke up. "We were supposed to meet in the city to get our nails done, but my mom let me hold her car so I decided to come and pick her up. Persia, I tried calling you, but kept getting the answering machine."

Michelle looked at Persia.

"Oh, right. I forgot to turn my ringer back on this morning," Persia said, still not sure what to make of Rissa popping up at her house. "We were just about to sit down to breakfast, so maybe it's best I catch up with you later."

"Persia, don't be rude," Michelle scolded her. "It won't be any trouble to set another place for . . . I'm sorry, I never caught your name."

"Larissa, but everyone calls me Rissa." Rissa smiled innocently.

"Well, Rissa, you're more than welcome to stay for breakfast if you like. Are you hungry?"

Rissa looked at Persia and smirked slyly. "Starving. I've been running on E all day."

"Okay, well Persia will show you to the bathroom to get cleaned up and then you can join us in the dining room." Michelle walked through the swinging doors back into the kitchen.

Richard lingered for a few seconds, trying to figure what to make of Persia's guest before mumbling something under his breath and walking into the kitchen to help his wife bring the food out.

As soon as they were gone, Persia tore into Rissa. "Bitch, you must've lost your last damn mind, rolling in here." She grabbed Rissa by the front of her shirt and gave her a little shake. "What the fuck are you doing at my house?"

Rissa looked down at Persia's hands. "First of all, you best get your mitts off me before me and you get to tussling and breaking up the nice shit yo' people got in this living room."

Persia grudgingly released her grip on Rissa.

"Thank you." Rissa smoothed her clothes over. "Persia, believe me I wouldn't be here if I didn't have to, but it was either me or Chucky. He's been trying to reach you all night and he wigged out when he couldn't get a hold of you. Plus the last batch of drugs he bought was some weak shit so he can't get his head right the way he wants to. You know how crazy he can get when he's geeking."

Persia knew all too well how Chucky could get when that monkey started crawling on his back and he needed a fix. "Chucky's addiction is no longer my problem."

"Shit, Chucky's addiction is all our problems. The fact that he's still got your ass in a sling is proof of that," Rissa capped. "Look, Persia, don't shoot the messenger. I'm sure you'd rather me be here playing nice then Chucky running up through this bitch making a scene."

"Well I can't just dip out on my family like that. We're just about to eat breakfast," Persia told her.

"Then I suggest you eat fast. Chucky is waiting on us."


Persia ate her breakfast in relative silence, only speaking when spoken to. Every time she looked across the table and saw Rissa smiling, eating her food, and chatting with her parents Persia wanted to pounce on her and beat the brakes off the girl. Yet she held her tongue. Chucky's bullshit was starting to hit way too close to home and she needed to nip it in the bud, but to do that she would need a trump card and Rissa's simple ass might prove to be just that.

"So, where exactly are you from, Rissa?" Michelle asked.

"I'm originally from Philadelphia, but I live in New York now. I'm up here for school," Rissa lied, shoveling food into her mouth like she hadn't eaten in days.

Michelle pretended not to notice, but Richard was giving her a look of disgust.

"Must be exciting, living in a new place," Michelle said.

"It has its moments, but I'm used to moving around a lot." Rissa scarfed down a pancake, hardly taking the time to chew. When she was done she started eyeballing the rest of the pancakes that were sitting in the middle of the table.

"Help yourself," Michelle told her, noticing Rissa staring at the pancakes.

"Thanks!" Rissa happily grabbed two more pancakes with her bare hands and dropped them on her plate.

Richard was about to say something, but Michelle silenced him with a look.

"Man, these sure are good! What brand are they?" Rissa asked.

"Excuse me?" Michelle didn't understand the question.

"I mean what kind of pancake mix do you use?" Rissa clarified.

Michelle chuckled. "I've never used boxed pancake mix a day in my life. I make them from scratch."

Rissa looked surprised. "You made these from scratch? Shit, Persia, you didn't tell me your mom was Betty Crocker!"

"Rissa, watch your mouth," Persia checked her.

"Sorry, old habits I guess," Rissa said, embarrassed. "All my mama did was cuss in our house."

"Well we don't use that kind of language in this house," Richard told her.

"So, what do your parents do?" Michelle asked.

Rissa shrugged. "Beats me. I never met my dad and my mom died when I was young."

Michelle covered her mouth. "Oh, I'm so sorry."

"It's cool. My sister has been looking after me since I was a kid. We've gotten along okay," Rissa said.

"So, what courses are you taking?" Richard asked.

Rissa gave him a puzzled look. "Huh?" she asked with a mouth full of pancake.

"You said you're up here for school so I was wondering what your major was," Richard clarified.

"Oh, umm, I'm taking business courses," Rissa stammered.

"Really?" Richard leaned forward, elbows on the table and chin resting on his knuckles. "Where?"

"I go to BMCC." Rissa blurted out the first school that came to mind. She had once met a girl from New York who said she went there.

Richard raised an eyebrow. "You moved from Philadelphia to attend a community college? Interesting."

"Richard, stop interrogating the poor girl and let her eat," Michelle cut in.

"I'm not interrogating her, sweetie. Just trying to get to get to know Persia's new friend," Richard said with a smile. It was clear that he saw through her bullshit. Luckily for Rissa, Richard's cell phone rang. He looked at the screen and frowned. "Excuse me, I have to take this." He got up from the table. "I hope you have a good reason for interrupting my breakfast," Persia heard Richard say as he walked out of the room.

"You'll have to excuse my husband, Rissa. He's extremely protective of Persia and our home," Michelle said apologetically.

"It's all good. You can never be too careful who you let in your house these days," Rissa said.

"Mom, I gotta get dressed so me and Rissa can head into the city. You know how Saturday traffic can be on the expressway." Persia wiped her hands on a napkin and got up from the table. "Do you need me to help you clean up before we go?"

"No, baby. I've got it. You and Rissa go ahead."

"Thanks. Love you, Mom." Persia kissed her mother on the cheek.

"Love you too." Michelle patted her daughter's cheek. "It was nice meeting you, Rissa. Don't be a stranger. Persia doesn't have many friends, but the few she does are always welcome here."

"Thank you, ma'am. I really appreciate that," Rissa said sincerely.

"Let's go, Rissa," Persia said forcefully.

Rissa followed Persia to the kitchen door and spared a glance back at Michelle, who was sitting at the table smiling warmly at her. She liked Persia's mother. She was a kind soul, kinder than anyone else she had met since she had been in New York, or anyone she'd ever met in her life for that matter. She felt bad about being at Persia's house under false pretenses, and for the first time since riding off with Chucky and her sister she began to question herself.

As Persia and Rissa were about to head up to her room they passed Richard in the living room. He was dressed in blue jeans and a white shirt, slipping into a black blazer. He was moving fast and had an irritated expression on his face. When he noticed Persia and Rissa he hurriedly buttoned his jacket and smoothed it over in the front.

"Everything okay?" Persia asked.

"Yeah, I just gotta go out and handle some work-related stuff," Richard said.

"But it's Saturday," Persia pointed out.

Richard mustered an awkward smile. "Oh, right. One of my students needs to complete an extra credit assignment so they can graduate on time and I promised I'd help them out."

"I wish they had teachers like you at St. Mary's," Persia said.

"They do, you just have to stop giving them a hard time long enough to find out which ones are which. I'll be back in a couple of hours. Do you need me to bring you back anything?"

"No, I'm fine. Thanks for asking though."

"Okay, you kids have fun in the city." Richard walked out the door.

"Hey, Persia, I thought you said your daddy was some kind of professor?" Rissa questioned.

"He's not my daddy, he's my stepfather," Persia corrected Rissa. "And he is a professor. Why do you ask?"

"Then he must teach at a rough school for him to need to take a pistol with him," Rissa said.

Persia looked at the girl as if she was crazy. "Richard is a square, and the last person in the world who would ever touch a gun. Are you high or something?"

"No, I'm sober and I've been around enough dudes who pack to know a concealed gun when I see one. I spotted the holster on his belt when he was putting his jacket on," Rissa insisted.

"Rissa, I don't have time for whatever hallucinations your withdrawal is causing. I know Richard, and he doesn't do guns. He wouldn't even know which end to hold if you handed him one."

"Whatever you say, Persia."

"Look, just come on so I can get dressed and go see what that pain in the ass Chucky wants." Persia led the way up the stairs. "And try not to steal anything while we're in my room."

# CHAPTER 19

It didn't take Persia too long to get dressed. She traded her sweats and T-shirt for a tight-fitting shirt, leggings, and construction Timberlands. She ran a comb and bumping iron through her hair and splashed on some lip gloss, puckering her full lips in the mirror to make sure they had just the right amount of shine to them. A quick sift through her mother's jewelry box scored the perfect accessories: a pair of puffy bamboo earrings that were almost as old as Persia. She wasn't trying to get fly, but she wanted to make sure she looked cute in a hood sort of way. She knew what Chucky liked and wanted to look the part. Not to please him, but to grab his attention. It was time to show her one-time lover that he wasn't the only one who knew how to play mind games.

As she was getting dressed her phone rang. She thought about picking it up, but then decided against it. It was probably Chucky looking to harass her further. She let the machine pick up and was surprised to hear Vaughn's voice come over the speaker.

"Hey, Persia, it's Vaughn. Listen, I was just checking on you to see if you were feeling better."

Vaughn paused for a minute as if he was trying to think of something else to say. "Ah, well, I've got to dip back to Philly, but I'll be back in New York later this week. We're playing the Giants at home next weekend. If you maybe wanted to hook up for dinner after the game or something . . . I dunno, just give me a shout when you can I guess. Okay, bye."

"He sounds a lot smoother giving television interviews than he does leaving messages," Rissa joked.

"What he sounds like ain't none of your concern," Persia snapped.

"For someone who is supposed to be just a friend, you sure sound defensive."

"Whatever, bitch. Let's just go." Persia grabbed her keys.

It had been decided that Persia would drive Rissa's car back into the city. Rissa claimed it was because she was tired after the big meal Michelle had made, and wanted to relax instead of fighting traffic on the expressway. Persia knew better though. She had been watching Rissa twitch and constantly keep wiping at her nose for the last few hours. Persia hadn't been free from her monkey that long where she couldn't recognize the 400-pound gorilla climbing up Rissa's back. She hadn't gotten her wake-up high and the sickness was starting to kick in. This was as good a time as any for Persia to make her play.

"You okay?" Persia asked from behind the wheel.

"I'm good," Rissa assured her, blowing her nose into a wilted piece of tissue.

"If you're feeling sick and you need me to pull over—"

"I said I'm good!" Rissa snapped.

"Umm hmm." Persia turned her attention back to the road. "Your mouth says one thing, but the fact that it's fall and all the windows are rolled down yet you're still sweating says something else."

Rissa touched her fingers to her face and they came away damp.

"You ain't had your medicine today, have you?" Persia asked. It was a rhetorical question that Rissa's body language had answered a long time ago.

"No, but I'm good. I dabble here and there, but I don't need to get high just to function. I'm not like Chucky and my sister," Rissa said proudly.

"Not yet, but how long do you think it'll be before your pet habit turns into a raging monster?" Persia asked.

"Listen to you. You danced with the devil for a few months and now you think you can school a bitch who has had it bad all her life. What you supposed to be, some kind of counselor?" Rissa asked sarcastically.

"Nah, I'm just somebody who has already visited the bottom of the barrel you're about to scrape so I've already seen what's down there waiting," Persia said seriously. "I don't know you real good, but you seem okay. You're not bad looking, and got a decent head on your shoulders, so I gotta ask: how did you manage to get caught up with a piece of shit like Chucky?"

Rissa shrugged. "I'm just rolling with my big sis. When she decided to ditch Philly with Chucky I left with them."

Persia gave her a look. "That's a great line to use if the police ever question you about your relationship with him, but you gotta come a little better with me. How long have you been fucking Chucky behind your sister's back?"

"You bugging out, I'd never do my sister like that!" Rissa declared.

"I hope you've got some other hidden talent that I don't know about because you're a poor liar. I see the way you look at Chucky; it's the same way I used to look at him before I found out who he really was. Don't bullshit a bullshitter."

Rissa looked at her, wondering if Persia was just that intuitive or if she was just that transparent. "It ain't what you think. I ain't no skank bitch who would step over her family for some dick, especially if it was someone she cared about."

"So you're saying Maggie doesn't really care about Chucky?" Persia questioned.

"No, I'm not saying that. It's just that for Maggie everything is a come up. We was barely making it in Philly until Chucky came along with all his flash and talk about cash. He was slinging big game and big dick and Maggie saw him as our way out of Pennsylvania, but I saw something else. For all his faults, Chucky has his moments where he can make you feel like you're the only girl in the world. You've been with him so I'm sure I don't have to tell you."

"Indeed you don't. I'll be the first to admit that me and Chucky had some good times, but we had more bad ones than we did good. I loved that man more than I loved myself, and in the end all I got for my love was a few broken ribs and a cracked skull. Look, I ain't judging you, Rissa. The heart wants what the heart wants. I just don't wanna see you end up like I did."

"I won't," Rissa said.

"Why, because you think Chucky loves your pussy more than he loves getting high?" Persia laughed. "Tell yourself whatever you need to if it helps you sleep at night, but you and I both know you're really not that naïve. You've been on the streets long enough to know that people like Chucky don't change."

"Even if I were to leave Chucky, I know my sister wouldn't and I can't abandon her. We're the only family we've got left."

Persia glanced at her. "I'm going to tell you something, and I don't want you to take it the wrong way, but your sister is a fiend. She's out there, maybe to the point of no return. Yeah, you guys roam the country together like two gypsies, but she's leaving you in spirit. Every time she puts that pipe to her lips she drifts further and further away. One day you're gonna wake up and find yourself alone out here in the world."

"Bullshit, it's always been me and my sister. We all we got. I love my sister and she loves me," Rissa said.

"Right, you show somebody how much you love them by getting them hooked on the same shit that's fucking your life up," Persia said sarcastically. "That ain't no knock on your sister, she's sick and in her own way by her giving you drugs that is showing you love, but that doesn't make it right. I don't doubt that Maggie means well, but for long as she's on that shit she's going to be incapable of loving you in the way you're looking for it. You're still young and ain't too far strung out to where you can't turn it around, but in order to do that you're gonna have to stop being a follower and learn to become a leader."

"You're just trying to fuck with my head to get me on your side because Chucky is blackmailing you," Rissa accused her.

"Honey, trust and believe you couldn't help me out of my situation even if you wanted to. Chucky is a vengeful bastard and he isn't gonna stop until he gets what he wants from me, or somebody kills him; either way I just want this all over with. You can take my advice or don't, and honestly I don't give a fuck either way." Persia turned her attention back to the road ahead. By Persia planting the seed of doubt in Rissa's head it was the first crack in the foundation of the plan Chucky was building. Before it was all said and done she would bring the whole thing down around his ears.

Persia had assumed that they'd be going into Manhattan to meet Chucky, but Rissa had directed her to Brooklyn, Flatbush to be exact. Traffic was horrible on the congested block and Persia ended up parking the car two blocks away and walking to the spot where they were to meet Chucky.

It had been awhile since Persia had stretched her legs in the hood, especially Brooklyn. There was a time when she loved coming to Brooklyn. Persia lived in Long Island City and was a Harlem girl at heart, but there was something she loved about coming to Brooklyn. It was very different than either of the places she had grown up and sometimes when she went there it felt like she was in a different city all together. The shopping, the food . . . Persia always got sucked up in it. Karen and her girls from uptown didn't like coming to

Brooklyn. They didn't like leaving the block at all for that matter, but Marty was always down to take the ride with Persia.

Thinking about her friend made Persia sad. Marty was a white girl, but she had a universal soul. Everyone who came into contact with her loved her. She was young, rich, and sexy and down for whatever. Marty was a reckless girl who lived carefree and as she pleased, but in the end it was her wild ways that proved to be her undoing. Persia often wondered, if she hadn't left with Chucky that night and stayed with Marty and Sarah, would things have ended up differently, or would she have been a victim too?

Persia pushed away the thoughts of her deceased friend and busied herself window shopping in some of the stores along the strip they were walking. As she was looking in the window of a boutique at a killer dress, she spotted a familiar face. "No way," Persia said and stepped inside the store.

Inside the store, Meeka was sitting on a stool trying on a pair of boots. She turned her foot this way and that trying to make up her mind about buying them, when she felt someone standing over her. She looked up and her chocolate-painted lips smiled when she saw Persia.

"Now this is a surprise." Persia bent down and hugged Meeka. "What are you doing in Brooklyn?"

"Trying to find the bargains. What are you doing so far from that mansion you live in?" Meeka shot back.

"There you go gassing it." Persia laughed. "I'm out here meeting a friend for lunch, but I saw you in here and you know I had to come shout my girl out."

Meeka shook her head. "It's a damn shame that the only time we run into each other lately is at funerals or by accident. We gotta do better."

"You ain't lying about that. I still got the same phone in my bedroom with the same number. You need to hit me up so we can hang out," Persia suggested.

"Word, I'm gonna do that. As a matter of fact, let me see if they got a pen in here so you can write my cell number down." Meeka pulled out her Nokia flip phone.

"Oh, you got a cell phone now? Let me find out you blowing up and getting all Hollywood on me," Persia teased her.

Meeka laughed. "Nah, I ain't Hollywood just yet, but I did run into some good fortune." Meeka asked the salesgirl who had been helping her with the boots to get her a pen and she scribbled her number down on a torn sheet of paper. "You better make sure you call me, too."

Behind them Rissa cleared her throat, reminding Persia that they had business to attend to.

Meeka cut her eyes at the rude girl. "This broad with you?" She sized Rissa up.

"Ah, yeah, this is my homegirl Rissa," Persia introduced her.

Meeka nodded in greeting, but Rissa just rolled her eyes. "Some bitches," Meeka mumbled. "Well I ain't gonna hold you up. If you're gonna be in Harlem later, hit me up."

"I'll do that," Persia promised, folding the piece of paper and putting it in her purse.

Meeka watched Persia and the girl she called Rissa leave the store. It seemed to be quite the coincidence that Persia randomly bumped into Meeka, but it wasn't. Meeka had been camped outside Persia's house for the past couple of hours. She punched in a number on her cell phone and waited.

"I don't like that bitch," Rissa said once they had left the boutique.

"You don't even know her," Persia pointed out.

"Yeah, but I know her type. I can't put my finger on it but something doesn't feel right with her. Her whole little greeting just felt so phony," Rissa said, shaking off the chill that had crept over her.

"I've known Meeka since I was a kid; she's one of my oldest friends. And you're one to talk considering that bullshit-ass front you put on in front of my mother," Persia capped.

"It wasn't bullshit; those pancakes really were good." Rissa smirked. "But seriously, your mom seems like a nice lady. You're lucky you have someone who cares about you."

"We've both got people who care about us, Rissa, it's just a matter of recognizing it and doing right by the people who have done right by us," Persia replied.

"Whatever." Rissa jammed her hands into her pockets and walked ahead of Persia.

The two of them continued walking past the shops and bodegas until they arrived at a small Jamaican restaurant. Persia followed Rissa in and spotted Chucky and Maggie sitting at a table in the back that had booth-like seats. It was near the window and gave him a view of the street. This was so that he could see anyone coming and going. When you had as many enemies as Chucky did you always had to err on the side of caution.

All it took was one look at Chucky to see that he was geeking. He was sweating heavily and his nose ran like he had a bad cold. When he spotted Persia, Chucky quickly got to his feet, eyes flashing with anger.

"So I gotta send Rissa all the way to that white-ass neighborhood you live in, instead of you just picking up the phone?" Chucky asked in an angry tone, causing a few of the other diners to look in their direction.

"First of all, lower your voice, Chucky. I'm standing two feet away. I can hear you just fine," Persia checked him. "And second, I turned my ringer off when I came in because I'd had a rough night and needed to sleep."

"What's the matter, boyfriend ain't giving you no dick?" Maggie snickered.

"Fuck you, crack whore. Unlike your unwashed ass, I'm selective about my dick. It takes a certain kind of man to satisfy my needs." Persia glanced at Chucky. "So we gonna stand here yelling at each other or are we gonna sit down so you can tell me what the hell you want?" she asked Chucky.

He glared at her for a few more seconds before retaking his seat, and motioned for her to take the seat on the other side of the table next to Rissa. To Chucky's surprise Persia slid in on the side next to him, purposely letting her thigh brush against his.

"Ain't you never heard the expression three is a crowd?" Maggie snapped at Persia. She didn't like how close she was playing Chucky.

"Then get your ass up and move to the other side," Persia capped back.

Furious, Maggie sprang to her feet and grabbed one of the forks off the table. "Bitch, I will blind you for trying to talk tough to me!" She lunged at Persia, but Chucky quickly got between them.

"You two knock it the fuck off." Chucky pushed them apart.

"Chucky, you better put a muzzle on your little pet dog before I spade that ass." Maggie waved the fork threateningly.

"You ain't gonna do shit but fall the fuck back like I just told you to. Go sit next to your sister and cool the fuck off." Chucky gave her a little shove.

Maggie's head reared back as if she had just been slapped. "Really, Chucky? You gonna choose this bitch over me?"

"Relax, Maggie. I ain't choosing nobody. You know me and Persia got business to discuss that ain't for everybody's ears so I ain't trying to be shouting across no damn table." He reached out and touched Maggie's face lovingly. "Now have a seat."

Maggie sat down next to Rissa, but continued to stare daggers at Persia.

"Look, Chucky, I didn't come here to fight with nobody. You asked to see me and so I'm here," Persia said, shrugging off her jacket so that Chucky could get a good look at her in the tight-fitting shirt.

"So how'd everything go last night with lover boy?" Chucky asked.

Persia thought about telling him how Ramses had shown up and ruined their date and how he was likely hot on Chucky's trail to kill him as they spoke, but instead she answered with a shrug. "Nothing fancy. He took me out to eat, but the food didn't agree with me so he took me home."

"Did you fuck him?" Chucky asked.

Persia rolled her eyes. "How many times do I have to tell you Vaughn and I have never had sex? For as ashamed as I am to admit it, you're the last man I was with."

Chucky grinned. "Don't nobody lay pipe like old Chucky."

Maggie snorted like she was about to say something slick, but Chucky's cold eyes silenced her.

"You know if I ever plan on getting more than dinner out of him I might end up having to fuck him," Persia said offhandedly. "You can't ever expect something for nothing. You taught me that."

"Well you hold off on giving homeboy that sweet pussy of yours for a minute. I intended to have you bleed him, but there's been a change of plans," Chucky said.

"Oh great, another one of Chucky's plans," Maggie said sarcastically.

"Maggie, if you keep opening that big-ass mouth of yours I'm gonna put something in it, and it ain't gonna be my cock," Chucky threatened.

Maggie got ready to say something else, but Rissa placed a calming hand over hers. Maggie looked at the worried expression on her sister's face and swallowed her words.

"Smart girl." Chucky winked at Rissa. "Like I was saying, in light of recent developments we're gonna have to speed things up a bit. I need y'all packed and ready to blow town at a moment's notice. After this last robbery, we're outta here. For now I just need you all to kick back and lay low while I handle the details."

"Are we done here? Because I'm ready to go," Maggie asked with an attitude. She hadn't gotten high in a few hours and felt her itch coming on.

"Yeah, we're done," Chucky told her, getting up from the table.

"Hey Chucky, I rode out here with Rissa and really don't feel like fighting with the bus. Do you think you can give me a ride?" Persia asked sweetly.

Chucky recognized the look she was giving him. It was a look he hadn't seen in a while and it caused his lower regions to stir. "Sure, I can do that."

"Oh hell no!" Maggie spoke up. "I need to get right and ain't nobody got time to be making no detours while you drop Ms. Prissy off. Let that bitch follow the yellow brick road back to Oz."

Persia's eyes narrowed to slits. "I ain't gonna be too many more bitches, Maggie."

"I just call it like I see it," Maggie said smugly.

"So do I, thirst monster!" Persia snapped back.

"Look, I've had about enough out of the both of you. Maggie, you can ride back to the pad with Rissa while I drop Persia off. Here." He dug in his pocket and tossed a small bag of cocaine on the table. "This should keep you calm until I get back."

Maggie and Rissa both scrambled for the bag of cocaine. In the end it was Maggie who came out victorious when she delivered a sharp elbow to her sister's gut and snatched the cocaine. Maggie cradled it in her hand like it was the most precious of things, oblivious to the fact that she had just knocked the wind out of her sister to claim it. If she hadn't been so preoccupied with the bag of cocaine she would've noticed the murderous look her sister was giving her.

# CHAPTER 20

Persia sat in the passenger seat of Chucky's BMW watching the traffic. Every so often she would glance over at Chucky, who couldn't seem to stop playing with his nose. Whenever he would catch her looking, she would just offer a weak smile. She couldn't help but to wonder if he knew how bad she wanted to shove him out into traffic. Being around Chucky repulsed her, but she had to play nice in order to get what she wanted and that was to be rid of him.

"So you gonna tell me the real reason you cracked on me for a ride, or you gonna keep with that 'I don't feel like dealing with the bus' lie?" Chucky asked as he dipped his car in and out of traffic.

"You swear you know me, huh?"

"Of course, I know you inside and out." Chucky laid his hand on Persia's leg, expecting her to move it, but she didn't.

"To be honest, I wanted to get some time to talk to you alone. Since you've been back them two junkie bitches you roll with are always glued to your hip," Persia said.

"Maggie and Rissa are okay. They're a means to an end," Chucky told her.

"Seems like more than that to me, especially with that Maggie broad. She acts like you belong to her. Is that your new girl?" Persia asked, but Chucky didn't answer. "Now it all makes sense. No disrespect, but I never would've figured her for your type. You've always liked 'em young and fine, not old and washed up."

"Call it what you want, but Maggie done held a nigga down through some rough times," Chucky defended her. "And since when did you care who I keep time with? You act like you hate me."

"I don't hate you, Chucky. I just can't stand your ass," Persia said with attitude.

Chucky laughed. Persia trying to act tough always amused him. "I see you've developed a stink-ass attitude since last time we ran together."

"Getting left to die in a crack house has a way of souring you on certain shit. And we ain't running together; you're blackmailing me," Persia corrected him.

"Blackmail is such a dirty word. I'm just helping you to help me."

Persia shook her head. "You can be such a dick sometimes. I don't understand how I ever fell for a muthafucka like you."

"Because you were used to fucking with little boys and I came and put this grown man dick on you," Chucky boasted.

"You sure are big on yourself, huh? I ain't gonna lie and say the sex wasn't good, but it wasn't the only reason I was with you. You were everything I wanted in a man: handsome, charming, and about your paper. I can still remember the day you first got at me, looking all good in your shiny red car and matching sweater," Persia recalled. "You couldn't tell me shit when I was riding shotgun through the hood with you. We were the envy of everyone on the block."

Chucky silently reminisced about the kinder days when he was still on top of the game. He was the man in the hood, but had fucked it all up because he had gotten greedy and sloppy. He looked at his reflection in the rearview mirror and what he saw staring back at him hurt. "Funny how shit can change overnight." He sighed.

"My mom always says the people you see on the way up are the same ones you see on the way down."

"Don't be so quick to count me out, Persia. I got plans, big plans," Chucky told her.

"I hope your plans are bigger than this nickel-and-dime shit you've been pulling with those two zombies you're running around with," Persia said sarcastically.

Chucky looked at her. "Make fun of me all you want, but this shit here is only a temporary arrangement."

"For as fucked up as it sounds, I actually believe you," Persia said to Chucky's surprise. "Chucky, you might be a shitty boyfriend and a scumbag of a person, but one thing I can't take away from you is the fact that you know how to get money. Remember that time when you took me with you to make that big pickup for Ramses? Man, that was the most cash I had ever seen at one time. And after that you took me to that strip club in the Bronx. When you walked in the room they treated you like a superstar."

Chucky recalled the moment, almost to the point where he could see the flash of the strobe lights and smell the whore stink. "Yeah, that was a good night."

"That was the first time we ever had sex in your car."

"Yeah, and you were screaming so loud that cop rolled up on the car like I was in there killing you." Chucky laughed as he recalled the incident.

"I was screaming because you were trying to destroy my insides with that horse cock of yours. Long before I was a slave to any drug, I was a slave to that third leg." Persia rested her hand on Chucky's lap and let her fingers brush across his dick. She could feel his hardness through his jeans. "For as ashamed as I am to admit it, even with all the rotten shit you've done to me I still get a little wet when I think about your dick." She gave it a little squeeze and felt the car swerve a bit.

"Cut that shit out before you make me crash, Persia," Chucky warned.

"You used to like for me to play with it while you drove and now you're acting all scared," Persia teased him while undoing his belt. His dick was so hard that she had trouble pulling it out of his pants.

"What the hell are you doing?" Chucky asked nervously, trying to focus on the road.

"Fucking with your life like you're fucking with mine." Persia spat in her hand and gripped his dick tightly.

When Persia tugged at his dick, Chucky's foot involuntarily tapped the gas pedal and the car lurched forward. He had to quickly change lanes to keep from rear-ending the car in front of them. "Persia, you're going to get us killed!"

"No, I'm not. You've got it all under control like always, right?" Persia began stroking him with both hands. Persia could tell by the strained look on his face that he was almost there, so she turned it up and began stroking him feverishly. "That feel good to you, baby?" she whispered in his ear, licking his lobe.

Chucky wanted her to stop, but her warm hands wrapped around his cock felt so good. His eye began to twitch as the blood rushed into his penis. A car horn blared behind them when Chucky drifted into the center lane. "Please stop."

The minute Persia heard him say "please" she knew she had him on the ropes. "Why should I?" she taunted. "Isn't this what you want, a woman willing to risk it all in the name of pleasing you? Admit that I'm the best bitch you ever had. Tell me you love me!" Persia demanded, running her thumb over the pre-cum that had started leaking from the head of his dick while keeping up her stroke.

"I love you! Sweet Jesus I love you!" Chucky cried out as his dick exploded in a spray of thick white jizz. Chucky yanked the wheel to one side, skipping over three lanes of traffic before skidding to a stop on the shoulder of the road. He sat there, foot still pressed firmly on the brake and panting. "I always knew you were kinda off, but now I'm convinced that you're just plain crazy. What the hell has gotten into you?"

"The devil," Persia replied, smiling sweetly while she wiped the cum from her hands onto the carpet of his BMW.

The rest of the ride back to Long Island City was a relaxed one; at least, it was for Chucky. He wore the unmistakable look of a man who had busted a nut: glassy eyes and a slack-jawed grin. He no doubt felt like the man, and that's exactly what Persia wanted. An overconfident man was more prone to mistakes.

She had Chucky pull over at the bus stop a few blocks away from her house. It wasn't like he didn't know where she lived, but she didn't want her mother or Richard seeing the car and asking questions she wasn't ready to answer just yet. For a few minutes she and Chucky sat in silence, listening to the quiet purr of the car engine.

"Thanks for the ride," Persia said.

"Nah, I should be thanking you." Chucky looked down at the dried cum on his pants. "For what's it's worth, I really do still care about you and I wanna make things right between us."

"I honestly don't see that happening. I've changed and so have you. You're not the man I fell in love with anymore," Persia said sadly.

"But I can be," Chucky declared. Feelings and plans be damned, there was no way he was letting Persia slip through his fingers again. "Dig, I know you look at me and all you see is a strung-out nigga who used to be somebody, but I'm about to crawl out of this hole. This last robbery I got planned is gonna be the start-up money for me to get back where I need to be and that's on top. I want the throne again, baby, and I want you to be sitting on the one beside me."

"I got a good life now, Chucky," Persia told him.

"And I wanna give you a better one! Persia, you been with me, you know me. All I need is a strong backbone and I'm right back in the game."

Persia sat there in silence, measuring Chucky's words. When she looked into his eyes they were pleading, begging her for another chance to fuck her life up. It was a rare moment of vulnerability for Chucky and she had no intention of wasting the moment. "What about Maggie and Rissa?"

Chucky shrugged. "Some people come into your life for a reason and some a season, and it's looking like Maggie's and Rissa's seasons are about to pass. You say the word and after this job they'll disappear."

Persia read between the lines of what he was saying. She wasn't sure if she was flattered or afraid of the fact that Chucky was willing to kill for her. It sounded good, but the fact that Chucky was so willing to kill the last two friends he had left in the world told her that he was still the same selfish bastard who was only concerned with himself. It was at that moment that any reservations Persia had about what she was planning for Chucky were put to rest. He deserved what he was about to get and then some.

"We'll see," Persia said, neither committing to nor rejecting his offer.

"I won't disappoint you. I promise. When we pull this last heist, we're gonna blow town and set up somewhere nice," he promised.

"And what is this latest caper you keep talking about? If you mean what you say then you can't keep secrets from me like I'm one of your crack whores."

"I thought you'd never ask; especially since you're gonna play such an intricate part." Chucky smirked.

There was something about the look in his eyes that made Persia nervous.

"We gotta blow town quick so this piecemeal shit ain't gonna work anymore," Chucky continued. "So instead of plucking apples, we're gonna make off with the whole tree and you're gonna provide the ax to cut it down."

"You said you were gonna pull a robbery; what's this other shit you're talking about?" Persia asked, not sure she really wanted to know.

"I'm talking about a home invasion, baby girl. One thing I've learned watching these young athletes is that they ain't too smart. The first things they blow their money on are jewels and cars. I'll bet where Vaughn lays his head is a treasure chest of shit waiting for a hungry nigga like me to come and take it from him. We're gonna hit your boyfriend's pad and you're going to help us," Chucky revealed.

"Wait a second, Chucky. Trying to milk Vaughn out of a few dollars is one thing, but setting him up to get robbed is going too far. I won't do it. I don't care what kind of dirt you have on me at this point or what you do with it, but I won't let you hurt Vaughn," Persia told him.

Chucky laughed. "Baby, you think them pretty words and that near fatal hand job you gave me give you some say-so in what I do? Nah, shorty. Just like I gotta prove I'm committed to you, I need you to prove you're committed to me. Now there's two ways we can go about this: the first involves you just showing me where Vaughn rests his head and I take what I want quietly, or I run down on this pussy in the streets and do it noisily. Me and Vaughn might get to talking and it'll come out that you and I got a dirty history. Maybe our little home movie even helps to reinforce the idea I put in his head that you've been helping me plan it all along."

"That's a damn lie!" Persia shouted.

"Yes, but who do you think Vaughn is gonna believe: the quiet girl he thinks he knows or the one he sees on camera sucking an eight-ball off my dick?"

"But I don't even know where Vaughn lives," Persia pointed out, hoping to derail his plan.

"Which is why after your next date you're going to get him to take you back to his house. He's going to invite you in, expecting to deflower you and that's when I'm gonna stick that little rich nigga for everything he's got."

"You haven't changed at all!" Persia accused him.

"Oh, but indeed I have." He clamped his hand around Persia's jaws. "The one thing I've learned during my time in exile is that words are no longer enough to prove loyalty; it's deeds that bind us." He kissed her roughly on the lips then pushed her away. "I'll be in town for a few days getting shit ready, but don't keep me waiting too long for your answer. With or without you that nigga is meat." He threw the car in gear and peeled off.

Persia had a lot to think about on the walk from the bus stop where Chucky had dropped her to her house. Once again Chucky had proved to be two steps ahead of her. There was no way she planned on helping Chucky with his plans to hurt Vaughn, but he had to believe that it was a possibility in order to buy some time. Finding out Persia was an ex-addict was something Vaughn might've been able to get past, but that video tape of her fucking and sucking for drugs going public would be a catastrophe of nuclear proportions. It would not only hurt Vaughn's heart, but there was no telling what effect it would have on his career. Persia had seen enough athletes in the news to know how nasty the press could be, and she refused to subject Vaughn to that. Chucky was playing dirty pool and as a result she was forced into a place of desperation.

# CHAPTER 21

When Li'l Monk finally came back outside he found Droopy right where he left him, guarding the stoop. He didn't notice Li'l Monk come out of the building because he was preoccupied trying to gain the attention of some young girls who were walking by with a series of catcalls. One of them turned around and gave Droopy a dirty look before throwing her head back and continuing on her way.

"Fuck you too, bitch!" Droopy yelled after her.

"Why you curse that girl out like that?" Li'l Monk asked.

Droopy sucked his teeth. "Stuck-up bitch acting like she's all that."

"Why, because she didn't want to stop and talk to you? If I were a girl I wouldn't stop and talk to a nigga making all kinda funny noises to try to get my attention. Women are people, not house pets," Li'l Monk scolded him.

"You only saying that because you got a girl and Sophie got that ass trained," Droopy teased him.

"Li'l nigga, can't nothing or nobody tame this wild animal." Li'l Monk pounded his chest. "I treat Sophie with respect because she's my lady and deserves to be respected, but even before her I was always mindful of how I treated broads. My mother taught me from young that a woman you choose to lie with should be a reflection of you. The same respect you command for yourself should be given to your woman."

"I hear you talking, Li'l Monk. When I find somebody I choose to be with I'll take heed, but right now I'm just trying to fuck, ya heard?"

Li'l Monk shook his head sadly at Droopy's ignorance. He sometimes forgot how young he was until he opened his mouth and said something dumb. "Walk with me to the Spanish restaurant. I'm starving."

Li'l Monk and Droopy walked the couple of blocks to the restaurant, talking about the day's events. It seemed like every few feet someone was stopping Li'l Monk to shake his hand, or shout him out. The neighborhood respected Omega, but they loved Li'l Monk. He was no doubt a man of the people and it showed wherever he went.

A car horn beeped twice and Li'l Monk turned in time to see Ramses's SUV riding past. His eyes locked with Ramses, who was sitting in the back seat. Li'l Monk expected Ramses to blank him again, but this time he at least acknowledged him with a nod, to which Li'l Monk nodded back. For that brief second when their eyes locked Li'l Monk felt something pass between them. He couldn't put his finger on exactly what it was, but it was definitely something. Li'l Monk was tired of playing guessing games and decided he would confront Ramses the next time the opportunity presented itself.

Of course the Spanish restaurant was crowded when they arrived. The line stretched from the counter and out the door. When the old Dominican woman who served the food spotted Li'l Monk, she quickly waved him forward. Li'l Monk was one of their regular customers. She liked him because he was always respectful and tipped well. She didn't need to ask what he wanted because he got the same thing every time he came in: roast pork, red beans, and yellow rice. The favoritism didn't set well with the people who had been waiting in line, but only one of them was foolish enough to say something.

"Yo, what the fuck? I been standing in line for like ten minutes and you gonna serve this nigga first?" a man barked. He was short and stocky with hard eyes.

"Calm down, I'll get to you in one minute," the old Dominican woman told him, while continuing to make Li'l Monk's plate.

"Fuck that, my money is just as green as his. This muthafucka ain't the president!" the stocky man shouted.

"I'll be out of your way in a second, my man. Just be cool," Li'l Monk said coolly. He thanked the woman and took his bag of food off the counter, leaving her a generous tip.

"He needs to before we have a misunderstanding," Droopy added.

The stocky man looked down at Droopy. "Who the fuck is you supposed to be, his bodyguard?"

"No, I'm the nigga who'll blow your fucking face off!" Droopy pulled the Beretta and pointed it at the stocky man. The old Dominican woman screamed behind the counter and people who had been in line waiting for their food scattered out of the way, as Droopy tried to draw a bead on his target. The stocky man went scrambling out the door screaming like a girl.

"Give me that." Li'l Monk snatched the gun from Droopy and grabbed him by the scruff of his hockey jersey. "Sorry about that, *mami*," he apologized to the old Dominican woman, and shoved Droopy toward the front door. "Have you lost your fucking mind?" he shouted at Droopy once they were outside.

"Man, he was disrespecting you so I stepped to that pussy!" Droopy declared.

"How, by getting mad that I skipped him in the line? Droopy, you drew an illegal gun on a man in an establishment that we visit just about every day. Being young and naïve is one thing, but the shit you did was plain fucking stupid."

"I'm sorry, Li'l Monk. I was just trying to show you that I'm with you and will pop that thang without hesitation!" Droopy said emotionally. He was trying to be tough, but his feelings were clearly hurt.

Li'l Monk sighed, realizing that Droopy was too naïve to see the wrong in what he'd done. "Droopy." He placed his hand on his shoulder reassuringly. "One of the things I love about you is your loyalty to me and this thing of ours. You're big on heart, but still have a lot of growing and learning to do. Take the rest of the night off."

"C'mon, I know I fucked up but don't take me off the money," Droopy pleaded.

"You can get back on the money tomorrow, but for the night you need to relax and reflect. Here." Li'l Monk dug in his pocket and pulled out his money. He peeled off some bills and handed them to Droopy. "Go catch a movie or whatever the fuck it is that teenagers do these days. Just get off the block for a while."

Droopy sadly accepted the money. "You know this ain't right. Can I at least have my gun back?"

"Bye, Droopy." Li'l Monk folded his arms and stared him down.

"This is some bullshit," Droopy mumbled and slunk away.

Li'l Monk ambled down the block, eating his food and lost in his thoughts. In his pocket he felt his cell phone vibrating. Careful not to get any grease on it, Li'l Monk eased the phone out of his pocket and checked the caller ID. It was Sophie. He had been ducking her calls all day and knew if he continued to do so she'd likely show up on the block. "What's up, baby?" he answered the phone.

"Damn, I was beginning to think your phone was broken since I been calling you all day long," Sophie said.

"Oh, my bad. I been in the house 'sleep all day," Li'l Monk lied.

"Really? Because when I bumped into your dad this morning he said he hadn't seen you all night," Sophie shot back.

"Man, you know half the time that dude be so high he don't know if he's coming or going. Anyhow, what's good with you?" Li'l Monk changed the subject.

"Worrying about your ass. I heard you and Omega got into a shootout at the strip club, so when I didn't hear from you I started getting worried."

Li'l Monk shook his head at how the story had been twisted yet again. "It wasn't a shootout, just a little scuffle, and I'm fine."

"What were you doing at a strip club anyhow?"

"I was having some drinks with my partner. What, I'm not allowed to go to strip clubs?" Li'l Monk asked defensively.

"Li'l Monk, you're my man, not my kid. You're free to go wherever you like as long as you carry yourself accordingly. I only asked because I know you don't care for strip clubs so I found it odd that you went, that's all. You're acting all suspicious and shit. What the hell is your problem?"

"Nothing, just a lot of bullshit happening on the block." Li'l Monk quickly recovered.

"Then maybe you need to come in out of the cold for a while. Why don't you come over and see me. I'll make us some dinner and we can watch a movie," Sophie suggested. There was a pause. "You still there?"

"Yeah, I'm here, babe. I was reading something. Sure, I'll swing by there tonight," Li'l Monk told her. His tone was flat not because he didn't want to see her, but because he was more preoccupied with putting together a good alibi to explain his whereabouts from the night before.

"Don't sound so enthused about it," she said sarcastically.

"I'm sorry, ma. My mind is just elsewhere lately," Li'l Monk admitted. "Maybe spending a few hours in your arms are what I need to take my mind off this bullshit."

"That's the Li'l Monk I know and love."

"You need me to bring anything?" he asked.

"No, I got some Absolut in the freezer and the weed is already on deck. Just bring some cigars with you."

"Got you. See you in a little bit." Li'l Monk got ready to end the call, but her voice stopped him.

"I love you."

Li'l Monk smiled. "I love you too." He placed the phone in his pocket and started making his way to the store. Hearing Sophie's voice was just what Li'l Monk needed to bring his focus back and remember the things that were really important to life. The thought of hurting Sophie hurt him more than the thought of losing her. She was a good girl and deserved a man who was going to do right. He was human and had made a mistake, but it was one he knew he would never make again. What happened between him and Tiffany would be a secret he took to his grave.

Li'l Monk proceeded to run up in the bodega, and grabbed some cigars and a pack of Skittles because he knew Sophie loved them when she was high. As an afterthought he grabbed two Guinness stouts. He planned on loving Sophie down that night and wanted a little extra kick. As he was coming out of the bodega he bumped into Neighborhood.

"Sup wit' you?" Li'l Monk greeted Neighborhood while using his teeth to pop the cap from one of the Guinness bottles.

"Out here trying to get on my feet, if you know what I mean?" Neighborhood scratched his face.

"What you telling me for? You know I don't hand to hand no more; go see one of them niggas around the corner," Li'l Monk told him.

"I would but I'm in a position of financial disposition, feel me?" Neighborhood quipped. "Think you could spare few coins to ease my pain?"

Li'l Monk frowned, digging in his pocket. "Neighborhood, I don't see how you keep that oil burner of yours lit with no source of income. I told you if you need some paper in your pockets I'll let you knock off a few packages." He handed him a few dollars.

"No, thank you! Leaving a crackhead to watch over cocaine is like leaving a rapist in a room full of drugged women and then wondering why half of them ended up fucked. I'd rather beg and hustle for my get-high than run the risk of having a gorilla like you on my back, or worse that damn Droopy. I just seen him and a bunch of them little dusty project kids trying to tie firecrackers to the tails of stray cats." He shook his head sadly.

"I told that knucklehead to get off the block for a while," Li'l Monk grumbled. He wasn't happy about being disobeyed.

"Now you should know better than that." Neighborhood snickered. "A young boy like that, all he knows is the hood. Where's he gonna go to get off the block?"

"I never thought about it like that," Li'l Monk said honestly.

"That's what ya got me for." Neighborhood winked. Suddenly his face got very serious and his eyes landed on something just behind Li'l Monk. "I'm about to take a walk and I think it'd be a good idea if you did too."

Li'l Monk turned around and saw a blood red tricked-out Jeep sitting on large chrome rims pulling to a stop at the curb. Three men got out, all looking like they meant business. One was an older dude, and another was younger and wore his hair in cornrows. From their body language Li'l Monk knew they were soldiers. Leading the pack was a light-skinned dude who wore his hair in long, loose braids fitted with red rubber bands at the ends. From the description Li'l Monk had gotten from the streets, it had to be the kid they called Swann.

"Fool-ass boy, what you still standing there for? Let's scat while we can!" Neighborhood urged.

"A nigga will never chase me off my own block." Li'l Monk put his beers down and squared up. He had his Desert Eagle and Droopy's Beretta so he was feeling froggy.

"Suit yourself." Neighborhood walked off.

"You Li'l Monk?" one of the men with Swann asked. He was an older dude, wearing jeans and a blazer.

"Since the day I was born," Li'l Monk replied. His hands were folded behind his back, one on each pistol.

Swann stepped forward and sized Li'l Monk up. "We didn't come for all that, so why don't you take it easy. They call me Swann." He extended his hand.

Li'l Monk looked down at his hand, but didn't shake it. "I know who you are, and you obviously know who I am, so this leaves me to wonder what you doing on the wrong side of the tracks?"

"I was hoping we could have a conversation without all the theatrics," Swann told him.

Li'l Monk shrugged. "So talk."

Swann looked over his shoulder at the older man with him, who just shook his head. They knew Li'l Monk was testing them. There was a brief and silent exchange among the trio before Swann turned his attention back to Li'l Monk. "A'ight, fuck it. I'm hoping we can come to some type of understanding over recent events."

"Your boys was trying to get at my partner so we did what we had to do," Li'l Monk said as if it was that simple.

A confused expression crossed Swann's face. "Huh? You think I'm here to talk about that shit between you and Nut? Man, I ain't stunting that shit. Ain't nobody die; it is what it is. I'm talking about this thing with ya peeps Pharaoh and Ramses."

"Then this is something you should be discussing with one of them," Li'l Monk told him.

"I would if it were them that their street soldiers rallied around. From what I get from everybody I speak to Ramses and Pharaoh tend to the chickens, but it's you and you alone who guards the hen house."

Li'l Monk snorted. "I can't speak on what you've heard. I'm just a loyal soldier."

"Modest, I like that. Okay, I'll cut right to it then. This tension between us and y'all ain't good for nobody's pockets. It needs to end before somebody gets hurt."

"Maybe if y'all hadn't started it we wouldn't have to finish it," Li'l Monk spat.

Swann and his boys exchanged confused glances. "Is that what Pharaoh and Ramses are feeding y'all? That we started this?" He gave a hearty laugh. "I heard Pharaoh had y'all over here drinking the Kool-Aid, but I didn't know it was true. Young homie, let me school you to something: the Clarks didn't start this war, Pharaoh did!"

The accusation hit Li'l Monk like a physical blow. As far as any of them knew it was Clarks who had cast the first stone and Pharaoh's crew was responding to the threat.

"The dumbstruck look on your face tells me you ain't versed in your history, so allow me to give you a quick recap," Swann continued. "Your boy Pharaoh's grip on the city ain't what it used to be; it's actually been slipping for years. Don't get me wrong, his name is still strong out here, but it's more from his legacy than anything he's done in the last ten years. When Poppa became boss of bosses, everybody fell in line behind him, including your Pharaoh. Like the good old kings of Europe, Poppa allowed every man to keep his land and titles in exchange for their loyalty. As a reward he flooded their neighborhoods with some of the purest drugs they'd ever tasted and everybody got rich. Everybody went along with the program except Pharaoh. See, he was always a greedy muthafucka who wanted it all for himself. We warned Poppa that Pharaoh was gonna be a problem and that it'd be best to clip him early, but Poppa wasn't a war lord. All he wanted to do was make money. So instead of having Pharaoh killed, he made him an outcast by cutting him off from that bomb-ass coke he was hitting everyone else and leaving him to fend for himself. Pharaoh was welcome to keep whatever territories he already controlled so long as his business didn't overlap with Clark business. When Poppa was killed and the big chair went to Shai, Pharaoh saw it as an opening to make his play. Instead of him stepping up like a man, he cut a backdoor deal with the Italians to try to dethrone Shai and start a war in the streets. He figures when the smoke clears his sneaky ass will be the last man standing."

Li'l Monk shrugged. "Awesome story."

"It's not just a story; it's cold truth. You got no reason to believe me, but ask any one of these old timers and they'll confirm what I've said to you about what kind of man Poppa Clark was and what he wanted for the city," Swann told him.

"Okay, even if it is true, it's nothing new. Niggas been warring over territories for years. What makes this situation so different?"

"The difference is, this is a conflict that Pharaoh doesn't have a snowball's chance in hell of winning. Pharaoh still thinks it's the nineties when he was king shit and hogging up the whole meal, but this is a new era. The game is the same, but the players are different and all of them want what the Clarks want, simply to make money. Pharaoh is forcing a lot of hands with his all-or-nothing stance and it isn't going to end well. We got the muscle, the guns, and the blessings of every major player on the board. Pharaoh's ego has finally proved to be his undoing, but that doesn't mean stand-up cats like you have to go down with him."

"So what, I'm supposed leave Pharaoh hanging and get down with y'all?" Li'l Monk asked sarcastically.

"It beats dying," Swann shot back. "Li'l Monk, when this goes down, and trust me this is going to happen, Pharaoh will put out the call to arms and it's you who the soldiers will rally behind. You have the power to help end this shit before it starts."

"Look, Swann, I understand your position, but you have to understand mine. When I was out here starving, it was Ramses and Pharaoh who put food in my stomach. I don't know how they do it where you come from, but where I come from we stand on loyalty. That being said, I'm gonna pass on your offer and y'all niggas do what you gotta do," he said, tightening his grips on the pistols.

"You gotta be about the dumbest nigga in the world," the younger dude who was with Swann said. "Swann, I don't know why you ever trying to reason with these knucklehead-ass niggas. I say we just get to knocking these muthafuckas off, starting with him!"

Li'l Monk took his hands from behind his back, brandishing the pistols. "I'm ready to die about mine; are you?"

Swann's men drew their guns, prepared to open fire, but Swann didn't move. The tension in the air was so thick you could feel it on your skin. Swann regarded Li'l Monk, searching his face for signs of fear and hesitation. He was clearly outgunned but the look in his eyes said he didn't care. True to his word, he was sincerely ready to die over what he believed.

There was the soft sound of someone whistling the old tune "Camptown Races." From the shadows emerged a rugged-looking man with dark eyes and a shotgun slung over his shoulder like he had an open carry license. For the first time since he was a kid, Li'l Monk was happy to see his dad. A few feet behind him stood Neighborhood, looking scared shitless. Li'l Monk thought he ran off, but he had gone for reinforcements.

"Is there a problem here?" Monk addressed the crew.

"Nah, ain't no problem, old head." Swann raised his hands in surrender. "We were just having a little chat with this young man."

Monk studied Swann and smirked. "Since when you need guns to chat?" He leveled his shotgun and cocked the slide. "I suggest you boys keep it moving before I start feeling talkative myself."

The youngest of the group, the one with the cornrows, took a step forward but Swann held him back. "You got that one. We were just leaving."

"A wise young man," Monk sneered.

Swann motioned for his people to fall back. He reached in his pocket and handed Li'l Monk a piece of paper with a number scribbled on it. "If you happen to change your mind, give me a call."

Monk stood there, still cradling the shotgun, watching Swann and his crew get back into the Jeep. The young one who wanted to pop off was glaring at them from the back seat. Monk responded by blowing him a kiss. "What was that all about?" he asked his son once the danger had passed.

"Just some hood shit," Li'l Monk downplayed it.

"I'm a crackhead, not a fool. I can see Shai sending Swann to handle some hood shit, but not Angelo. He's old school and a serious cat." Monk was speaking about the older man who had been with Swann. He hadn't said at the time but he recognized him from when he was a soldier under Poppa Clark. "Shoot straight with me, junior," Monk demanded.

"He wanted to talk about that shit with Pharaoh," Li'l Monk told him.

"Boy, didn't I tell you to keep your nose out of that mess? Ain't nothing you can do about that but try to keep from getting killed when it jumps off."

"That ain't what Swann thinks," Li'l Monk shot back. He hated when his father tried to treat him like a kid.

"Oh yeah, and what exactly is it that Swann thinks?" Monk asked.

"He thinks that I can help to squash it, because me and Omega are the muscle and the soldiers respect us."

Monk looked at his son seriously. "And what do you think?"

"I think that war ain't no good for either side. I'm just out here trying to get a dollar. I don't wanna die out here over no bullshit." Li'l Monk said honestly.

Monk nodded in approval at the answer. "Maybe your ass is actually out here learning something on these streets. War is a nasty business, but unfortunately it's a part of the game you've chosen to play. If you don't want no part of it, I suggest you hang up your pistols and square up."

Li'l Monk laughed. "And go back to starving? No, thanks."

"Well you can't have it both ways, Li'l Monk. You either stand tall or get your ass out of the way," Monk told him.

Li'l Monk nodded. "Pretty sound advice."

"That's what fathers are for. And on that note, I got moves to make. I got people to see and stashes to snatch."

"Before you go, can I ask you something, Dad?"

It was the first time Li'l Monk had called him Dad since he was a kid, so Monk knew whatever it was had to be weighing heavily on him. "Sure, son."

"What kind of man was Poppa Clark?" Li'l Monk asked, thinking on what Swann had said to him.

It was an odd question. "I never met him personally, but from what I hear he was a class act. They don't make 'em like Poppa Clark anymore. Why do you ask?"

"Just wondering, that's all."

Monk could tell there was more to it, but didn't press the issue. "Okay."

"And thanks for holding me down tonight," Li'l Monk said sincerely.

"Anytime, son. I was never there to teach you to play catch or no shit like that, so the least I can do is be there to put a hole in a nigga from time to time. You gonna be okay?"

"Yeah, I'm heading over to Sophie's for the night," Li'l Monk told him.

"That might not be a bad idea. I can sleep better knowing you're lying up in some pussy, rather than worrying about you lying in a ditch. These streets don't love nobody, especially us Monks." Monk started walking off, but Li'l Monk called after him.

"Do you think I'm doing the right thing by standing with Pharaoh in this?" Li'l Monk asked.

Monk pondered the question before answering. "I think you already knew the answer to that question before you asked it," he replied before disappearing into the night.

# CHAPTER 22

Ramses lounged on the front steps of his East Harlem brownstone, enjoying the nighttime breeze and a mild. It had been a hectic few weeks for him and it was the first time he had actually been able to relax.

Things within the organization were becoming increasingly turbulent. Their new relationship with the Italians had helped to alleviate some of the pressure, but Mr. D being murdered had caused a hiccup that was threatening to turn into a stinking belch that they would all have to smell. As if that wasn't bad enough Poppito's emissary, Felix, was becoming impatient with their futile investigation into Petey's murder. Ramses could remember a time when he and Pharaoh would've told both parties to eat a dick and arm up rather than be diplomatic about it, but they no longer had the luxury that came with being a superpower in the drug game. Their team was still strong, but their strength depended heavily on their alliances and business relationships. Times were changing and they had to adapt or risk becoming extinct. It was a bitter pill, but one that they had to swallow whether they liked it or not.

"I'm about to run to the store, do you need anything?" Estelle asked, coming down the front steps of the brownstone. She was an older woman with salt-and-pepper hair, and kind of on the portly side.

"Nah, I'm good," Ramses said.

"Okay, I'll be back in a little while. Keep an eye on the roast I got in the oven. Don't let it get all dry. You know I hate a dry roast," Estelle said.

"Sure thing," Ramses agreed.

As Estelle was walking down the block, King Tut came walking up. Tut gave her a smile and curt nod before continuing on to meet Ramses. "Yo, Ramses, I didn't know you still lived with your mom."

"Don't be a wise ass. That wasn't my mother; it was my housekeeper," Ramses lied. In truth Estelle was his wife and best kept secret, since very few people other than Pharaoh knew that he was married. Ramses didn't hide Estelle because he was embarrassed. In fact, he loved her more than anything, which was why he kept her hidden away. In the game he played love was a liability that your enemies could use against you. "So what happened with that thing I had you look into?"

King Tut shook his head sadly. "Your suspicions were right about our boy George double dipping. He's sucking Clark dick, but it's worse than that."

"Well don't keep an asshole in suspense, spit it out, li'l nigga," Ramses demanded.

"Not only was George in bed with the Clarks, but he was also the one behind whacking Petey," King Tut told him.

Ramses's eyes got as big as saucers. "Are you sure?"

"I'm more than sure. I got proof." Tut pulled out the small recorder and pressed play.

The first voice Ramses heard was Tut's: "I always took you for a stand-up dude, but that's some real bitch shit. To top it off, you dropped a body on Ramses's streets without getting the nod. You're out of pocket, old man."

The next voice was unmistakably George's: "This thing that's brewing between Pharaoh and the Clarks ain't got nothing to do with me. I'm just out here trying to make a dollar and they came with a better offer. Ramses of all people should be able to understand that. This wasn't personal; it was all business."

Ramses sat there with a stunned expression on his face. He had known George for a long time, long enough to even consider him a friend. George had always been a sneaky son of a bitch, but killing wasn't in his character. He figured he knew George pretty well, but listening to Tut's recording told Ramses that he didn't know George as well as he thought. "Dirty muthafucka!"

"That's the same shit I said, boss. I thought George was an okay dude until all this shit," Tut said, faking sadness at George's betrayal.

"Did you whack that piece of shit?" Ramses asked.

"Nah, I maimed him a bit but I didn't want to take his life without getting your okay first. I know you two have history," Tut said.

"Our history ain't got nothing to do with the future. I want that chicken frying sack of shit dead," Ramses declared.

"I'll get right on it," Tut promised.

"No, this kill will go to Felix and his people. It should make them feel better getting to snuff the life of the man who was behind Poppito's nephew's death."

"You're a brilliant man, Ramses." Tut smiled.

"You better damn well know it. Nobody can pull a fast one on me," Ramses spat.

Tut had to keep his laughter bottled in after the statement. Ramses thought he was so smart, but Omega proved to be smarter. It was his idea to record the confrontation with George then doctor the tape to make it appear that he was also behind Petey's murder. Tut didn't think Ramses would go for it, but thankfully he did. Once George was dead, King Tut and Omega would be in the clear.

"What's up with Omega?" Ramses asked, as if he was reading Tut's mind.

"Ah, I dunno. I haven't seen him today. You want me to track him down?"

"No, just curious. How's he been acting lately?"

Tut shrugged. "Same old Omega, out here chasing this paper."

"You and Omega been getting pretty tight lately, huh?"

"Yeah, that's my dawg," Tut said proudly.

"Glad to hear it, because you two may find yourselves spending a lot more time together. I need solid young soldiers out here holding down the fort in prime areas of operations, especially Lenox and Seventh," Ramses told him.

This surprised Tut. "But Omega and Li'l Monk run those areas."

"Whoever I say runs those areas is who runs those areas," Ramses corrected him.

"So you saying Li'l Monk is out?" Tut asked excitedly.

"Don't get ahead of yourself, King Tut. Li'l Monk is still a part of this organization and therefore family, unless I say different. All I need to know is that if your number is called do you have the balls to step up?"

"Fo sho, Ramses. Anything you need, say the word and I got you," Tut said eagerly.

"That's good to know. For the time being you just keep your eyes open and your ears to the streets. Anything comes up, you bring it to me directly," Ramses told him.

Their conversation was broken up when a white Rolls-Royce coasted to a stop in front of Ramses's brownstone. The windows were too heavily tinted to see who was inside, but Ramses knew who it was.

"I gotta go handle something right quick." Ramses got up from the steps.

"Is that Pharaoh? Man, I'd love to meet that dude." Tut made to approach the car, but Ramses grabbed him by the back of his neck.

"Didn't I just get done telling you not to get ahead of yourself?" Ramses snarled.

"Chill out, Ramses. I was just trying to pay my respects," Tut said in a nervous tone.

"You get to praise the Pharaoh when I say it's time and not a minute before. Until then, you stay in a child's place and do what the fuck I told you." Ramses shoved him away.

"A'ight, you got that." Tut smoothed his clothes over. "Whatever you say, boss."

King Tut stood there on the curb, watching Ramses as he stepped off the curb and got into the back of the Rolls. Normally he would've been upset about a man putting his hands on him and plotting revenge, even a man as important as Ramses, but not that day. For as much of a savage as Tut was he was also a very good observer and his visit with Ramses, coupled with the shifting pieces on the chessboard, confirmed what he already suspected: things were about to change within the organization. Now all he had to do was figure out how to use the unrest to his advantage.

Pharaoh was lounging in the back of the plush vehicle, smoking a big cigar and sipping cognac from a crystal glass. Instead of his usual three-piece suit he was wearing a black blazer, white shirt, and blue jeans. "Trouble in paradise?" he asked, staring out the window at King Tut who was still standing on the curb.

Ramses looked out the window. "Nothing I can't handle," he assured him.

"Funny, you keep saying that but you have yet to make me a believer." Pharaoh blew a cloud of smoke in the air. "There is an infestation of flies in my kingdom, yet instead of swatting them my right hand remains still."

"Pharaoh, you act like I've been out here sitting on my ass. In the last couple of weeks we've recruited twenty new soldiers and taken over some promising new territories. We're fortifying the kingdom so when it goes down with the Clarks, we'll be ready."

Pharaoh gave him a look. "I'm not talking about the Clarks. I'm talking about some unresolved issues that you've been sitting on for far too long. It doesn't look good when people are allowed to spit in my face and aren't disciplined properly. Why is that piece of shit Chucky still alive?"

"Because we haven't been able to track the slippery bastard down," Ramses replied. "I ran into the girl he used to run around with, Persia, and I planned on having some of our people pay a call on her. I'm not going to let them hurt her, but if we put a good enough scare into her she'll likely be able to tell us where to find that cocksucker."

"I already know where he is. Chucky is right here in New York, pissing on my head and telling me that it's raining. And you know what? I didn't have to pressure an innocent girl to find out!" Pharaoh said sharply.

Ramses was stunned. "I had no idea."

"Exactly my point. You are supposed to be my eyes on the streets, but apparently your vision is getting piss poor. You need to handle that, Ramses, or I'll turn to someone who can."

"I'll take care of it," Ramses promised.

"Like you took care of Li'l Monk?" Pharaoh asked with a raised eyebrow.

Ramses lowered his eyes. "Pharaoh, I—"

"Let me save you the trouble of trying to lie to me for the sake of buying time," Pharaoh cut him off. "I understand how this particular situation can be difficult for you. You've developed a fondness for Li'l Monk, almost like a father and son bond. As a parent, I get it, truly I do, but it doesn't change what has to be done."

"Pharaoh, we still don't even know if it was Li'l Monk who was responsible for what happened to Mr. D," Ramses pointed out.

"You're right, we don't, but considering the evidence it's not something I'm willing to bet my life on. Are you?"

Ramses was silent.

"I didn't think so. I don't like it anymore than you do, but when you weigh what we stand to lose by harboring him versus what we stand to gain by putting this kid in the dirt and making the Italians happy I think you'll agree that Li'l Monk is expendable."

"I guess so," Ramses said softly.

"Don't look so sad, Ramses. You seem to be fond of King Tut; you can make him your new adopted son," Pharaoh said sarcastically.

"Whatever, man. I'll take care of it," Ramses said with an attitude. He felt horrible about what Pharaoh was making him do, but he didn't have a choice.

"You've told me that once before, yet Li'l Monk still lives. So I've put the matter in more capable hands."

"What the fuck is that supposed to mean?" Ramses asked.

Pharaoh sat back and smiled. "You'll find out when you read the morning paper."

# CHAPTER 23

After his father had gone Li'l Monk started making his way to his car. Sophie didn't live too far away, but he didn't feel like walking. The streets were hot and so was he.

As he was walking he spotted a car riding down the block. It was an old-model Chevy Nova with a rusted side panel. He wouldn't have paid it any mind except that he noticed it was full of white faces. They were either police or some downtown crackers trolling the ghetto to score drugs. Either way Li'l Monk wanted no part of them. Li'l Monk stopped and twisted his face into a mask of anger and glared at the car. The white boys took the hint and sped off.

"Junkie muthafuckas," Li'l Monk grumbled and got into his Bonneville. Sunken low in his seat, Li'l Monk slowly coasted through the streets of Harlem. Driving always brought him a measure of peace. In the confines of his car there were no corner boys to dictate orders to, no Omega pestering him about money or bitches, and no junkies begging for a high. It was just him and the streets. He had just turned on his radio and was about to turn to the oldies station when his cell phone went off. With a frustrated sigh, he flipped it open and took the call.

"Damn, nigga, where the fuck you been?" Omega's voice came over the line.

"I been in the hood; where the fuck you been? I ain't seen you since I left Stacy's."

"That's because I was still there until about an hour ago," Omega informed him.

"What the fuck could you possibly have been doing over there for damn near twenty-four hours?" Li'l Monk asked.

"What the fuck you think I was doing? After you left Stacy called over some of her dancer friends and we had an orgy that was out of this fucking world! I ain't never had a bitch suck my dick from the back before until today!"

"Sounds like you had a good time," Li'l Monk said in an uninterested tone.

"Would've been better if my dawg had been there. Why'd you break out like that without saying anything?"

"I had some shit to do," Li'l Monk said. He wanted to tell him about what had happened with Swann, but didn't want to bring it up over the phone.

"I don't know what you had to do that was more important than climbing back inside Tiffany's fine ass. She was pissed that you left her hanging," Omega told him.

"I'll bet she was, but seeing how y'all had an orgy I'm sure there wasn't no shortage of dicks to replace me. So how was the pussy, O?" Li'l Monk asked with an attitude. He wasn't sure why, but the thought of Tiffany fucking someone else irritated him.

"I wouldn't know because I didn't hit it and it wasn't for lack of trying," Omega admitted. "You must've really put it on that bitch, because she wasn't checking for anybody but you."

"She might as well have gone ahead and done her thing, because what happened between us was a one-time thing. I slipped and bumped my head, but I'm back to my senses now and it's all about Sophie."

"I hear you talking, nigga, but somebody better deliver that memo to Tiffany. She was all in her feelings because she felt like you played her, taking the pussy and running like you did." Omega laughed.

"She'll get over it, or she won't. I don't give a fuck," Li'l Monk said. He felt bad about hurting Tiffany's feelings, but not bad enough to offer her an explanation. She knew what it was when they lay down together. Besides, it wasn't like he'd ever see her again so he wasn't sweating it.

"But fuck that broad. Where you at now? I came across some bomb-ass hydro and me and some of the homies are about to go straight to the moon. Come through the block."

"Nah, y'all have fun with that. I'm gonna go check my lady and kick back for the night," Li'l Monk told him.

"Fuck it, have it your way but if you change your mind you know where to find me," Omega told him and ended the call.

Li'l Monk tossed his cell phone back onto the passenger seat and turned his attention back to the road. He pulled to a stop at a red light at the intersection of 123rd and Lenox and waited patiently for it to change. While he was waiting he happened to look out the window toward the corner bodega and spotted a familiar face, Charlie. He was one of several young men involved in a dice game. Li'l Monk had been trying to call Charlie since the funeral and had even popped up at his house, but he could never seem to catch up with him. It was obvious to him by then that Charlie was avoiding him, but for the life of him he didn't know why. There was no time like the present to find out.

When the light changed, Li'l Monk pulled through it slowly and double parked his car on the block, just off the corner. He killed the engine and jumped out, and walked up on Charlie. "Sup, my nigga?"

Charlie turned around, startled to see Li'l Monk standing behind him. "What's good, Li'l Monk?" He extended his hand nervously. Li'l Monk didn't bother to shake it.

"You're harder to catch than a crackhead," Li'l Monk said.

"Oh, you know since my sister was killed I been in the crib. Kinda wanna keep it close to home so I'm there for my family," Charlie said, flashing a goofy smile.

"Is that right? Funny because I've been calling your house and your mom always says you're not home. I even popped up a time or two and got the same thing. I'm starting to feel like you're avoiding me."

"C'mon, man, why would I be avoiding you?"

"That's what I'm trying to figure out. Let's take a walk. I need to holla at you about something."

"It's your roll, Charlie. You gonna shoot or keep talking to your girlfriend?" a big-lipped kid with a nappy afro called out.

Li'l Monk glared at the big-lipped kid, but didn't reply to his comment. "Charlie, somebody knocked Mr. D off," he told him.

"Who?" Charlie fronted like he didn't know who Li'l Monk was talking about, but it was a weak front.

"Nigga, you know who. The Italian I took you with me to see," Li'l Monk said. "Look, this ain't the time to play games. That dead guinea has got a lot of people looking at me sideways and I need to find out what happened."

"What's that got to do with me?" Charlie asked innocently.

Li'l Monk knew Charlie was bullshitting him and he was starting to get angry. "I ain't in the mood for you to be fucking around. I need to know if you told anybody about the old man or the safe. Don't lie to me either, Charlie."

The big-lipped kid with the afro walked up and tapped Charlie on the shoulder. "Yo, y'all niggas is holding up the game. Either roll the dice or forfeit the bread."

"Homie, I apologize for holding up what y'all got going on, but I'm gonna need you to give us a minute," Li'l Monk told him.

"And I'm gonna need y'all to take this lover's spat somewhere else. I got money on the floor, so if you ain't betting then you need to get the fuck up outta here and let Charlie get back to the game," the big-lipped kid shot back. By then the other players in the dice game were watching the exchange.

"Listen, I know you're out here trying to put on for these nobody muthafuckas, but it's a bad night to play tough guy. Let me finish my conversation and I'll be out of your way," Li'l Monk said calmly. He could feel his blood boiling and was trying to control his rage.

"You gonna let him talk to you like that, Blood?" a nameless face instigated from the sidelines.

The big-lipped kid took Li'l Monk's calm demeanor for weakness and decided to show off.

He ambled up and stood nose to nose with Li'l Monk, spitting a razor from his mouth into his hand expertly. "You got about five seconds to get the fuck from around here or I'm gonna make you uglier than you already are, and that's my word."

"That's your word, huh?" Li'l Monk sized him up.

"Straight like that." The big-lipped kid tossed the razor from one hand to the other, taunting Li'l Monk.

Li'l Monk looked from Charlie, who was clearly terrified, back to the big-lipped kid. "Have it your way then," he said, before snuffing the big-lipped kid. The blow landed with so much force that the big-lipped kid flew clean out of his shoes and landed six feet away. Several of the players from the dice game surged forward like they were going to jump Li'l Monk, but when he pulled his gun they froze. "What? Y'all feeling brave." He swept the gun back and forth over the crowd, causing the once tough guys to cringe. "I'll light this whole fucking block up!"

"Li'l Monk, be cool," Charlie laid a calming hand on Li'l Monk's shoulder, which turned out to be a bad move.

Li'l Monk grabbed Charlie's arm and twisted it to the point where Charlie thought he was going to break it. "You little worm muthafucka, who are you to tell me anything? Now me and you are

about to take a walk and have us a little chitchat."
He backed down the block, dragging Charlie along
and keeping his gun trained on the dice shooters.
He shoved Charlie into the passenger seat of his
Bonneville and peeled off.

"What the fuck was that all about?" Charlie
asked, rubbing his arm.

"That was about me trying to help your bitch ass
out and you almost getting me killed!" Li'l Monk
snapped.

"I told you I don't know nothing about what
happened with that old man," Charlie insisted.

Li'l Monk backhanded Charlie so hard that
his head snapped back into the headrest, and
blood leaked from his nose onto the seat of the
Bonneville. "Bullshit you don't. I've known you
all your fucking life so I know when you're lying.
I looked out for you, tried to put you back on
your feet, and you repay me by putting my life in
danger?"

"Li'l Monk, you got it wrong, man," Charlie
insisted.

Li'l Monk picked his gun up off his lap and
pressed it to Charlie's cheek. "Then tell me right."
He glanced at Charlie then back to the road. "What
would make you double-cross the only nigga in the
world to ever show you love?" His voice was heavy
with emotion.

"It was all Chucky!" Charlie blurted out.

The mention of Chucky's name shocked Li'l Monk to the point where he swerved and almost hit another car. "Fuck is you talking about? Chucky has got a death sentence hanging over his head. Ain't no way he'd be fool enough to show his face back in the city."

"You say that because you don't know Chucky," Charlie shot back. With a heavy heart he went into telling Li'l Monk about how he had turned Chucky on to the safe in Mr. D's apartment and the scheme he'd come up with to take it off. "We were just supposed to take the money. I was never down for no murder."

"Damn, do you realize what your thirst has done?" Li'l Monk slammed his fists on the wheel. His mind turned end over end, processing what Charlie had just confessed and trying to find a way out of it. Just then, something struck him. "Charlie, one thing is nagging at me and I just can't shake it. When Chucky snuck back into New York he knew that there weren't many people he could trust, so he had to be careful about who he let in on his schemes. My question is, when did the two of you get that cool?"

Charlie was caught off guard by the question and when his answer didn't come quick enough, Li'l Monk gave him another whack. This one was to the mouth with the back of the gun and knocked one of Charlie's teeth out.

"You been in bed with this nigga since before I took you to Mr. D's, haven't you?" Li'l Monk pressed him.

"You don't understand, man," Charlie murmured with his hand over his bloody mouth. "You and me, we go back to free lunch. We was two poor-ass kids together and when you starting rising to the top you didn't look out for me!" Charlie said emotionally.

"Bullshit, man. There was never a time when I saw you and didn't break you off," Li'l Monk reminded him.

"Break me off?" Charlie snorted. "I'm a grown-ass man, Li'l Monk. Fuck breaking me off; we were supposed to eat together. When you hooked up with Omega, I was out of the picture. You had somebody to get money with, why couldn't I? You left me out here with nobody. I didn't have nobody." He wept.

Li'l Monk wanted to bash Charlie's skull in, but it wouldn't change anything. He didn't know what he felt more, anger at Charlie for jamming him up or hurt that his friend had crossed him. Li'l Monk and Charlie had been best buddies since they were kids, more like brothers than anything. Had it been anyone else, Charlie would've already been dead, but even having crossed into a dangerous situation, Li'l Monk still couldn't bring himself to harm Charlie. He still had love in his heart for his adopted little brother.

"You hurt me, Charlie. You hurt me deep," Li'l Monk said, sticking his gun between the driver's seat and the center console.

"I know, and I'm sorry." Charlie sniffled, while wiping the tears from his eyes with the backs of his hands.

"You're sorry, all right, the sorriest sack of shit I ever laid eyes on. You and me are done. You hear me, Charlie? We're fucking done!" Li'l Monk growled.

"I know, man, and I don't blame you."

"Who else was in on this besides you and Chucky?" Li'l Monk asked.

"He had two broads with him. Maggie and Rissa were their names," Charlie said.

"I usually don't kill bitches, but I think in this case I might have to make an exception. I'm gonna handle all parties involved, but before I do, your punk ass is going to help me bring some closure to this. First I'm going to take you to Ramses and you're gonna spill your fucking guts and clear my name. Then you're going to tell us where we can find that piece of shit junkie Chucky."

"Man, if I talk, I'm dead," Charlie said.

"If you don't talk, you're dead." Li'l Monk patted the gun. "You've been a bitch all your life. The least you can do is stand up and be a man for once," he spat.

He stopped at a red light and a car pulled up next to them on the passenger side. Li'l Monk spared a casual glance at it, before turning his focus back to the red light, waiting for it to turn green. Something about the car nagged at him, so he looked again and spotted the rusty panel on the side. It was the same Chevy Nova he had seen earlier. Before his brain could process it, one of the back windows rolled down and the barrel of a shotgun came out. He didn't even have a chance to shout a warning to Charlie before the shotgun kicked and reduced Charlie's head to pulp.

# CHAPTER 24

Persia sat on her living room couch aimlessly flicking the channels on the sixty-two-inch television. Her eyes were fixed on the screen, but seeing nothing. Her mind was more fixed on the drama in her life rather than the drama on TV.

When she came in the house the first thing she did was peel her clothes off and take a hot shower. After washing the soot from the day off her body, she grabbed the scrub brush she used to clean the tub and scrubbed her hands until they were raw. She wanted to obliterate any traces of Chucky's semen from her hands. If she had been smart she'd have ripped his dick off and tossed it to the wind, but revenge was a dish best served cold and slow.

While she dried off she checked her answering machine's messages to see who and what she had missed while she was out. There was a message from Asia, wanting to know where the hell she had been all day and one from Sarah just checking in on her. She started to call her back, but when she noticed the time she decided against it. Sarah was in enough hot water as it was and phone calls in the middle of the night wouldn't do much to help her get back into her parents' good graces.

Persia scanned through the rest of the messages, half listening to most of them, but none were from Vaughn. She was kind of hoping that he had called back, but after not hearing back from her after the earlier message he'd chalked it up and headed back down to Philadelphia. Vaughn had likely washed his hands of her and Persia couldn't say that she blamed him. He had been going out of his way to woo her, but Persia had been acting like a world-class bitch. Vaughn probably thought she was an unappreciative sack chaser, never knowing that she was dealing with him from a distance because she was trying to protect him.

After she finished drying herself and checking her messages Persia changed back into her sweatpants and T-shirt, and went downstairs into the living room. Her mother had gone to bed already, which was a good thing for Persia. She really didn't feel like sitting through another one of her mother's question-and-answer sessions. Michelle had a sixth sense and could always tell when something was up with Persia. All her life her mother had been her biggest supporter, and always seemed to have the knack to make everything okay when it came to Persia's problems. She wanted to pour her soul out to her mother and tell her everything that was going on with her, but Michelle had been carrying the burdens of her only seed long enough.

Persia was eighteen, a woman, and it was time for her to start cleaning up her own messes.

Persia heard the front door open and a few seconds later Richard rounded the corner of the foyer. His black blazer was hanging over his arm and his cell phone was in his hand. Standing under the overhead light Persia could see the worry lines etched in Richard's face. Something had him stressed out. When he looked up and noticed Persia sitting there he straightened his face.

"I'm surprised to see you're still up," Richard said by way of a greeting.

"Surprised to see you're just getting in," Persia shot back. "That student of yours must've needed quite a bit of help."

For a second a confused look crossed Richard's face but then he remembered what he'd said before he left the house. "Oh, I had some other things to take care of after that. Has your mom gone to bed already?" He changed the subject.

"Yeah, you know Mom is an early bird."

"Indeed she is. I'm still a little wired from the day myself so I'm gonna stay up for a few. Mind if I sit?" Richard nodded at the empty space on the couch next to Persia.

"Sure." Persia slid over to give him a bit more space.

Richard tossed his blazer on the arm of the chair and sat down. "So, how was your little outing into the city?"

"Eventful," Persia said in a less-than-happy tone.

"I can only imagine. Your new friend Rissa seems like quite the character. Where did you say you met her again?"

"She's a friend of a friend," Persia told him.

Richard didn't miss the fact that she had side-stepped his question, but he didn't press it. "What kind of design did you get on your nails?" He reached for her hand but Persia snatched it back. "Sorry, didn't mean to invade your space."

"It's not your fault. I guess I been a little on edge lately," Persia said honestly.

"We've noticed. Your mom said she wanted to have a talk with you about your recent mood swings. I told her to leave it alone and to let you open up about whatever is going on when you're ready. Is everything okay with you?"

Persia was hesitant. There were things going on in her life that were likely beyond the scope of anything Richard could relate to, but she didn't have anyone else to talk to and felt like she was going to explode if she kept everything bottled in. "I'm just having guy trouble I guess." It was neither the truth nor a lie.

"Oh, I didn't know you were dating again; at least, not seriously," Richard said.

"There's this guy I've been seeing for a little while now."

"Not another street dude I hope," Richard said.

"God no! He's a square," Persia assured him.

"Sounds like my kind of guy. Anybody I'd know?" he asked.

"I doubt it. He's from New York, but lives in Philadelphia now."

"So this is a long-distance relationship then?"

"Something like that. Philly isn't that far so he comes to New York all the time to see me," Persia told him.

"A man who is willing to drive from state to state to see you sounds like a keeper."

"Oh, he is. He's so nice and a perfect gentleman. I like him a lot, and he's crazy about me. He wants us to be exclusive."

Richard looked confused. "So why the long face?"

"I'm afraid to commit to him. This guy has really got his stuff together, and my life is a mess and I don't wanna track dirt into his," Persia said sadly.

Richard did something unusual and placed his hand over Persia's. "When are you gonna stop dragging that heavy ball and chain? Yes, you've made mistakes in life, and you'll likely make plenty more before it's all said and done, but you can't let what you did dictate what you'll go on to do. That's no way to live. Your past is called the past for a reason. Leave it behind you."

"I'm trying, but it's hard to keep my past behind me when it keeps jumping out in front of me. No matter how hard I try I can't seem to outrun it," Persia said with tears dancing in the corners of her eyes.

"Then stop running and start fighting. The only way you'll be able to finally lay your demons to rest is to kill them. You've got to put whatever is troubling you in the ground and bury it once and for all," Richard told her.

"What if I'm not strong enough?"

Richard gently lifted her chin and looked her in the eyes. "Sweetie, you are far stronger than you think. Strength is a trait all the women in your family carry. It's in your blood. Take it from someone who knows."

Richard had been speaking metaphorically, but to Persia his words rang quite literally. It was time for her to exorcise her demons once and for all.

"Thank you, I really needed to hear that just now." Persia gave him a big hug. When she inhaled a somewhat familiar scent tickled her nose. She sat back and gave Richard a curious look. "Have you been smoking?"

# CHAPTER 25

Li'l Monk floored it and the Bonneville jumped through the red light, nearly getting sideswiped by a bus. Blood covered the windshield making it hard for him to see in front of him, but there was no time to clean it off. He whipped the car through traffic trying to evade whoever was chasing them. Li'l Monk heard the shotgun kick again and his rear window exploded in a spray of glass. He made a hard right trying to shake them and saw a woman step out into traffic at the last minute. He yanked the wheel trying to avoid hitting her and lost control of the car, running up on the sidewalk and crashing into a street light. The seat belt cut into his shoulder as his body was thrown forward and his head hit the steering wheel with so much force that he thought he cracked his forehead.

The world swam in big, beautiful colors and for a few seconds Li'l Monk wasn't sitting in what was left of his mangled Bonneville, but walking hand and hand through a field of flowers with Sophie. The vision faded when he heard the screeching of tires. He glanced around, dizzily trying to get his bearings. The front was completely ruined and there was glass everywhere. Poor headless Charlie had gone through the windshield and was splayed out on what was left of the hood. The only thing that saved Li'l Monk from being thrown from the car too was the fact that he was wearing his seat belt. Through a haze of pain, he looked up in his rearview mirror and saw the shadows of several men getting out of the Nova behind him. If they trapped him in the car, he was as good as dead.

Li'l Monk tried to retrieve his pistol, but it was stuck between the seat and now crumpled center console, leaving him defenseless. When he tried to get out of the car the seat belt held fast. Li'l Monk tried to pop the release but it no longer worked. He grabbed a piece of the windshield's glass and cut through the fabric, opening a nasty gash in his hand in the process. Li'l Monk's hand was bleeding like a stuck pig and would probably need stitches, but he was free. He pushed the car door open and spilled out onto his hands and knees.

"He's still alive!" he heard one of the men shout.

Fighting against the pain, Li'l Monk got to his feet and took off running. Every step he took sent a wave of pain through his body, but his adrenaline kept him on his feet. Li'l Monk rounded the corner and cut down a dark block. All he had to do was make it to the next block, which was well lit and full of people. Whoever was after him wouldn't dare gun him down in front of so many witnesses . . . or so he hoped.

Behind him Li'l Monk could hear the footfalls of the men pursuing him. They were getting closer. Willing himself on, Li'l Monk sped up. He could see the lights of the bodega on the next block. He was almost there. Li'l Monk was mere feet from the corner when someone stepped out into his path. He tried to stop, but his momentum carried him forward. There was a sharp pain in his gut as something hard slammed into it and sent him spilling onto his face. Li'l Monk rolled over onto his back and saw a masked man standing over him, holding a shotgun.

"Where are you going when the party is just getting started?" the man wielding the shotgun taunted him.

"Jesus, that fucker is fast!" Another of the masked men joined them. He was breathing heavily from the chase.

"Yeah, he's fast, but I'm smart, which is lucky for you lugs. Told you splitting up was a good idea," said the man wielding the shotgun.

"What do you want, a fucking cookie?" A third masked man appeared. "Whack this spade so we can get the fuck outta Harlem."

"Okay, no need to get your panties in a bunch." The masked man pointed the shotgun at Li'l Monk. "Say night-night, you ugly son of a bitch."

"You first," Li'l Monk replied, before firing his heel outward as hard as he could. When Li'l Monk's boot made contact with the man's kneecap, the bone snapped like a twig. The masked man collapsed, howling in pain as he crashed to the ground and the shotgun went flying. Li'l Monk crawled on top of the screaming man and yanked the mask off. It was one of the Italians he had seen with Frankie the Fish at the steak house. The Italians would've never made a move against him without first getting Ramses's okay. Once again he had been betrayed by someone he trusted. Mad with rage Li'l Monk wrapped his hands around the downed man's neck and snapped it.

The other three masked men surged forward and found Li'l Monk ready for them. When the first one got within arm's reach, Li'l Monk grabbed a fistful of his testicles and squeezed. The masked man let out a high-pitched shriek.

"That's right, you little guinea bitch, scream for daddy." Li'l Monk applied pressure. He was trying to rip the man's nuts off when something crashed into his back and sent him back to the ground. One of the men had blindsided him with a baseball bat.

The masked men began stomping Li'l Monk viciously and taking turns hitting him with the bat. After what he had done to their comrade, shooting him was no longer acceptable. They planned to beat him to death.

Li'l Monk curled up into a ball trying to protect himself as best he could, but it was futile. He could feel the light fading. As he was taking what he was sure were his last breaths his mind went to Sophie. She was going to be pissed when he didn't show up to eat the dinner she'd prepared for him.

"I'm afraid I can't let you do what it is that you're planning," a voice called from behind the Italians. They turned to see a tall man wearing a tattered overcoat. On his head he wore a hood that obscured his face in shadows.

"Take a hike, buddy. This ain't your business," one of the masked Italians said, retrieving the shotgun from the ground.

"Anytime a white boy spills the blood of an innocent black man on these streets, it becomes my business," he said in a tone that was somewhat familiar to Li'l Monk. "You chumps look real bad ass, jumping a wounded man." Two machetes slid down from within the sleeves of his jacket. "Let's see if I can help make this a fair fight."

The Italians surged forward toward the hooded man. When he moved it was like watching a leaf falling from a tree, graceful and steady. The first to reach him was a man who had hit Li'l Monk with the baseball bat. When he swung the bat the machete met it midair, and cleaved not only the wood but the lower half of the man's face. Never breaking his motion the hooded man brought the second machete around and buried it in the space between his neck and his shoulder. Planting his foot on the Italian's chest, the hooded man pushed, freeing his machete and sending the body flying into the second Italian who had been advancing on them, knocking him to the ground. Before he could crawl from under the corpse the hooded man struck with the other machete and ended him.

The masked man holding the shotgun was just bringing the weapon into play, hands trembling as he took aim. Before he could squeeze the trigger, one of the machetes sailed end over end and buried itself in his chest. The hooded man casually strolled over and regarded his would-be killer. The man who had been previously holding the shotgun was on the ground, clutching at the machete handle and howling in pain. When the hooded man removed the machete, blood shot up from the wound like a fountain.

"You're dead . . . fucking dead," the bleeding Italian rasped.

The hooded man expertly twirled the machete. "We've all got to leave this world at one point or another, but some of us must go sooner than others." He brought the blade down and cut off the Italian's head.

Li'l Monk lay on his side, racked with pain and floating in and out of consciousness. He watched through a haze as the hooded man cleaned his blades on the clothes of the dead Italians before stalking slowly toward Li'l Monk. Li'l Monk's brain screamed for him to get up and run, but he had not the strength left. If this was to be his time, there wasn't much he could do about it. The man knelt next to Li'l Monk and pushed his hood back, revealing his face.

"You?" Li'l Monk croaked before succumbing to his wounds and passing out.

# PART IV

# *TRIPLE CROSS*

# CHAPTER 26

Omega hit the block early that morning. He had been bullshitting around and partying the last few days and needed to get back to business. He needed to check in with all the trap houses and make sure the corner boys had what they needed and understood where it needed to go. Something that used to take a few hours at best would likely take double the time that day because he didn't have Li'l Monk to split the duties with. He hadn't heard from Li'l Monk since the night before, and something about it bothered him. It wasn't beyond Li'l Monk to disappear for a day or so at a time when he was with Sophie, but something about this time felt different.

The news he'd gotten from Ramses didn't help. He'd heard that Chucky was back into town. Chucky had been like a virus that they just couldn't seem to get rid of. His very existence drove Ramses mad because Chucky being his protégé was a constant reminder of his failure. He wanted Chucky exterminated at all costs, but it had not proven to be an easy task. Chucky was as slippery as a snake and just as deadly. He was a man who knew how to carry a grudge and he had never been a fan of Li'l

Monk. If Omega didn't hear from Li'l Monk by that afternoon he was going to go looking for him.

He had Paulie, Blue, and Dre with him that day. Omega didn't like them being so close when he was handling sensitive business, but Ramses had insisted. He felt like it was time for them to come in off the corners and learn the trade under Omega. Omega never could figure out why Ramses seemed so big on the trio. Granted, he had hand-picked them but they weren't the sharpest knives in the drawer. Omega didn't feel like they were ready, but Ramses did.

Lately Ramses had been recruiting heavily to thicken their ranks. When Omega first joined Pharaoh's army it had been a privilege to be a part of it, but lately it seemed like they were letting anyone in who didn't mind dying. Times were definitely changing, but Omega wasn't sure if they were for the better or worse.

When Omega was done making his rounds he decided to kick back on the block for a few hours so his presence was felt. He hadn't been a fixture on the block lately and needed to remind everyone he was running shit on that strip.

"You see this shit?" Paulie pointed at something in the newspaper he was reading. "It says they found some white boys chopped up in Harlem last night."

"Word, where at?" Omega snatched the paper so he could see for himself. It was an article about a multiple homicide that had occurred the night before on the east side of Harlem. According to witnesses they saw two cars speeding across 120th Street, with someone firing a gun from one of the vehicles. They recovered one of the cars and several dismembered bodies, but the other car allegedly involved in the chase was nowhere to be found. What really caught Omega's attention was the last line in the article. According to reports one corpse discovered at the scene was identified as an associate of the Parizzi crime family.

"What's the matter, O? You know them or something?" Dre asked, noticing the peculiar look on Omega's face.

"Nah, man." Omega handed the paper back to Paulie.

A taxi pulled to a stop at the curb a few feet away. Omega stepped off the stoop, smiling and rubbing his hands together. Stacy stepped out of the taxi, wearing a miniskirt that didn't leave much to the imagination and a cropped jacket. He had called her to come through and keep him company while he was hanging on the block. His gleeful smiled faded when Tiffany got out of the taxi after her. Seeing her irritated Omega because he knew the only reason she was on the block was because she was hoping to bump into Li'l Monk. Omega gave Stacy a look that said he didn't approve of her bringing Tiffany along, to which Stacy shrugged her shoulders as if to say she hadn't had a choice.

"Well, well, how you ladies doing?" Blue asked, adjusting the brim of his baseball cap.

"Better than you," Stacy capped and leaned into Omega.

"You're one cold bitch, Stacy," Blue told her.

"Watch your mouth, nigga!" Omega checked him.

"My fault, O. I didn't know you was claiming that," Blue said.

"I ain't claiming nothing but this hood, but when you see a lady in my presence you show the proper fucking respect," Omega spat.

"He didn't mean nothing by it, O," Dre spoke up, as always trying to be the voice of reason.

"Word to mine, Ramses got some of you li'l niggas feeling yourselves, but don't forget who still runs this hood." Omega adjusted the front of his pants where he kept his gun tucked. It was a simple gesture, but the message he was trying to convey wasn't lost on the new recruits. Omega was an easygoing guy who loved a good time, but he wasn't above killing to get his point across.

"So, what's up, baby? What's ya name?" Blue turned his attention to Tiffany.

"Tiffany," she said flatly, folding her arms and looking everywhere except at Blue.

"Damn, don't tell me this one belongs to you too, Omega?" Blue asked.

Omega raised his hands. "Nah, I got no papers on that one, bro. She just doesn't seem to be feeling you."

"That's because we haven't gotten to know each other yet." Blue draped his arm around Tiffany.

Tiffany knocked his arm away. "Nigga, didn't your mama ever tell you it's not polite to touch women without an invitation?"

"I like her. She's a firecracker." Dre laughed.

"Omega, you seen your friend today?" Tiffany asked, ignoring everyone else.

"Nah, I ain't seen Li'l Monk," Omega told her.

"That's who you out here making sad eyes over? Li'l Monk?" Blue asked in disbelief. "Shit, baby, you need to be keeping time with a real nigga and not some zoo escapee."

Everyone laughed at Blue's joke, but the laughter was quickly drowned out by the thunderous sound of Omega's palm making contact with Blue's face. Blue stumbled down the stoop, holding his cheek and looking at Omega in wide-eyed shock.

Omega bounced down the stairs, and grabbed Blue by the front of his shirt, shaking him like a rag doll. "I done told you li'l niggas before about disrespecting my comrade." Omega pulled his gun and placed it to the side of Blue's head. "The next time I gotta check you, you're gonna check out, feel me?"

"You got it, O. You got it," Blue said fearfully.

"Now get the fuck off the block until I tell you that you can come back." Omega shoved him.

"But Ramses said we gotta play the block," Dre spoke up.

"I don't give a fuck what Ramses said. I'm out here right now. Matter of fact, if you feeling some type of way you can bounce with the nigga!" Omega barked. "Yo, all y'all new niggas get from around me right now." He waved his gun dismissively.

Dre wasn't feeling the way Omega was talking to them and his facial expression said as much. "A'ight, boss." He nodded. Dre slowly backed away with Blue at his side. The whole time he was glaring at Omega. He would see how tough he talked when his security blanket was ripped away from him.

"You handled them niggas like a real G, baby," Stacy said excitedly. "I'll bet he'll think twice before he gets smart with you again."

"Stacy, close your mouth. Don't comment on shit you ain't got nothing to do with," Omega checked her. He knew he had overreacted and it had been wrong of him to put his hands on Blue, but he was angry. The young boys were out of pocket for cracking jokes on Li'l Monk and he didn't want them to think it was okay to disrespect someone who outranked them, especially someone he considered a brother.

When Omega heard his cell phone in his pocket he quickly fished it out and answered it, hoping it was Li'l Monk. A look of disappointment crossed his face when he heard Huck's voice on the other end.

"Sup wit' you, youngster?" Huck asked.

"Not too much, everything good?" Omega questioned. He found it was odd that Huck was calling him instead of Ramses.

"All depends on who you ask," Huck replied. "Our mutual friend needs something done and it's gotta be done tonight."

"You ain't said nothing but a word. Give me the details and it's done," Omega assured him.

"The groundwork has already been laid. Tut has got it all mapped out. All you gotta do is be there to make sure he doesn't fuck it up," Huck told him.

Being asked to defer to Tut on a mission for Ramses raised Omega's eyebrow. It was both a slight and suspicious that Ramses would let Tut in on organization business before Omega and he wanted to point it out, but he held his tongue. "Okay, what's the business?"

"We're bringing closure to that immigration problem. We know who snuck old boy across the border," Huck informed him.

He knew without Huck having to say that he was speaking about the situation with Petey. Tut had already told him that Ramses had gone for the ruse and they were in the clear. Still, he wasn't sure how to take the fact that Ramses had called Tut's number to handle it instead of him. "A'ight, I'll make sure I get with Tut. Any word on Chucky?"

"We're on top of that too. Within the next few days most scores should be settled."

"Solid." Omega nodded and ended the call. A broad smile crossed his face. Figuring out a way to distance himself from Petey's murder had been giving him nothing but grief, but in a while he wouldn't have to worry about it. A part of him felt bad for what was about to happen to old Chicken George. The old man had always been okay by Omega, and he never charged him for his chicken dinners. Still, technically George was a traitor and would be dealt with accordingly. Somebody had to take the fall and it was better George than Omega.

Omega was in the process of dismissing Stacy and Tiffany so he could go find King Tut and get the lowdown, when he spotted Sophie coming down the block with her friend Tasha. Sophie had a worried expression on her face.

"Sup, Sophie? Everything cool?" Omega greeted her.

"I don't know, but I'm trying to find out. Have you seen Li'l Monk?" she asked.

"No, I spoke to him last night and he told me he was going over to your place," Omega told her.

"He was supposed to, but he never made it. I've been calling him all night and all day, but I keep getting the voicemail."

Omega frowned. "That ain't like him at all. Maybe he got locked up."

"You know I called all the precincts and hospitals I could think of before I dragged my ass all the way out here. I'm starting to get worried. Have you heard anything in the streets?"

Omega thought back to the newspaper article he'd read about the dead Italians and wondered if there was any connection. "Nah, I haven't heard anything. I'm gonna have a few of the homies put their ears to the streets to be on the safe side, but I'm sure wherever he is, my nigga is good. Li'l Monk is a soldier."

"Yeah, he's a soldier, but he's also my man and I'm worried sick," Sophie shot back.

"So, you're Li'l Monk's girl?" Tiffany looked Sophie up and down.

Sophie returned the stink looks. "I'm sorry, do I know you from somewhere?"

"Nah, y'all don't know each other. Shorty ain't from around here," Omega cut in. "As a matter of fact, the both of these young ladies were just leaving."

"What? But we just got here!" Stacy protested.

"And now you're just leaving." Omega gave her a cold look.

Stacy knew better than to argue. "Okay." She wisely got off the stoop. "Can you at least give us cab fare?"

Omega pulled some bills from his pocket and shoved them into Stacy's outstretched hand. "Here." He didn't even bother to count them; he just wanted to be rid of the girls.

"You gonna come by later?" Stacy asked.

"I'll call you," Omega dismissed her.

Stacy frowned at the dismissal, but didn't say anything for fear of scaring off her new meal ticket. "Okay. Let's go, Tiff."

"Yo, when you see ya peeps tell him to holla at me," Tiffany said to Omega. Before leaving she gave Sophie one last dirty look before smiling and walking away.

"What the fuck was that all about, Omega?" Sophie asked once the girls had gone.

"Pay them chickenhead bitches no mind. Dig, you go back to the crib in case he calls or comes by. I'm gonna hit the streets and see if I can get a line on Li'l Monk."

"Thank you." Sophie hugged him. "I don't know what I would do with myself if something happened to Li'l Monk."

"Don't you worry none. Ain't nobody stupid enough to try Li'l Monk, but if by chance some fool does get it in his mind," Omega said, tapping his waist where he kept his gun, "there's gonna be a storm of fire and brimstone, and that's my word!"

# CHAPTER 27

Li'l Monk awoke with a gasp, like a drowning man who had just broken the surface of the ocean and was taking his first sips of life-giving air. A heavy fog was wrapped around his brain and it took a few seconds to orient himself. He was lying on a cot in a windowless room that smelled of musty, stale water. Li'l Monk propped himself up on his elbows and looked around. It took a minute for his eyes to adjust to the darkness giving him even minimal visibility.

The room wasn't very big, slightly larger than a walk-in closet. There was a writing desk propped up against the wall, and an adjoining door leading to another room. Inside Li'l Monk could hear the sound of running water. He wasn't alone. It was just then that Li'l Monk remembered the car chase and the Italians who meant to kill him.

Going into survival mode, Li'l Monk rolled off the cot and to his feet. He must've gotten up too fast because the room started spinning. He pitched forward onto one knee, using his hand to keep him from falling. As soon as his palm touched the ground, fire shot up through his hand and sent a numbing pain through his whole arm. The pain was so intense that Li'l Monk cried out.

Behind him a door swung open and the room was flooded with light, temporarily blinding him. Li'l Monk could feel someone behind him and he tried to get up, but was still very weak. A pair of strong hands grabbed him under his armpits and helped him back to the cot, where he collapsed on his back. Li'l Monk looked up and found the man who had introduced himself as Kunta standing over him.

"Easy, little brother. You've been through the wringer. Don't overexert yourself too soon," Kunta said in a soothing tone.

"What the fuck happened?" Li'l Monk rasped.

"Somebody decided that it was your time to die and I convinced them otherwise," Kunta said.

"The Italians," Li'l Monk said, remembering the face he'd seen under the mask.

"All white faces look the same to me so I cannot speak to their country of origin, but I can tell you where they now rest. I dispatched the men who sought to harm you, but more will come."

"I know, which is why I gotta get outta here and back in the streets." Li'l Monk sat up. "If niggas think they can make a play on my life and I ain't gonna get back they've got another think coming." He tried to stand and the dizziness returned.

"You're barely well enough to walk, let alone mount a counterstrike," Kunta told him. "Besides, going off on a killing spree in broad daylight is like throwing stones at the penitentiary."

"Daylight? How long have I been unconscious?"

Kunta looked at the cheap wristwatch he wore. "Almost eleven hours."

This surprised Li'l Monk. He felt like he had only been out for a few minutes. "Damn."

"Those men did quite a number on you. Had I not shown up when I did you might not have awoken at all."

"I guess it's a good thing you came along when you did. How did you find me anyhow?" Li'l Monk asked.

"I've been following you," Kunta admitted.

Li'l Monk frowned. "For what?" he asked.

"Let's just say I had a feeling you would be needing my help, and I was right. You've run afoul of some very nasty people. Luckily the men they sent for you were amateurs, little more than thugs with pistols, but I fear the next men they send at you won't be."

"Let them come and they'll get sent back in bags like the last ones," Li'l Monk capped.

"I admire your bravery, little brother. You are a man who does not back down from a fight, and that's admirable, but you have to know how to pick your battles. I've seen you in action, and I'll admit you're good, but not good enough to take on an entire mafia family on your own. You'll need help and a plan."

Li'l Monk wanted to argue his point, but he knew Kunta was right. With the blessings of Ramses the Parizzis had marked him for death, and the fact that several members of their crime family had been shipped back to them in bags probably didn't help make things any better. They would continue to hunt him until he was either dead or could find a way to clear his name. Neither could be accomplished in his current state. He needed to regroup and come up with a plan.

"Not to sound ungrateful of anything, but why do you even give a shit? I mean you hardly know me yet you've put your ass on the line to help me. Why?" Li'l Monk wanted to know.

Kunta weighed the question. "Because I owe it. Not to you personally, but to someone who cares very much about the well-being of you and your father."

"Face," Li'l Monk said remembering what Kunta had told him during their first meeting. "What exactly is your connection to my uncle?"

"I'm afraid that's a complicated story," Kunta said.

"Well, it's like you said; I can't make a move until nightfall so I've got time to listen."

"Very well," Kunta began. "I came to this country as a young boy of twelve. My parents had come to America several years prior to try to build a life for us better than the one we had in the Congo and sent for us when they were established. I was thrilled with the prospect of coming to America, which was supposed to be the land of dreams; but all I found were nightmares. My family and I had escaped the oppression of the soldiers who routinely raided our village only to find ourselves equally oppressed by the street gangs and drug dealers who preyed on the American ghettos. My father was an electrician in Africa, but in the United States he made his money as a street vendor. It was a less-than-modest living and we were barely able to keep up with our portion of the rent for the two-bedroom apartment we shared with my aunt and several of my cousins. I had a very rough time during my first years in America. I was skinny, poor, and didn't speak much English, which made me an easy target for bullies. It seemed like I was in a fight every other day. I won a couple, but lost most of them. Still, I never backed down. Eventually word got around that the new African kid on the block had heart. It was my unwillingness to back down that landed me in prison."

"What happened?" Li'l Monk wanted to know.

"As I said earlier, my father made his money as a street vendor. Sometimes he would let me work with him at his stand so I could learn the value of earning my way in the world. He mostly sold CDs and books, but from time to time he would come upon stuff that people had thrown away and fix them up for resale. Americans are so wasteful that they throw things away at signs of the slightest glitch and my father turned other people's trash into his treasures.

"He'd restored and sold a laptop to one of the neighborhood dealers. The laptop worked fine when he left with it, but two days later he brought it back, broken, and claimed my father had tried to cheat him. My father was a great many things, but he was no cheat. The dealer demanded his money back for the broken laptop, and when my father refused the dealer his friends started beating him. My father warned me to stay out of the fight, but I couldn't just stand by and watch. I grabbed the baseball bat my father kept behind his stand and started swinging. I wasn't trying to hurt anyone. I just wanted to get the men off my father, but I accidentally hit one of them in the head with the bat and put him in a coma," he said sadly.

"You did what you had to do."

"And this is what we tried to explain to the police to no avail. They didn't see it as a young boy trying to defend his father; they saw it as one black man trying to kill another, which I've come to find is the norm in this country. I was arrested for attempted murder and sent to the city jail until my next court date. Being that I was sixteen at the time they were trying me as an adult. My family couldn't afford to hire a lawyer so my life was placed in the hands of a public defender. They were offering me ten years on the attempted murder, but the public defender told me he could get them to reduce the attempted murder to a lesser charge if I signed a piece of paper outlining what I had done. I knew little to nothing about my legal rights so of course I jumped at the chance and signed the paper. What he failed to explain to me was that the lesser charge, assault with a deadly weapon, still carried prison time. Instead of going home to my family, as I thought I would be, I was put on a bus and sent upstate to begin serving the three-year sentence I was given. I thought the time I spent in the city jail was bad, but it was nothing compared to what I was forced to endure in the state prison. I was a baby being thrown into a cage with grown men and was forced to do some things that I am not proud of in order to survive."

"Did your family ride the bid out with you?" Li'l Monk asked.

"In the beginning, yes. My mother and father visited me whenever they could and sent me clothes and commissary when they had the money to spare, which wasn't often. A little over a year into my bid I found out that my father had been shot and killed on his way home from work one night. The police said it was a robbery gone wrong, but I had other suspicions. My mom held it down for as long as she could, but after a while it got to be too much and she moved back to Africa with the rest of the family. I was left alone in a strange country."

"What'd you do?"

"What any other teenage boy who felt abandoned would've done; I raged. Until then my parents and wanting to get home to them were the only things that kept me sane while I was in prison. With my father dead and my mother gone I had nothing left to care about, so I became just what the prison system was designed to make us: a savage. I stopped being the prey and became a predator. I was fighting, stealing, and had even snuffed out a life or two. The way I was carrying myself it would've only been a matter of time before someone killed me or I ended up getting more time added to my sentence. I didn't care though. I was just ready for it to be over one way or another. I was too far gone to care about life or anything else anymore and that's when I met Face.

"Because of my age and the fact that I hadn't finished high school while I was on the streets the prison made me take a GED course. Face was the teacher's assistant. The chick who taught the course didn't give too much of a shit how many of us passed or not, she was just there to collect a check, but Face was different. He seemed to take a genuine interest in the young men in the class and he was one of the few people who wanted us to succeed."

Li'l Monk chuckled. "That's Face all right, always wanting to save muthafuckas who don't wanna be saved."

"Indeed, Face is a good man. At first I thought he was just some kiss-ass inmate who was just trying to get some time knocked off for good behavior, but after asking around about him I found out Face was the genuine article. He had been a boss in the streets and was well respected in the prison. One night there was an incident where a dude tried to press me for my sneakers and I cut his face. I found out later that he was a gang leader and his homies had marked me for death. I was ready to go out fighting, but Face stepped in and squashed the beef for me. I didn't ask him to, yet he had done it anyway, which meant that I was now indebted to him. I expected him to try to make me his bitch or some kind of flunky, but that wasn't what Face had in mind for me. In return for saving my life he wanted me to get my GED."

Li'l Monk looked surprised.

"I was baffled by this too, but I did as he asked. I spent every free moment I had with Face. He studied with me, we worked out together, and he even taught me how to box a little. Face became like my surrogate father and I learned a great deal from him. In the end, not only did I pass the GED test with one of the highest scores in the prison, but I also learned what it meant to truly be a man.

Because the changes I had made within myself and the fact that I passed the GED test, the parole board looked favorably upon me and I made parole my first time up. I literally owe my life and my freedom to Face."

"Man, that's some heavy shit!" Li'l Monk said, digesting the story Kunta had just told him. "So, how does my father play into this? You said Face sent you to find him."

"Yes, I have a message that I am to deliver to him from Face."

"Why couldn't he deliver whatever the message is over the phone or write a letter?" Li'l Monk wondered.

"I'm afraid prison has made him a somewhat paranoid man. He was worried about the message being intercepted. He was very specific about me delivering it to him in person."

"So, what's the message?" Li'l Monk asked.

"I'm afraid it's for your father's ears only. Face was very specific about that. Even I do not understand the meaning of the message, but he said that your father would," Kunta told him.

"Then I guess we need to find dear old dad. Maybe whatever Face has to tell him can help me out with all this shit I'm in."

"It's a possibility, but we won't know until your father makes heads or tails of the information.

Before we begin tracking him down, I suggest we try to find a solution to the more immediate dilemma, which is the price on your head. Tell me, what could you have possibly done to put you in the crosshairs of the mob?" Kunta asked.

"I was dumb enough to try to help a friend in need," Li'l Monk said and went on to tell him the short version of how he had tried to help Charlie and how he had double-crossed him by taking Chucky back to the house and the murder of Mr. D.

Kunta shook his head sadly. "Sounds like you need to make better choices in friends, little brother. Your kindnesses have placed you at a disadvantage, wedged between two very powerful enemies but with the resources to see you dead."

"Tell me something I don't know," Li'l Monk said sarcastically. "I know how Pharaoh's organization is run so that may give me an edge, maybe even a fighting chance. It's the Parizzis I'm worried about. The Italians have got a reach that goes far beyond the streets. Getting them off my back ain't gonna be so easy."

"Then we must clear your name. Maybe we can force your friend Charlie to tell what he knows."

"That'd be kind of hard to do now considering what's left of his head is now decorating the uphol-stery of my car. I was on my way to make him come clean when the guineas rode down on me."

"Then we'll need another way." Kunta got up and began pacing the small room. "Is there anyone else who can attest to what this Charlie's told you? Maybe one of his accomplices?"

"That bitch-ass nigga Chucky and the two broads he's been running with. Charlie said their names are Maggie and Rissa. The problem with that is Chucky has got a bigger price on his head than me. Ramses has been trying to track him down to kill him for months, but hasn't had any luck. Besides that, Chucky hates my guts. He'd rather die than help me."

"Then he just might have to," Kunta said seriously. "Chucky may be the only card you have left to play. Worst case scenario he refuses to talk and we instead present his head to the Parizzis and hope it buys you a pass. Do you have any idea where we can lay hands on Chucky?" Kunta asked.

Li'l Monk thought long and hard on it. "No, but I know someone who might. Do you have a phone I can use?"

# CHAPTER 28

Persia got up earlier than usual that Sunday. She had a lot to do and not a lot of time. It was going to be a full day.

After her talk with Richard the night before her wheels had started to spin and for the first time she could see the path she needed to follow very clearly. Persia had been through so much that she still bore the scars and it had been fucking with her psychologically. She had become a victim of her own self-pity and she had forgotten who she was and what kind of stock she came from. Persia was no weak-ass chick who broke down in the face of adversity; she was a fighter. Richard was right when he had told her that a cold world bred hard men, but what Persia had come to understand was that it bred even colder women. It was time to close the curtain on this sideshow.

She hit Vaughn up earlier, hoping that she would be able to catch him before his morning walk-through. He was playing in a big game the next day against the Giants, one of their biggest division rivals, so there was no doubt he would be busy with team activities. Luckily she was able to catch him.

Vaughn was surprised to hear from Persia, but even more surprised when she asked if his dinner

invitation for after the game still stood. Vaughn
did her one better and invited her to come and
watch him play. He offered to send a car for Persia
to bring her to the stadium in New Jersey, but she
declined, opting to take public transportation. The
car service would've been more convenient, but
Persia wanted to show him that she was capable of
doing for herself, so he never got it twisted about
her character or her intentions for him. Vaughn
protested, but he understood and respected it.
They ended the call with him telling her he'd leave
two tickets at the box office for her.

After hanging up with Vaughn she felt a mixture
of guilt and apprehension about her pending meeting with him. She really liked Vaughn, but there
was no way they'd be able to move forward until
she laid her cards on the table. If he cared for her
like he professed to then he should understand, or
so she hoped. Either way the lies she carried were
getting too heavy. She needed to shed their dead
weight, not just for Vaughn but for the sake of
being able to move on with her life.

Wanting to tell Vaughn the truth was the main
reason she wanted to see him, but not the whole
reason. She knew that on the night of such an
important game cameras would be all over Vaughn,
and her being seen with him would be the glue that
held her real plan together. All the dominos were
set up, now all Persia had to do was set them in
motion.

No sooner had she put the phone down on its cradle than it started ringing again. She looked at the caller ID, but didn't recognize the number. It was probably Chucky calling to see if she had made up her mind about going along with his plan. She started not to answer, but knew that if she didn't he would only keep calling or, worse, send someone to her house again. "What?" she answered with an attitude.

"Uh, hi, can I speak to Persia please?" A familiar voice came over the line.

"Li'l Monk?" Persia asked in surprised.

"Yeah, this is me. Did I catch you at a bad time or something?"

"No, thought you were this other asshole I've been ducking. What's up? I'm surprised to hear from you."

"I need to ask you something. Now I know it's a sore subject for you and trust me I wouldn't be asking if I had a choice."

"What's going on?" There was something in the tone of his voice that unnerved her.

"When is the last time you saw Chucky?"

The line went silent.

"Persia, you still there?"

"Yeah, I'm still here." Her voice came back on the line. "Why are you asking me about Chucky?"

Her response gave Li'l Monk pause. The fact that she answered his question with a question instead of saying she hadn't seen him meant he had likely made contact. "Listen, I got it on good authority that Chucky is back in New York. If he is, I know you're one of the few people he'd reach out to."

"I wish I could help you, but I have no idea where Chucky is," Persia lied.

"Persia, how long have we known each other?" Li'l Monk asked.

"Since we were babies."

"Right, and in all this time we've never lied to each other. No matter how bad it was, we were always able to tell each other the truth. Just like you know me better than anybody, I know you better than anybody, which means I can tell when you're hiding something. Now I'm going to ask you again, and I want you to think long and hard on it before you answer. Has Chucky reached out to you?"

She could tell by the sense of urgency in his voice that something was wrong and it had to do with Chucky. She started to spin another lie about having not seen Chucky when suddenly an idea formed in her head. "Yes," she finally admitted.

"I need to get a line on this nigga ASAP, and it's a matter of life and death," Li'l Monk insisted.

"I'm sorry I lied when you first asked but I'm scared. I know there's a lot of bad blood between you guys and Chucky and I just don't wanna get caught up. I don't want Ramses coming after me because of what I done with Chucky in the past."

This part was true. She knew that Ramses had passed a death sentence on Chucky for what he had pulled and anybody else who was involved would likely go along for the ride.

"Look, baby girl, I ain't never let nobody hurt you before and I don't plan on letting anybody hurt you now. I can fix all this shit. I just need to know where I can lay hands on this pussy," Li'l Monk told her.

"Okay, I'm going to hold you to that promise. The last time I saw him was in the Bronx. I don't have an exact address, but I can get it for you. I'll just need a little time," Persia told him.

"Time is something that I don't have a lot of, but I'll take my blessings where I can get them. Thanks, Princess P. I owe you big time for this," Li'l Monk told her and ended the call.

Persia felt like a weight had just been lifted off her shoulders. Li'l Monk's call had completely changed her game plan. Until she had spoken to him she had it in her mind that the only way out of her dilemma would be to kill Chucky on her own. Persia was no murderer, but she was desperate. If killing him was the only way to break his hold on her it was a risk she was willing to take, but Li'l Monk had unknowingly given her an alternative.

Since they were children Li'l Monk had been so smitten with her he would do anything she asked of him, including commit murder. She could've given Li'l Monk the address to the apartment where Chucky was staying, but she had to cover her ass first. There was no doubt in her mind that Li'l Monk would waste no time in getting after Chucky once she turned him loose so she needed to make sure all her ducks were in a row first, which meant insulating herself from any- and everybody who was involved. When the shit hit the fan she didn't want any of it splattering on her.

She was sure Li'l Monk could take care of her Chucky problem, but Ramses was still an issue. Even with Chucky gone there was no guarantee that Ramses wouldn't want to settle up with her for the part she'd unwittingly played in his she-nanigans. She would need to find a way to give him second thoughts about coming after her and this was where Vaughn came in. She would use his celebrity as her shield and send a message to Ramses or anyone else that harming her would be bad for business. With Persia in the spotlight with Vaughn, the risk of trying to kill her would no longer be worth it.

A part of her felt bad about manipulating Li'l Monk the way she was, but she had limited resources and had to use whatever was at her disposal, including the people close to her.

When Persia came downstairs her mood had improved considerably. She was going to go out and buy herself a new outfit for her date the following night. She wanted to make sure she looked good for Vaughn and the cameras. As she crossed the living room she noticed the door to Richard's study was cracked. From inside she could hear him on the phone speaking harshly to someone. Persia was shocked because Richard rarely used foul language, but he was launching a profanity-laced tirade that would have made Redd Foxx proud. Persia crept to the door and peeked inside.

"What the fuck is that supposed to mean to me?" Richard paced back and forth while talking on his cell phone. "Nigga, that ain't on us if it didn't go how it was supposed to. You tell them sweat suit–wearing muthafuckas they gotta wear that." He listened for a minute. "Yeah, yeah, I know it's still gotta be handled. Tell you what, put them three new niggas on it. The knuckleheads from Lenox. Tell them I got ten stacks on this pussy's face."

Listening to Richard was like listening to a total stranger. The man raging on the cell phone wasn't the bookish man her mother had married. He was someone else.

Richard looked up and noticed Persia standing in the doorway. "I gotta call you back," he said and abruptly ended the call. "Hey, Persia, I didn't see you standing there." He smiled sweetly. It was as if someone had flipped a switch and turned the rage off.

"I haven't been standing here long. I just walked up," Persia lied. "You okay?"

"Just some bullshit I have to deal with," Richard said as if it was no big deal.

"More work-related issues?"

Richard looked down at his cell phone. "No, this is personal."

"Okay," Persia said, picking up on the fact that it was clearly something he didn't want to talk about. "Is Mom around?"

"She said she had some errands to run in the city. Is there something I can help you with?"

Persia was hesitant. "Well, I hate to ask but do you think I could borrow a few bucks?"

"Sure, honey. How much do you need?" he asked, retrieving his wallet from his pants pocket.

"Whatever you can spare is fine. I need to buy an outfit for tomorrow night. I'm going to a football game."

"A football game?" Richard asked surprised. "I could never get you to watch the games on TV and now you're going to one?" He handed her some cash.

"Let's just say I've recently acquired a new appreciation." She accepted the money. "Thanks." She hugged him and started back toward her bedroom.

Richard called after her. "After the game, see if you can get Vaughn to sign a football for me."

Persia was stunned. She had worked hard to keep her relationship with Vaughn a secret from her family until she realized how serious they were going to get. "How did you find out?"

"I was browsing a sports Web site to get the game scores and came across a picture some paparazzi caught of you two coming out of a movie theater. I believe it was taken the same night you lied and told your mother and me that you and Asia were going to the library."

Persia lowered her head in shame, having been caught in a lie. "Are you going to tell Mom?"

"No, I'll leave that to you, whenever you feel like the time is right, so long as you don't wait too long."

Persia nodded. "That's fair. Thank you."

"Anytime. You just let Mr. Tate know that at some point we'll be expecting Vaughn to come and present himself like a respectable young man who's courting a young lady. I may not be your biological father, but I still love you like a daughter. Never forget that."

"I won't," she said and bounced up the stairs.

For the first time in a long time things were finally starting to look up for Persia. Within the next forty-eight hours all of her problems would be solved and she wouldn't have to lift a finger. All that was left for her to do now was set the table and ring the chow bell.

She picked her phone up from the cradle and dialed the necessary number. It barely rang twice before the caller picked up. "Okay, I'm in. I wanna see you tonight so we can go over the details."

# CHAPTER 29

The first thing King Tut noticed when Omega came to pick him up was the sour expression on his face. He was sitting behind the wheel of his car, sucking the life out of a blunt and scowling. Something was clearly troubling him. He wasn't sure what it was, but he had a pretty good idea.

"What up, why you looking like somebody kicked your dog?" Tut asked, getting into the car.

"I can't find this nigga, Li'l Monk," Omega told him.

"And tell me again why that's a bad thing? Shit, I don't know how you can stand looking at his ugly mug all day," Tut joked, but Omega didn't laugh. "Don't stress it, O. He's probably laid up with that chick of his. Isn't that usually where he disappears to whenever something important needs to be handled?"

"Nah, he ain't over there. Sophie said he was supposed to come over last night but he never showed up," Omega said. "I'm starting to get worried."

King Tut was silent for a while, regarding Omega. He was no doubt stressed with Li'l Monk being missing, which was to be expected, but there was business to be handled. "I know this ain't the best time to bring it up, but we need to handle that piece of business with Felix." He changed the subject.

"Right, how did it go when they got the news?" Omega asked.

"Well your little plan went off without a hitch. Ramses bought the story about George," Tut informed him.

"Just like I knew he would." Omega beamed proudly. "Telling Ramses that George was behind it wouldn't have been enough; he would've needed proof. That doctored recording was just what we needed to tip things in our favor."

"But how did you know he wouldn't want to check it for authenticity?" Tut asked.

"Ramses is old school, and cats his age ain't hip to the miracles of modern technology. Besides that, he's so arrogant and sure of his hold over us that it probably never even entered his mind that we'd dare try to fool him. I'm loyal to Ramses, but I'm more loyal to myself."

"You are fucking brilliant, O!" Tut stroked his ego.

"I told you that I'd figure a way out of it; all you had to do was trust in ya boy. How did the wetbacks take it?" He was asking about Felix and the men Suarez had sent to find out who killed Petey.

"Not well at all. Man, them spics was hotter than fish grease when we broke the news. It didn't help that the dude we fingered as the shooter was an affiliate of Pharaoh's. They're still suspicious of us, which is why we gotta go along for the ride to clean up the mess. They want us to help whack one of our own as a show of good faith."

"Fuck it, if it takes helping them get rid of George to put us all in the clear then he can consider his ass gone. The sooner we get this shit handled the sooner I can get in these streets and find Li'l Monk. I got a bad feeling about this."

King Tut frowned. He looked like he wanted to say something, but held his tongue.

"What? You got something to say, spit it out, Tut."

"I'm just thinking, man. I know Pharaoh and Ramses say we aren't officially at war, but anybody with eyes can see what's going on. They're moving in on us. I hear a few of them been playing the hood pretty close, and what if Li'l Monk got caught slipping?" King Tut knew the theory was a farfetched one, but he couldn't very well say what he really suspected. He was testing Omega to see where his head was at before deciding whether to tip his hand as to what he picked up on when he spoke to Ramses.

The thought of Li'l Monk being murdered by the Clarks filled Omega with rage. "That's my word if

I find out one of them touched my brother, I don't give a fuck what Pharaoh says, I'm gonna ride on them bitches!" He punched the steering wheel.

"And be the one responsible for officially igniting the war without Pharaoh's blessings?" Tut questioned. "That might land all of us in the dog house."

"If that's the way it plays out then so be it. Li'l Monk is my brother and if somebody has touched him there ain't nothing short of God that's gonna stop me from taking down his killer and I don't give a fuck what Pharaoh says. Blood will answer for blood!" Omega declared.

King Tut sat back and listened as Omega went into a tirade about what he would do to the persons he found were responsible if something happened to Li'l Monk. He understood his hostility, but felt like Omega wasn't seeing the bigger picture and that might prove to be a problem.

King Tut could tell based on his cryptic conversation with Ramses that Li'l Monk had done something to fall out of favor with Pharaoh, and his spot was about to be up for grabs but it never occurred to him that Ramses would have him killed. Having Li'l Monk knocked off was either a very bold or desperate move on Ramses's part. The pressure was on him and he was cleaning house. Li'l Monk being gone opened up the lane for King Tut to step up. Someone would have to be promoted to fill the void Li'l Monk would leave behind and that someone would be King Tut. If they played their cards right King Tut and Omega could put themselves in position to be the future of Pharaoh's army, but it would never work if Omega wasn't willing to charge Li'l Monk's death to the game. Omega was too loyal to Li'l Monk not to let his death go and therefore would likely present a problem down the line, unless of course he also found himself removed from the equation too. This would make Tut the next logical choice to be Ramses's right hand in the streets. For as appealing as the idea of being Omega's partner was to Tut, the prospect of being the last man standing appealed to him more.

King Tut placed a reassuring hand on Omega's forearm. "You know ain't never been no love lost between me and Li'l Monk, but if you insist on riding for him then I'll ride with you," he said in his most sincere tone.

Omega looked at Tut and nodded. "Good looking out. I really appreciate that."

"That's what friends are for, O." Tut patted him on the back, planting an imaginary knife in it.


It was a relatively short drive from Harlem to Westchester, where they were to meet Felix and his men. The rendezvous point was at a gas station that was about a mile from George's house.

Felix wasn't hard to spot, sitting in a big Hummer sitting on chrome. There were several Hispanic men standing around the vehicle, talking among themselves and watching traffic. Though there were no weapons visible, there was no doubt the men were armed.

No sooner had Omega turned his car into the gas station, than Felix's men had their car surrounded, guns appearing in their hands as if by magic. Tut looked like he was about to reach, but Omega gave him a look and stayed his hand. After what seemed like an eternity of waiting, Felix appeared from the Hummer and strolled over.

He was an average-looking man with a kind face and a receding hairline. As he had been the first time Omega and Tut had met him, Felix was dressed in a white shirt and black slacks. The difference was this time his outfit was accessorized by two big guns holstered under his arms like they were legal. "*Retirarse.*" He ordered his men to stand down in Spanish and they obediently complied.

"What was all that about?" Omega asked, getting out of the car.

"You can never be too cautious when handling poisonous snakes," Felix told him. "You boys had us waiting so long I was beginning to think that you were backing out of our agreement."

"Nah, man. We're all in," Omega assured him. "Listen, this is the plan—"

"No, it is you who should listen," Felix cut him off. "You two are here as proof of your boss's loyalty to our cartel, but it is I who will be calling the shots on this mission. In the meantime, keep your mouth shut and try not to get shot."

Omega trailed Felix's Hummer in his car to the block where George lived and parked a half block down. The sun had gone down so they had the cover of darkness on their side. Felix's men filed out of the Hummer, checking their weapons and conferring with their leader for last-minute details. Felix barked orders in Spanish dispatching his men this way and that. He was like a general and they were his loyal soldiers.

Felix motioned for Omega and King Tut to follow as he and two of his men crept across the lawn of George's house. In the shadows, Omega spotted the men Felix had sent ahead positioning themselves to cover any possible exits. There would be no escape for George. As he stood just outside George's front door, Omega saw a woman pass one of the windows. He hadn't counted on anyone being home except for George and the presence of the woman gave him pause.

"Hold on, man," Omega called after Felix. "It just occurred to me that we never checked the house to see if anybody else is there with him." He wanted to gauge Felix's temperature before he mentioned the woman he'd just seen.

"Have you come here to stall or prove yourself?" Felix asked with an attitude.

"Nah, I ain't stalling. I'm just saying; we should make sure there aren't any women or children in the house before we move forward with this. George is a player in the game so I'm down for killing him, but I ain't with clipping no innocents," Omega told him.

Felix gave a throaty laugh. "My friend, I don't know how Pharaoh does things, but in our cartel there are no innocents, especially when the blood of our family has been spilled. Anyone who is in that house with him will soon wish they'd found somewhere else to be tonight," he said before kicking the door in and storming the house.

George sucked down his third cigarette in the last fifteen minutes. It had been a rough day for him. Between the pain in his burned hand and the throbbing headache that he couldn't seem to shake, George was in a foul mood.

Ever since Tut had popped in on him it seemed like things were going from bad to worse. He knew that it had been a bad idea to take the deal Swann had laid on the table for him, but the way things were going with Pharaoh he didn't have much of a choice. The product was getting less and less potent and some of George's faithful customers were beginning to go elsewhere. It wasn't just George who was seeking a new supplier. Word on the street was quite a few of Pharaoh's drug outlets were getting fed up with him cutting the product trying to earn a few extra dollars.

Pharaoh's drugs weren't the only thing getting weaker. Rumor had it that his hold on the streets was slipping. Of course Pharaoh was still strong enough to crush a middleman like George, but the bigger fish were circling his pond. It was only a matter of time before someone took a chunk out of his ass. George couldn't say he didn't see it coming. Most of the other old timers had gotten into bed with Shai when he took over for Poppa, but because of George's friendship and loyalty to Ramses, George sided with them. It was like eating crow when he had to go, hat in hand, to Swann to take Shai up on his original offer. He felt bad about doing Ramses like that, especially with all that his old friend had done for him, but he had to do what was best for his business. He had planned on telling Ramses himself and hoped that his friend would understand; but that sneaky-ass King Tut had let the cat out of the bag before he had a chance, and now George found his among the many names on Ramses's shit list.

He reached for the glass of whisky that he'd had sitting on the nightstand, but found it empty. The same was true for the bottle sitting next to it. He had been in his room since he'd gotten out of the hospital, popping pain killers and drinking. As severely as his hand was burned it'd be a long time, if ever, before he fried chicken again. It was just one more thing he had to pay King Tut back for when he caught up with him.

George slipped his robe on and made his way downstairs to fetch another bottle of whiskey from the cupboard. When he entered the kitchen he found Hugo, one of the security personnel he'd hired, sitting at the table sipping a cup of coffee and eating a piece of chicken. Hugo was a large man, who wasn't the sharpest knife in the drawer, but he knew how to handle himself in tough situations.

"Hugo, did I hire your big ass to sit around and eat up my food or make sure nothing happens to me and mine?" George asked with an attitude.

"My bad, boss man. Dooley and John are making the rounds, and Claire ordered some pizzas for dinner. Everything is under control so I was just taking a little break," Hugo told him, cleaning the chicken bone and dropping it on the plate among the half a dozen or so others he'd devoured.

"Well, break yo' ass up from my table and go do your job," George snapped. Hugo mumbled something under his breath and went to do as he was told. Hugo was a good man and George hadn't meant to be so harsh with him, but his nerves were on edge. After King Tut had outed him, Ramses had been blowing his phone up. He knew what he wanted, but wasn't quite sure what to say to him just yet. He and Ramses had been friends, but after finding out what George had done he wasn't sure where they stood at that point. Ramses was a man who didn't take betrayal well, so George didn't want to take any chances and brought in some extra muscle.

As George was rummaging through the cupboard for a bottle of whiskey, Claire came into the kitchen. Claire was a girl half George's age, who didn't have much ambition but could fuck and suck like she was put on earth to do it. She had started out as his mistress, but was promoted to live-in girlfriend when George's wife found out about them and left him.

"Claire, did you move my bottle? I know I put it in this cabinet and, now that I'm looking for it, I can't find it," George fumed.

"Yes, I put it in the liquor cabinet where it belongs," Claire told him.

"Damn it, why you always moving my shit? You know I hate when people move my shit around," George snapped.

"I moved it because there's no need to hide your liquor in here like some relapsed drunk. Unlike your ex-wife I'm not on you about how much you drink, so there's no need to hide your bottles anymore," Claire shot back. "Why are you in such a damn pissy mood today?"

"What kind of mood would you be in if somebody went upside your head then tried to deep fry you?" George asked.

"I told you about being out there trying to play with them young niggas. You way too old to be still trying to sell drugs, especially when you own a business. Why don't you stick to frying chicken and leave the crack game alone?"

"Shit, with the way you like to shop and sniff coke I'd have to keep that restaurant open twenty-four hours a day just to keep the lights on. Instead of your worrying about what the hell I'm doing you need to be tending to my boy," George told her, referring to the two-year-old son he had with Claire. His son was one of the few reasons he still kept her around.

"Junior is fine. He's upstairs sleeping, so please don't wake him up. I don't know who keeps me running more, you or him." Claire rolled her eyes. "And, speaking of junior, I need to go out and get him some stuff so I'm gonna need some money."

George gave her a look. "Didn't you just hit me for some shopping money the other day?"

"Yes, but that was for me and this is for him," she said.

"Okay, go upstairs and look in—"

"I know, top drawer, third from the right," Claire cut him off.

George shook his head. "You're slicker than a pig in shit. I don't even know why I keep you around."

"Because nobody sucks your dick like I do." Claire kissed him on the cheek and headed upstairs to take her cut.

After dealing with Claire, George found he needed a drink more than when he had first come downstairs. He left the kitchen and headed into the living room where the liquor cabinet was. Dooley and Hugo were standing near the front door talking among themselves and John was just coming back downstairs after having checked the upper level of the house. For as much grief as George gave the three of them, he couldn't deny the fact that they were on point. Having them at their positions filled him with a feeling of safety. That feeling lasted all of ten seconds before everything went to shit.

# CHAPTER 30

When the front door burst open, the door swung forward and clocked Dooley in the back of the head, stumbling him. Just as he was trying to right himself, several slugs ripped through the door and Dooley's back. He pitched forward and his lifeless body landed at George's feet.

At the sight of the corpse at his feet, George backpedaled so fast that he tripped and fell through the glass coffee table. Pain shot through his burned hand when he instinctively tried to use it to break his fall. Lying there, nursing his wounds, George watched in shock as several Hispanic men rushed into his home. At first George thought it was a robbery, as he had no problems with the Latinos, but all the pieces fell into place when he saw King Tut slither across his threshold. The Latinos hadn't come to take his goods; they had come for his life.

Hugo moved with the speed of a man half his size when he drew his big .45 from his jacket and let it rock. The paintings on the walls shook as Hugo fired at the invaders. The .45 shells that had been intended for Felix tore through one of his shooters who had jumped between him and the bullets. The Latino's body spun like it had just been hit by a car before one more slug hit him in the back and carried him into Felix. They landed awkwardly on the floor, with Felix pinned and at Hugo's mercy.

Before Hugo could finish what he started, King Tut intervened and shot him twice in the leg, dropping the big man to one knee. Tut stepped forward, placing the hot barrel of his gun against Hugo's forehead. He made eye contact with Felix, before popping Hugo in the skull, splattering blood all over himself and Felix. There was a terrified look on Felix's face, as he had never come that close to death before. An unspoken understanding passed between them. Felix was now in King Tut's debt.

Ignoring the pain in his hand, George pushed himself to his feet and took off running across the living room trying to get to the kitchen where he had a pistol stashed. He bobbed and weaved, trying to avoid the gunfire of the Latinos who were laying siege to his home.

Jay popped up seemingly out of nowhere, firing two 9 mms and covering George's escape into the kitchen. The guns spit fire, backing Tut and the Latinos back toward the front door. He was their last line of defense, and doing an adequate job until Omega crept up on his blindside. He let off two shots, hitting Jay in his jaw and temple, ending him.

Omega started to rush into the kitchen to finish George off when he remembered the woman he'd seen, who wasn't accounted for among the dead. "Y'all get George. I'm gonna make sure ain't no surprises waiting for us upstairs." He bounded up the stairs.

George burst into the kitchen in a dead run. His heart thundered in his chest as he heard the sounds of gunshots and screams coming from the living room. There wasn't much he could do for Hugo and the others, but at least he could save himself. George had almost reached his stash spot, when the back door came crashing open and another Latino appeared, firing his gun.

Swinging the stainless steel refrigerator door open George hunkered down and used it as a shield. Bullets peppered the door, as the Latino advanced. He moved in for the kill and that's when George popped up holding the .25 he kept stashed in the vegetable bin.

"Die, muthafucka!" George roared, firing the .25. It took every bullet in the small gun's clip to finally drop the Latino. He was just popping in another clip when something heavy hit him in the back of the head, sending him spilling to the floor. George looked up and found himself staring down the barrel of King Tut's gun.

"Time to pay the piper, old timer," Tut taunted him.

"So this is how it goes down? As long as me and Ramses been friends he's gonna have me taken out of the game all because I switched suppliers?" George asked in disbelief.

"Afraid you got it wrong, Chicken George. This is about that boy you murdered," Tut informed him.

George was confused. "What the hell are you talking about? I didn't kill anybody."

"No, but I told them spics out there you did," Tut informed him.

"You set me up?" George asked in disbelief. "Why?"

Tut shrugged. "Somebody had to take the fall," he said before pulling the trigger.

Just then Felix and his remaining men came into the kitchen. When he saw Tut standing over George's corpse, holding a smoking gun, he became angry. "You killed him before I had a chance to question him, you stupid little fucker!" he snapped. "I wanted to find out who else was involved in Petey's murder."

"Look, man, he smoked one of your boys and was about to smoke me." Tut nodded at the .25 on the floor next to George's body. "I didn't have a choice."

Felix glared angrily at Tut. He had seen the man in action and somehow doubted that George had posed that much of an immediate threat. There was no time to argue about it as the police would surely be on the scene soon. "I'll deal with you later," he told Tut. "*Nos vamos*," he said to his men, letting them know it was time to leave.

"I'll catch up. I gotta go check on my boy," Tut said and started toward the upstairs bedrooms.

Omega crept down the upstairs hallway, with his gun at the ready. He went from room to room checking for threats and the woman he had seen earlier. He knew that if Felix found her first she was as good as dead and he didn't want it on his conscience.

From the bedroom down the hall he could hear muffled sounds, like someone was crying. With his gun raised, he kicked in the door and darted inside, sweeping the room for threats. The room was decorated with cartoon characters on the wall and a toddler bed in the corner. He didn't see anyone and was about to go and check a different room to see if the sounds had been coming from somewhere else when he spotted a closet. Omega crept to the door and placed his ear against it. The sounds he had heard were coming from inside. Raising his gun, he snatched the door open.

Claire was inside the closet, huddled in the corner and holding a small child in her arms. When she saw Omega her eyes went wide with fear. "Please don't kill me! I have a son!"

"Keep your voice down," Omega shushed her. "I ain't gonna kill you, but if those guys downstairs hear you they sure as hell will. Stay in the closet

and count to one thousand before you come out.
Do you understand?"

Claire nodded.

"Good, start counting." Omega backed away
from the closet. He was about to step out into
the hallway when he heard a thunderous bang
right before something slammed into his back.
Staggered and using the wall to brace himself,
Omega turned around and found the same woman
he had tried to save seconds earlier holding a
smoking gun. Claire fired again, this time hitting
him in the chest and dropping him.

Omega lay on the ground, staring at the ceiling
and feeling his life drain away. The first law of the
jungle was self-preservation and he had broken
that law when he put himself in jeopardy trying
to save the woman. He watched helplessly as she
stood over him and pointed the gun at his face.

"If you niggas thought you were gonna come in
here and harm me and mine then you got the game
fucked up," Claire said.

"But, I tried to save you," Omega rasped.

"That was your bad, not mine." Claire fingered
the trigger.

Omega closed his eyes and waited for the end.
He heard the shot and braced for the impact of the
bullet, but felt nothing. When Omega opened his
eyes he saw Claire standing there with a strange
expression on her face. He wasn't sure what had

happened until he saw the red spot in the middle of her forehead, followed by a trickle of blood spilling out. Claire rocked once then fell over dead. A few seconds later, King Tut appeared in the room.

"How bad are you hit?" Tut knelt beside Omega and checked his wounds. They looked bad.

"I need to get to the hospital," Omega told him fighting to catch his breath.

"Yeah, you probably should. If you don't get those wounds tended to you're probably gonna die." Tut stood up and wiped his hands on his pants.

"You gotta help me. I need a doctor." Omega extended his hand, but Tut just stood there.

"Sorry, O, but there's only room enough for one lion in the jungle." Tut turned to walk away, but stopped short. He knelt next to Omega and whispered to him, "Before you kick the bucket the least I can do is give you a little bit of closure on a couple of things. Li'l Monk isn't missing, he's dead. The punch line to that joke is that it was Ramses who ordered the hit. I'm just sad that it wasn't me who got to air-hole that ugly muthafucka." He laughed. King Tut dug in Omega's pocket and took his car key. "You don't mind, do you?" he asked sarcastically. "Of course you don't. It's not like you'll be needing a car where you're headed. See you in the afterlife, my friend." He patted Omega on the cheek and left him to die.

Omega's last thoughts were that Li'l Monk had warned him about King Tut and he didn't listen.

Felix and his men were waiting near the front door when King Tut came back downstairs. He expected Omega to follow, but there was no sign of him. "Where's your boy?"

"Bitch got the drop on him," King Tut said faking sadness.

"I'm sorry for your loss," Felix said sincerely.

King Tut shrugged. "It's all a part of the game, man. Let's get outta here before we all end up in prison." He walked past Felix headed back to where Omega had left the car.

Felix stood there for a few moments longer, watching King Tut stroll off as if he didn't have a care in the world. He spared a glance back at the stairs, contemplating if he should take a look to verify Tut's story, but decided against it. Whatever really happened between Tut and Omega wasn't his business. He had accomplished what Poppito had ordered him to do, which was avenge Petey's death, so his work was done.

As Felix and company were pulling away from the block, the pizza delivery guy was turning into the driveway of George's house. He was late because he had stopped to get some weed along the way then got held up in traffic. He made hurried steps to the front door, hoping the woman who placed the order hadn't called back because he would surely get fired and he needed his job.

He raised his hand to knock on the door and noticed that it was open. "Pizza delivery," he announced himself and stepped in the house. When he crossed the foyer and entered the living room he dropped his pizza boxes. The house looked like a scene out of a horror movie. He was about to run out and call the police when he heard what sounded like a child crying somewhere upstairs. Against his better judgment he went to investigate.

When the pizza delivery guy made it to the bedroom at the end of the hall he saw something that he would never forget. There were two corpses in the bedroom, a woman and a man. Both of them had been shot. Near the woman, tugging at her arm and trying to wake her up, was a small child. He was crying uncontrollably and sitting in a pool of his mother's blood.

Careful not to step in any of the blood the pizza delivery guy crossed the room and went to attend to the child. The child clung to his mother for dear life as the delivery guy scooped him in his arms. "Easy, little man. Everything is going to be okay," he tried to calm the child as he carried him back across the room. A house full of corpses was no place for a child. As the pizza delivery guy was leaving, something grabbed his leg, startling him. Apparently, not everyone in the house was dead.

"Help," Omega gasped weakly.

# PART V

# *WRATH*

# CHAPTER 31

Ramses sat on a bench in Central Park, puffing on a big cigar and lost in his own thoughts. Huck was at his normal position, at Ramses's side, holding him down. With them were also three hired guns. Ramses hated traveling in such large entourages but in light of all the dead bodies dropping around him he wasn't taking any chances. His well-laid plans were slowly going to shit and there was no shortage of people to point the finger at, including Pharaoh.

He had discovered that Pharaoh had taken it upon himself to give the Italians his blessings to murder his former protégé Li'l Monk. Ramses didn't like it, but he knew it would eventually have to be done. The problem was the Italians had botched the job and woke a sleeping dog. The Italians' mistake had been approaching Li'l Monk as if he was just some common street thug. If Ramses had been consulted he could've warned them to be prepared to deal with a monster. Not only did Li'l Monk dispatch several Parizzi soldiers, but he had spit in the face of Frankie the Fish by dismembering them. That bit of information surprised Ramses. He knew Li'l Monk was lethal with a gun, but had never known him to handle blades. The idea that Li'l Monk might've had help had crossed Ramses's mind, but it was highly unlikely. Li'l Monk had no one else to turn to, Ramses had seen to that when he made him an outcast.

The problem Ramses now faced was that Li'l Monk was still alive, and probably none too happy about finding out he'd been crossed. It was like kicking a rabid dog and then not being fast enough to run away. Pharaoh had dispatched some of their new recruits to claim Li'l Monk's head, but Ramses had little faith in them being successful. If he had been a betting man he'd have laid everything he had on Li'l Monk chewing those young boys up and spitting them back out. When he was done feeding on the appetizer, he would come for the main course and Ramses planned to be ready.

Just then the person he had been waiting for came strolling down the path as if he didn't have a care in the world. The shooters who were with Ramses surged forward forming a wall between King Tut and Ramses.

King Tut looked the shooters up and down before turning to Ramses. "Is this how you treat all your soldiers when they march home in victory?"

Ramses nodded at his shooters and they moved to the side to let King Tut pass.

"That's more like it." King Tut brushed past the shooters to Ramses.

"I hear the chickens have been cooked." Ramses ignored his comment and cut straight to the chase.

"Yeah, man, deep fried, fricasseed, baked and barbecued; that nigga is a meal," Tut said proudly. "Poppito has his nephew's murderer, your relationship with the Puerto Ricans has been salvaged, and Petey's turf is free to come under new management. Everybody is happy."

"Except Omega," Ramses pointed out. "What the fuck happened out there?"

Tut frowned. "O got caught slipping. He was trying to save this broad and her kid and the bitch ended up smoking him," he said. Sometimes the best lies were hidden in the truth. "After she dropped Omega, I dropped her and got out of there."

"You sure that's how it happened?" Ramses asked suspiciously.

"Ramses, I seen it with my own eyes. Why you acting like my word ain't no good?" Tut asked.

"Because if Omega is dead I'd sure like to know who that is they pulled them bullets out of up there in Westchester," Ramses said.

"Omega lived?" King Tut gasped, not able to hide his shock.

"I don't know if you'd call the condition he's in living, but he ain't dead," Ramses informed him.

"What'd he say?" Tut asked nervously.

"Nothing, yet. Last I heard he was just out of surgery. It's touch and go right now and nobody can say for sure if he'll make it."

"Damn, can we see him?" Tut asked, faking concern.

"Not unless you're a lawyer. Omega is now the prime suspect in a multiple homicide. Even if he survives his injuries, he's probably gonna have to do some time. Our ranks are getting real thin out here real fast. Omega was a good soldier and losing him is gonna hurt."

"With all due respect, Ramses, Omega ain't the only good solider you got riding for you," King Tut told him.

Ramses regarded him. "So what you saying?"

"I'm saying I'm ready to step up," Tut said confidently. "With Omega getting taken off the streets like that, these young boys need a leader now more than ever. You don't get somebody out there to call the shots and the streets are gonna be thrown into chaos. You don't wanna sit on this too long, Ramses. Moves have to be made."

Ramses knew King Tut was trying to leverage him, but he also knew that he was right. Li'l Monk and Omega were the glue that held the team together and with them gone the soldiers would start tearing each other apart for corners and leave the entire organization in disarray. It would make them ripe for the plucking for their enemies. "Even if I were to give you the nod, what makes you think those loyal to Li'l Monk and Omega will follow you?"

Tut rubbed his hands together greedily. "I'll make them an offer they can't refuse: get with the program or get missing."


Ramses's talk with King Tut left him with some unanswered questions and a bit of a dilemma. When he'd first brought King Tut into the fold he sought to remake him in his image, but it would seem that Tut was turning out to be another failed experiment. He was the most unlike the others Ramses had tried to school. Benny had been weak-minded, and Chucky greedy, but King Tut was ambitious . . . too ambitious for Ramses's tastes. He was a man who didn't mind stepping on toes to get what he wanted, and Ramses wasn't sure how well that sat with him.

Omega getting shot and Tut managing to escape was too convenient for Ramses's tastes. There had to be more to it, but Ramses wouldn't be able to find out until he had a chance to hear Omega's side of the story. There was no way he would attempt to visit him with all the police around and his connection to the crime, but Ramses had already assigned a lawyer to the task. Once he heard back to see if the stories matched up he'd know better

how to proceed, but in the meantime he needed to
hook up with Pharaoh to figure out what they were
going to do about Li'l Monk. He was a problem
they were going to have to deal with sooner rather
than later.

Ramses whipped his cell from his pocket and
dialed Pharaoh's number. "It's me; we need to
talk." He listened for a few seconds. "Yeah, I know
the place. I'll meet you there at ten."

"How do you think Pharaoh is going to take the
news about Omega?" Huck asked once Ramses had
hung up with Pharaoh.

Ramses shrugged. "Probably won't make him
much of a difference, so long as we find someone to
replace him before it starts affecting our profits."

"Ain't we gonna at least see what the charges
against Omega are looking like before we name a
successor?" Huck questioned.

"No need. He was caught with his hand in the
cookie jar. Even if they don't hit him for the mur-
ders, he's still looking at time. The only question
now is how much. Tut should be capable of holding
it down, at least temporarily."

Huck frowned. "Before you handed the keys to
Omega and Li'l Monk they were vetted over time.
They proved themselves to be solid young dudes,
and loyal."

"Except Li'l Monk," Ramses reminded him.
"I would've given him the world, but it wasn't
enough."

Huck gave Ramses a funny look. "You trying to convince me or yourself? C'mon, man, we been in the street long enough to know a real nigga from a creep. Li'l Monk might've been a lot of things, but disloyal wasn't one of them. How many times has he handled business without question or taken one for the team? A man can't fake those kinds of characteristics."

"You think sitting by and watching this has been easy for me?" Ramses snapped at his friend. "I don't like it any more than you do, Huck, but it's what has to be done to keep the peace. You and I know how much losing Li'l Monk is going to hurt us, but Pharaoh doesn't give a shit. To him, everybody is replaceable."

"Even us?" Huck shot back.

Before Ramses could answer the question, a man in a hooded jogging suit appeared on the path in front of them. He accidentally bumped into Ramses as he was passing, which got him snatched up by Ramses's shooter. They slapped the man across his face and tossed him to the ground before drawing their guns on him.

"Why don't you watch where you're going?" Ramses snapped.

The man raised his hands in surrender, showing the tattoos on the backs of them. "My apologies, boss. I don't want any trouble," he said in a thick accent. He sounded as if he was of African descent.

"You want me to teach this nigga some manners?" one of the shooters asked, hoping Ramses gave him the okay to pop off.

Ramses thought about it for a minute. "Nah, let this immigrant muthafucka go on his way."

"Thank you, boss man, thank you." The jogger scrambled away, thankful for his life. The jogger waited until he was a safe distance away before stopping. He spared a glance over his shoulder to make sure the men weren't pursuing him. From his pocket he fished out the wallet he'd lifted when he collided with Ramses, and smiled triumphantly.

# CHAPTER 32

Droopy had been having an eerie feeling in his gut all day. It started out that morning when he popped into the local bodega to grab the newspaper. Droopy liked to read the sports section. As he was thumbing through it he came upon an article about a shootout on the east side the night before that had resulted in a car crash. He skipped the details and continued to the scores from the previous night's basketball game.

He shoved the paper into his back pocket and made his way to the block to report for his shift. Normally he would check in with Li'l Monk to receive his package, but he wasn't around so he had to get his package from whoever was running the strip that day, which happened to be Dre. Droopy sat on the stoop while he waited for the runner Dre had sent to get his package. While he was out there he overheard Dre having a conversation with someone on the phone. He wasn't sure what it was about, but Dre seemed to be elated by whatever news he had just received. During the conversation Droopy heard him say something about "wetbacks" but didn't pay it any mind. After receiving his package, Droopy went about the business of selling drugs.

It had been hours since Droopy had started his shift and there was still no sign of Li'l Monk. His big homie had been on his mind heavily since he'd last seen him the night before. He had been pissed that Li'l Monk had made him shut it down early, but he understood he was just trying to look out for Droopy. Droopy had never had anyone be kind to him, which was why he was always trying so hard to impress Li'l Monk. Droopy suffered from a Napoleon complex. He had always been the runt of the litter and constantly felt the need to prove himself. To gain respect in the streets you had to be willing to go further than anyone else.

Once Droopy had finished running through the package he had, he went back to the building to get another one. Dre was still out there, but now he had his boys Blue and Paulie with him. Dre was cool by himself, but tended to turn into an asshole when his boys came around. Droopy never cared for them, especially Blue, because he was always fucking with him.

"I need another package," Droopy told Dre.

"Bet." Dre nodded and sent a fiend off to get him another one.

"Omega ain't around yet?" Droopy asked.

"Why you keep asking about Omega? We handing out the packages," Blue told him in a nasty tone.

"Yo, I'm getting a little tired of you thinking you can talk to people any kind of way, my nigga. This is Omega and Li'l Monk's strip and I only take orders from them!"

"Ain't nobody seen Li'l Monk in days and it'll be kinda hard for Omega to give any orders from ICU," Paulie said with a smirk.

Droopy was stunned. "What?"

Dre gave Paulie a dirty look for his harsh delivery. "Omega got shot last night," he told Droopy in a softer tone.

"What happened? Is he okay? What hospital is he in?" Droopy fired off questions.

"Easy, shorty. He ain't dead, but he's in bad shape and they don't know if he's gonna make it. Other than that we really don't know what happened," Dre lied. He really knew the whole story and then some, but there was no sense in tipping Droopy off until he was sure whose side he was on.

"Damn, this is fucked up," Droopy said sadly. Hearing Omega got shot only made him more frightened about Li'l Monk's disappearance. For all he knew he could be somewhere dead. "That's my word, if I find out who laid hands on my people I'm gonna murder them," he said emotionally.

"I feel you shorty and I'm with you." Dre draped his arm around Droopy. "Right now we just gotta hold our heads until we know what's what. When it's time for the bodies to start dropping, you'll be the first to know. In the meantime, those of us who are left gotta stick together. We gotta hold it down for Omega and Li'l Monk."

"I need to take a walk to clear my head. If y'all find out anything, let me know," Droopy said.

"You got it," Dre promised. Dre stood there, watching Droopy walk off with his head hung low and his emotions on his sleeve. A sly smirk appeared on his face.

"You think that li'l dude is gonna be a problem?" Blue asked.

"Nah, I doubt it," Dre said. "He's in his feelings right now, but once we knock Li'l Monk out the box and we're out here running shit with King Tut he'll either get over it, or join his partner in the dirt."

"Straight like that," Paulie chimed in.

"Let's take this walk to the store for some cigars. I'm trying to smoke before we bag up the rest of this work," Dre said, before leading the way to the corner store.

A few seconds after Dre and his boys had gone, Neighborhood appeared in the doorway of the building. He looked in the direction Dre and the others had gone in and shook his head sadly. Something wicked was coming.


Droopy made hurried steps up the block with his brain racing. If Dre thought the story he fed him would be enough to satisfy his curiosity he had another think coming. Droopy was young, but he was no fool and an excellent judge of character. Li'l Monk and Omega conveniently coming up missing around the same time was no coincidence. They knew something that they weren't telling and Droopy intended to find out what. He wasn't sure what was going on, but what he did know was that if they had anything to do with it, he was gonna body them.

The first thing Droopy had to do was find a payphone, which was easier said than done. With the growing popularity of cell phones, payphones were becoming extinct. He had to walk nearly six blocks to find one that worked, cursing himself the whole time for not investing in a cell when he started hustling. He dropped some change in the phone and dialed one of the few numbers he knew by heart: Li'l Monk's. He had tried to call him from the payphone on the block earlier, but kept getting the voicemail. To his surprise, someone picked up, but it wasn't Li'l Monk.

"Hello?" a female voice answered.

"Who is this?" Droopy asked.

"Nigga, you called my phone," the girl said with an attitude.

"Shorty, you know damn well that ain't your phone. It belongs to a friend of mine. Stop playing games and tell me where Li'l Monk is. I need to speak to him," Droopy demanded.

"Look, you disrespectful li'l nigga, I don't know nobody named Li'l Monk. I found this phone near the park so it's mine now. Possession is nine tenths of the law," she said and hung up.

"Fucking bitch," Droopy said to the empty line and slammed the phone down. He was about to call her back and demand she turn Li'l Monk's phone over to him when her words came back to him and hit him like a ton of bricks. With nervous hands he retrieved the newspaper from his back pocket and began flipping through the pages. He stopped when he came across the article about the shooting. The picture was blurry, and the car was mangled but it was the right make and color. Dropping the paper, he took off running as fast as he could.

Big Monk sat on his living room couch in an almost comatose state. Every few seconds he would reach up and touch his face with his fingertips because he could no longer feel it. He had been snorting high-grade cocaine and drinking whiskey all morning, courtesy of a liquor store he had robbed the night before. Hunting had been slow in the streets and he needed some quick cash to get high before the sickness set in. He found an out-of-the-way liquor store that seemed to be an easy enough mark . . . or so he thought.

The two Puerto Ricans working in the store put up one hell of a fight. They gave him so much of a run that Monk had to kill them both in order to keep them from killing him. He couldn't understand why the men were willing to die over the $1,500, but as he was raiding the refrigerator where they kept the wine it all became clear. The liquor store was a front for a cocaine spot. All told Monk made off with six ounces of white, and a case of whiskey for his troubles. Monk had planned on hitting the streets to try and sell off most of the cocaine, but he hadn't managed to pull himself off the couch yet.

From behind his ear Monk pulled a McDonald's straw, which was sliced in half to make it shorter. He didn't even bother to separate lines from the mound of cocaine on the table; he just jammed one end of the straw into his nose, the other end into the pile, and went for broke. His head snapped back, one nostril clogged with cocaine and his eyes as wide as if someone had just stuck him with a live wire. He was just about to treat his other nostril when he heard banging.

Moving off pure reflex, Monk was on his feet with his shotgun in his hands. His eyes whipped around the room nervously like there was someone else in the apartment with him. The banging continued and only then did he realize it was coming from the front door. He stalked across the living room, trying to get his legs to cooperate. The cocaine had him so charged that it felt like all his muscles contorted at one time. His movements felt awkward and almost robotic, but his trigger finger was fluid. Monk aimed the shotgun at the center of the door and leaned in to check the peephole. When he saw who was standing on the other side, he frowned. He undid the locks, snatched the door open, and buried his shotgun into the intruder's chest.

"Give me one reason why I shouldn't lullaby your little ass," Monk demanded.

Droopy swallowed hard, looking down the barrel of the shotgun. "It's about Li'l Monk!"

# CHAPTER 33

The sun had barely set and Li'l Monk was in the streets. Kunta had advised him to wait until he was feeling a little stronger, but time was a luxury Li'l Monk didn't have. The plan was for them to split. Li'l Monk needed Kunta to hit the streets to do some reconnaissance for his preemptive strike. Li'l Monk's enemies would see him coming from a mile away, but nobody knew Kunta's face. Kunta didn't like the idea of separating, but Li'l Monk wasn't in a negotiating mood. While Kunta was off playing spy, Li'l Monk had to go home to retrieve some of the things he would need.

Going home was risky because Li'l Monk wasn't exactly sure where he stood. Ramses had given the green light to have him killed, and knowing Ramses this wasn't an impulse decision. Killing Li'l Monk was a big move that couldn't have been made without support and preparation. Li'l Monk had no way of knowing who else was in on it and until he could find out there was no one he could trust, not even Omega.

Thankfully his block was quiet when Li'l Monk appeared. Aside from a few random stragglers, nobody who knew him was around. He slipped into the building and bounded up the stairs to his apartment. Before putting his key in the door he took a second to listen. He wasn't too worried about any surprises waiting for him inside his apartment because most knew his dad was crazy as hell and always armed, but after narrowly escaping the Italian hit men he didn't want to take any chances. Once he was sure nothing was fishy he went inside.

Big Monk wasn't at home, but from the looks of things he had left in a hurry. There was cocaine all over the table and a half-empty whiskey bottle. His father was a careless man about life, but never when it came to his drugs. If he had left his stash out in the open like that then whatever he had rushed off to do must've been extremely important. He just hoped that his father came back soon because he needed him to link up with Kunta. With any luck, whatever message Face had sent could help to put an end the deadly game Li'l Monk found himself forced to play.

When Li'l Monk was passing the kitchen he noticed the answering machine light blinking on his house phone. Normally he didn't check it, because only bill collectors called the house phone, but he was in dire need of information and thought there might be something on the answering machine that he could use. The first four messages were from bill collectors, as he had expected. He was about to abandon the answering machine when he heard Sophie's voice come over the speaker.

"Hey, Li'l Monk, it's me again. I've been trying to call your cell phone since you stood me up last night, but haven't been able to reach you. Standing me up was not cool and your ass had better either be dead or in jail or I'm fucking you up. And while I'm venting, who is the light-skinned bitch I saw on the block asking about you earlier? Bitch kept giving me dirty looks like she had something to tell me. I'm telling you, if I find out you been out here in the streets fucking with these dirty-ass groupie hoes you better stay missing because I plan on killing you!"

It didn't take a rocket scientist to know who Sophie was talking about: Tiffany. In light of everything going on the last thing Li'l Monk needed in his life was women troubles. He had no idea why Omega would've had Tiffany on the block, especially after what had happened, but he planned on checking him about it when he saw him. Li'l Monk continued listening to Sophie's rant, trying to figure out what he was going to say to her when he saw her. Toward the end of her message she said something that shook him to the core.

"And what's up with your boy Ramses? He pulled up on me while I was chilling in front of my building and started asking me all kinds of ques-

tions about you. You and I both know that Ramses
has barely ever said two words to me and now he
wants to chop it up like we're all friendly. I might
be paranoid, but it didn't feel right. Li'l Monk, all
this stuff is starting to make me nervous. You need
to get with me and let me know what's going on
before I draw my own conclusions."

Li'l Monk's hands shook with rage as he listened
to Sophie's message for a second time. He was a
soldier and had made his choices in life, but Sophie
was a civilian and therefore off-limits. Ramses had
crossed the line when he tried to press Sophie. The
fact that Ramses had approached Sophie himself
meant that by now he realized the Italians had
botched the job and he was getting desperate.
Desperate men were unpredictable. It was now
clear to Li'l Monk that bartering for his life was out
of the question. Ramses and Pharaoh had to die.

Li'l Monk went into his bedroom and stripped
off his soiled clothes, changing into some fresh
ones. He grabbed a pair of black jeans, black boots,
and a black T-shirt. Stealth would be important,
but not as important as his accessories. From the
back of his closet he grabbed an old police-issued
bulletproof vest he'd scored from a crackhead and
strapped it on before donning his black T-shirt.
He'd lost his Desert Eagle in the car crash so he'd
need another weapon and knew just where he
could get one.

He crept into his father's room, which was a mess of dirty clothes and empty liquor bottles as always, and headed for his closet. After moving several piles of dirty laundry out of his way, Li'l Monk searched the floor until he found what he was looking for: a small notch carved into the wood. He gave it a gentle tug, exposing the trap door beneath that hid his father's treasure chest. Over the years Big Monk had sold off most of his hidden arsenal to help feed his drug habit, but there were still a few toys left that would help. He selected a chrome P89 with a black rubber grip, a shotgun that looked like it had seen better days, and a small .38. As an afterthought he also took a large hunting knife. It would come in handy if he found himself in close quarters. Now armed to the teeth he was ready to go to war.

When Li'l Monk opened the door to leave he was surprised to find someone standing on the other side. His hand instinctively went to his gun, but he paused when he realized it was Neighborhood. The old fiend's eyes got as wide as saucers when he saw Li'l Monk.

"Damn, nigga, you look like you just seen a ghost," Li'l Monk said.

"I did, baby boy, I did." Neighborhood pulled him in for a hug. "I'm glad to see you're okay. I been hearing some real bad stuff in these streets about you."

"Well you're about to hear some worse shit before the night is over," Li'l Monk told him. "What're you doing here? You looking for my pops?"

"Technically yes, but it's about you. Can I come inside for a minute? These walls got ears and what I got to say might get me killed." Neighborhood looked around nervously.

Li'l Monk didn't feel like entertaining Neighborhood right then but he'd piqued his curiosity. He stepped to the side and let Neighborhood into the apartment. "Say what you gotta say and make it quick. I got shit to do."

"I'll bet, especially with that price on your head," Neighborhood told him.

"And what do you know about it?" Li'l Monk asked suspiciously.

"Not too much, man. Only what the streets are saying. I hear you're on Ramses's shit list."

"I'm gonna be on more than his shit list when I catch him."

"Li'l Monk, I know you're built Ford tough, but taking on Ramses is a tall order. Maybe it's best you get low until all this blows over," Neighborhood suggested.

"You know better than that. Monks don't run from no fights; we finish them. Now if you've come to tell me what I already know, which is Ramses is trying to have me killed, you're wasting my time."

Li'l Monk opened the door, letting Neighborhood know it was time for him to leave.

"I can dig it, Li'l Monk. You gotta do what you gotta do, but let me ask you something: how much is it worth to you to know the name of the next person they're gonna send at you?" Neighborhood rubbed his hands together greedily.

Li'l Monk thought on it for a few seconds before pulling his gun and putting it to Neighborhood's head. "I'd say it's worth your life. Stop fucking with me, old man, and start talking."

Neighborhood smiled nervously. "Well since you put it that way, this bit of information is on the house."

# CHAPTER 34

"So what you gonna do with your part of the money?" Blue asked. He was hunched over a small glass coffee table, sifting through a pile of cocaine with two playing cards.

"I would buy a phat-ass chain and a car!" Paulie said, lighting the weed.

Dre looked up from his position at the dining room table where he was chopping big rocks into smaller ones. "You sound dumb as hell. The bounty is only ten stacks, and we splitting that three ways. What kinda car you gonna get with thirty-three hundred dollars?"

"A beat-up-ass hooptie." Blue snickered.

Paulie took a deep pull off the L and let out the smoke. "Fuck the both of y'all. If I catch him and get the drop, I ain't gotta split shit."

Dre laughed, shoveling small bags of crack into a Ziploc. "Nigga, stop acting like you wouldn't shit your pants if you bumped into him in a dark alley."

Paulie stood up and began strutting around the living room with his chest poked out. "Broad day or in the dark, if I run into him it's on." He pulled a .22 from his pocket and flashed it.

"Man, quit lying and pass the weed." Blue snatched the blunt from him.

"Yo, at least wash your hands before you hit that. I don't need no coke on the end of the blunt." Dre reminded him of the cocaine residue still on his hands.

Blue looked at his fingers, which had stained the end of the blunt with white powder. He shrugged before placing the blunt between his lips and hitting it anyway. "In the mouth or up the nose, a high is a high."

Paulie looked from one bickering friend to the other and shook his head. "I should've known I couldn't talk to you two clowns about no real nigga shit. There's a nigga running around disrespecting our team and y'all act like smoking weed is more important than taking this fool's life!"

"Allegedly," Dre said. All eyes in the room turned to him for an explanation. "I been hearing some things lately, like maybe this situation ain't what certain people are trying to make it out to be."

"Like a setup or something?" Blue asked.

Dre shrugged. "Dawg, I don't know, but something about it doesn't feel right."

"Dawg, you killing me with this conspiracy theory shit." Paulie waved him off. "We're being offered a nice piece of change and a seat at the table for this job, so ain't nothing to debate about. All I need to know is that the boss wants him dead and he's willing to pay for it. Who he is and what he's done is irrelevant. Fuck Li'l Monk!"

At that moment something heavy slammed against the door. By the time any of the young men realized what was going on, the second kick had landed and the door came off the hinges. Now standing in their foyer, wearing a trench coat that until that moment concealed the shotgun he was carrying, was the topic of their discussion.

"Fuck me? Nah, nigga, fuck you!" Li'l Monk barked and opened fire.

Blue had made it halfway to his feet when the spray of buckshot knocked off his Dodger cap, as well as half of his dome. Dre made a break for the kitchen, but didn't get far. Li'l Monk jerked the trigger again and peppered the back of his leg with the shotgun, dropping him just between the kitchen and the living room. When he turned toward Paulie, he took a slug from the .22 high in the chest, knocking him to the ground and dislodging the shotgun.

Paulie advanced on Li'l Monk, holding his gun sideways like they did in the movies. His prey was wounded and at his mercy, so he was trying to savor it. Had he been a seasoned killer, he'd have picked Li'l Monk off from deep with the gun, but he was a novice. As soon as Paulie was close enough, Li'l Monk came up holding the P89 he'd borrowed from his dad. Paulie with the braids opened his mouth to say something and Li'l Monk put a bullet in his throat.

Li'l Monk tore his black T-shirt down the middle, exposing the vest he was wearing beneath it and the ruined .22 slug lodged in the chest plate. "Stupid muthafucka," he mumbled, ripping the slug free and tossing it. He stalked into the living room, gun sweeping back and forth while on point for surprises. Blue was right where Li'l Monk had dropped him, but Dre was gone. It wasn't hard to track him down, because his ruined leg had left a bloody trail.

Li'l Monk found him crawling through the kitchen, trying with all his might to get to the kitchen counter and the gun resting on it. His outstretched fingers had just grazed the butt of the gun when Li'l Monk pulled him back.

"Not so fast." Li'l Monk dragged him by his ruined leg back into the living room.

"Please, don't kill me, Li'l Monk," Dre begged.

"I'm sure somebody will punch your ticket one of these days, but that honor won't go to me." Li'l Monk picked him up by the front of his shirt and held him against the refrigerator. "Lucky for your maggot ass I need you to live, at least until I get what I want." He pressed his gun against his forehead. "I'm going to ask you some questions and you're going to give me some answers. If you think about lying, I'm going to give you a headache that aspirin won't be able to help you with." He tapped the gun against the kid's forehead. "Who else was in on this little plan to take my life?"

"I don't know, man. We got the word from Ramses. He said if we knocked you out the box then we could have your spot," Dre confessed.

"Pussy nigga, you couldn't hold my dick let alone my spot!" Li'l Monk snapped. "But that's beside the point. Did Omega know about all this?"

"If he did know, he never said nothing to us. If you plan on shooting him too, you can find him in the ICU at some hospital in Westchester," Dre confessed.

Li'l Monk slammed Dre against the refrigerator hard enough to knock the magnets off. "Y'all niggas touched my family?" he snarled.

"It wasn't us!" Dre protested. "Omega is the big homie. All any of us know is that him and King Tut went to handle something and only one of them came back in one piece."

"Damn," Li'l Monk cursed. His being marked for death and Omega getting taken out the game weren't coincidences. Pharaoh and Ramses were cleaning house.

"That's all I know, I swear, man!" the kid with the shaved head told him.

"I believe you, which is why you still have your fucking head. I'm gonna let you live, but I want you to take a message back to your boys for me. I didn't start this family feud, but I'm gonna finish it. You tell those cocksuckers Ramses and Pharaoh that I'm coming and I'm going to keep wasting their soldiers until Pharaoh stops hiding and comes out onto the dance floor so we can settle this like gangstas. That faggot you works for thinks he's a god, but I'm going to show the world he is indeed mortal when I make him bleed!"

"You got it, Li'l Monk, anything you say. I'll tell him," Dre fearfully agreed.

"Yeah, I know you're gonna deliver my message, Dre, but you're gonna have to write it down. I don't know how well your mouth will work after I break your jaw," Li'l Monk told him before proceeding to viciously pummel him.

Li'l Monk stepped out of the building and breathed deeply. The night air felt good in his lungs, especially after the light workout he'd had in the apartment. Sadly he had expected more from the men Ramses had selected to replace him and Omega. Dre and his crew were little more than flunkies, and hardly capable of running an organization. This meant they weren't the head of the snake. Li'l Monk had a feeling if he turned over enough rocks, he'd find King Tut hiding under one of them. It was just one more blood debt he'd have to settle.

The burner phone he had gotten from Kunta vibrated in his pocket. "Speak," he answered. Li'l Monk listened intently as the caller on the other end spoke. "Good looking out, Princess P." He ended the call. Barely able to contain his excitement he pressed send on the only number stored in the phone and waited. "Yeah, it's me. A little birdie just whispered in my ear and told me where to find Chucky. It's time to end this."

# CHAPTER 35

For the last year or so Chucky had been having shit luck. He'd been beaten, humiliated, stripped of his rank, and damn near killed. To boot he had a drug habit that was becoming harder and harder to control. Yes, it had been a rotten year for Chucky but the phone call he'd gotten from Persia that morning was a sign that things might actually be about to change for the better.

Ever since he had dropped Persia off the day before she had been on his mind heavily. The minute he let her walk off he cursed himself for not just kidnapping her ass and keeping her close to him until he did what he had to do and could blow town. He knew that getting her to double-cross her new man was a long shot. Vaughn was a million dollar athlete who could give Persia everything and Chucky was a junkie trying to recapture his greatness. It wasn't even a fair fight. This was why his heart filled with so much joy when she called him and said she was in.

Chucky had to admit that getting Persia to set up Vaughn hadn't been in his original plan. He knew the broken condition he'd left Persia in the last time he'd been in New York and expected to come back to find her still the floundering mess he'd left behind, but to his surprise Persia had really started pulling it together. The tipping point was coming across the picture with her and Vaughn in the newspaper. After all he had put her through Persia had bounced back and it was killing Chucky. Looking at her and Vaughn shining made him think of himself and Persia and what they could've possibly been if he hadn't fucked it up. He couldn't stand to see her happy without him so he looked to find some company for his own misery.

Chucky had no illusions about the slim chances of him convincing Persia to rip Vaughn off. At best he figured he'd fleece her for whatever few dollars he could pressure her into scrambling together, but to his surprise she was receptive to his advances. This made him hopeful. With enough money and enough of a head start he and Persia could start over somewhere else where their pasts didn't matter and he could show her the man he was capable of being as opposed to the monster she'd come to know. This was where it got complicated. Before he could focus on a future with Persia, he had to do something about the present. Persia had made it clear that before they could explore the road of life he had to cut his extra baggage, which meant Maggie and Rissa had to go, and he had to be creative about how he gave them their walking papers.

Persia had said she wanted to come through later on that night to go over the details of their plan so he didn't have a lot of time, but for what Chucky planned he would only need a few hours. He changed out of the sweatpants and T-shirt he had been wearing most of the day and changed into something more befitting him: a pair of Timberlands and nice sweater and a brand new pair of jeans Rissa had boosted for him from Macy's. He wanted to make sure he looked good for Persia when he saw her. After giving himself the once-over in the mirror he was ready to put his plan into motion.

When he came out into the living room he found Rissa and Maggie sitting around the table talking. He reasoned they must've been talking about him because they abruptly stopped when he walked into the room. "What y'all out here doing? Plotting on killing me?" he joked.

"No, we plotting on getting off E," Maggie said. From the slight twitch in her eyes Chucky knew she was starting to geek.

"Damn, y'all hoovered up all the shit we came up on last night?" He faked an attitude. Chucky knew damn well the few grams he had set out for them wouldn't be enough to float Maggie and Rissa for the whole day. He needed them thirsty for what he had in store.

"Don't say 'y'all' because I barely had any," Rissa said with an attitude. She had been acting more moody than usual since she had come back from Persia's house.

"If you're slow you blow, bitch." Maggie wiped her nose with the back of her hand. "Don't worry though, Chucky. I saved a taste for you." She dipped in her bra and pulled out the small amount of cocaine she had hidden from her sister.

"And that's why you're my down-ass bitch." Chucky kissed her on the forehead.

"It ain't enough to cook, but we can snort it," Maggie said while emptying the contents onto the tabletop.

Chucky looked at the coke and frowned. "That ain't gonna do much but take the edge off. I was thinking we could have us a little party." He walked over to the refrigerator and removed a box of cereal from the top. He dug inside and removed the brown paper bag he had stashed in there and threw it on the table.

Maggie grabbed the bag and tore it open. Inside there was a small bundle of cocaine. "You sneaky bastard, you've been holding out!"

"I wasn't holding out. I was making sure you two thirsty bitches didn't smoke or snort up all the shit and leave us with nothing for our celebration."

"What are we celebrating?" Rissa asked, eyeing the drugs hungrily.

Chucky took a seat at the head of the table. "Ladies, tonight is our last night in New York. By tomorrow we'll be moving on to greener pastures."

"About damn time. I'm about sick of this place and everybody in it," Maggie said.

"By tomorrow night, we'll be in the wind, but first I got some last-minute stuff to take care of. Y'all hold it down while I'm gone."

"Where you going?" Maggie asked, emptying the cocaine onto the table. She couldn't wait to cook it up so she could smoke.

"None of your damn business," Chucky snapped.

Maggie's eyes narrowed to slits. "You must be going to see your precious princess, considering you're all dressed up." She looked him up and down.

"Maggie, don't start your shit, not tonight."

"Yeah, that's it. Whenever someone mentions Persia your ass gets all defensive and shit," Maggie capped.

"And what's it to you if I am going to see Persia? You jealous?" Chucky taunted her.

Maggie laughed. "Of that square bitch? Never! But it is kinda fucked up that you'll try to put your unwashed cock in my mouth whenever the mood strikes you, but you get all spiffy for her."

"It's all a part of my plan," Chucky said.

"Plan my ass." Maggie snorted. "That little bitch ass got you sprung!"

"You better watch your step, Maggie," Chucky warned.

"What's the matter? Does the truth hurt? You know, you've been going on and on about this plan of yours, but so far I ain't seen you do shit but chase this bitch who you claimed ruined you. You know when I first hooked up with you, Chucky, I thought you had some real potential, but now I ain't so sure. This bitch has got your brain all scrambled. Shit, you've got your head shoved so far up her ass that you might as well wear it as a hat!" Maggie sat back and folded her arms triumphantly. Her moment of victory was short-lived.

Chucky moved like a blur, slapping Maggie with so much force that she flew over the back of the chair and crashed to the floor. Rissa moved to get between them, but Chucky shoved her out of the way sending her flying into the refrigerator. Chucky grabbed Maggie by the throat and lifted her off her feet, shaking her like a rag doll. "You trump-mouthed bitch, I think you need a reminder of who the fuck I am!" He slapped her again.

"Get off her, Chucky!" Rissa screamed.

"Shut your fucking mouth before you get a taste of this medicine too!" Chucky snapped at Rissa. Chucky grabbed Maggie by the jaws and began to apply pressure. "You think you're hot shit, but don't forget that when I dragged your ass out of Philadelphia you were sucking cock for dime bags!

If it weren't for me you'd probably be dead or in jail! I made you so I got no problem breaking you. Never forget that." He released her and Maggie crumbled to the floor.

Rissa scrambled across the floor and hugged Maggie to her. "You're a fucking monster, Chucky!" she spat.

"I guess it takes one to know one, or haven't you seen yourself in the mirror lately?" Chucky laughed. "Now like I was saying, I got some business to handle but I'll be back in a few. You bitches hang tight, and try to save a little coke for me." He grabbed his jacket off the couch and stormed out of the apartment.

Long after Chucky had gone, Rissa continued to cradle her sister. Normally it was Maggie trying to protect her, but this time the roles were reversed. She looked down at Maggie. She had a bruised cheek and a bloody lip, but she wasn't hurt too bad. Rissa had seen her in a lot worse shape. "You okay?"

"Yeah, Chucky hits like a bitch," Maggie joked, pushing herself off the floor. When she stood, her legs felt weak and she had to grab on to the table for balance.

"You sure you don't need me to take you to a hospital or something?" Rissa asked in a concerned tone. She reached for Maggie to help steady her, but her sister pulled away.

"I said I'm fine damn it." Maggie eased into the chair. Her jaw was killing her and her back hurt from when she fell.

"I should've stabbed that nigga when he hit you. Who the fuck does he think he is?" Rissa fumed.

"That wasn't about nothing. Couples fight all the time. Chucky was just mad; he didn't mean nothing by it."

"That bruise on your cheek says he meant plenty by it," Rissa countered, sitting across the table from her sister.

"I don't know why you're making such a big deal about this. It ain't like this was the first time me and Chucky got into it and I'm sure it won't be the last." Maggie grabbed a club flyer from the table and began chopping through the cocaine. Between her aching body and her thirst she didn't have time to wait for it to cook so she was going to snort it.

"So, does that mean you're supposed to just sit around and be his punching bag?" Rissa shot back. "You don't have to take this shit from him."

Maggie rolled up a dollar bill and treated herself to one of the lines of coke she'd carved out. "And what do you suggest I do? Go back to turning tricks in North Philly, or sit around and wait for some white knight to rescue me like you're doing?" She cleared her nostrils. "I hate to break it to you, baby, that shit is a fantasy and this"—she pointed to the coke—"is my reality." She took another bump of the coke. "And yours too." She extended the rolled-up dollar bill to her.

"I don't want any," Rissa refused. She could feel her jones coming on, but wanted desperately to keep her head on straight.

Maggie looked at Rissa suspiciously. "What the fuck is eating you?"

"Nothing, I just wanna talk to my big sister without my head being all fucked up for once," Rissa said.

"Is that right?" Maggie made another line disappear. "So tell me." She snorted to clear her nasal passages. "What exactly do you wanna talk about, little sister?"

"This!" Rissa motioned around at the apartment. "You ain't gotta put up with this shit. What's to stop you from picking up and leaving him? What's to stop us from just putting Chucky and all his shit behind us?"

Maggie lit a cigarette and exhaled a cloud of smoke. "Simple: I ain't got no money, no place to go, and no desire to do more than to just make it from one day to the next. Chucky might not be the best man, but he has his uses. Though I'm sure I ain't gotta tell you that."

"And what's that supposed to mean?" Rissa asked defensively.

"C'mon, Rissa. You can't bullshit me. I used to change your shitty Pampers, so I think I know you better than anyone. You think I don't see the way you look at Chucky and the way he looks at you? I know y'all been together."

"I can explain."

"Nah, baby girl. You don't owe me no explanations. That Chucky can be quite the charmer when he's after something."

"How long have you known?" Rissa asked shamefully.

"For a while now," Maggie said, snorting another line. She pinched her nose, as this one stung a bit.

"How come you never said anything?" Rissa asked.

"What good would it have done? For as much as either one of us might hate to admit it, we're two peas in Chucky's pod. The only difference between me and you is that I'm an old fool and you're a young one." Maggie laughed, and a sneeze came out.

"So what now?"

Maggie shrugged. "We play the hands we're dealt and see how the game ends."

"But we don't have to play. We could run away, just me and you!" Rissa said.

"And where are we gonna go? We ain't got nothing, and nobody except Chucky. I'm a washed-up old fiend who's probably gonna die with a pipe to her lips or a gun to her head."

"Don't say that." Rissa's eyes welled with tears. She had never seen her sister look quite so broken.

Maggie placed a hand over Rissa's. "This is my truth, and I've come to accept it. I've made a mess of my life, and if you stay around me you're gonna make a mess of yours too. You're still young enough to go out there and do something in the world."

"I won't leave you, Maggie," Rissa told her.

"Then that's too bad, because I don't have any plans on going anywhere. This is where I choose to be." She snorted another line. "You gotta get free of this bullshit. Go out and be somebody. If not for yourself then do it for me. Promise me you'll make something of yourself."

"I promise," Rissa said with tears in her eyes. She had seen her sister beaten down before, but never broken. She reflected on Persia's speech about her sister being too far gone to save, and for as much as she hated to admit it, she was right.

"Now before you go galloping off into the sunset," Maggie said, and slid the coke toward Rissa, "take one last ride with your big sister."

Rissa stared down at the cocaine. She had promised herself she would try to stay straight, but it looked so white, so pure, so inviting. What could one little bump hurt? "One last ride." She took the rolled-up dollar from Maggie and treated her nose. She wouldn't realize how prophetic her words would be until it was too late.

# CHAPTER 36

The hospital emergency room was especially busy that night. There were more than a dozen people waiting to be treated for this or that, and more seeming to pour in. The influx of patients kept the doctors and nurses busy running back and forth. In the back of the emergency room a fight broke out between a girl and her boyfriend, which required all three of the security guards who were on duty to break it up. Had they not been so preoccupied with the fight one of them might've noticed the man dressed in the long trench coat slip past them.

He got on the elevator and before the doors could close he was joined by an orderly pushing a laundry cart. The orderly gave the man in the trench coat a curious look, but tried not to stare. The man in the trench coat smiled at the orderly as the elevator doors closed. When the doors opened again, on the floor that housed the intensive care patients, the man in the trench coat stepped out, wearing the orderly's uniform, and pushing the laundry cart.

The duty nurse at the front desk barely spared the orderly a glance as he pushed his cart past her, whistling "Camptown Races." At the end of the hall there was a police officer. He was supposed to be guarding the room of the patient he had been assigned to, but he was more interested in trying to get the phone number of one of the nurses. When the orderly approached with the laundry cart, the cop gave him an irritated look for interrupting his flirting session.

"Gotta change the bedding in there." The orderly flashed his best slave grin, all tooth and gums.

The cop mumbled something before motioning for him to go inside while he turned his attention back to the nurse.

The orderly pushed the cart to the side and crossed the dimly lit hospital room. He stopped at the foot of the bed of the lone patient in the room and looked him over. The young man appeared to be in pretty bad shape, with tubes running in and out of his body and an oxygen mask over his face. His body was a mess of bloody bandages, some of which were starting to leak into the bed sheets. The orderly picked up his chart and gave it a quick look. The patient had suffered multiple gunshot wounds and a collapsed lung. He didn't look in any condition to get up from the bed, let alone cause any kind of trouble, but one of his hands was cuffed to the bed rail.

Placing the chart back in it's place, the orderly walked around to stand at the head of the bed.

He regarded the patient for a while. He looked so peaceful; lying there all bandaged up he looked more like the child he was than the thug the streets had made him. The orderly leaned over and placed a tender kiss on the patient's forehead and his eyes fluttered open. It took a minute to focus, but when he realized who it was standing over him, his heart was gripped with panic.

"Remember me, muthafucka?" Big Monk sneered down at Omega.

Omega's free hand flapped around trying to find the call button that was lying on the bed next to him. Before he could snatch it up, Monk grabbed it and ripped it from the wall.

"Now why you wanna go and break up our little party before we've had a chance to talk?" Monk removed the oxygen mask from Omega's face and leaned in to whisper, "The last time I saw you, you were sitting on my couch rolling a blunt, and do you remember what I told you that night?"

Omega remained silent. He just glared hatefully at Big Monk.

"Let me see if I can refresh that memory of yours." Monk slammed his fist down onto Omega's stomach. When Omega opened his mouth to scream, Monk clamped his large hand over it. "I told you that if anything happened to my son I was going to hold you personally responsible. I thought we had an understanding and then I hear that somebody is out there trying to kill my one and only child. Did you know about them trying to put my boy to sleep?"

Omega shook his head frantically that he didn't.

Monk slammed his fist into Omega's gut again. "Don't lie to me, boy. I ain't in the mood. You touch my child?"

"No, Li'l Monk was my brother. I'd never cross him," Omega croaked.

"Then who did?" Monk pressed him.

Once again Omega went silent.

"Oh, you think I'm fucking around, huh?" He ripped the cord loose from the television and looped it around Omega's neck. "If you're willing to die for whoever you're trying to protect, I'm more than willing to kill you for who I'm trying to protect. Give me a name, muthafucka!" He began strangling him.

Spots danced before Omega's eyes as he tried to catch his breath. He was trying to call for help, but couldn't get the words out over his shrinking windpipe. Omega thrashed violently in the bed as Monk choked the life out of him.

"You're gonna sing, little songbird, or you're going to die!" Monk said sinisterly. "I want a name!"

"Ramses!" Omega was finally able to croak out.


It had been a long day for Huck. He had been running back and forth all day handling organization business. Had it been twenty years ago he could've gone for days without rest, but he was an old man and couldn't hang like he used to. When he got home he had never been happier to see the small house that he owned in Yonkers.

Huck had quite a bit on his mind, mostly to do with Ramses. He had known him a long time and had never seen him as rattled as he had been over the last couple of weeks. Though he wouldn't admit it, the business with the Clarks was starting to take a toll on him. Huck had gone to his friend on more than one occasion and suggested that they all sit down and hash out an amicable agreement rather than all-out war, but his advice fell on deaf ears. He was committed to the will of Pharaoh even if it meant sacrificing them all in the name of his ego.

In Huck's opinion Ramses had been making some very questionable moves, one such was the assassination of Chicken George. The minute Huck heard the story King Tut came back with he knew it was bullshit. George might've been guilty of trying to double dip with the Clarks to try to increase his profits, but him having Petey killed made no sense. George sold a moderate amount of cocaine out of his chicken shack to make some extra money, but he had no designs on being a boss. Encroaching on someone else's territory wasn't just pointless, it also wasn't in George's character. He was a greedy son of a bitch, but he was no killer. In Huck's gut he knew there was more to the story than King Tut was telling, but Ramses took him at his word and authorized the murder of a man they had known for over twenty years. It made Huck wonder how Ramses would react if someone ever pointed the finger at him for something? Would their friendship be enough for him to see reason, or would the will of Pharaoh dictate his movements?

The slaying of Chicken George troubled Huck, but not as much as what Ramses was trying to do to Li'l Monk. Li'l Monk was a good soldier, and one of the few who Huck could actually say he liked. He was a young man of principles and honor, things that you didn't see often with his generation, yet Pharaoh had ordered him gunned down like a common dog without any real proof that he was guilty. The sad part was that Ramses was willing to go along with it. When he saw a man who always had a voice in the organization start following orders blindly Huck knew they were approaching the end of an era. The game he had once loved so much was dying in his arms and he wasn't sure how much longer he'd be able to stomach it.

After setting his alarm system Huck went upstairs to shower and change into his pajamas. He was too wound up to sleep, so he decided to make himself a snack and watch television. He whipped together a sandwich and grabbed a beer before going into the living room and cutting on the TV. *King of New York* was playing on cable, which was one of his favorite movies, so he decided to settle in and watch it until he got tired.

Huck had just settled into his favorite chair when he realized he felt a breeze on his neck. His living room window was open, which was odd, because Huck never left the house without making sure the windows and doors were locked. He closed the window and settled back in front of the television. When Huck picked up his beer to take a swig, he realized that it was now half empty. He was just trying to figure out what was going on when he heard someone whistling an old tune that he was familiar with, "Camptown Races." Huck's first instinct was to go for his gun, but in his heart he knew it was already too late.

"Had I known you were coming by, I'd have made sure to stock something a little heavier than beer," Huck said, not bothering to take his eyes off the television.

Monk emerged from the shadows, holding his trusty sawed-off. "Been awhile, Huckle Buck." He called him by his full nickname.

"Not long enough if you ask me."

"Then it's a good thing I didn't ask you," Monk shot back. He came to stand between Huck and the television. "I take it that you know why I'm here?"

Huck looked from the shotgun to Monk's hard face. "Indeed I do."

"You touch my boy, Huck?" Monk asked.

"Nah, Monk. I never touched him. As hard as it might be for you to believe, I was actually quite fond of him. He kinda reminds me of you when you were out there on top of your game," Huck told him with a smirk.

"Yeah, he's just like his dad as far as being about his business. He's also like me when it comes to making bad decisions when it comes to who to trust." Monk slapped Huck with the butt of the shotgun and knocked him off the chair. "That boy loved Ramses more than he loved me and what'd it get him, Huck? What'd it get him?" he barked emotionally.

"It got him the same thing it will eventually get all of us in the end: fucked when we've outlived our usefulness!" Huck spat.

Monk's eyes flashed with rage. He snatched Huck to his feet, and delivered a vicious backhand across his face, sending him flying into the television. Before Huck could get to his feet, Monk was over him with the shotgun. "Fuck, nigga, I'm gonna kill you!"

Staring down the barrel of the shotgun, Huck eased back. He rested on one elbow, wiping the blood from his lip with the back of his hand. "Damn, I'm surprised at you, Monk. You gonna come in here and gun down an unarmed man? Shit, the Monk I knew from back in the day had more honor about him than that. He'd at least give a nigga a fighting chance. I guess that pipe done stripped you of your honor as well as your dignity."

Monk gave Huck a knowing smirk. "I see your game, old timer, and I'm more than willing to play it." He propped the shotgun against the wall. "Get up and show me something."

Huck pushed himself up and brushed the broken glass from his pajamas. He rolled his shoulders and took a fighting stance. "You know those fists of yours were legendary in the streets. Some say they're made of iron." He danced on the balls of his feet.

"Well now you'll get to see firsthand before you leave this world," Monk told him and moved in.

Huck was far more agile than one would've thought for a man of his age. He met Monk's bull charge with a flurry of punches to the face, with most of them connecting. The blows would've dropped most men or at least slowed them down, but Monk ate them like dinner mints. Huck saw Monk rear back to strike, and had braced himself but was ill-prepared for the force of the blow that landed on his side. It was like being shot at close range with a gun. Huck had to take a few steps back, trying to catch his breath.

"I guess the pipe ain't took everything from me," Monk sneered. He faked low and when Huck instinctively went to protect his midsection, Monk fired a left hook at his face. Huck raised his arm just in time to deflect the blow, but it came with a cost. A smile spread across Monk's face when he felt the bone in Huck's forearm snap. Monk laid into Huck hitting him with vicious combinations, trying to break every part of Huck that his fist made contact with. He kept hitting him until Huck crumbled like a sack in the corner, bleeding and gasping for air.

"I see there's some truth in every legend." Huck hugged his broken ribs, coughing blood onto his pajamas.

"So it would seem." Monk picked up his shotgun and went to stand over Huck. He leveled the barrel with Huck's face, and fingered the trigger.

Huck looked down the barrel of the shotgun with sad eyes. He knew without question that his time on earth had come to an end. "I never laid a hand on that kid!" he declared.

"You might as well have. Then at least you wouldn't have died for nothing," Monk told him before blowing Huck's brains all over the wall.

After dispatching Huck, Monk went into his kitchen and grabbed a garbage bag. He then proceeded to make his way through Huck's home, taking anything he could find of value. Once he had picked Huck's place clean he was ready to make his exit. As an afterthought he went back and took the gold watch and pinky ring off Huck's corpse. "Don't see too much need to be flossing in hell." He laughed to himself. With his loot slung over his shoulder like Santa Claus Monk walked out the door whistling a happy tune.

# CHAPTER 37

Chucky cruised the streets in his BMW wearing a shit-eating grin. The sun was shining, he had a few dollars in his pocket, and for once one of his plans seemed to be working. Life was indeed good and by the end of the night it promised to get better.

Maggie starting that argument and causing him to come across her chin couldn't have come at a better time if he planned it. She would no doubt be pissed that he'd slapped her around and be looking for a way to spite him. The most obvious way would be for her to use up all the drugs before Chucky came back, which was all the better, at least for Chucky.

Simply telling Maggie and Rissa that it was the end of the road for their relationship wouldn't have done. After dragging them up and down the coast, tying them to all his schemes, abruptly ditching them wouldn't go over well. There was nothing worse than a woman scorned, especially when the woman had enough dirt on you to bury you. Maggie and Rissa had seen and heard too much to leave them dangling in the wind. The two girls and the secrets they carried had to be buried.

In order to accomplish his task Chucky had to reach out to an old fiend who used to cook up for them named Butch. Had Butch not been a degenerate addict he could've been a world-renowned chemist. The man had an intimate knowledge of chemicals and could whip up just about anything given the proper materials, including a lethal drug cocktail, which was what Chucky had commissioned him for. He had Butch whip him up a batch of cocaine cut with several things, including beuthanasia, a chemical used to euthanize animals. Maggie and Rissa would never see it coming until it was too late. All Chucky had to do was wait then go back to the apartment and clean up the mess.

Of course Butch was suspicious, but the $5,000 Chucky promised him for the cocktail put all his apprehensions to rest. Just like any other addict his greed trumped his morals. He planned to make the cocktail for Chucky, take his money, and the minute he was gone he intended to double-cross him by calling Ramses to try to collect on the price on Chucky's head. It was a greasy move on Butch's part, but he figured it was no greasier than whatever Chucky was planning to do with the poison cocktail. Butch thought he was slick, but Chucky was slicker. Instead of the $5,000 Chucky had promised him, he paid Butch with two bullets to the head. Chucky had learned from his mistake with Karen that murder was best committed with no accomplices.

He had some time to kill before going back to the apartment so he set about to handle some last-minute errands. It had been ages since his car had been cleaned so he took it to the carwash. While they were cleaning his car Chucky went to the store across the street to grab some beer, cigarettes, and a newspaper. He wanted to see what time the football game was the following night so he could plan accordingly. Persia had promised she would have Vaughn's address for Chucky when she came by that night and he planned to hit Vaughn in his home after the game. From there he and Persia were going to jump on the I-95 and head for Florida. It was as good a place as any to start their new life.

While he was in the store he tried calling Charlie again. He had been trying to reach him since the night before but his cell phone kept going to voicemail. It was unlike Charlie to not answer his phone, especially when Chucky was calling. He was the only friend Charlie had left in the world, if you could call someone like Chucky a friend. Initially he thought that maybe Charlie had a change of heart and had snitched, but quickly pushed the thought out of his mind. Charlie might not have been the shooter, but he had taken Chucky to the apartment, which made him just as guilty and he would've been just as dead. It had to be something else. As Chucky stood in the line waiting to pay for his purchases and flipping through the newspaper he realized what that something else was.

Inside the newspaper he found an article about a shooting that had occurred in Harlem, leaving several people dead. Among the listed dead was Charles Parker, aka Charlie. Chucky damn near dropped his beers when he read the name. According to the article, Charlie had been found missing most of his head so he had to be identified by his fingerprints. Charlie's death was just one more sign of Chucky's fortune turning. Though he doubted Charlie would ever tell anyone about his involvement in the killing of the old Italian, he planned on killing him anyhow instead of taking chances. With someone having done the job for him Charlie was no longer Chucky's problem.

Though Charlie being killed solved a problem for Chucky, it also raised a series of questions. Who was the killer? The other corpses at the scene were identified as associates of the Parizzi crime family. It was possible that they were the ones who had murdered Charlie, but if that was the case, who had murdered them? From the brutal way in which they were all killed, Chucky had his suspicions as to who was responsible. If he was right then his little blame game hadn't worked as well as he'd hoped. For as much as Chucky was tempted to tangle with his old nemesis one last time it wasn't worth risking. He might've survived the first attempt on his life, but it would've only been a matter of time before somebody put that rabid dog down. It was just too bad he wouldn't have the pleasure of doing it himself.

When Chucky figured enough time had elapsed for the cocktail to take effect he started making his way back to the apartment. On the way he stopped at the hardware store to grab some things he'd need: trash bags, gloves, and cleaning supplies. It would've probably been easier for him to leave them where they were and find another hideout, but he didn't have the time or the cash to rent another apartment. Besides he didn't want to raise suspicions with Persia over the sudden move.

Chucky was smiling and whistling a happy tune when he turned down the block to his apartment building. The smile quickly faded when he got to his building and found it crawling with police.

It didn't take Li'l Monk long to find the building Persia had given him the address to. It was a rundown tenement, wedged between two buildings that looked just as shitty. It was a sleazy neighborhood and just the right kind of place for a piece of shit like Chucky to be hiding.

Gaining access to the building was easier than he'd thought it would be. The lobby door was broken. After taking a cautious look around Li'l

Monk slipped inside the building. The lobby reeked of urine and there was no elevator, so he would have to walk up the three flights to Chucky's apartment. As he reached the stairs he noticed two unsavory types loitering at the bottom. They both looked high out of their minds. They watched Li'l Monk as he passed, but he avoided making eye contact with them. He would just be another nameless face to them.

He tiptoed up the broken stairs, stepping over trash and broken paraphernalia. The dilapidated building that Chucky now called home was a testament to how far he had fallen. Didn't matter; he'd fall even further when Li'l Monk sent him to hell. Kunta wanted to make Chucky confess, but Li'l Monk liked the idea of presenting his head better.

When he reached Chucky's apartment door, he placed his ear to it and listened. He could hear a television playing inside, but no voices. This gave him pause. Persia had assured Li'l Monk that Chucky would be home that night, but what if she was wrong? He had come too far to turn back so he decided to take a gamble.

Li'l Monk kicked the front door in then rushed the apartment, sweeping his gun back and forth in case there were any surprises waiting for him. He found himself standing in a small, dingy living room. In a corner, on a snack table, sat the small television he'd heard playing. Moving cautiously, he headed toward the bedroom. The door was partially cracked, but no one appeared to be inside. The house appeared to be empty. Li'l Monk was walking back toward the front door, dialing Persia to let her know that her information had been bad when he spotted something in the kitchen. He hadn't seen them when he first passed the room because he hadn't been looking on the floor.

There were two females: one young and one older. Li'l Monk reasoned that these were the women who had been traveling with Chucky. There were no visible wounds on them, but they both had blood coming from their noses and mouths. Li'l Monk took one look at the overturned chairs they'd been sitting on and the coke on the table and knew what had happened. The two junkies had taken a lethal trip, more than likely sponsored by Chucky. If he had killed them then that meant he was more than likely in the wind by then. With him gone and the girls dead, Li'l Monk had no hope of clearing his name.

Li'l Monk pulled out the burner to call Kunta so he could break the news. It was time to put plan B into action, which was to kill as many of his enemies as he could before they took him out. He was walking toward the door to make his escape when he heard what sounded like coughing. Li'l Monk rushed back into the kitchen and realized that one of the girls, the younger one, was still alive! She

was trying to turn over on her side, coughing out
clots of blood onto the floor. Li'l Monk knelt beside
her and checked her pulse. It was weak, but still
there. She looked up at him in wide-eyed horror
and tried to crawl away, as if she knew his face and
what he was capable of.

"Don't worry, I'm not going to hurt you. I'm
going to get you some help," Li'l Monk told her,
while dialing 911 on the burner phone. If the girl
managed to survive there was still hope for him
to clear his name. "Yeah, I just found a girl who
overdosed. Send help, quick!"


Chucky sank as low in his seat as he possibly
could as he slowly coasted past the crime scene. A
small crowd of onlookers had formed just outside
the yellow tape barrier the police had erected
around the front of his building. Two of the paramedics were coming out with a zipped black bag
on a gurney. At least Chucky knew his cocktail had
worked. He waited for them to bring a second body
bag out, but instead saw Rissa on a stretcher. The
paramedics were working feverishly trying to keep
her alive.

"Fuck!" Chucky cursed. He had planned everything perfectly; how could it be that Rissa had
survived? More importantly, how did the paramedics know to come there? He had stolen both

Maggie's and Rissa's phones before he left so there was no way they could call for help, and it sure as hell wasn't one of the neighbors. It was then that Chucky spotted the answer to his question.

He almost didn't see him there, standing among the crowd of spectators. At first Chucky thought it was impossible and his eyes were playing tricks on him, but he knew they couldn't be. He'd know Li'l Monk's gorilla-like profile anywhere. Li'l Monk stood there long enough to watch the paramedics load Rissa into the back of the ambulance, before fading into the crowd.

If Chucky knew Li'l Monk as well as he thought, he knew that it was more than likely Li'l Monk's tenderhearted ass who had stumbled upon Rissa and Maggie and called the ambulance. Once again Li'l Monk was fucking up his plans by putting his nose in things that didn't concern him. Just then something occurred to Chucky: how the hell did Li'l Monk even know where to find him? Rage filled his heart as he realized that he had been set up, and there was only one person who could've been responsible.

# CHAPTER 38

"This shit had better be worth it," Asia said to Persia across the back seat of the Lincoln Town Car.

"I promise, it will be. And thanks for the ride," Persia said. She was going to take public transportation, but decided that she was dressed far too cute to be hopping off trains and buses in her new outfit, so she called in a favor. Since Vaughn had left two tickets she invited Asia to attend the game with her, in exchange for getting a ride in her family's Town Car to the arena.

"It's me you should be thanking," Basil said from behind the wheel. He was Asia's cousin and personal driver for their family.

"Don't worry, Basil. I'll see if I can get you some tickets to the next game," Persia promised.

"Fuck the tickets, I'd rather have cash," Basil shot back. Unlike Asia who had grown up in high society with her mother's people, Basil was from her father's side and had grown up around gangsters.

"Hush, Basil, and watch the road or I'll tell Mother who it really was smoking weed in her Mercedes," Asia threatened.

Basil mumbled something and rolled up the tented visor between them.

"So." Asia turned back to Persia. "You've finally decided to come clean with Vaughn, huh? I think you're making the right decision."

"I hope so, Asia. I'm nervous as hell, which is part of the reason I'm bringing you along. If Vaughn does flip out he won't make too much of a spectacle in front of an audience." Persia laughed.

"Sweetie, you're just being paranoid. I'm sure Vaughn will understand," Asia assured her.

It took longer to get into the parking lot of MetLife Stadium than it did to drive to the arena from Long Island City. Basil dropped them off a few yards from the main entrance and told Asia to call when they were ready to leave. Since the tickets were already waiting for them they didn't have to wait in the long line with the others. They were directed to a special window where they picked up their tickets and one of the security personnel escorted them up to one of the skyboxes overlooking the field.

Persia and Asia felt like rock stars when they entered the room. There were other people there, friends and family of the players, but all eyes were on the two young girls. There was food set up and an open bar, which Asia helped herself to. She was only seventeen and had no business drinking, but being that she was a guest of Vaughn no one questioned her about ID.

After loading up on some of the complimentary food and drinks, Persia and Asia reclined in the theater-like seats to watch the game. There was a huge window through which they could see the entire field below, but there were also several televisions set up playing the game. Persia squealed loudly when she saw Vaughn take the field, which drew her a dirty look from one of the other girls who had also been in the skybox. Asia wanted to step to the girl, but Persia stopped her. Nobody could steal her joy that night, even some hating-ass broad in a pair of knockoff Gucci shoes.

Persia was in especially good spirits. Not only was she getting to see her new man play for the first time, she had finally ended the game her old man was trying to play. By then she was sure Li'l Monk had caught up with Chucky and gotten rid of him and it was good riddance as far as she was concerned. She wanted to feel bad about setting a man up to be killed, but she didn't. Chucky was a parasite and a piece of shit who had gone out of his way to make her life miserable. Whatever he got he deserved as far as she was concerned. The only thing she felt bad about was putting Li'l Monk in harm's way to get the job done. The only thing that brought her even a sliver of peace was that she knew Li'l Monk had been looking to kill Chucky anyhow. All she did was connect the dots for him. She hoped that her childhood friend survived the mission, for both their sakes. If Li'l Monk failed she would have to find another way to get rid of Chucky, but she was confident that Li'l Monk could pull it off and finally free her from Chucky's hold.

Pushing thoughts of murder from her mind, she turned her attention back to the field. It was an extremely close game, with the Eagles getting hammered most of the way, but Vaughn managed to lead his team on a late game drive that put them in position to kick a game-winning field goal. It wasn't the prettiest win, but it was a win nonetheless.

Just after the game several security personnel came to the skybox to escort guests of the players down to a waiting area near the locker room. The waiting area was packed with player entourages and media outlets looking to catch some last-minute pictures and post-game interviews. Among the people escorted downstairs with Persia and Asia was the girl with the knockoff shoes who had been giving them dirty looks upstairs. From the way she kept cutting her eyes at Persia and Asia you'd have thought they were waiting for the same man.

"Persia, you know that girl or something?" Asia nodded at her.

"Not that I know of. She's been reckless eyeballing me since we got here," Persia said.

"Yes, I've noticed and I'm not feeling it. Look I'm not trying to cut up at your man's place of business and all, but I think it's only fair to warn you that if she opens her mouth I'm going to run up in it," Asia declared.

"And while you're in her mouth I'm gonna be in her ass," Persia added. That night was too big of a night for Persia to have some groupie bitch fuck it up.

Persia ignored the girl and busied herself watching the tunnel to wait for her man. As the players marched out past her she couldn't help but to think how much bigger they were in person than they appeared on the television. After what felt like forever Persia finally spotted Vaughn coming out of the tunnel, laughing and joking with one of his teammates. He had changed out of his uniform and was now wearing a dark blue suit and a black shirt. As soon as he stepped out of the tunnel the media was on him, shoving cameras and microphones in his face.

Persia beamed proudly as she watched Vaughn field questions about the game. He allowed them about ten minutes before excusing himself and making his way toward where Persia was standing. He smiled proudly when he saw her, but his smile faded when the girl with the knockoff shoes stepped into his path. She said something to Vaughn that Persia couldn't hear, but the look on Vaughn's face said it wasn't pleasant. It was then that Persia decided she had seen enough and moved to intervene.

"Look, shorty, I keep telling you that I ain't got a nickel in that dollar," Vaughn was telling the girl as Persia walked up. When he spotted her, a guilty look crossed his face.

"Sup, Vaughn? Everything okay?" Persia asked him, looking the girl up and down.

"Yeah, babe, everything is cool." Vaughn leaned in and kissed Persia, making it clear what time it was between them. "You about ready to go eat? I'm starving."

"Don't you wanna finish your conversation first?" Persia said in a less-than-sincere tone.

Vaughn smiled because he saw the jealousy peeking out of Persia and he thought it was cute. "It ain't really my conversation to have, which is what I was just explaining to this young lady." He motioned toward the girl with the knockoff shoes. "Lady," he said to the girl, "the only thing I can tell you is that I'll give him the message when I see him. It ain't my place to get involved, and this ain't the place for no ratchet shit to go down."

"Well if your friend would stop ducking my calls I wouldn't have to pop up at his job," the girl shot back.

Vaughn shrugged. "Again, it ain't my business. Now I hate to be rude, but I'm running late for my date with my lady." He looped his arm around Persia's waist. "Now if you'll excuse me." He escorted Persia out of the waiting area leaving the girl with the knockoff shoes standing there looking stupid.

"What was that all about?" Persia asked when they were outside in the team parking lot.

"Some bullshit. That's some crazy-ass broad one of my teammates was knocking off over the summer who thought she was special."

"Oh, so that's what y'all athletes do, make girls think they're special then leave them stranded and half crazy?" Persia asked with an attitude.

Vaughn looked at her seriously. "You need to slow your roll, ma. I can't be held accountable for what the next man does. I'm only responsible for my actions. When I say something I mean it. Do you understand that?"

"Yeah, okay," Persia said.

"Now if you're done with the third degree, I'd like to get something to eat before I faint from starvation."

"I'm hungry too," Asia added. "I could go for a good lobster or maybe a steak."

"I was thinking of something a bit closer to my roots." Vaughn smiled.

Instead of taking Persia to a fancy restaurant like he normally did, he surprised her by taking Persia and Asia to Sylvia's in Harlem. It was funny because though Persia was a child of Harlem, she had never eaten in the restaurant. She had heard mixed opinions about the food so she wasn't quite sure what to expect. Vaughn claimed it was one of his favorite places to eat when he was at home, and took the liberty of ordering for Persia and Asia since it was both their first times. He had the beef ribs, while Persia opted for the smothered pork chops. Asia didn't eat pork or beef so she had the fried chicken.

To Persia's surprise the food was actually quite tasty. It reminded her of Sunday meals her mother used to cook for her at home. The way Asia cleaned her chicken bones you'd have thought it was her first time ever having soul food. After dinner they ordered desserts and coffee while they sat around and talked. Asia noticed that there was something clearly lingering between Persia and Vaughn that needed to be said so she took that time to excuse herself and go to the lady's room.

"Vaughn, I'd really like to thank you for treating me to another wonderful night," Persia told him.

"It was my pleasure, doll. I was really glad to hear from you, too. You know, for a minute I was starting to think that I was wasting my time by pursuing you," he said sincerely. Vaughn had just about given up on Persia until he'd gotten the call from her.

"I know. I've been a real bitch and I'm really sorry about that, Vaughn. There's just so much going in my life right now that I feel like my head is screwed on backward. I needed to sort some things out before I could seriously entertain the idea of getting into a relationship. I didn't want to come into it with excess baggage or secrets. That's kind of why I wanted to talk to you tonight. You know I really like you right?"

"Wait, is this the part when you break it to me that you were really born a man?" Vaughn joked.

"Stop playing, I'm trying to be serious here!" Persia swatted him on the arm.

"Okay, my bad. I'm listening."

"My life hasn't exactly been roses. I've had some ups and some downs, but I'm trying to get it all together. Like I said, I really like you, but I don't want to build the foundation of whatever it is that we have here on lies, so I feel like I should tell you the real truth about me and my past and let you decide what you want to do from there."

Vaughn took her hands in his from across the table. "We've all got a past, but it shouldn't affect our futures. Whatever you've done or whoever you were before we met doesn't matter."

"But it does!" Persia got misty-eyed. "You've got your life together and are going to go on to do great things, and I don't want my mistakes to get in the way of that. There's something I need to tell you and I'm not sure how it'll make you look at me afterward."

"Persia, you're my boo. There's nothing you can tell me that'll make me look at you differently."

"Even if I told you that I'm a former drug addict?" Persia blurted it out. She expected Vaughn to be mad, or possibly get up and storm out and tell her that he never wanted to see her junkie ass again, but instead Vaughn just sat there, staring at her with a smirk on his face. "Well aren't you going to say something?"

Vaughn shrugged. "What is there to say?"

"I dunno. Say something . . . anything!"

"Okay, since we're laying truths on the table, I might as well lay mine out. I already knew about your addiction," Vaughn informed her.

Persia couldn't hide her shock. "Wait, what do you mean you already knew?"

"I'm young, but I'm no fool. I know a man in my position has to protect himself against certain things. Do you think I would've gotten involved with you without first knowing what I was getting into? I had some people check into your history when we started dating."

"You had people spying on me?" Persia asked in an offended tone.

"No, I didn't have anyone spying on you but I did have some people do a background check. Now before you get all indignant and accuse me of violating your privacy, or whatever else is running through your mind just hear me out. As professional athletes we find ourselves moving targets and everybody wants to take a shot. From the family members who feel like you owe them something when you make it, to the skanks looking for a come up, everybody wants a piece of your brand and your bank account. I see athletes get caught slipping all the time. I mean look at that crazy shit with the girl at the stadium. That dude is in for a world of grief all because he was careless. I worked too hard to go out like the next dumb nigga who's willing to put his dick in anything warm and wet."

"So do you have people look into all the girls you date?" Persia asked.

"No, only the ones I plan to get serious with." Vaughn smiled at her.

"So if you knew, why didn't you say anything?"

"Because I didn't want to make things awkward between us. I figured you'd tell me in your own time, and you did," Vaughn told her. "I'm famous, but I'm also from the hood so I know what time it is. My mother got high, my father got high, and I had a bunch of other relatives who were strung out. It doesn't make them bad people, they just made some mistakes, much like you did. You were a young girl involved with a snake-ass nigga and got in over your head. You did it, and overcame it. Simple as that."

"So you still wanna be with me, even knowing that one day my past could come up and tarnish your image?" she asked.

"I'd be lying if I said the media and public opinion couldn't sometimes be cruel, but I don't give a shit about what other people think or say about me.

My job is to take that field week in and week out and give my all to my team and the organization. Outside of that anybody with an opinion about Vaughn Tate and what he does off the field can go to hell. I'm willing to take the heat if you are too."

Persia couldn't stop the tears that had forced their way out of her eyes. She had carried the burden of that secret for so long, thinking that Vaughn wouldn't want her if he knew who she really was. Not only did Vaughn accept her for who she was, he wanted to add on to who she was trying to become. Persia was so full of emotions that she couldn't find the words so she let her actions speak for her and jumped into Vaughn's lap, planting kisses all over his face.

"Thank you for understanding," Persia said between kisses.

"No, thank you for being honest." Vaughn kissed her on the lips.

"Get a room, why don't you?" Asia joked when she rejoined them at the table.

"Sorry about that," Persia said, embarrassed.

"No need to be sorry, sweetie. I take it everything worked out like I said it would?" Asia asked.

"Yes, it did. And thank you for helping me find the courage to be honest."

"That's what friends are for; at least, real friends." Asia smiled. "Well, it's getting late, and I've got school tomorrow."

Persia looked at her watch and saw that it was just after midnight. "Wow, I didn't even realize. It's almost a shame to end such a perfect night, but I know you've got to get back to Philadelphia, Vaughn."

"I'm not due to be back until the team meeting tomorrow to watch game tape, so maybe the night doesn't have to end so soon, unless you've got a curfew or something," Vaughn said suggestively.

"My mom is likely asleep already," Persia told him. She knew what he wanted and she was finally ready to give it to him.

"Asia, do you need a ride?" Vaughn asked.

"No, I'll call Basil and have him pick me up. You kids have fun, and don't do anything I wouldn't do," Asia said playfully.

"Whatever, heifer. I'll call you after school," Persia said, getting up from the table.

"Make sure you do, because I want all the dirty details," Asia told her.

Vaughn stood and held out his elbow to Persia. "Shall we?"

"Absolutely," Persia said taking his arm.

Vaughn, Persia, and Asia waited outside until Basil arrived and Asia was safely in the car. After Asia had gone Vaughn and Persia headed to his SUV and pulled out into traffic. Vaughn and Persia were so caught up in the anticipation of their long-awaited night that they never noticed the red BMW following them.

# CHAPTER 39

By the end of the night Li'l Monk was running on fumes. He hadn't had a chance to eat or sleep and his whole body ached. For as much as he wanted to just get some rest there was still too much left to do.

His hopes had rested on finding Chucky at the apartment Persia had sent him to, but they were dashed when he arrived to find no sign of Chucky and one of the girls who knew the truth dead. Out of options he switched to his plan B, which was where Kunta came in.

Li'l Monk had Kunta shadowing Ramses all day. He knew that after he started tearing shit up in Harlem it would force Ramses to take action, but he couldn't make a move without conferring with Pharaoh first. Knowing Pharaoh the way he did he wouldn't talk business on a phone so they would have to meet in person. If Li'l Monk planned on killing Pharaoh, he would first need to know where to find him.

Li'l Monk and Kunta arranged to meet on 114th Street near Morningside Park. When Li'l Monk arrived, he found Kunta already there, sitting behind the wheel of a car he'd stolen to get around for the day.

"How'd everything go?" Li'l Monk asked.

"Just as you said it would," Kunta informed him. "After I lifted Ramses's wallet I went and staked out his home. He returned there shortly after his meeting with King Tut, but he only stayed for a few minutes. I followed him to a diner out in Queens where he met with a man in an expensive suit."

"Pharaoh," Li'l Monk said in disgust. "Did you happen to get a look at him?"

"Sadly, I did not. He was wearing a large brimmed hat that obscured his face, so I was never able to get a clear look, but I can tell you he was light skinned."

It wasn't much, but it was more than Li'l Monk had to go on when he started. "So what happened after the meeting?"

"They got into two separate cars and left. I already knew where Ramses was going so I figured it best to follow the other man. I tailed his car out to Queens where his Rolls-Royce pulled into a parking garage. It came out a few minutes later, and I was about to continue following until I noticed that the man in the suit was no longer in the car, but slipping away on foot. I followed him for several blocks into a residential neighborhood where he entered a large house through the back door."

"You mean to say you know where Pharaoh lays his head?" Li'l Monk asked in disbelief.

"If this man I followed was indeed this Pharaoh, yes. I do not know the address, but I'm sure I could find the house again if we went out there," Kunta said confidently.

"Kunta, I could kiss you!" Li'l Monk grabbed him in a bear hug.

"Li'l Monk, I am fond of you, but not that fond," Kunta joked.

"So, where was this house located?" Li'l Monk asked, already making plans in his mind.

"Long Island City," Kunta told him.

"What?" Li'l Monk asked, not really understanding. He didn't know much about Long Island City, other than the fact that it was where Persia had moved to when Face took them out of Harlem. What were the odds that Pharaoh and Persia coincidentally lived in the same neighborhood? "I need you to show me."

An hour later Li'l Monk and Kunta were riding in the car they had stolen through the neighborhood where Kunta had followed Pharaoh to. The whole time Li'l Monk had been putting different scenarios together in his head, none of which ended well. What he was thinking was impossible, it had to be. When Kunta pulled to a stop and pointed to the big house across the street Li'l Monk's heart sank.

"Kunta, are you absolutely sure?" Li'l Monk asked, hoping it had been some kind of mistake.

"Yes, I'm sure," Kunta insisted. "What's the matter? Do you know this place?"

"I thought I did, but these days I don't know what I know anymore," Li'l Monk said sadly.

"So what now, do we go in and kill Pharaoh?" Kunta asked.

"Not yet. Let's head back to the city. I need you to find my father and relay Face's message; after that you're done. You've been more of a help than you know, Kunta, and I really appreciate it," Li'l Monk told him.

"Little brother, we've come too far together for me to abandon you now. I gave my word I would look out for you," Kunta told him.

"And you have. You've honored your promise, but I have to go at it alone from here," Li'l Monk said.

Kunta didn't like it, but he had learned in his short time around Li'l Monk that he was a man who could not be swayed once his mind was made up. "As you wish," he reluctantly agreed and pulled away from the house.

The ride back to the city was a somber one, and Li'l Monk had much to think about. If what Kunta was right about what he was saying the situation has just gotten way more complicated. Before he did anything he needed to be absolutely certain that the person he was about to murder was indeed Pharaoh, and there was only one person he knew of besides Ramses who could make a positive ID.

# CHAPTER 40

Vaughn took Persia to the Times Square Marriot, where he had rented a suite for the night. It seemed like as soon as they arrived the paparazzi were on them snapping pictures. Persia hadn't known where they were going before they got there so she had no clue how they knew. It was like they had GPS trackers on celebrities and always knew where they would be. Vaughn smiled and played it up for the cameras while Persia tried to hide her face.

"No need to be shy, baby." Vaughn pried her hands away from her face so that the cameras could get a shot of her. "You're with me now." He planted a kiss on her lips for all to see. After fielding a few questions and posing for a couple more pictures, Vaughn whisked her into the elevator.

Persia pressed her back against the wall and exhaled. "Jesus, do they ever quit?"

"Nah, they don't. Some of them can be real pushy about it, but for the most part they're okay."

"I don't know how you can keep your sanity with people jamming cameras in your face twenty-four hours a day," Persia said.

"It's all a part of the life. After a while I got used to it and you will too." Vaughn put his arm around her.

"So you must plan on keeping me around for a while, huh?"

"As long as you wanna be kept," he said seriously. "I wasn't bullshitting when I said I wanted you to be mine, Persia. Now I get the chance to show you how serious I am." He kissed her.

They had barely crossed the threshold of the suite before Vaughn and Persia were all over each other, kissing and fondling. It had been so long since Persia had given herself to a man willingly that she almost couldn't contain herself.

Vaughn scooped Persia up and carried her into the bedroom of the suite, where he laid her gently on the pillow-top bed. He looked at her hungrily as he tore out of his expensive suit and tossed it on the floor as if it was a dollar store T-shirt. Persia made to take off her clothes, but Vaughn stopped her. "Allow me," he said and began to slowly strip her. When Vaughn beheld her naked body his eyes misted up and for a minute she thought he was going to cry.

Persia reached up and pulled Vaughn on top of her. She had a fire raging between her legs and needed his throbbing cock to put it out. She wanted the dick, but he wasn't quite ready to give it to her. Vaughn kissed her tenderly, staring at her lips then working his way down her body. He flicked his tongue over her nipples until they stood just as erect as his dick. He continued kissing her, making his way down her stomach and found his way to her love nest. When Vaughn's tongue slipped inside her, Persia gasped as if she had just been touched with a live wire.

Vaughn's tongue explored every inch of her insides, causing her eyes to roll back in her head. Every time she came she felt like she died a little bit. "I want you inside me, Vaughn," she panted.

"Ask me nicely." He toyed with her clit.

"Please, baby, let me feel it," she begged.

Vaughn took a minute to grab his pants from the floor and grabbed a condom from his pocket. He took his time rolling it over his erect dick, before hovering over her. Balancing himself on his powerful arms he slid inside her. Granted, he wasn't as well hung as Chucky, but what he lacked in size he made up for in technique. His pole slipped in and out of her, slowly, giving her long and deep strokes. "You like that, don't you?" he asked, already knowing the answer.

"Oh I love it." Persia moaned. "Damn I love this dick."

"I'm gonna make you love me like you love this dick." Vaughn told her before flipping Persia onto her stomach and entering her from behind. He gripped her about the waist and began plowing into her in a steady rhythm. "Shit, Persia. Oh shit," he rasped, letting her know that he was about to cum.

"That's right, say my name, say my name," Persia demanded and started throwing it back, getting turned on by the sound of her ass hitting against his washboard stomach. She winced when she felt Vaughn's nails digging into her sides, but she didn't ask him to stop. She was dancing somewhere between pleasure and pain and it felt good to her.

They came at the same time, with Vaughn collapsing on top of her. They lay there for a few minutes, feeling each other's heartbeats and basking in the moment. Once Vaughn was done emptying himself, he rolled off her and lay on his side, breathing like he had just run a marathon.

"That was fucking awesome!" Vaughn said.

"You weren't so bad yourself," Persia said jokingly. She was silent for a few minutes after, as the realization of what she had just done set in. Persia wasn't a virgin, but she was no loose girl either. She could count her sex partners on one hand and still have fingers left over. Giving her body to someone was a big deal for her. "So what does this mean?" she asked him.

Without her having to elaborate, Vaughn knew what she meant. "It means you now belong to me and I belong to you, if that's what you want."

"Vaughn, since I was a little girl all I ever wanted was someone who I could care for and who would care for me with no strings attached."

"I don't care about you, Persia, I love you," Vaughn told her.

"Don't say things you don't mean, Vaughn."

Vaughn propped himself on his elbow and looked her directly in the eyes. "I never say things I don't mean. From the minute I saw you at the club with that clown-ass nigga you were with I knew that I loved you, I just never thought it would be possible for me to have you."

"Well you've got me and you're stuck with me." Persia pinched his nipple playfully.

Vaughn pulled Persia to him and kissed her on the forehead. "I wouldn't have it any other way."

Persia buried her face into Vaughn's chest so that he wouldn't see the tears falling from her eyes. After what she had been through with Chucky she had given up on love or ever finding her happy place, but Vaughn had shown her there was still hope. With these thoughts in mind she drifted off into a peaceful sleep.

Persia felt like she had just drifted off when she was awakened by a heavy knocking on the hotel suite's door. She lifted her head from the pillow and looked at the clock. It was 5:00 a.m. Her mother was going to shit a brick about her staying out all night.

The banging on the door continued.

She woke Vaughn. "You expecting somebody?"

"Hell no," Vaughn said, rubbing the sleep from his eyes. He got out of bed and slipped on his pants before going to the door. "Can I help you?" He looked through the peephole.

"Hotel security, sir." The man on the other side flashed something that looked like a badge, but the movement was too quick for Vaughn to clearly make it out. "We've had some complaints about screaming coming from the room."

Vaughn smirked confidently figuring someone had heard Persia screaming when he was tearing that ass up. "We're good in here, thanks," Vaughn said through the door.

"Okay, sir, but we're still going to need you to open the door so we can ensure that there's no one in the room being harmed," the voice on the other side replied.

Vaughn sucked his teeth in frustration before opening the door. "Listen, man, I told you we're good. Ain't nobody hurt."

"Not yet they ain't," the man said before clocking Vaughn upside the head with the butt of his gun, knocking him out. He stepped over Vaughn and went into the bedroom where Persia was still stretched out naked.

When Persia saw the man appear in the bedroom doorway she gasped in horror. "Chucky?"

"Yeah, bitch, it's me. I'll bet I was the last person you expected, especially after you sent your little guard dog to kill me."

"Wait, I can explain!"

"Explain it to God when you see Him, you traitorous whore!" Chucky grabbed her by the hair and dragged her out of the bed.

# CHAPTER 41

Vaughn awoke with a splitting headache. He was lying face down on the floor of his hotel suite trying to remember how the hell he got there. He went to push himself up from the floor and realized he couldn't move his hands, because they were bound behind his back. It was then he remembered the fake hotel security and being cold-cocked.

"Glad to see that little love tap I gave you didn't do too much damage. Wouldn't want you not to be able to play in next week's game," a voice called from somewhere behind Vaughn.

Vaughn craned his neck and saw the man who had identified himself as hotel security standing over him. Upon closer inspection he realized that it wasn't the first time he'd seen him. It was the same dude he had seen in the club with Persia the night they first met. "What the fuck is this?"

"What the fuck does it look like?" Chucky snapped.

"Look, if it's cash you're looking for I got about fifteen hundred dollars in my wallet. Take it and get the fuck out of here," Vaughn told him.

Chucky kicked Vaughn in the ass so hard that he slid a few inches across the floor. "What the fuck am I supposed to do with fifteen hundred funky-ass dollars? See, in the beginning it was about money, but now this shit is all about karma." He grabbed Vaughn by one of his arms and dragged him into the bedroom. He tossed him into the corner next to Persia, who was sitting in a chair with her hands tied in front of her. She wasn't naked anymore, instead wearing one of the hotel's bathrobes. Her eyes were red and swollen from crying.

"Baby, did he hurt you?" Vaughn asked in a concerned tone.

"No, I'm okay," Persia told him.

"For the moment." Chucky stalked over. "And what the fuck was you supposed to do if I did hurt her, pussy?" He kicked Vaughn in the gut.

"Leave him alone! This is about me and you, not Vaughn!" Persia shouted.

"You made it about him when you brought another nigga into our relationship," Chucky snapped.

"Relationship? You're blackmailing me; we aren't in a fucking relationship!"

"Stop being all muthafucking technical about the shit! You know what I mean." Chucky began pacing the floor. "I can't believe you. I'm out here risking my life and my freedom so I can build a future for us, and this is how you do me? You gonna give another nigga my pussy after all I've done for you?"

"The only thing you've ever done for me is ruin my life. For the love of God, Chucky, why can't you just leave me alone?" Persia sobbed.

"Because I can't!" Chucky snapped. "You don't think I've tried to get your tramp ass outta my system? I don't know what the fuck it is, but you've got more of a hold on me than any drug ever did. I'm sick over you. In the beginning it was just about payback for what your daddy did to my brothers, but then it turned into something else."

"What does my father have to do with any of this?" Persia asked confused.

Chucky swooped in and grabbed her by the cheeks. "Don't play stupid, bitch!" He rained spittle in her face. "Your daddy gunned my brother down like a dog on the street! Don't act like you didn't know. You were there. We both were."

"You're out of your mind. I don't know anything about . . ." Persia began, then her words trailed off. Her mind went back to when she was a little girl on the playground. She had been talking to her father, telling him what she wanted from the store when the car pulled up and she saw a man holding a gun. In her mind she could see the muzzle flashes, before the man who had been trying to kill her father hit the ground. Everything was a blur after that, but she could remember as she was being pulled away from the crime scene seeing a boy in the back seat of the car. He was staring at Persia's father with hateful eyes, the same hateful eyes that were now locked on her. "The boy in the car. It was you, wasn't it?"

"Yes," Chucky said emotionally. "I loved my brothers more than anything and your father and Monk took them from me."

"So you put me through all this over something that happened over thirteen years ago that I didn't have anything to do with?" Persia was stunned. Chucky had made her life a living hell since the day he walked into it and now she understood why.

"It had everything to do with you! I wanted to hurt your daddy the same way he hurt me and I knew there was only one way to do it. I had to touch the thing he loved most in the world: his precious princess," Chucky told her.

Persia's head spun as none of it made sense. "I don't understand. Why not just kill me?"

"I had planned to, but first I wanted you to suffer," Chucky admitted. "I wanted to break you down until there was nothing left of daddy's little girl and then I was going to snuff your lights out. Then something happened that I never expected. I fell in love with you," he said sincerely.

"If this is how you treat people you love, I'd sure hate to see how you treat people you don't," Vaughn said from the ground.

Chucky knelt down and put his gun to Vaughn's head. "You shut your fucking mouth! You don't know what you're talking about."

"I know it takes a bitch-ass nigga to break down a good woman," Vaughn spat.

Chucky laughed and removed his gun from Vaughn's head. "Is that what she has you thinking, that I'm the only monster in this movie? You got a high football IQ, but you're short on common sense. How well do you really know this bitch you're trying to defend?"

"If this is the part where you drop the bomb on me about Persia being an ex-addict, save your breath. I already know and it don't mean shit to me," Vaughn said.

"I see she's told you some of her secrets, but has she told you all of them?" Chucky taunted Vaughn.

"Chucky, don't," Persia pleaded.

"What's the matter, Princess P? You don't want your boy toy to know that in addition to being a crack whore, you're also a murderer? Well I should say attempted murderer since your pet dog missed his mark."

"Fuck are you talking about?" Vaughn asked.

"I'm talking about your bitch trying to have me clipped. Tell him, Persia. Tell Vaughn how you tried to have me killed."

Vaughn looked at Persia. "Baby, is that true?" When Persia lowered her head in shame instead of denying it, Vaughn knew that it was. The revelation surprised Vaughn. He had always known Persia was from the street, but he never would've expected that she had it in her to try to have a man murdered.

"Don't look so sad, Vaughn. You ain't the only one this sneaky bitch played for a sap," Chucky taunted. "In fact, I probably did you a favor by busting in here like this. I'm a poor nigga and she tried to have me killed when she was done with me, so there's no telling what she'd have done to a rich nigga like you once you let her get close."

"Fuck you, Chucky! I wish Li'l Monk had murdered your ass!" Persia spat at him.

"Well he didn't, which is good for me and bad for you." Chucky pulled her off the chair and started pulling her toward the door. He stopped and picked up Vaughn's pants and began going through the pockets.

"Where are you taking her?" Vaughn asked. He struggled against his restraints but couldn't get free.

"Me and my bitch are about to take a little road trip." Chucky took Vaughn's cash then threw the wallet at him.

"Please don't do this," Persia pleaded with him.

Chucky yanked her to him and kissed Persia roughly. "I told you, baby. You belong to me and nobody else. Now let's go." He pulled her behind him.

"I'll find you, Persia! I promise, I'll find you and make this nigga pay!" Vaughn raged. He struggled against his restraints but couldn't free himself.

He felt so helpless knowing Chucky was about to abscond with the woman he loved and there wasn't anything he could do about it.

Chucky pulled Persia along toward the front door, thinking of how great life was going to be for them. Even though she had tried to have him hit, he forgave her. In Chucky's twisted mind she was just being a scorned woman and trying to pay him back for what he'd done. It didn't matter; they would get through it like they got through everything else. Persia was in her feelings over Vaughn, but once he got her down to Florida and showed her what kind of man he would really be she would forget all about her boy toy.

Chucky had just twisted the handle of the hotel door, unlocking it, when it came flying open. He was barely able to move out of the way to keep the door from hitting him in the face, but he couldn't avoid the heavy boot that crashed into his chest and sent him flying into Persia, knocking them both onto the floor.

Persia hit her head on the arm of the sofa when she fell and for a few seconds the room spun. Through the haze of pain she saw several armed men and a woman come into the room and fan out. When she looked closely at the girl she thought her eyes were playing tricks on her. "Meeka?"

Meeka moved toward Persia with a knife in her hand and Persia instinctively scrambled back. "It's okay, I'm not going to hurt you." She knelt down and cut Persia free, while she watched her with frightened eyes. "Are you okay?"

"I don't understand, what is all this? How did you find me?" Persia rattled off questions.

"Because she's been following you for the last couple of days," the leader of the group spoke up. He was a handsome man, dressed in a black turtleneck and black pants. Holstered under his arms were two large guns with rhinestone handles.

"Following me? Why would you be following me?" Persia asked.

"To get to him." Meeka nodded at Chucky who was just beginning to stir.

Chucky was trying to crawl for the gun he had dropped when Frankenstein grabbed him by the back of the neck with one of his massive hands. He lifted Chucky in the air and began to squeeze.

"Careful, Frank. We don't want to damage our parcel," Christian warned.

"Found another one." Boogie came out of the bedroom, pushing Vaughn in front of him. He had cut his legs free but left his hands tied. He shoved Vaughn, causing him to fall onto the floor near Persia. "Oops." He snickered.

"Boogie, is it too much to ask of you to show even the slightest bit of tact from time to time?" Christian asked, clearly irritated.

"Sorry, boss." Boogie said sarcastically. He was actually hoping Vaughn fell hard enough to hurt himself. Boogie had lost a stack by betting on the Giants the night before.

"Are you okay?" Persia touched Vaughn's face.

"Yeah, I'm good, but would you care to tell me what the hell is going on?" Vaughn looked at the armed men in the room.

"I'll spare you the boring details, but the short version of it is that there is a price on Chucky's head and my associates and I have come to collect," Christian said flatly. "The reason I had Meeka following you around is because I knew that wherever you were, Chucky wouldn't be far behind and it would seem that I was correct."

"So are you going to kill us too?" Persia asked fearfully.

Christian gave a throaty laugh. "Sweetie, I'm a businessman, not a monster. Normally I would've been forced to take you out as well, because witnesses can make things unnecessarily complicated, but you've been given a pass. I promised your friend Meeka that no harm would come to you and I am a man of my word."

Persia looked at Meeka. "I guess I owe you."

"Regardless of what I've chosen to do with my life, I'm still the same girl you used to run around and get into trouble with. We're friends and that'll never change."

"Thank you." Persia hugged her.

"I think we've taken up enough of your time, kids. We best be going. Chucky has a date with destiny."

"I ain't going nowhere! Get the fuck off of me!" Chucky struggled helplessly in Frank's grip.

"Frank, would you please shut him up? I can't even hear myself think." Christian clutched his head dramatically.

"With pleasure," Frank said and slammed Chucky face first into the wall, knocking him out. Frank then stuffed Chucky in the large laundry sack he was carrying and tossed him over his shoulder.

"Thank you. Boogie?" He turned to the man with the thick glasses. "Could you please call Ramses and tell him we've got something that belongs to him."

"Sure thing." Boogie pulled out his cell and stepped to the side to make the call.

"So what now?" Vaughn asked.

"Well, we can handle this one of two ways: you can call the police and tell them what happened, and in that case I'll have to disappoint poor Meeka by paying you both a second visit. Or you can forget we ever met and go about your life as if this never happened," Christian said.

"Then I guess you were never here," Vaughn said.

"You are a wise young man, Mr. Tate." Christian smiled. "Come children, let's go." He led his entourage toward the door. He stopped short and turned to Persia. "Please be sure we get invitations to the wedding. After all, we are extended family now," he said and left.

"What did he mean by that?" Vaughn asked Persia.

"I have no clue."

# CHAPTER 42

Li'l Monk sat outside the house Kunta had brought him to, chain smoking cigarettes. His mind was a jumble of thoughts and none of them were good. When he'd set out on his mission of revenge against those who had wronged him, he knew that he would have to leave his feelings on the table to do what needed to be done, but it didn't make it any easier on him, especially the step he was about to take.

There was a thumping sound coming from the trunk of the car, snapping Li'l Monk out of his daze. His passenger was getting restless. He reasoned that he couldn't blame them considering the ride was involuntary. Normally such barbaric tactics would've gone against his moral code, but in matters of life and death morals sometimes went out the window. It would all be over soon.

It was just before daybreak when there was finally signs of movement in the house. A woman came out wearing spandex, a pullover fleece, and track sneakers. She took a few moments to stretch on the front steps before taking off into a brisk jog down the block. He was glad she was gone because Li'l Monk wasn't sure if he had it in him to do what he had to do while she was in the house. Checking the clip in his P89 to make sure it was full, Li'l Monk slid out of the car and started across the street.

As luck would have it the woman neglected to lock the front door when she had gone for her jog. Li'l Monk turned the knob and slipped inside. The house was relatively dark except for the first pink rays of the sun that were just starting to shine through the picture window. Li'l Monk moved silently across the living room, making his way to the stairs. He knew the master bedroom was located on the second floor. He crept up the stairs, passing a room with a closed door. Li'l Monk took a second to peek inside. The bed was empty and still made, meaning it hadn't been slept in. He wondered where the occupant was. Had she known that the shadow of death would pass over her house that night, and made it a point not to be there? And if she had, would she have tipped him off? It was a bit late to worry about it by that point.

Li'l Monk continued to the master bedroom and found the door cracked open. He peeked inside and saw a lump lying under the covers. He had caught Pharaoh slipping! He had waited for that moment for so long and now that it was at hand, he found himself nervous. "Get it together," he whispered to himself as he approached the bed. "This the front desk with your wake up call, muthafucka!" he snarled and dumped four shots into the bed. When he snatched the covers back to deliver a head shot he didn't find a body, only a few shot-up pillows. He had been duped!

Li'l Monk ducked just as something whistled through the air where his head would've been. He turned and found himself confronted by a man wearing pajamas and holding a baseball bat.

"You picked the wrong house to rob, buddy!" Richard swung the bat again.

Li'l Monk dove out of the way just as the baseball bat smashed through the nightstand. He was trying to get to his feet, but Richard was on him again. This time when he swung the bat, his strike rang true and hit Li'l Monk in the arm, knocking his gun into the hallway, and tumbling down the stairs. Richard swung again, but this time Li'l Monk was ready. He grabbed the bat midswing and a struggle ensued.

Their fight spilled out into the hallway and Richard pinned Li'l Monk's back to the staircase banister. Richard was far stronger than he looked. Li'l Monk kneed him in the balls, and yanked the bat free. Before he could swing it, Richard tackled him and sent them both spilling down the stairs and into the living room. Luckily for Li'l Monk Richard took the brunt of the fall and was slow to get up. This gave Li'l Monk time to recover his gun. Richard had just managed to get to his knees when Li'l Monk pressed the P89 to the back of his head.

"Game over, Pharaoh."

\*\*\*

Richard sat at the base of the stairs with his hands tied to what was left of the banister. He was scared to death, but tried his best not to show it. "What's this all about?"

"I think you know what this is about, Pharaoh," Li'l Monk told him.

"Why do you keep calling me that? I don't know any Pharaoh," Richard said. He was rewarded by a slap in the mouth from one of Li'l Monk's powerful hands.

"You know just what I'm talking about, pussy. I know everything now, including how you tried to have me killed!" Li'l Monk spat. "I was loyal to you and Ramses and the one time I needed y'all on my side you threw me to the dogs, and I just wanna know why? I worshiped you niggas and as a reward you tried to off me!"

"Kid, I'm a teacher not a killer. I have no idea what you're talking about," Richard insisted.

"I've got to give it to you, you're good. I would've never guessed that a square-ass nigga like you was really the notorious Pharaoh. You're better at keeping your secrets than you are your word. Does Ms. Michelle know what you've been up to? How about Persia? How are they going to feel when I smoke your ass and everything comes out?"

"Listen," Richard began in a calm voice. "I can prove to you who I am. If you go upstairs and grab my wallet off the table, my driver's license is inside. That'll prove I'm not who you think I am."

"I've got a better idea. Hold tight for a second." Li'l Monk walked out the front door.

Richard knew he didn't have much time. He wasn't sure where Li'l Monk had disappeared to, but he knew that he wouldn't be gone long. If he didn't get free by the time he came back, it was game over. He had just managed to free his hands when Li'l Monk came back, but he wasn't alone. There was a woman with him. Her hands were tied and there was a pillowcase over her head. At first he thought that it might've been Persia, but he could tell from her hands that the woman was too old to be his stepdaughter. He had no idea who it was, but he wouldn't have to wait too long to find out.

When Li'l Monk saw that Richard had freed one of his hands his eyes flashed with anger. "What, were you planning to run off? Were you gonna leave your family here to take your medicine for you? You're just as much of a coward as you are a snake, so let me see you crawl on your belly." Li'l Monk shot him in one of his legs.

Richard howled in pain, clutching his bloody leg. "You shot, me! You fucking shot me!"

"That's just a flesh wound. Before I take you from this world I want you to admit it. Admit it to me and yourself who you really are, Pharaoh!" Li'l Monk demanded.

"I keep telling you, I'm not Pharaoh!" Richard whimpered.

"Well I know someone who'll say different." Li'l Monk snatched the pillowcase from the woman's head and revealed that it was Queen, the old timer he had seen at the funeral. He remembered Neighborhood telling him that she was one of the few people who had ever seen Pharaoh's face.

Queen blinked, letting her eyes adjust and looked around the room. When she spotted Li'l Monk holding the gun, she began backpedaling. "Please don't kill me."

"Calm down, Ms. Queen. I ain't gonna kill you," Li'l Monk assured her. "I apologize for my rough handling of you, but I didn't think you'd come with me willingly."

"Well if you ain't gonna kill me what the hell do you want?" Queen asked suspiciously.

"I need you to identify someone. Who is this?" Li'l Monk pointed at Richard.

Queen squinted and studied Richard's face. "He looks familiar, like I might've seen him somewhere before, but I can't say that I know him."

"Lady, I ain't in the mood for games. Neighborhood told me that you can identify Pharaoh," Li'l Monk said.

"I can and that isn't him," Queen said honestly.

Frustrated, Li'l Monk grabbed Queen by the back of the neck and forced her down in front of

Richard. "Maybe you need to look a little closer. Stop playing with me; we both know this is Pharaoh."

Queen laughed. "Is that what you thought? Fool-ass little boy, if you had simply asked me I could've told you that Pharaoh died nearly ten years ago. I know because I was at the funeral."

Li'l Monk was stunned. Richard had to be Pharaoh, all the clues pointed to it. There was no way he could've been wrong. "Well if Pharaoh is dead then who the fuck has been carrying his name?"

"I think I can answer that for you," a voice called behind Li'l Monk. All eyes in the room turned and they saw Michelle standing in the doorway holding a gun. "Good to see you again, Li'l Monk." She greeted the youngster in a kind voice. When she turned to Queen her face soured. "I wish I could say the same about you, Mother."

Li'l Monk was so stunned that you could've knocked him over with a feather. He stood there looking back and forth between Richard and Michelle, pointing a gun, trying to get his brain to process what his eyes were telling him. "What the fuck is going on?"

"I'll be happy to explain, but first I'm going to need you to put the gun down," Michelle told him. When Li'l Monk didn't comply, she pointed the gun directly at him. "That wasn't a request. I was there when you came into the world, Li'l Monk, so please don't have me be the one to take you out."

Li'l Monk placed the gun on the floor and kicked it away.

"Thank you," Michelle said and stepped into the living room. She walked over to Richard, who was still on the floor clutching his leg. "Are you okay?"

"This little nigga shot me!" Richard grunted.

"Well it serves you right for being so fucking careless. I always told you that ego of yours was going to be our undoing," Michelle scolded him.

"Wait, you mean to say that you're Pharaoh?" Li'l Monk asked her in disbelief.

"Yes, and no. These days Pharaoh is just a name, one that I inherited when my father died," Michelle confessed.

Now it was Queen's turn to look surprised. "You're the one who's been running around carrying Pharaoh's name? I thought it was just some street nigga running around impersonating him."

"No, Mother. No street nigga could accomplish what I have over the years. Only one who carried the blood of the Pharaoh could've carried his name, and who better than his baby girl?" Michelle smirked.

Queen's eyes watered. "I knew the ghost of my no-good baby daddy lived somewhere but I had no idea that it was within my own daughter."

"Bitch, miss me with those crocodile tears!" Michelle snapped. "You never gave a shit about my father or me; all you ever cared about was his money."

"That's not true. I loved your father," Queen insisted.

"Bullshit. If you did, you'd have allowed me a chance to get to know him instead of lying about who he was all those years," Michelle accused her.

"Can somebody please help me to make sense of this?" Li'l Monk asked.

"Of course. You've always gone out of your way to protect my daughter so at the very least I owe you an explanation." Michelle sat on the arm of the chair. "You see, growing up I never had any contact with my father, other than the checks he would send to my mother once per month, which she smoked or snorted up every chance she got. I didn't meet him for the first time until shortly before he died. We talked for a long time and it was then that he revealed everything to me, about him being married, my mother keeping me away from him and more importantly who he really was. Imagine my surprise when I found out the man who I always thought was a deadbeat was actually a wealthy kingpin."

"And an adulterer," Queen added.

"Old woman, if you open your mouth one more time I'm going to shoot you in it," Michelle warned her. "As I was saying, my father was a man who lived with many secrets, including the fact that he was terminally ill. No one knew except those closest to him, including his brother Ramses. It was Ramses who came to me with the idea of carrying on the front that Pharaoh was still in control of everything. See, Ramses had always been a good soldier, but he was no leader. He knew that he wouldn't be able to fill Pharaoh's shoes. He needed someone to step up to carry on the legacy, which is where I came in. Face had taught me everything he knew about running a criminal organization, so I had the knowledge but I was the wrong gender. Being that I was a female I couldn't pass myself off as a man if there ever came a time when Pharaoh had to show his face. By then Face was already in prison for killing that boy and I was married to Richard. He would make the perfect front man and because we were married he could never testify against me. I would let Ramses run the business, and Richard would impersonate Pharaoh while I played the good housewife and raised my daughter. It was the perfect plan, but the problems started when Richard and Ramses got beside themselves. Richard had started believing that he was really Pharaoh instead of a puppet, and started making bad decisions, like cutting the side deal with Italians to go against the Clarks and sacrificing you."

"Baby, you don't understand. Li'l Monk had to go! He killed Mr. D and was going to fuck everything up with the Italians!" Richard explained.

"Horse shit, Richard," Michelle shot back. "Li'l Monk is one of the few among our ranks who truly understands honor. Men like him don't kill for petty change, they kill to protect what they love and to defend what they believe in. If you hadn't been so busy playing God and really paying attention to the pieces on the chessboard you might know that!" she snapped.

"Li'l Monk." She turned to him. "You were always loyal to my family and my organization and you didn't deserve what Richard tried to have done to you. For this, I am truly sorry. Had I known what was going on behind my back with Richard and Ramses I'd have intervened sooner."

"It's all good, Ms. Michelle. Call off your goons and we'll call it even," Li'l Monk told her.

Michelle nodded. "You have my word, your name will be cleared."

"So you mean to tell me you're just gonna let this little nigga slide? How is that going to look on me within the organization if I let Li'l Monk slide?" Richard asked heatedly.

"My dear husband, this organization is no longer your concern. You were never built to be a boss and I was wrong for trying to heap the responsibility on you. It's time for someone else to wear the face of the Pharaoh." She looked at Li'l Monk.

Li'l Monk raised his hands. "Look, I'm flattered that you think so highly of me, but I've seen what comes with sitting in the big chair and I'll pass. I'm content just to get money."

Michelle laughed. "Don't be so quick to pat yourself on the back. You are a born leader, Li'l Monk, but you're still young. There is much you still have to learn about life and the world before you can walk a mile in the king's shoes. I have someone else in mind for that."

"Okay, well if we're done here I'm gonna go ahead and leave y'all to sort the rest of this out." Li'l Monk started for the door, but froze when Michelle pointed her gun at him. "What's this? I thought you said my name would be cleared."

"It will, but that still doesn't change the fact that you now know my family's darkest secret." Michelle stood up. "I'm afraid you know too much to simply ride off into the sunset."

Mrs. Schultz was taking her dog for his morning walk as she always did around that time. As usual her path took her past the Chandler house at the end of the street. She didn't know what it was about their lawn that her dog loved so much, but it was one of the only places she could get him to relieve himself. Her dog had his leg up, pissing on Michelle's roses, when she heard gunshots coming from inside. She snatched her dog and made hurried steps down the street while calling 911 on her cell phone.

# CHAPTER 43

It was the wee hours of the morning when Monk finally made it back to Harlem from Huck's place. He had stopped off in the Bronx to see a fence he knew to try to get rid of some of the stuff he had ripped off. He got a few dollars for the items, but felt like he could've gotten more if he had time to negotiate. The only reason he settled for what the fence offered was because he didn't want to lug the heavy garbage bag full of stolen merchandise all the way back to Harlem on public transportation.

When Monk got back to his apartment to stash his loot the first thing he noticed was that his bedroom door was open, and he always closed it before he left. He drew his gun and made his way into the bedroom. He noticed that the clothes he'd had on the floor of his closet were now pulled out and tossed onto the bedroom floor. Upon further inspection he saw that his hiding place had been tampered with and several of his weapons were missing. There was only one person besides him who knew where he kept his stash: Li'l Monk. He breathed a sigh of relief knowing that his son was still alive, but the fact that he had raided his stash for guns meant that he was in trouble. Monk had to find him before Ramses did.

When Monk rolled around to the strip where the young boys hustled he noticed that there wasn't a soul in sight. None of the young dope boys who frequented the block were out that night, which meant they all knew that death was coming. It didn't matter. No matter what rock Ramses or his minions sought to hide under, Monk would find them and dispatch them.

Monk was cutting across a back alley when he felt the hairs on the back of his neck stand up. He stopped and spared a glance over his shoulder, but saw nothing except for a cat chasing a rat across the alley. Shrugging it off, he kept walking. As he neared the mouth of the alley he heard soft footfalls behind him. Monk stopped, and spun holding his shotgun.

"You got two choices: show yourself or meet your Maker," Monk said to the darkness.

A few seconds later a shadowy figure appeared, wearing a tattered hood over his head. He began walking slowly toward Monk, but when the old timer pumped his shotgun, the shadow froze.

"That's far enough, partner. Let me see your hands," Monk ordered. The shadowy figure raised his hands to show Monk that he wasn't armed. "Okay, now step out here where I can see you and do it slowly. I'd hate to have to blow your fucking head off by accident."

"As would I," the shadowy figure said in a thick accent. He took measured steps toward Monk, keeping his hands in plain sight. "Trust me, I mean you no harm."

"Most niggas who start a sentence with 'trust me' usually aren't to be trusted, so I think I'll be the judge of that. Now I don't know you and obviously you don't know me or you wouldn't have been dumb enough to follow me into this alley. Or maybe you do know me and just think you're better than the last few hitters who've tried their hands with old Monk."

"I am no hitter," Kunta said, and removed his hood so that Monk could see his face, "simply a messenger. My name is Kunta. Perhaps you've heard of me?"

"Yeah, my boy told me you paid a call on him recently. You responsible for his disappearing act?" Monk leveled the shotgun at Kunta's face.

"Yes, but only from his enemies, not from this world. Your son is alive and well, but for how long only God can say. I fear he's gotten himself into a most dire situation," Kunta said sadly.

"So I've heard," Monk said in a sour tone. "Where's Li'l Monk now?"

"Hunting those who are hunting him," Kunta said. "This Pharaoh wants him dead and it is my hope that I can help to prevent that from happening."

"Then what the fuck are you doing here talking to me, instead of putting in work with my boy?" Monk asked.

"For reasons that I cannot explain, Li'l Monk has chosen to walk the last mile of this journey alone. By morning the men who wish to harm Li'l Monk will be dead or he will," Kunta said honestly.

Monk grabbed Kunta by the neck and slammed him against the wall. "You trying to be funny, li'l nigga?"

"No, I'm being honest," Kunta said in an even tone. "I understand your anger, truly I do, but in the little time I've come to know your son he doesn't strike me as someone who can be deterred when his mind is made up about something."

Monk gave him one last shake for good measure before letting him go. Monk wanted to tear Kunta's head off, but he couldn't deny the truth in his words. If Monk wanted someone to be angry at all he had to do was look in the mirror. Monk had no illusions about what kind of father he had been to Li'l Monk when he was growing up: a shitty one. He had taught him to fight, survive on the streets, and even kill, but during the times when his son really needed a father, Monk was never there. The guilt of knowing his son may possibly die because of his shortcomings was tearing him to pieces.

It took Monk a few minutes to compose himself enough to formulate words without yelling or breaking down and crying. "You said earlier that you were a messenger." His voice was heavy with emotion.

"Yes. I bring word to you from our mutual friend, Face," Kunta said evenly.

At the mention of his old crime partner's name, Monk gave Kunta his undivided attention. "What'd he send you to tell me, how disappointed he is in me for fucking up everything we built?"

"Nothing quite so intimate, but it's extremely cryptic. So much in fact that I have no idea what it means," Kunta admitted.

"Well don't keep an asshole in suspense. Spit it out," Monk demanded.

"He said to tell you when you finally feel your back touching the bottom of the barrel look to Exodus 2." Kunta relayed the message as it had been given to him.

At that moment, all the alcohol and cocaine Monk had consumed over the last few hours disappeared and for the first time in years he found himself completely sober.


Chucky awoke disoriented, and with a throbbing pain in his forehead from where it had hit the hotel wall. He looked around and realized that he was in a warehouse, but where he didn't know. When he tried to reach up to see if he had a knot on his head he realized that he couldn't move his arms. He looked down and saw that he was handcuffed to a chair. "What the fuck?"

"For a minute I was beginning to think that Frank had been a little too rough with you and that you might sleep through all the fun." Christian appeared in front of him.

Chucky looked at him with defiant eyes. "What, is this supposed to be the part where I beg you for my life? I don't know what you thought, but I'm a muthafucking gangster. So if you're gonna kill me then do it and let's get this shit over with."

"And where would be the fun in that?" Christian patted him on the cheek. "There is someone here who would very much like to have a word with you. Meeka, could you show our guest in, please?"

"Got you." Meeka went off to do as Christian had asked.

When Chucky saw who Meeka had escorted back into the room all the blood drained from his face. "Ramses!" he gasped.

"Been a long time, Chucky." Ramses stalked toward the chair. "A real long time."

"Ramses, this is all a big misunderstanding. I planned on paying your money back once I got on my feet," Chucky pleaded.

Ramses punched Chucky in the face as hard as he could. "Bitch-ass nigga, you still think this is about money? This is about honor, which is something you lack!" He hit Chucky again.

"Ramses, before you do whatever it is you've got planned for Chucky, I'd like to discuss the matter of payment," Christian interrupted.

"Right, right." Ramses backed up. "Pay this nigga," he told one of his goons.

The goon stepped forward and tossed the duffle bag he was carrying at Christian's feet. Christian knelt down and looked inside. "Is it all here?"

"Every dime," Ramses assured him. "You can count it if you want."

"I don't think that'll be necessary. You seem like a trustworthy enough type. He's all yours." Christian handed the bag off to Meeka.

"I want to thank you, Christian. I've been trying to lay hands on this nigga for damn near a year." Ramses was talking to Christian, but looking at Chucky, cracking his knuckles. "I think before I kill you I'm going to have a little fun. You junkie piece of shit, you don't know how many nights I lay awake dreaming of this moment."

"Too bad the moment is going to be short-lived," Christian told him.

Frank appeared as if by magic behind Ramses's goons and grabbed them both by the necks. With a flick of his wrists he snapped their spines as easily as pencils and let them fall lifelessly to the ground. Ramses made to reach for his gun, but Christian had the drop on him, placing one of his rhinestone pistols to Ramses's head.

"You set me up?" Ramses asked in disbelief.

"Not entirely. I'm a firm believer in honoring my contracts, including the one that has been placed on you. A mutual friend of ours sends their warmest regards," Christian told him before shooting Ramses in the head.

"What the fuck, Christian? I thought we were supposed to kill Chucky for Ramses, not the other way around." Meeka looked at Ramses's corpse. She didn't understand what was going on.

"Calm yourself, my little rose. Ramses has always been the target, but we needed a way to draw him out so we could dispatch him. Chucky was simply bait. I knew he was the one person Ramses hated enough to step out of his comfort zone," Christian explained. "Cut him loose," he ordered.

As Boogie removed Chucky's handcuffs, Chucky sat there looking at Ramses's body at his feet. He had come close to dying on many occasions, but never that close. He stood, rubbing his wrists. "Man, for a minute I thought I was a goner."

"Oh, make no mistake, you're still going to die, just not on behalf of Ramses," Christian told him. "Hold that muthafucka," he ordered.

Boogie and Frank grabbed Chucky by the arms and held him so that he couldn't move. "Wait, but you said you were using me as bait to draw Ramses out."

"I did and you have, but ending your life has nothing to do with money. This is about you being a lowlife muthafucka who preys on young girls."

Christian drew one of his rhinestone guns. Just then he had a thought. "Hey, Meeka, I know I said I'd never ask you to take a life again unless it was absolutely necessary, but I figured you might want this honor." He extended the gun to her.

"For what he did to my friend Persia, absolutely!" Meeka took the gun from Christian.

"Wait a second. Meeka, you know me! How many times did I come through the block and lay paper on you girls or get you high when y'all were fucked up?" Chucky tried to jog her memory.

"Yeah, I remember what you did for us, but I also remember what you did to us. This is for Persia and Karen," Meeka spat before pulling the trigger and ending Chucky's reign of terror.

"Good job, little rose." Christian took his gun from Meeka and kissed her on the forehead.

"Christian, can I ask you something?" Meeka asked.

"Sure, baby. What's up?"

"You said that Chucky was only the bait and Ramses was the real target. So that leaves the question: who put the money up for the hit?"

Christian didn't answer; he just smiled.


Monk squinted against the rays of the early morning sun, wishing he'd thought to invest in a pair of sunglasses. He couldn't remember the last time he'd been awake that early, let alone out in the world. He was tired and cranky, but it was a big day for him so he didn't complain. He was leaning on the hood of the minivan he had driven that day. It was hardly his style, and had it been stolen he'd have selected something with a bit more flash, but it was a rental.

He checked his watch for the hundredth time, wondering if he'd gotten the time wrong. He'd been waiting outside for nearly forty minutes and there was still no sign of his passenger. The sound of the front gate buzzing drew Monk's attention. Several men came out and walked into the parking lot to greet their peoples, but none of them was who Monk had come for. When the gate starting closing again Monk figured that he had gotten his information crossed and was about to leave, but just then the gate stopped and one more person came out. It had been years since he had seen him, and he had put on a little weight and grown a beard but Monk could still recognize his closest friend.

"My nigga!" Monk smiled and threw his arms open.

"What's up with you, baby boy?" Face hugged him. "Thanks for coming to pick me up."

"It was the least I could do. I'm glad to see you're out . . . finally."

"Yeah, I'm out and I don't ever plan on going back. That prison shit is for the birds," Face said, tossing the parcel he'd come out with into a trash can. The only thing he held on to were his pictures and the letters Michelle and Persia had been writing him over the years. "I'm glad you were able to decipher the message I sent by my young boy, Kunta."

"Exodus 2: it was the page in the Bible you sent me where you wrote all your lawyer's information down," Monk said. "When I called him this morning I thought he was bullshitting me about you getting out, but here you are in the flesh. One thing I can't figure out is why you sent such a cryptic message instead of just calling me or writing a letter?"

"Because neither of those routes is one hundred percent secure," Face told him. "When you see what I've got lined up for us you'll understand why I kept everything so cloak and dagger."

Monk shrugged. "If you say so. Now that you're out, what you wanna do? I got some bitches we can pay a call on if you wanna get some pussy, but knowing your ass you probably want to stop by and see your family. It's been a long time."

"Indeed it has, but I don't wanna do either just yet. Take me through Harlem right quick. I wanna survey the kingdom I left behind," Face said, getting into the passenger seat.

"Whatever you say, Face, or should I refer to you as Pharaoh now?" Monk teased and walked around to the driver's side.

# EPILOGUE

After what had happened that night in the hotel suite Vaughn wouldn't have wanted anything else to do with Persia, but he was surprisingly understanding. It would take awhile for him to get over being beaten, robbed, and damn near killed, but he loved Persia enough not to give up on her. Despite his success, Vaughn was still a young dude from the trap so he understood more than most how people, places, and things could sometimes derail even the best laid plans.

Persia was never able to make the formal introduction that she had promised Richard because when she got home she found out that he was dead. According to the statement her mother had given to the police, it was a robbery gone wrong. Some men had broken into their home while Michelle was out for her morning jog, and Richard surprised them. He was shot dead in their living room and the killers had escaped. Persia took Richard's death hard, but not as hard as her mother. When Persia's father went away, it was Richard who stepped to the plate and held the family down. It would be a long and hard road for Michelle, but Persia planned on being there for her. Michelle had carried Persia when she was going through hard times and it was time for her daughter to shoulder the load. It was the least she could do for the woman she owed everything to.

After what had happened to Richard in their Long Island City home, there was no way they could still live in it. There were too many painful memories for them, so Michelle decided to sell it and bought a smaller one in Pennsylvania. This worked out for Persia since she would be starting classes at Temple University that fall. It would allow her to be closer to her mother and Vaughn. She couldn't say that she had chosen to attend Temple because Vaughn played ball in Philly, but she couldn't say she didn't either. Happiness was a fleeting thing for the women in Persia's family, and she wanted to enjoy hers for as long as she could. For as gloomy as the last few years of her life had been she deserved a little sunshine.

Frankie the Fish sat in the back of the Italian delicatessen with several of his men, eating sandwiches and playing cards. They were arguing over the game when a young man with oily black hair, wearing a track suit came in. He leaned in and whispered something into Frankie's ear.

"Okay, show them in," Frankie said, wiping his hands with a napkin.

A few seconds later the young man in the track suit came back in with a brown-skinned girl trailing him. She wrung her hands nervously, and her eyes were trying to look everywhere except at Frankie.

"I usually don't take visitors without appointments, but my associate says you have some pertinent news that had to be delivered to me personally," Frankie told the girl.

"Yes, sir," the girl said sheepishly.

Frankie motioned for her to have a seat at the table. She was hesitant, but the young man looming behind her let her know she didn't have a choice in the matter. After some contemplation, she took the seat.

Frankie leaned in and looked at her with eyes so cold they made her flesh crawl. "Who are you and what's so important that you would interrupt our card game?"

It took the girl a few seconds before she finally found her voice. "I apologize, Mr. Frankie. I wasn't even sure if it was a good idea to come, but my sponsor seemed to think it was a good idea. Making amends for the wrong I done is a part of the recovery process. My name is Rissa, and I have information about what really happened the night your uncle was killed."

*Several months later*

The death of Ramses had changed things in the hood, but not to the point where hood business wasn't still hood business. The faces had changed, but the game remained the same. Several young men sat on the stoop of one of the trap houses that had once been run by Omega and Li'l Monk, having a heated debate.

"Man, you bugging. That nigga is dead and stinking," one boy was saying to the other.

"That ain't what I heard. They say Pharaoh got him and turned Li'l Monk into one of his army of the dead," the other boy shot back. "They say he still creeps through the hood when the sun goes down, collecting souls for the Pharaoh."

Just then King Tut came out of the building. He looked down at the young men and frowned. "Fuck is you li'l niggas out here doing? If you ain't getting money get the fuck off my stoop!" he snapped. The little boys took off running, fearful of the almighty King Tut. Tut shook his head, watching the kids bend the corner. With Ramses no longer on the board he had to go out on his own and try to make the best out of a bad situation. He had cut a deal with Felix and Poppito and he was now running things on the streets. The block didn't seem the same without the likes of Omega and the others, but Tut reasoned that the show must go on.

King Tut walked to the corner store to get some cigars and a pack of cigarettes. He had his head down, lighting a cigarette, when he felt someone standing in front of him. When he looked up to see who it was, his face went white like he had just seen a ghost.

"What's the matter, Tut? Ain't you happy to see me?" Li'l Monk asked.

Tut opened his mouth to reply, but no words came out.

"Omega sends his best from behind the wall." Li'l Monk let the shotgun rip, hitting King Tut in the chest, sending him flying through the bodega window. People screamed and scattered, trying to get out of the way of the mad gunman. Li'l Monk ignored them, stepping through ruined window, over the glass and rubble to get to King Tut. Tut was a mess of blood and guts, but he was still breathing. Li'l Monk knocked his front teeth out when he shoved the shotgun barrel in his mouth. "Long live the muthafucking king," he said before blowing Tut's head off.

Li'l Monk tucked the shotgun and strolled causally down the block. Long after he was gone you could still hear the echo of the song he was whistling, "Camptown Races."

END